BIG BAD WOOL

LEONIE SWANN

Translated from the German by Amy Bojang

Allison & Busby Limited
11 Wardour Mews
London W1F 8AN
allisonandbusby.com

First published in German under the title *Garou* in 2010.
This edition published by Allison & Busby in 2025.

Published by arrangement with Soho Press, New York,
with the assistance of Rights People, London.

Copyright © 2010 by Leonie Swann.
English translation Copyright © 2025 by Amy Bojang.

The moral rights of Leonie Swann to be identified as the author of
this work and of Amy Bojang to be identified as the translator of
this work have been asserted in accordance with the Copyright,
Designs and Patents Act 1988.

All characters and events in this publication,
other than those clearly in the public domain,
are fictitious and any resemblance to actual persons,
living or dead, is purely coincidental.

All rights reserved. No part of this publication may be reproduced,
stored in a retrieval system, or transmitted, in any form or by
any means without the prior written permission of the publisher,
nor be otherwise circulated in any form of binding or cover
other than that in which it is published and without a similar
condition being imposed on the subsequent buyer.
A CIP catalogue record for this book is available from
the British Library.

First Edition

ISBN 978-0-7490-3213-5

Typeset in 11/16.5pt Adobe Garamond Pro by
Allison & Busby Ltd.

By choosing this product, you help take care of the world's forests.
Learn more: www.fsc.org.

Printed and bound in the UK using 100% Renewable Electricity at
CPI Group (UK) Ltd, Croydon, CR0 4YY

EU GPSR Authorised Representative
LOGOS EUROPE, 9 rue Nicolas Poussin, 17000, LA ROCHELLE, France
E-mail: Contact@logoseurope.eu

DRAMATIS OVES

Miss Maple	*The cleverest sheep in the flock, maybe even the world.*
Mopple the Whale	*The fat memory sheep.*
Sir Ritchfield	*The old lead ram, still has the best eyes in the flock.*
Othello	*The new lead ram, black, four-horned and determined.*
The Winter Lamb	*A young outsider in search of his name.*
Ramesses	*A nervous young ram full of good ideas.*
Zora	*A Blackface sheep with a weakness for the abyss.*
Heather	*An outspoken young sheep.*
Cloud	*The wooliest sheep in the flock*
Cordelia	*An idealistic sheep.*
Maude	*Has the best nose in the flock.*
Lane	*The fastest sheep with the longest legs for miles.*

DRAMATIS OVES

Melmoth — *Ritchfield's twin; difficult to forget.*

Willow — *The second most silent sheep in the flock.*

? — *The most silent sheep in the flock.*

The Unshorn Ram — *A shaggy stranger.*

DRAMATIS CAPRAE

Aubrey	*A little black goat bursting with mad ideas.*
Megara	*The goat with the black ear.*
Amaltee	*A young grey goat.*
Circe	*A young red goat.*
Calliope	*A young brown-white mottled goat.*
Cassandra	*An old blind nanny goat.*
Bernie	*A legendary billy goat.*
Calypso	*A nanny goat, who mostly keeps to herself.*
The Goat With Only One Horn	*A sceptic.*

DRAMATIS PERSONAE

REBECCA	*The Shepherdess.*
MUM	*Her mother.*
THE JACKDAW	*Pascal, the master of the chateau humans, has a bit of a limp*
HORTENSE	*Smells of violets and looks after the little humans.*
MADAME FRONSAC	*The housekeeper; Mum calls her the Walrus.*
MONSIEUR FRONSAC	*Is always watching.*
MADEMOISELLE PLIN	*Estate manager, hair always scraped back severely.*
PAUL THE GOATHERDER	*Doesn't say a word.*
YVES	*General dogsbody.*
THE GARDENER	*Guards the apple orchard.*
ERIC	*Makes goat's cheese.*
ZACH	*A top secret agent.*
DUPIN	*A policeman.*
THE VET	*Not very popular with the sheep.*
THE SHORT WALKER	*A winter visitor.*
THE TALL WALKER	*Another winter visitor.*

DRAMATIS CANIDAE

Tess   *The old sheepdog.*

Vidocq   *A Hungarian sheepdog.*

The Garou   . . .

PROLOGUE

Over and done with it.
It was always nice afterwards.

He liked to just stand there, leaning on a tree listening to the thrill of the chase seep into the snow. Like blood. The sky and the rush of the forest above him, the ground beneath him. Surveying the scene in front of him.

Everything was so peaceful. No fear. No hurry. He felt free. Newly born. Surprised to have hands – they were so red – and legs and a body.

During the hunt everything felt so disembodied; there was just a front and back, tracks and prey and speed. Life and death. Four legs or two? It didn't matter. And sometimes they got away. Rarely. That was a good thing. All was well.

A robin landed on a branch. So pretty, so close, so alive. He loved the forest. No matter what had happened, no matter what might happen, the forest took him in, and he became an animal like all the other animals. If it had been nighttime, he would have howled at the moon out of sheer joy.

But it wasn't nighttime, and that was a good thing too. It was broad daylight, and the colours shone.

And time was slipping away.

He sighed. The time afterwards was always too short.

He would soon start to freeze. He had to go back. Wash his hands white in the snow. Put on some gloves. A different pair of boots. Double back. Cover his tracks. Start thinking again. About groceries and tax returns and about her, of course. Always her. About the things humans think about.

He needed to take a suit to the cleaners. He had run out of aftershave. A plant in his bedroom was looking a bit sad. Maybe it needed watering? He didn't know much about plants. He had work to do. And he needed to have lunch. Mushrooms fried in butter and fresh bread! Some crusty bread would be nice.

He took a final look at the scene in front of him – the fox again! The fox was an interesting accent – then off he went, on his two legs, changing a little with every step.

He couldn't help but smile as he stepped out of the forest. Sheep! The chateau looked so much more interesting with snow and sheep. They were so white – all except one. The black sheep put him on edge.

He carried on along the fence towards the chateau, surreptitiously seeking out her window. He couldn't help it.

Nothing.

Deep inside him the creature curled up into a sated, contented little ball and went to sleep.

1

THE SILENCE OF THE LAMBS

'And then what?' asked the winter lamb. 'Then the mother ewes brought them to safety, away from the man with the little dog. And they found a . . . a . . .' Cloud, the woolliest sheep in the flock, was at a loss.

'A haystack!' Cordelia suggested. Cordelia was a very idealistic sheep indeed.

'Yes, a haystack!' said Cloud. 'And the mother ewes ate while the lambs rolled in the hay – and fell silent!'

The sheep bleated enthusiastically. The repeated telling of the story of *The Silence of the Lambs* had resulted in a few changes, and it had gained a little something each time.

Rebecca the shepherdess had read the book to them in the autumn when the leaves were already yellow, but the sun was still round and ripe and robust. The sheep could no longer say why the book had given them the creeps back then, during those first cold silvery autumn nights. Only Mopple the Whale, the fat memory sheep, still remembered that hardly any lambs, and precious little hay, had featured in the book that Rebecca had read to them on the sun-warm steps of the shepherd's caravan.

The wind drove wisps of snow between their legs, the bare branches at the bottom of the meadow fence shivered and the story was over.

'Was it a big haystack?' asked Heather, who was still young and didn't like it when stories ended.

'Very big!' said Cloud confidently. 'As big as . . . as big as . . .'

She looked around for something big. Heather? No. Heather wasn't particularly big for a sheep. Mopple the Whale was bigger. And fatter. Bigger than all of the sheep was the shepherd's caravan standing in the middle of their meadow, even bigger than that was the hay barn and biggest of all was the old oak growing on the edge of the forest that had shed countless crunchy, bitter brown leaves in the autumn. It had been a devil of a job grazing around all of those leaves.

Flanking their meadow was the orchard to the right, and the goats' meadow to the left. Behind the two meadows was the forest, strange and susurrant and far too close; in front of them the yard with stables and dwellings, smoking chimneys and humans making a racket; and right next to them, close and grey and solid as a pumpkin, the chateau. The slight incline up to the forest gave the sheep an excellent view of it.

'As big as the chateau!' said Cloud triumphantly.

The sheep marvelled at the size of the chateau. It had a pointy tower and lots of windows and blocked the sun far too early each evening. A haystack would have made a welcome change.

Something made a bang. The sheep gave a start. Then they craned their necks curiously.

Something had been chucked out of the window of the shepherd's caravan. Again!

The flock launched into action. Quite a few Things had been chucked out of the shepherd's caravan just recently and sometimes they turned out to be interesting. A pan of only slightly burnt porridge for instance, a houseplant, a newspaper. The houseplant had made them feel bloated. Mopple was the only one who had enjoyed the taste of the newspaper. Today wasn't a bad day: in front of them in the snow lay a woolly jumper. Rebecca's woolly jumper. *The* woolly jumper. The sheep liked this jumper more than all the others. It was the only item of clothing they understood. Beautiful and sheep-coloured, thick and fleecy – and it smelled. Not just vaguely of sheep like most woolly jumpers, but of certain sheep. Of a flock who had lived by the sea, grazed on salty herbs, trodden sandy ground, breathed well-travelled winds. If you sniffed very carefully, you could even make out individual sheep. There was an experienced, milky mother ewe, a resinous ram and the scraggy shaggy sheep from the edge of the flock. There were dandelion and sun and seagulls calling in the wind.

The sheep drank in the jumper's woolly aroma and sighed. For their old meadow in Ireland, for the vastness and the grey thrum of the sea, for the cliffs and the beach and the gulls, and even the wind. It was quite obvious by now: the wind was supposed to travel – sheep were supposed to stay at home.

The door of the shepherd's caravan opened and Rebecca the shepherdess stomped angrily down the steps, her lips pursed. She retrieved the jumper from the snow, bringing their pleasure in the comforting aroma to an abrupt halt.

'That's it!' she muttered, frowning dangerously and brushing snow crystals off the knitted wool. 'That's it! I'm chucking her out! This time I really am going to chuck her out!'

The sheep knew better than that. All sorts of Things were chucked out of the caravan, but not *her*. She barely moved at all, but when she did, she was surprisingly quick. The sheep doubted she would even fit through the window of the shepherd's caravan.

Rebecca seemed doubtful too. She looked down at the jumper and sighed deeply.

A familiar face appeared in the milky glass of the caravan window, strangely soft-edged and wide, staring disapprovingly down at Rebecca and the sheep. Rebecca didn't look up. The sheep stared back, fascinated. Then the face had disappeared again and the caravan door opened. But nobody came out.

'From now on, that stinking thing stays out of the house!' came a moan from the caravan.

Rebecca took a deep breath.

'It's not a house, Mum,' she said in a perilously quiet voice. 'And it's definitely not *your* house. It's a caravan. *My* caravan. And the jumper doesn't stink. It smells of sheep! That's normal when it gets wet. Sheep smell like sheep when they get wet as well! Sheep always smell like sheep!'

'Exactly!' Maude bleated.

'Exactly!' the other sheep bleated. Maude had the best nose in the whole flock. She was well-versed in smells.

An icy silence drifted out of the shepherd's caravan. 'And they don't stink!' Rebecca hissed. 'The only things that stink around here are your . . .'

She broke off, sighing again.

'Little bottles!' Heather bleated.

'And the goats!' Maude added for the sake of completeness.

The sheep could sense the silence in the caravan condensing into a little dark cloud. And the cloud was thinking.

'Who cares?' Mum shrieked. 'I don't care if they smell of sheep! They can spend all the livelong day standing around smelling of sheep out there! But not in here. Sheep have no business being in here!' Her voice softened. 'Really, Becky, all I'm asking for is some basic hygiene!'

Hygiene didn't sound like a bad thing. A bit like fresh, green, gleaming grass.

'Hygiene!' the sheep bleated approvingly. All apart from Othello, the new jet-black lead ram. Othello had spent his younger years in a zoo, where he'd seen — and above all smelled — a few hygienas from a distance and knew that they were nothing to get excited about. Not in the slightest.

Rebecca lowered her hands, and a jumper sleeve that she'd only just lovingly cleaned landed back in the snow again. She looked lost, a bit like a young ram who didn't know whether to run away or attack.

'Attack!' Ramesses bleated. Ramesses was a young ram himself, and usually plumped for running away.

Rebecca lowered her head, crumpled the jumper to her chest and puffed herself up. She wasn't particularly big. But she could make herself very big when she wanted to.

'This is my caravan. And they're my sheep. And this is my jumper. And nobody here needs your permission to smell of sheep. And I don't need your advice. Dad left me all of this because he trusted me, and d'you know what? I'm not making a bad job of it!'

The sheep could sense something in the caravan changing. The cloud expanded, getting clearer and wetter. Then it started to rain.

'Your faaather!' Heather whispered into Lane's ear.

'Your faaaaather!' came a groan from the caravan.

'Great. Well done, Rebecca!' muttered Rebecca.

The shepherd's caravan sighed deeply, then Mum appeared in the door. It didn't look like she was just standing there. It looked like she was stuck to the doorframe like a rather elegant slug, neat and brown and gleaming. Water was running out of her eyes, blurring her face.

The sheep looked at her, unsettled.

By now the sheep were convinced that Mum had brought the rain, in her ocean-blue handbag perhaps, or maybe in her little shiny metal case, possibly even in the pockets of her immaculate coat. The rain had been her ally when she had knocked on the door of the shepherd's caravan – the rain and homemade sloe gin.

Rebecca had opened the door, and Mum's words had begun to patter down: longing, daughter, what sort of backwater was this, from now on I'm only flying first-class, daughter, worried, only for the holidays, you look thin, and I brought you some sloe gin.

Rebecca's arms had drooped. 'Mum!'

It hadn't exactly sounded welcoming, but Mum and the rain had stayed all the same. It hadn't rained at all before that, not for the entire autumn – at most a thundery shower that made the frogs in the chateau moat croak with delight. That was it.

From then on there was nothing but rain. It dripped in the hay barn. The ground was muddy and slippery, especially down at the feed trough. The concentrated feed tasted damp. The little stream on their meadow was now a brown torrent, and Mopple the Whale had fallen in while hunting down a riverbank herb.

'Panta rhei,' said the goats at the fence.

First it rained. Then it snowed. Then the sloe gin was chucked out of the window. It wasn't particularly slow. Some other Things followed. Some of the banished items were fetched back into the caravan by Rebecca, some by Mum and some by nobody, and Mopple ate the newspaper and that night he dreamed about a human with a fox's head.

It was all connected somehow – but the sheep didn't know how.

'It's got nothing to do with Dad,' Rebecca said, softly this time, putting on the jumper. 'It's about you and me. You're a guest here, and I want you to act like a guest. That's all. Okay?'

'Okay,' Mum snivelled, dabbing her eyes with a white cloth.

'Okay!' the sheep bleated. They knew what was coming next: cigarettes. Mum on the caravan steps, Rebecca a bit farther up the hill, leaning on the wardrobe that, for some unknown reason, resided under the old oak.

Smoke and silence.

The sheep were silent, too, scraping in the snow, grazing damp winter grass or at least acting as if they were. They were all waiting for something that was about to happen. Something you might not be able to see, but could definitely smell.

There was a strange sheep on their meadow. He had been there before them, not on the sheep's meadow, but in the apple orchard and on the narrow strip of pasture between the meadow and the edge of the forest. Now he was in with them and spent day after day loitering about near the fence. Whenever Rebecca leaned on the wardrobe smoking, the strange ram froze. He didn't move a muscle, not an ear, or an eyelash, not even the tip of his tail. But he smelled. Smelled of purest, blindest panic.

The whole thing made the sheep nervous.

In general, the strange ram wasn't a fearful sheep. He wasn't scared of Tess, the old sheepdog who spent most of her time sleeping on the steps of the caravan. Nor was he scared of Othello's four black horns. But he was scared of Rebecca when she leaned on the wardrobe smoking and looking out across the meadow. He was scared senseless.

Finally, Rebecca stubbed out her cigarette, carefully put it in her pocket and walked back down towards the shepherd's caravan. The strange ram relaxed and started muttering to himself. The other sheep waggled their ears and tails in an attempt to shake off the silence.

The strange ram got on their nerves. He didn't really smell like a sheep and what's more, he didn't look like a sheep either. More like a big, cumbersome moss-covered stone.

Miss Maple, the cleverest sheep in the flock and maybe even the world, claimed he was a sheep all the same. A lonely sheep that nobody had shorn for years, with a great mass of stiff, felted grey wool on his back – and a story that nobody knew. He was amongst them, but not with them, he was running with a flock, but not their flock. Sometimes they got the feeling that the strange ram couldn't see them at all. He could see other sheep though, sheep that nobody else could see.

Ghost-sheep. Spirits.

The real sheep didn't look at him. Apart from Sir Ritchfield.

'I think . . . it's a sheep!' Ritchfield bleated excitedly. The old lead ram was currently taking a keen interest in the question of who was a sheep – and who wasn't.

The others sighed.

Yet again they were wondering if the trip to Europe had really been such a good idea after all.

They had inherited the journey from George, their erstwhile shepherd. One day he had just been lying lifelessly on their pasture, pinned to the ground by a spade. The sheep themselves had had nothing to do with it – well, not that much anyway – but they had inherited a trip to Europe and the shepherd's caravan, and along with it came Rebecca, George's daughter, who had to feed them and read aloud to them. It was in the will.

But then there must have been some kind of mistake. The Europe George had told them about was full of apple blossom, with herby meadows and peculiar long bread. Nobody had said anything about honking cars, dusty country lanes and buzzing gnats, nothing of snow and ghost-sheep, let alone goats.

The sheep blamed the map. Rebecca had brought a colourful map that she spent inordinate amounts of time constantly gazing at during their travels, and the map evidently knew nothing about Europe.

Three sheep had distracted Rebecca in a meadow of sunflowers while Mopple the Whale had snatched the map from the steps of the caravan, and eaten it in its entirety, even the hard shiny bit made of card. And sure enough: a woman had turned up a few days later, her hair severely scraped back, full of flattery, offering the sheep somewhere to stay. Before long they'd said goodbye to the exhaustion of travelling life and had a meadow again, a hay barn, a feed store and this time even a wardrobe. But it wasn't their meadow.

'Remind me why we're here again.' Mum sighed, smoking her second cigarette, still stuck in the doorway like a slug. Tess had managed to squeeze past her and was greeting Rebecca on the steps of the caravan, her tail wagging. Rebecca crouched and scratched Tess behind the ears. Tess tried to stick her greying muzzle into Rebecca's armpit.

'I'm here because the sheep need somewhere to overwinter,' Rebecca said. She had already explained it a hundred times, first to the sheep then to Mum, sometimes to herself as well. 'The pasture's good; the rent's cheap. It's idyllic. I was asked. Why you're here, I don't know.'

The sheep knew why Mum was there: she was a parasite. Rebecca had secretly told them once while she was giving them their hay. 'She acts like she's well-to-do, but she's broke. Hardly surprising given her job! So, she throws together some sloe gin and holes up here for weeks on end. Just for the holidays? Pah! You'll see. I've got no idea how I'm going to get rid of her.'

Not through the caravan window, that was for sure. Mum blew smoke down at Rebecca and Tess, eyeing the chateau critically.

'We should get out of here. Look around you, darling! Look at this godforsaken place – not to mention all the nutters.'

'Hortense is all right,' Rebecca said.

'No style,' said Mum with contempt. 'I thought French women were supposed to have style. What's the deal with the goatherder over there? He spends the whole day wandering through the forest and doesn't say a word when he walks past. It's just not normal! Have you noticed the way the others keep their distance from him? There must be a reason for it.'

'They keep their distance from us too,' Rebecca said.

Tess had rolled onto her back and was getting a belly rub from Rebecca.

'There's a reason for that,' Mum said. 'You don't understand people, Becky. Just like your father. You've never been interested in people. I always have been. I've got the *sense*. I can *see*. Idyllic? The cards say something quite different!'

The sheep cast meaningful glances at one another. Card Things often said something different. Like the shiny map made of card, until Mopple had eaten it. All of their problems had started with the map.

'Do you know which card has been turning up in all of my séances for the last two weeks?'

Rebecca sighed, standing back up and stretching like a cat. 'The Devil!' the sheep bleated in chorus. It was always the same.

'The Devil!' Mum screeched triumphantly from the steps of the shepherd's caravan.

Rebecca laughed. 'That might be because you have three Devils in your deck, Mum. And you took out Justice and Temperance!'

Tess did a doggy stretch and slipped past Mum's slippers, back into the caravan.

'And? The cards just have to be adjusted a bit to suit modern life, that's all. Since I removed Temperance, my success rate is seventy-five percent! Do you know what the others . . .'

Rebecca waggled her hand back and forth as if she were shooing away invisible – and very cold-hardy – flies, and Mum sighed.

'Be honest, darling, do you really feel comfortable here?

When he comes tomorrow, ask the v—?'

Quicker than a fox, Rebecca darted up the caravan steps and put her hand over Mum's mouth.

'Are you out of your mind?' she hissed. 'Do you have any idea what will happen if you say that word? It'll be like unleashing the devil!'

'The devil!' the sheep bleated.

If anything was going to be unleashed around here, it was usually the devil.

* * *

That evening the sheep spent longer than usual standing in front of the hay barn looking out into the night. The yard buildings nestled up to the chateau, seeking refuge. The apple orchard was silent. The smell of smoke and new snow was in the air. The shadow of an owl glided soundlessly over the meadow towards the forest.

Did they feel comfortable here? Cloud maybe. Cloud was the woolliest sheep in the flock and she felt comfortable anywhere. Wool and comfort went together. Sir Ritchfield seemed to like it too because there were lots of conversation partners who didn't run away: the old oak, the wardrobe, the stream, sometimes the unshorn stranger, and if he was lucky, a goat or two. In fact, Ritchfield's loud and one-sided conversations were rather popular with the goats, and quite often a whole gang of them gathered at the fence, giggling and gambolling.

The others weren't so sure. Something wasn't right. A single forgotten apple still hung in the orchard, red as a drop of blood. You could see it, but not smell it. Maybe it was time to eat some more card, so that they could move on. But what sort of card?

'What was she about to say?' Miss Maple asked suddenly.

'Who?' Maude asked.

'Mum,' Maple said. 'Before Rebecca covered her mouth.'

The sheep didn't know and fell silent. A crescent moon hung over the meadow like a nibbled oatcake.

'Rebecca seems really panicked,' said Miss Maple. 'As if something's about to happen. Something terrible.'

'What's the worst that could happen?' said Cloud, fluffing herself up.

'What's the worst that could happen?' the other sheep bleated confidently. Every day there was concentrated feed in the trough and they were read to on the steps of the shepherd's caravan. If the drinking pool was frozen over, Rebecca hacked through the ice with a pickaxe. If it snowed too much, they stayed in the hay barn. If they were bored, they ate or told stories. And awaiting them at the end of every story was a fragrant haystack.

The sheep looked out at the blue snow and felt like they could take on anything.

At that moment a sound cut through the silence, long and thin, distant and heart-wrenching.

A wail.

A howl.

2

CLOUD DISAPPEARS

Cloud was flying.

Not swaying majestically like a cloud-sheep as she did in her dreams; more like a dandelion seed, zigzagging back and forth with the changing moods of the wind. Straight across the meadow, over slushy snow and grass that was frozen solid, in a high arc over the stream, past the old oak – sparrows scattering – and up the hill.

Her legs were galloping frantically below her. Her ears were thudding. Her heart was fluttering in the wind. Faster! She'd left the others behind ages ago, but not him. He was right behind her, hard on her heels, an ominous glint in his eye.

The wind blew Cloud towards a swaying forest. Between the forest and the meadow was the fence.

It was always there, but for some reason Cloud hadn't reckoned on it today. Her eyes darted in all directions, panicstricken. Left along the fence into a corner? Right along the fence into a corner? The wind had other plans.

Without so much as taking a breath, Cloud galloped headlong into the wire.

A ringing in her ears, a dull ache in her neck. The fence yielded. One of the posts connecting the wires fell over. The sky toppled over.

But the next moment Cloud was back on her hooves and she turned her head. Her pursuer was panting up the hill, just a few sheep's lengths away. But the fence now lay flat in front of her, and she jumped over it. Another jump to the edge of the forest. Another and she was in the forest.

Suddenly, the rushing in her ears had stopped. Cloud was shivering. She felt as if she didn't have a single strand of wool left on her body. Completely naked. Absolutely freezing. A little bird landed on a branch high above her, and snow dusted down.

Cloud shuddered and cautiously trotted on.

Soon the half-dark of the forest enveloped her like a barn, and the panting had gone.

A snap here, a snap there, but otherwise silence. Maybe it was all just a dream after all.

The other sheep had watched Cloud's flight with mixed feelings.

On the one hoof, they were happy that the vet hadn't caught Cloud. On the other, they were next. One of them. Then another. And another. All of them eventually. The vet would hold them so tightly that they wouldn't be able to breathe for fear. He would hurt their hooves and their ears. He would stab them with a needle and pour foul, bitter liquid into their mouths. The vet was the most dangerous creature they knew. Now he was standing at the edge of the forest, his arms hanging limply at his sides, staring intently after Cloud.

Rebecca swore. She pushed her red woolly hat out of her face and scowled at the sheep. 'Stay there!' she hissed.

As if the sheep had a choice! Rebecca had shut them all in the pen. The pen was nothing more than a narrow and actually very well-liked piece of meadow – the piece of meadow with the feed trough on it. But sometimes Rebecca shut a gate, and then they were trapped, crowded together, shoulder to shoulder, right down at the yard fence, where the most humans went by. Why Rebecca insisted on always doing things with the vet was a mystery to the sheep.

Now the shepherdess was running up the hill, infinitely more elegantly than the vet, if not quite as elegantly as Cloud. The vet said something and opened his arms wide, as if to catch Rebecca. She shook her head. The vet reached for her wrist, but Rebecca gave him the slip and disappeared into the forest. The vet looked down at the sheep, peeved.

The sheep acted naturally.

The vet acted naturally too, looking at his feet, at his hands, at the sky and back at the sheep. Anywhere but the forest.

Then something strange happened.

Rebecca stepped out from amongst the trees and slowly retreated from the edge of the forest, backwards, her hand stretched out in front of her, as if she were trying to fend something off – a cheeky sheep maybe, or – like so often on their travels – a car or an angry farmer with a chewed stem of leek in his hand.

The shepherdess's eyes darted from left to right as if there were something there.

As if something were coming.

But nothing came out of the forest.

* * *

A little later their meadow was teeming with humans. They had roared onto the yard in three cars and swarmed out: two through the yard gate to the stables and houses and barns where the humans lived; two out around the yard buildings and chateau wall, where nobody lived; and most of them straight onto the meadow, where the sheep lived.

They went along the fence, searched the hay barn up on the hillside, disappeared into the forest, appeared again, carried Things to the edge of the forest and back from the edge of the forest, spoke to Rebecca, systematically zigzagged across the meadow, muddying the snow and treading the meagre winter grass even flatter than it already was.

The sheep were impressed. They hadn't expected such a thorough search for Cloud. So, this is what happened when things went 'too far' for Rebecca: she called humans with caps for help – and dogs. Two dark sheepdogs with equally dark voices sniffed their way across the meadow.

The sheep shuddered, too frightened and too penned in to panic properly. The eeriest thing about the sheepdogs was that they weren't the slightest bit interested in the sheep. Not even the strange sheep who once again obviously hadn't trotted over to the feed trough like the rest of the flock, and was now standing under the old oak enviably free, muttering and scenting the air, seemingly completely disinterested in all the excitement.

The sheep wanted out. They attempted protest bleats to start with – a tried and tested recipe against the evils of the world. If you bleated for long enough, something happened, usually the right thing. But Rebecca, who usually made sure that the right thing happened, just stood there wide-eyed, her arms drooping at her sides.

The sheep bleated and bleated. Eventually they stopped bleating and fell menacingly silent. But that didn't get anybody's attention either.

'That's it,' Maude said after a spell of fruitless silence. 'Let's run away!'

That plan appealed to the sheep. Rebecca would soon see how ridiculous a shepherdess looked without any sheep!

'But how?' Lane asked.

'Mopple should play dead again!' Heather bleated.

Heather liked it when things happened.

'Why does it always have to be me?' Mopple muttered, but they had already explained it to him many times before: Mopple was the biggest and fattest sheep in the flock. Unmissable and impressive when he lay on the ground with all four legs in the air.

It had already worked a few times before. The first time was when the apples in the orchard were ripe, and then once again during the hay harvest. Mopple lay lifelessly on the ground, and Rebecca rushed over to them in the meadow, horrified. The shock meant that she didn't close the gate properly behind her. The third time, Rebecca had grown suspicious and called the vet, especially for Mopple. All the same: playing dead was a tried and tested method of getting on the other side of fences.

Mopple slumped into the snow sighing, then thrashed his legs and died. The other sheep made a bit of space around him so that he could be seen, bleated dramatically and peered over at Rebecca out of the corner of their eyes. But Rebecca was sitting on the steps of the caravan wrapped in a blanket speaking to one of the capmen. Mum appeared behind her and pressed a steaming cup of tea into her hand. It was the first time the sheep had seen her doing anything useful. That showed just how serious the situation was.

Mopple flailed his legs theatrically. 'So?' he groaned from the ground.

'Nothing,' said Cordelia.

'Nothing at all!' said Ramesses.

'She can't hear anything!' said Sir Ritchfield, shaking his head.

'She's not looking,' said Zora.

'Maybe we *did* disappear,' Cordelia whispered. 'Before, when the vet came into the pen with us, we all wished we could disappear. Maybe it's happened!'

'I didn't wish I could disappear!' Heather muttered. 'I wished the vet would disappear.'

The vet *had* disappeared, pale and stealthy, straight after Rebecca had stumbled down the hill and anxiously talked to Mum and her talking device.

'Maybe they're looking for us,' said Lane. 'All of us!'

Bit by bit the strange humans seemed to settle down slightly. They abandoned the meadow and the forest and gathered in front of the shepherd's caravan. Three men drove away in a car with two dogs. The rest stood around unenthusiastically drinking the tea Mum had brewed in the caravan. One of them threw up. The meadow gate was open.

Now that it had quietened down a little you could hear Tess barking inside the caravan.

The usual humans ventured into the yard as well, curious and ominous as young crows. You barely saw them coming, but every time the sheep peered through the fence towards the yard, a few more had appeared: first, ruddy-faced Madame Fronsac, who always had food in her pockets. She was a potential source of fodder, and the sheep looked at her expectantly. But the rosy-cheeked woman didn't seem to be in the mood for feeding them today. She just stood there as if she'd swallowed something the wrong way, wringing her big red hands. Beside her, Monsieur Fronsac was doing what he always did: watching. Maybe a bit more sadly than usual. Yves appeared through the yard gate, an axe over his shoulder. The sheep wrinkled their noses. Yves was far from being an aromatic delight; he prowled around near the meadow with his axe too much, and he always grinned when he saw Rebecca. Grinned like dogs sometimes do, with their teeth but not their eyes. Rebecca had once told them that he was a 'dogsbody,' but even the youngest lamb could see that although he might grin like a dog sometimes, he certainly didn't have a dog's body. Not in the slightest.

The goatherder shuffled along the courtyard wall.

The gardener appeared out of the orchard, blonde Hortense and her violet scent wafted out of the chateau. Finally, some of the rarer creatures appeared. Chateau creatures that the sheep otherwise only caught fleeting glimpses of beneath their upturned collars. The woman with the severely scraped back hair who had offered the sheep somewhere to stay. The children. The children were sent away at once.

The rest kept their distance from the capmen and honked away in hushed tones, speaking the unintelligible language of the Europeans. All apart from the goatherder. He just clutched his crook, his hands white despite the cold, white as snow. The sheep were interested in the goatherder – not personally, but for professional reasons, so to speak. With reassuring regularity, he turned up at the goat fence with a sack of fodder, and they had tried to befriend him despite the strong scent of goat. All in vain. Even crazier than his goats, the sheep supposed.

Rebecca was still sitting on the steps of the caravan, leafing manically through her big book. The big book transformed the honks of the Europeans into some sort of sense, but it didn't seem to be doing a particularly good job of it today.

'*Pourquoi?*' squawked Rebecca. '*Quand? Qui?*'

Hortense came through the meadow gate towards her, enveloping the shepherdess in a cloud of ridiculous floral scent, but she didn't have the answers either. Then Madame Fronsac broke away from the other chateau humans, too, and lumbered up the hill to the shepherd's caravan. Mum called her 'the Walrus,' and only Othello, who knew the ways of the world and the zoo, understood why. The Walrus nervously honked something that Rebecca didn't understand.

'She says you should take your sheep and get away from here!' Hortense explained. 'In your place, she would leave right away! *Tout de suite*!'

'You see! I told you so! That's what I've been saying all along!' Mum droned from the caravan.

Rebecca fell silent, and Hortense shrugged awkwardly. And then, subtly, something between the humans changed.

They became stiller, but not quieter. The chateau humans backed a little farther away from the meadow fence, almost imperceptibly; Rebecca absent-mindedly tucked a wisp of hair behind her ear; Mum positioned herself on the caravan steps, fluttering her eyelashes. Tess barked even more loudly. All because another car had driven into the yard, bigger and blacker than any of the others.

The Jackdaw got out of the car. The Jackdaw was something like the chateau humans' lead ram, and he didn't really look like a jackdaw, not as small or colourful, and obviously he didn't have a beak. But something about the way he moved, sharp and quick and precise, reminded the sheep of the young jackdaw that had been on their meadow a while back. The jackdaw on their meadow had had a drooping wing.

The Jackdaw from the chateau had a limp. Not much of one, and most humans probably hardly noticed it, but the sheep knew, and the Jackdaw himself knew too.

One of the capmen approached him and said something.

The Jackdaw nodded, then he carried on towards the shepherd's caravan and gently placed his hand on the Walrus's arm. All of a sudden, the Walrus had tears streaming down her cheeks and was led away by Hortense and Monsieur Fronsac.

The Jackdaw stepped towards the pen and glowered at the sheep. The sheep gazed back uneasily. Up to now they had never taken him particularly seriously because of his limp, which presumably meant he was too slow to be a danger to them, but now they were penned in. The big gaunt face of the Jackdaw hovered over them, so closely that there was no escaping his eyes. Two hands casually nosed their way over the top slat of the fence, blackened by gloves, long and skinny like bird's claws, even in the gloves. The sheep were afraid one of those nimble hands was going to reach out and grab their wool, a hand that could not be avoided here in the pen.

The hand didn't come for them, but the Jackdaw's eyes followed them, a look of cold, piercing interest and something like annoyance – as if the sheep were to blame for something. Every so often his gaze flitted over to Rebecca, and the sheep disliked what happened to his eyes then even more. They became deep and narrow, dark and sparkling, like wells.

'Attack!' one of them bleated.

'Fodder!' bleated Mopple the Whale, who had got back on his hooves under the beady gaze of the Jackdaw.

Soon all of the sheep were bleating for fodder. Rebecca would have to open the gate. Fodder was the right strategy now. Fodder was usually the right strategy.

But Rebecca still wasn't moving.

'Well,' said one of the sheep. 'We're in a trap, huh?' They were in a trap! Mopple and Maude bleated in alarm.

Ritchfield coughed, and Ramesses sat on his haunches in shock.

'It's not really a trap,' Zora said soothingly. 'It's just a pen. Rebecca lured us in here. She'll let us out again. She has to. It's in the will.'

There were lots of important things in the will. Including that Rebecca had to feed them and read aloud to them. That none of the sheep were to be sold or 'slaughtered' – whatever that meant. The vet was in the will too. More's the pity. The sheep could have done without the vet.

'That's not a sheep!' Sir Ritchfield, the old lead ram, muttered. Nobody paid him any heed.

'Maybe we ought to hide,' Cordelia said.

'Where?' asked Heather sharply. 'In the feed trough, maybe?'

'That's not a sheep!' Sir Ritchfield repeated with conviction. The old lead ram was wedged between Lane and Zora, staring into the feed trough. And standing in the feed trough, staring back at him, was a little black goat.

The sheep gave a start. A goat in their midst! And nobody had picked up the scent!

'Attack!' the goat bleated, jumping onto Mopple's broad back. Mopple got the hiccups.

The others were shocked. It was a widely known fact that goats climbed trees. But climbing on sheep as well? It fit the mould, anyway. They tried to ignore the goat. That was easier said than done. The goat hopped from Mopple's back onto Maude, and then onto Lane. She jumped over Ramesses, cautiously arcing over Othello's black back and finally landed on Sir Ritchfield.

'Not a sheep . . .' Sir Ritchfield bleated. The goat lowered her head and whispered something in his ear.

'Pigs?' Sir Ritchfield bellowed anxiously. The goat sniggered.

Heather couldn't stand it any longer. 'What do you want?' she asked the goat. Ritchfield sneezed.

'Bless you,' said the goat. 'The vet.'

She sniffled delicately. 'I've got the sniffles. He's infected me!' The goat thumped Ritchfield's grey back with her front hooves. Ritchfield sneezed for a second time.

The sheep cast all-knowing glances at one another. Completely mad!

'The vet's gone,' said Mopple the Whale in an attempt to get rid of the goat.

'But he's coming back!' the goat said triumphantly. Now, unfortunately, that sounded almost too rational. The sheep fell silent and listened to Mopple's hiccups.

When the vet came back, they would be long gone. Somehow. Somewhere. Maybe in the shade of the old oak. Or underneath the shepherd's caravan. Or behind the feed store. Or – ideally – *in* the feed store. Or at a pinch, in the feed trough. Anywhere. Just not here in the pen.

'You don't really want the vet, do you?' Mopple gurgled after a while.

'No,' admitted the goat. 'I want adventure!'

'Here?' Mopple hiccupped agitatedly. 'On Sir Ritchfield?'

'Right here,' the goat confirmed.

Mopple decided to keep his distance from Sir Ritchfield in future. Hiccups were bad enough. You couldn't graze properly with the hiccups. Adventure was all he needed!

'I want to warn you,' said the goat. 'I'm going to warn you!'

'Too late!' Ramesses groaned. 'The vet has been and gone!' The goat shook her head.

'Snow?' Maude asked. 'More snow?'

'That too,' the goat conceded. 'Listen up!'

The sheep were aghast. Rebecca had forgotten all about them, their meadow was overrun with capmen, and a little black goat was standing on Sir Ritchfield giving a speech. About secrets, danger and adventure. About the moon, which – the goat claimed – was a giant goat's cheese. And most importantly, about a were-creature. A shapeshifter. A wolf that wasn't really a wolf. The little goat called him Garou. In short – it was about a whole host of things that the sheep had absolutely no interest in. They tried not to listen as best they could.

'I think we should work together!' the goat said in closing. 'The others think I'm mad,' she added proudly.

'Pigs!' Sir Ritchfield bleated, shaking his head.

'We think you're mad too,' Heather said.

'Superb,' said the goat. She hopped off Sir Ritchfield's back and landed in the far-too-empty feed trough. She started trotting back and forth in it, back and forth, to and fro, to and fro. The sheep gazed at her in fascination. She was so small. Her coat so shiny and black – even blacker than Othello. Her eyes were so yellow and strange, her little horns so sharp. And her scent!

The goat trotted and trotted, muttering things like 'they don't believe you,' 'not yet,' 'what did you expect of sheep?,' 'do you think we should?' and 'okay, then.' The sheep felt a bit dizzy from all the toing and froing.

Suddenly the black goat stood still.

'Today is your lucky day!' she announced. 'You get three wishes!'

'Concentrated feed,' Mopple bleated instantly. '*Hick!*'

'For the humans to leave,' said Maude.

'For Rebecca to let us out of the pen!' Heather bleated.

'For Cloud to come back!' Cordelia said – a bit too late. Shortly afterwards the last of the cap-men tipped the remains of their cold tea into the snow and returned to their cars.

'*Revenons à nos moutons!*' somebody said, and Rebecca suddenly looked over towards the sheep. Finally! Then they were fed after all, by a rather preoccupied shepherdess, who tipped in six buckets of fodder instead of the usual five, one of them straight onto the goat.

While they were all stuffing themselves, Rebecca went along the fence with the goatherder and checked the posts.

Then the gate creaked open and the sheep flocked back onto their bruised meadow.

Without Cloud.

The winter lamb hadn't trotted straight out of the pen like the others. He was still standing beside the little goat at the feed trough. They were about the same size.

'How did you do that?' the winter lamb asked.

'What?' the goat asked innocently.

'The thing with the wishes,' said the winter lamb.

'A goat spell,' said the goat.

'Really?' asked the winter lamb.

'No,' said the goat. 'Sheep only ever wish for what's going to happen anyway. Goats, however . . .' She looked at the winter lamb with her yellow goat's eyes. 'If you want something to happen, then you have to make it happen.'

'So, what would you wish for?' the winter lamb asked.

'A lot,' said the goat. 'I'd wish for a place where sweetwort always grows, and for the longest goat beard in the world and for a rotten apple to fall on Megara's head one day. But right now' – she cocked her head on one side, thinking – 'right now I'd wish for someone to come and gobble up the moon. The whole thing.'

She looked towards the gate where the shadow of the chateau was proceeding to climb over the fence towards the meadow, as it did every afternoon.

'I've got to go,' she said. 'I'm not here if you need me!'

The winter lamb would have liked to ask her a few things – above all her name.

That evening the sheep chewed on their winter grass even more listlessly than usual. Even Mopple. Everything smelled wrong. Too much like dog paws, powder and gumboots. Of human sweat and cigarette smoke. And of something else that the sheep couldn't make any sense of.

And far too little of Cloud.

'No sheep may leave the flock!' bleated Sir Ritchfield in distress.

'Unless that sheep comes back again!' said Cordelia.

'Why doesn't Cloud come back?' Heather asked.

'I wouldn't come back to a meadow full of dogs and caps either,' said Miss Maple. 'She's probably hiding somewhere. And maybe it's not that simple to find your way out of a forest like that. Too many trees.'

They decided to bleat into the forest as loudly as they could. Maybe Cloud would come out then!

'Cloud!' they bleated in chorus. 'The vet's gone! We're still here! Come back!'

But the forest kept its silence.

3

HEATHER CRAVES SOME WOOLPOWER

'She's lovely and woolly!' said Zora approvingly. 'For a human,' said Maude.

The others nodded. The shepherdess was obviously trying to set an example as far as woolliness was concerned. Maybe she was also trying to replace Cloud. She obviously wasn't woolly enough for that by a long shot.

Rebecca was sitting on the steps of the caravan, wrapped in a blanket, looking unusually large wearing two coats, one over the other, and underneath – the sheep could smell it – the beloved woolly jumper. She had the stalk-eyed contraption hanging round her neck. The stalk-eyed contraption was normally only deployed on bright days when long-legged birds stalked across the meadow, herons or storks with black beaks and once, in the autumn, a couple of cranes in a celebratory mood. Then Rebecca held the stalk-eyed contraption up to her eyes and claimed it made the birds bigger. It was clearly a figment of her imagination; the sheep could see perfectly well that the birds hadn't got bigger in the slightest, but the shepherdess seemed to be enjoying herself at any rate.

But today, with her blanket and the cold and the dusk, it didn't look like she was enjoying herself at all.

'I think you're overreacting!' Mum droned, passing Rebecca a Thermos from the caravan. 'Come in! You can't spend the whole night sitting out there!'

Rebecca took the flask from her.

'I know. But I'll sit here for as long as I can. I have to watch over them, at least for a little bit. You should have seen it, Mum! At first, I didn't even know what it was, if it was a human or an animal . . .'

'A deer,' Mum said. 'These things happen.'

'These things don't just happen!' said Rebecca, pouring herself some tea. 'Not like that! It was so messed up, so . . . Who would do such a thing? A dog? A fox? Hardly!'

Rebecca was shivering. 'Look how quickly they got here! Four cars, an inspector and dogs, the whole shebang. I mean who does all of that for a deer? It was as if . . . well, it was as if they'd been expecting it, you know.'

'Well, there's nothing else going on around here,' said Mum. 'I'm going to shut the door, okay? The cold's coming in.'

Rebecca nodded and sipped her tea. Then she grabbed the stalk-eyed contraption.

The sheep looked around for long-legged dusk birds, but there were none to be seen. None at all. Not even a chicken. In fact, Rebecca wasn't even looking at the meadow. Rebecca was looking up at the forest.

'Hopefully it doesn't get any bigger!' said Heather.

The sheep peered critically over at the trees. The forest was big enough!

'I think she's looking for Cloud!' said Ramesses. 'She's looking through the stalk-eyed contraption to make Cloud bigger! And when she's big enough, we'll be able to see her over the trees!'

It wouldn't have been such a bad plan, if the stalk-eyed Thing had worked, that is.

Miss Maple didn't say a word. She had the feeling that Rebecca wasn't looking for Cloud. Rebecca was looking for something else – something that mustn't, under any circumstances, get any bigger.

Rebecca sat on the steps of the shepherd's caravan drinking tea, making stalk-eyes, getting bluer and bluer with the advancing dusk. The sheep were grazing. The forest whispered mockingly. The chateau was silent. The door leading to the tower opened, and somebody came out, and because he had unusually light hair, the sheep could easily recognise him in the twilight – Eric. Eric didn't live in the chateau, but he often came by, in an old van, and put goat's cheese in the tower. Or took it out of the tower. The sheep liked the fact that he never did anything loud. They liked the goat's cheese less. Now Eric was just standing at the foot of the chateau looking over at the forest with a confused expression on his face. Rebecca waved. Eric waved back. Then he got into his old van and drove off.

After some considerable time, the caravan door opened again. A long strip of golden light fell across the meadow, right over Mopple the Whale. Mopple got the hiccups again. 'I've finished working now!' said Mum. 'Come in, darling, or you'll catch your death!'

Rebecca sighed. 'Good God, I really hope I find her! A

runaway sheep is bad enough, but now this! What if . . .'

'Sitting around out there isn't going to help. Come inside! Have a cuppa! If you want, we can read the cards . . .'

'Mum!'

'Well, when he comes tomorrow, just ask the v—' Rebecca leapt up from the steps knocking over her tea, but she didn't make it this time.

'. . . the vet,' Mum said. 'Ask him how best to . . .'

'The sheep didn't hear any more after that. The vet was coming back! With his sharp needle! Tomorrow! Ramesses was the first to lose his nerve, and galloped across the meadow in big panicked leaps. Maude and Lane darted after him, bleating. Soon the whole flock was running up and down the fence bleating their hearts out. They didn't really believe that running would help stave off the vet, but it felt good.

Miss Maple was the only one who had stayed by the caravan, and she was trying not to think about the vet. Rebecca and Mum were talking about something else. They were talking about it, and not talking about it at the same time.

The tea had melted a black hole in the snow.

Rebecca crossed her arms. 'Great!' she said. 'What do you think it's going to take to get them back into the pen again tomorrow?'

It would take fodder, thought Maple. Fodder and patience. Nobody could resist fodder. Except . . .

'He's a bit of an oddball,' said Mum, in an attempt to distract Rebecca from the bleating sheep.

'The vet?' Rebecca shrugged. 'It is a bit strange that he didn't take a look at it,' she muttered then. 'I mean, as a vet . . . He didn't even look at it! Not once. As if . . . as if he wasn't even curious. And he tried to stop me from looking.'

'He just didn't want you to see it.' Mum sighed.

'He didn't want anybody to see it. He didn't want me to call the police. As if something like that could be covered up. I would have found it the next time I checked the fence anyway.'

Rebecca hopped from one leg to the other. Tess leapt out of the caravan and danced around Rebecca. Danced and barked.

'There!' Mum pointed at Tess. 'She ought to keep a look out! I mean, what have you got her for?'

Rebecca stopped hopping.

'That's true,' she said. 'Tess would bark.' She frowned, her face blue in the twilight.

'She didn't bark!' she said then. 'It must have happened yesterday or this morning, and she didn't bark!'

'Because it wasn't on the meadow,' said Mum.

'It almost was!' said Rebecca. She rolled up her blanket and went up the caravan steps.

'Good night!' she said to the sheep, who were slowly settling down again. The golden strip of light crept back into the shepherd's caravan, and the door slammed shut.

The sheep stood in the snow, aghast. Good night! Easy for her to say! She wasn't going to be lured into the pen and vetted by the vet!

'I'm just not going to go into the pen!' Heather suddenly announced.

'But the feed bucket is in there,' said Mopple despondently.

'We just need woolpower!' said Heather. She'd heard Mum say it. With a bit of woolpower, anything was possible! Some of the sheep fluffed themselves up in an effort to give their wool a bit more power. Others looked sheepishly down at the ground. Cloud had been the sheep in the flock with the most woolpower – and the vet had chased her into the forest.

'We don't just need woolpower!' Maple said suddenly. 'We need a plan!'

'I'm certain that's a sheep!' declared Sir Ritchfield with utter conviction.

The strange ram was asleep, leaning on the fence near the apple orchard looking far from sheepy in the late evening light, more like a pile of leaves and moss, but Ritchfield seemed very sure of himself.

The sheep had surrounded the unshorn stranger on three sides and were trying to get him to talk. The unshorn ram might be shaggy, misshapen and matted, but he was undoubtedly the most strong-wooled sheep they had ever come across. And he knew something important: he knew how to not go into the pen, even when the feed bucket was being shaken and the tangy aroma of concentrated feed was wafting over the meadow. They just had to tease it out of him.

But how?

Up to now the sheep had always avoided speaking to the strange ram. The fact that he didn't seem to be able to see or hear them put them on edge. What if they accidentally bumped into him? Maybe they would pass through him as if through mist. The sheep found the whole thing creepy.

Othello cleared his throat. Nothing.

The strange ram had briefly glanced up when they had all turned up en masse where he was sleeping, like you'd glance at a gust of wind or a far-off sound. But now he was standing there, his eyes half shut again, relaxed and sleepy. It wasn't normal. It made the sheep doubt whether *they* were there.

'Hello, ram!' said Cordelia bravely. 'Welcome to our meadow!' It was rather late for a welcome greeting – but better late than never.

The unshorn ram didn't even move his ears.

'We don't want to disturb you!' Lane explained. 'We just want to be more strong-wooled!'

The ram's eyes shut a bit more. He muttered softly, not to them – to someone else, someone he seemed to know well. The sheep looked around – there was nobody there. Of course there wasn't.

'Ram!' Ramesses bleated. 'We don't want to go into the pen!'

The ram's eyes were shut. He was humming quietly to himself.

'I don't think he can speak,' said Cordelia.

'He can mutter,' said Heather. 'If he muttered a bit more loudly, he'd be able to speak!'

They decided to leave the rest of the discussion to Sir Ritchfield. Because he was hard of hearing, Ritchfield set a good example when it came to speaking loudly.

It took a while for Sir Ritchfield to cotton on.

But then, standing in front of the strange ram, he straightened up to his full lead-ram height, raised his imposing horns into the night sky and scraped in the snow with his hooves. The others watched him deferentially.

'Ram!' thundered Sir Ritchfield, with dignity. 'Some things are there. And some things are not there. And some things are only there sometimes. And it's not always easy to tell what's there and when it's there. Melmoth was there, and now he's not, and in some way, he is still there, and sometimes . . .'

Ritchfield broke off, staring thoughtfully at the pattern his hooves had made in the snow, and thought about Melmoth the wandering sheep, his twin, his brother, who had just disappeared over the cliff back then. All of a sudden, the strange ram's eyes were open, and for the first time the flock got the feeling that he noticed them.

'Tourbe,' he said. 'Farouche. Grignotte. Boiterie. Sourde. Tache? Aube?'

The sheep didn't understand a word of what he was saying.

'Aube?' asked the strange ram. 'Pâquerette? Gris? Marcassin? Pré-de-Puce?'

'He's mad,' said Heather.

Little wonder! All that wool all over him was enough to make a sheep go mad.

'Names,' muttered the winter lamb suddenly. 'They're all names.' The winter lamb himself didn't have a name. The sheep were only given names once they had lived through their first winter.

'Is that you?' he asked. 'Farouche Grignotte Gris Marcassin Tache? That many names?'

'Aube!' The unshorn ram nodded sadly.

The winter lamb looked at him respectfully. He would have liked to have said his name, if only he had one.

'I'm just me,' he said quietly.

'You're not them,' the strange ram said in surprise. 'But almost! Just as white. They were so white, you know. Aube, Farouche. Even Gris. Before. It's good that you're all white too.'

'Ehem,' Othello grumbled.

'Where are you from?' the unshorn ram whispered. 'Why?' His voice sounded like leaves in the wind. Thin and gentle and far, far away. 'Are you . . . back then? Before?'

'We're here,' said Othello. 'Now. That's the point.'

'You've got to get out of here!' the strange ram bleated agitatedly. 'Scatter! Every sheep for himself. Hide under trees. Hide in the shadows. And *if you see him, don't move.* No matter what you see! No matter what! Look away! If you run, you're his!'

'He can't mean the vet!' said Heather.

'This meadow is our pasture,' said Othello quietly. 'We're not running. We just don't want to go into the pen!'

The other sheep had backed away a bit. Now that the strange ram had become so agitated, he had started to emit a strong and not particularly sheepy scent.

'Where are the others?' he asked. 'Farouche? Aube? Pâquerette?'

'I don't think he's eating enough!' said Mopple quietly. And hiccupped.

Mopple the Whale ate too much.

'Where are the others?' Cordelia asked gently.

Heather sneezed. A snowflake had landed right on her nose. A second went in her eye like a cold teardrop. Snow again! The birds sat silently in the branches, fat, fluffy and dark like overgrown catkins.

The snow completely threw the strange ram. His eyes rolled. His entire moss-covered body began to shake.

'Hide, Farouche!' he bleated. 'He's coming! He's coming out of the wardrobe! Gris! Aube! Hide! Hide! *Quick*!'

He shoved past the other sheep and rushed along the fence at a strange, lumbering gallop, zigzagging across the meadow to the gorse bushes at the goat fence. He stopped there.

The other sheep's eyes darted in all directions, but there was nothing there. Just snow.

'Well, his nerves aren't very good,' said Zora finally.

'No,' said Othello.

'That's a brave ram. A very brave ram indeed.' Othello was a master of the duel. He knew what bravery was. Not the opposite of fear in any case. 'Something terrible happened to his flock. To Farouche and Aube and Pâquerette. And I think it happened here.'

'I think that was a . . . sheep!' Sir Ritchfield bleated suddenly.

The others sighed. Ritchfield was no spring lamb.

The sheep looked at one another. In their tales, Jack the Lad, who had got away unshorn, was a heroic figure, a legendary sheep who gave shepherds the runaround, escaped their shears by a hair's breadth and trotted into the sunset, his wool blowing wildly in the wind. A hero of woolpower. The unshorn ram, however, couldn't even explain to them how not to go into the pen.

'Hay barn!' said Othello, and the sheep trotted mutely over to the barn.

Only Mopple continued to just stand around in the snow, experiencing a rare loss of appetite. Mopple had a phenomenal memory, as big and fat as he was. Once he had memorised something, he never forgot it. *Hick.* Whether he wanted to or not. Not that he *believed* what the goat and the strange sheep had told them. *Hick.* It wasn't that. Only . . . it had all been crazy in the same way. It hung together like two plants coming from the same root. Somewhere deep down. You could taste it. *Hick.* And now it was sitting heavily in his stomach like . . . like . . . like bloat-grass. Sitting there fermenting. And the goat had granted their wishes. She couldn't be all bad. *Hick. Hick.* If only it hadn't been the wrong wishes . . . and as for these blasted hiccups!

He would have liked to speak to Miss Maple about it. Not

about the hiccups, about the rest of it. Miss Maple was so clever that it sometimes made you feel dizzy. Or Othello? Preferably Zora. Mopple liked speaking to Zora about things. She had horns and a pretty black face, and she was interested in the abyss – and roots. Mopple decided to trot over to her as soon as he had got rid of these idiotic hiccups.

There was in fact no hay in the hay barn, just yellow straw on the ground and – high above their heads – a window without any glass, through which snowflakes fluttered, but back in Ireland they'd slept in a hay barn and Europe shouldn't change that.

The barn stood in the middle of the young night, and the sheep stood in the barn, breathing. Zora turned her head to the window and looked at the stars. Sir Ritchfield coughed. Othello's front hoof scraped in the straw. Maude scented the air. The winter lamb scratched himself on a post.

Nobody was asleep. Nobody wanted to be chased across the meadow by the vet tomorrow. The night seemed colder without Cloud.

'Maybe we ought to hide after all?' Cordelia said thoughtfully.

They liked that plan.

'But where?' asked Maude.

'Behind the old oak!' Ramesses bleated excitedly.

The old oak was the only noteworthy tree on their meadow, and its location was practical, with three escape routes and the goat fence as rear cover. The sheep trotted off to try it out. But no matter how tightly they pressed together, the old oak's boot wasn't a particularly convincing hiding place, even in the dark.

'We could hide *on* the old oak!' Ramesses wasn't giving up that easily.

The others rolled their eyes.

They tried hiding behind the wardrobe – catastrophic! – behind the hay barn up on the hill – better! – behind the shepherd's caravan – meh – and finally behind the feed store. It smelled good behind the feed store, but they didn't feel particularly well-hidden. The problem was, every time they were hidden on one side, they were exposed on three sides. Maude claimed the best way to hide yourself was to scrunch your eyes tightly shut. They tried that too, but no matter how tightly Maude scrunched her eyes shut – the others could still see her clear as day.

'I've got it!' bleated Mopple the Whale, who had rejoined the flock. 'Let's hide *in* the feed store!'

'What if Rebecca comes into the feed store?' asked Lane. 'Then we'll be trapped!'

'She won't come into the feed store!' said Mopple. 'She only goes into the feed store to feed us. And if we're not there, she can't feed us!'

It was a splendid plan. There was only one catch: the catch on the door of the feed store. There was a lock on the catch. A lock that you could only open by counting. The sheep weren't particularly good at counting, but it was worth a try.

'Three!' said Heather. 'Eight!' snorted Othello.

'Four!' bleated the winter lamb.

The lock on the feed store didn't seem very impressed with their counting skills.

'Maybe we need to count *something*?' said Maude. 'Like . . . legs!' She looked down at her hooves. 'One . . . two. Two!' Maude looked proudly at the others.

'Two?' asked Lane. 'Just two?'

'It's got to be more than that!' said Cordelia.

'I can only see two,' said Maude stubbornly.

Miss Maple looked critically at Maude. 'Four,' she said then.

The lock didn't budge.

The sheep counted Sir Ritchfield's ears (two!) and Othello's horns (four!), they counted the knots in the door of the feed store (three!), the leaves on the old oak (three!) and the snowflakes fluttering from the sky (at least seven!).

But not a peep from the number-lock.

The door of the shepherd's caravan opened and Rebecca looked over at them suspiciously. The sheep made out they were only interested in the oatcake moon and Rebecca shut the door again.

The sheep trotted back to the hay barn, frustrated. There was no escape. The vet would turn up unbidden on their dream meadows brandishing some hoof shears, and tomorrow he would drag them out of the pen, one by one, apart from Maude, who had already had her turn with the vet before Cloud this morning.

'What if we don't hear the feed bucket?' said Othello suddenly.

'Ritchfield maybe . . .' muttered Heather.

'Nobody!' said Othello. 'The vet comes – we go. It's as simple as that.'

'But . . .' Zora bleated. 'This meadow is our pasture! We're not running! You said so yourself!'

'We're not running,' said Othello. 'We're just going away!'

The sheep looked at their lead ram with respect. 'What about Rebecca?' asked Lane.

'Rebecca will follow us,' said Othello.

That's how it had worked up to now: the sheep had trotted off in the direction that smelled the most appetising and Rebecca had followed, her face crimson.

'We'll wait until dawn. Then Rebecca can follow our tracks in the snow. We'll go into the forest and look for Cloud. And when we've found her, we'll carry on.'

The sheep fell silent. It was a bold plan. But it wasn't as attractive as the one involving the feed store.

'Where are we going then?' Cordelia enquired hesitantly.

'Away,' Othello responded.

'What if it snows?' asked Ramesses.

'It won't snow,' said Othello.

'What if we don't find Cloud?' asked Lane.

'We're going to find Cloud,' said Othello decisively.

The sheep looked impressed. Othello had thought of everything.

'And how do we get into the forest?' the winter lamb asked all of a sudden. 'Rebecca has only just checked the fence.'

'I'm not sure yet,' said Othello quietly. 'But we're getting into the forest.'

Mopple snored. Heather sneezed. Ritchfield muttered softly. A few lonely snowflakes danced down onto the sheep through the glassless barn window.

'I know how we could get into the forest,' bleated the winter lamb.

'I thought so,' said Othello. Nobody had less faith in fences than the winter lamb.

'We can't get through the wire fence,' said the winter lamb, his eyes gleaming. 'But there's a loose slat in the wooden fence between us and the goats. I saw the black goat slip through. And nobody checked the fence on the goats' meadow!'

Mopple fell silent. Ritchfield snored. It had stopped snowing outside.

4

SIR RITCHFIELD LEADS THE CHARGE

A half-moon was shining. Blue snow crunched. The air was as cold as the shearing blades. A little flock of ever-determined sheep cautiously drew closer to the nocturnal goat fence.

Othello the lead ram, Miss Maple because she was clever, Mopple because he had a good memory, Sir Ritchfield because he thought it was going to be an outing, and the winter lamb – nobody knew why. What if the goats were all asleep? But somehow, they couldn't imagine catching the goats doing something as normal as sleeping.

And sure enough, in the middle of the night, near the fence, stood three goats with curved horns, narrow faces and long, skinny necks. One dark goat, one grey goat and a blue goat with a black ear – at least that's what it looked like in the blue light of the moon. Standing there as if they had been waiting for the sheep to arrive.

Standing silently. Their eyes twinkling.

Time was of the essence. They had to get off the meadow before the humans awoke. Especially Rebecca. And morning was close. Not yet visible, but close.

One of the goats burped.

'I'm Maple,' said Maple. She wanted to tackle things diplomatically.

'Yes, and?' bleated the dark goat.

'I'm Mopple,' said Mopple. 'And that's Sir Ritchfield.'

'He's old and you're fat,' said the grey goat.

'I am not fat!' bleated Sir Ritchfield. The outing wasn't exactly going as he'd have liked.

'You're just imagining it!' bleated a goat with only one horn a little way away. The other goats didn't look over.

Othello snorted impatiently.

The goats snorted too. And sniggered.

'I'm Pan,' said the dark goat then. 'And the other two are Pan too.'

'I'm Pan too!' bleated a fourth, grey-blue mottled goat, who had curiously come closer.

The sheep stood mutely, marvelling.

'You want something,' said the grey goat. 'Sheep are always wanting.'

'Sheep are always wanting,' groaned the other three in chorus.

'Even at night!' added the blue goat with the black ear reproachfully.

'But we're not wanting,' continued the grey goat. 'We're Pan and we're not speaking to you. We only speak to ourselves. To nobody but ourselves.'

The sheep cast meaningful glances at one another. Completely round the bend! They had known all along!

'I'm Nobody,' said the winter lamb suddenly.

The goats peered through the fence with interest. 'Really?' asked the grey goat.

'Really!' bleated the mottled goat.

'Really!' said the blue goat with the black ear.

'We'll speak to Nobody,' said the dark goat patronisingly.

All four of them looked expectantly at the winter lamb.

The winter lamb thought for a moment.

'What if a sheep were to come onto your meadow?' he asked then.

'Scandalous!' bleated the grey goat. 'Outrageous!' breathed the grey-blue goat. 'There'd be a riot!' said the dark goat.

'*Vive la révolution!*' bleated a second grey goat that had appeared beside the four others.

'What about if it didn't eat anything?' asked the winter lamb. 'Not a single blade of grass? If it just went straight across your meadow into the forest?'

A cloud drifted in front of the moon and it went very dark. 'Into the forest?' asked the dark grey-blue goat.

'Why?' said the dark-grey goat.

'What for?' said the deep-blue goat with the black ear. 'Are you mad?' The five goats looked at the sheep with newfound respect.

A black-grey goat trotted closer, curiously.

'That's Pan,' the deep-blue goat with the black ear explained politely.

'That's not a sheep,' muttered Sir Ritchfield.

'That's a completely different matter,' said the dark-grey goat. 'It's all right, as long as it doesn't eat anything.'

'Nothing at all?' blurted out Mopple. The goats didn't even look at him.

'And what if it was several sheep?' asked the winter lamb. 'Like . . . all of them?'

The moon crept out from behind the cloud and the goats got paler.

'We won't eat a thing. We'll just cross your meadow tomorrow morning. No scandal. No riot. No *révolution*. What do you want in return?' asked the winter lamb.

'Us?' the grey goat said innocently.

'Us?' asked the dark goat.

'We're not wanting,' said the grey-blue goat with dignity.

'Goats are never wanting!' bleated the blue goat with the black ear.

'What do you want in return?' the winter lamb stubbornly repeated.

'Nothing!' said the dark goat. 'Nothing at all!' bleated the grey goat.

'Of course not!' said the blue goat with the black ear. 'Except . . .'

'. . . maybe . . .'

'. . . a . . .'

'. . . teensy-weensy . . .'

'. . . little something!'

The goats gambolled about excitedly. 'Done!' said the winter lamb.

'He might just make it,' Zora said in surprise.

'As long as he doesn't forget where he's going.' Mopple the Whale sighed.

'Goats,' muttered Othello.

'It's exciting though!' said the winter lamb, leaping in the air with all four legs like . . . well, like a goat!

The whole flock had gathered at the goat fence and was staring through the slats, mesmerised. The edges of the sky were already pale and Sir Ritchfield, the old lead ram, was carefully, but purposefully trotting across the goats' meadow towards the split tree, while his opponent, the blind nanny goat, zigzagged back and forth, more quickly admittedly, but without any sense of direction.

'Ritchfield! Ritchfield!' the sheep bleated.

It was actually quite simple. Simple, but mad. A race between the elders. If Ritchfield got to the split tree before the nanny goat, the sheep could cross the meadow without the goats raising the alarm. If not . . .

'Ritchfield! Ritchfield! Ritchfield!'

They had drummed it into the old ram that he had to get to the tree. Nothing more and nothing less. And they hoped beyond hope that he wouldn't forget his only task on the way.

The blind goat had become entangled in a gorse bush and was cautiously reversing.

'Ritchfield! Ritchfield!' the sheep bleated excitedly. Getting louder and louder.

Ritchfield stopped and listened. The sheep fell silent, aghast.

Ritchfield looked confused for a moment. Then he shook his head and trotted on towards the tree.

'Phew!' said Mopple.

'Ritchfield!' bleated Heather enthusiastically. The others shot her angry glances.

But the goat had freed herself from the thicket and was rushing across the meadow again. Still, if Ritchfield carried on as he was, she had no chance.

'Ritchfield! Ritchfield!' bleated the goats. They craned their necks, hopped in the air and were having a whale of a time.

'Ritchfield!'

Ritchfield stopped and listened again. 'Ritchfield!'

'That's mean!' bleated Ramesses.

'Goats,' groaned Zora.

Ritchfield waggled his ears and trotted on. Still making his way towards the tree.

'Unbelievable!' said Mopple. Ritchfield was going to do it! Just a few more sheep's lengths!

Suddenly, a stout young goat was standing between Ritchfield and the tree. A goat with long, sharp horns.

'The watchword?' asked the goat. 'The password? The code?'

But deaf Sir Ritchfield trotted on regardless.

'Stop!' the sharp-horned goat bleated in horror. Barely a nose away from the goat, Ritchfield came to a sudden halt and shook his head. He took a step to the left. The goat took a step to the right. Ritchfield took a step to the right. The goat to the left.

'Not a sheep!' Sir Ritchfield said, shaking his head.

'The watchword!' insisted the goat.

'The code! The code!' said the other goats, smirking.

'What?' Sir Ritchfield bellowed.

The blind nanny goat at the other end of the meadow stood still, tilted her head and listened. Then she made a run for it. Straight towards the tree.

'That's it.' Mopple the Whale sighed.

'PASSWORD!' the young goat bleated loudly, facing up to Ritchfield. But not loudly enough.

Ritchfield tittered bashfully. 'What's that you say? A duel? Why not? Why not indeed!'

Next moment the old grey ram was rearing up. His eyes were

gleaming, his hooves were dancing, and his horns were raised like mighty branches in the frozen air. Ritchfield snorted. The other sheep looked on in awe. Now they remembered why Ritchfield had been their lead ram for all those years.

Shrouded in clouds of breath, Ritchfield went backwards.

A single step at first. Then a second. Then a third. 'Ritchfield! Ritchfield!' the sheep bleated enthusiastically.

The stupid tree was forgotten. Ritchfield would show the goats what a fair duel looked like!

Ritchfield lowered his powerful horns and galloped off. The goat looked surprised. Then she reared up goat-style on her hind legs. Her sharp goat horns gleamed like ice. The sheep held their breath, but Ritchfield thundered on unperturbed. Next moment the goat had leapt aside and Ritchfield crashed full-force into the boot of the old split tree. A full, round thud resounded across the meadow. The blind nanny goat stood still and bleated.

'That's that!' said Othello contentedly.

There was no more time to waste. The sky was getting paler and more transparent, smoke was in the air and soon Rebecca's yellow caravan window would begin to glow and Mum would appear on the steps, smoking. One after another, the sheep squeezed themselves through the gap in the goat fence. There was a bit of commotion when Mopple the Whale got stuck, almost blocking their escape route, but Zora bit the rotund ram's rear and Mopple shot through the hole like some kind of overweight grasshopper.

Maude was the only one who didn't want to go. 'I'm not going across the goats' meadow!' she bleated. 'It stinks! And what's the point anyway? The vet already got me! What's the worst that could happen?'

The sheep didn't really know what might happen to Maude, but they didn't like the idea of just leaving her behind.

'But we're all going!' Heather bleated.

'Not any more!' Maude gave the goat fence her back.

But later when Othello did a round of the flock to make sure they were all there, Maude was standing on the goat side of the fence, a sheepish look on her face.

'What about him?' Zora asked looking over towards the gorse bushes. The strange ram had closed his eyes again and seemed to be sleeping. 'He's a sheep too!'

'But he knows how to not go into the pen,' said Heather.

'Still!' said Cordelia. 'He ought to come too!'

The sheep bleated half-heartedly over to the unshorn ram. Nothing.

Then they made to cross the goats' meadow. The scent was pungent. The goats were far away, blurry grey dots at the other end of the meadow. The sheep found the whole thing a bit creepy.

They met Sir Ritchfield under the split tree, and then continued towards the edge of the forest. The old grey ram was still rather stunned, but in high spirits.

'What a wonderful outing!' he bleated. 'Truly wonderful!'

'And that's just the beginning,' grunted Othello. The black lead ram checked every single post of the goat fence. Sniffed them. Leaned against them. Nudged them with his four black horns. One after the other.

'Good morning, Pan,' said Maple cheerfully.

A lone goat had appeared at the fence. On the wrong side. Over there. Outside. On the edge of the forest. A morning-white goat with a black ear.

'I'm Megara,' said the goat with dignity.

The winter lamb was amazed. Goats could just pluck names as they pleased – like leaves or buds or tufts of grass. 'How did you get out there?' asked Lane. Lane was an incredibly practical sheep.

'Oh, I'm not outside,' said the black-eared goat. 'I'm inside. You're outside!'

'What about if we wanted to be on the inside too?' asked Miss Maple.

The goat sighed. 'Wanting, sheep are always wanting! Just go through the fence!' The black-eared goat elegantly manoeuvred herself through the wire at a point where it wasn't properly attached to the post and was easy to move aside.

Othello abandoned the posts.

'Have you been into the forest before?' asked Heather.

The goat sniggered. 'The question is rather – has the forest been here before?'

Zora rolled her eyes and scrambled past the black-eared goat, the first through the wire. Cautiously. Sure-hoovedly. As if she were on the edge of the abyss. The forest was an abyss. It just went in rather than down. Zora's ears tingled with anticipation.

Panting bravely, Mopple squeezed through the wire behind Zora. Then Othello. Then Maple, Heather and Lane. Sir Ritchfield got caught up on his curved horns, but was still in high spirits. It took a while for them to free the giggling Ritchfield from the wire. Maude was afraid of the cold twang of the wire, Cordelia of the stillness behind it. Ramesses had a nervous sneezing fit. One sheep lost a tuft of wool to the fence; another was tripped up. They were all finally on the other side, the winter lamb last of all, full of dark thoughts. Now the goats were speaking to everybody!

He was Nobody and what good was it doing him? None at all. Not even with the goats.

The caravan window glimmered, and the sheep were on their way. Huddled together. Nervous. Into the forest they went.

'Oh, by the way,' the goat called after them, 'if you meet the Garou . . .'

'What then?' the winter lamb asked gloomily.

'Oh, nothing,' muttered the goat as the sheep disappeared between the tree trunks one after another.

'Nothing at all.'

5

AUBREY APPEARS

The fox was the only one who knew.

The human left tracks in the snow like all the other humans. He smelled like them and moved through the trees like them, tall and stiff and ridiculously upright; he made a racket like them and had little to no understanding of the undergrowth. Other humans nodded silently to him as if he were nothing special; sheep and goats barely raised their heads when he strode past, even the deer only turned their ears towards him, cavalier in their vigilance.

But the fox followed the tracks in the snow to untold pleasures.

He knew better than anybody else that something wasn't quite right with this human.

At the end of the tracks, the man had already finished and was just standing there, leaning on a tree. The fox licked his lips, hugged the ground, and waited.

Only once the human had turned and left, did the fox shoot out of his hiding place and bite ecstatically into the red snow.

Then something tickled his neck, like breath but more fleeting. The fox looked up, and a little way away, the human was standing between the trees, looking back.

They held each other's gaze for a while, like spider silk, fragile and tough and inescapable, and knew that they were there.

That made the human smile.

It made the fox alert – and cold.

The human walked on and the fox ate. He ate until the human had condensed to a tiny dot blundering between the tree trunks like a fly.

Then he dropped the prey, licked his lips one last time and followed the big-footed human tracks again. And barely even knew why. It was a feast for a fox – for lots of foxes. But this fox was grey-muzzled and cunning. Many summers and winters had smoothed his sleek coat, and the fox had become slicker and slicker, until he was able to move through the forest like a slippery fish through water. The fox swallowed the forest and breathed the forest with every step, every look, and he had to know something so that he could breathe. The fox had to make sure that the human had left the forest.

Every time.

It was still night in the forest, and as quiet as sleep. The whisper of the wind didn't dare enter, and the trees were silent.

The sheep were in awed silence too. Trees! There were so many! It came as quite a surprise to them. Until now they had only got to know trees in isolation, as harmless shade-givers with bark to be gnawed with impunity, and a boot to rub against until it was smooth and shiny and no longer offered a satisfying rubbing experience.

But here, everywhere was so full of trees – trunk upon trunk, a mighty flock, so tightly packed – that the sheep could only advance one behind the other, in twos or threes or singles, instead of in their favoured cluster formation. They didn't like it. Something could be lurking behind every tree trunk, and the sheep had the uneasy feeling that the trees themselves were lurking, like very patient cats lying in wait for very cautious mice. They progressed gingerly, hesitant and wary, but their hearts were galloping away. The sheep missed the sky.

After a period of silence between them – both forest and sheep – Zora plucked up the courage and picked some buds from a delicate branch at sheep's height. From then on, things were a bit more relaxed, still alert, but not without the occasional tasty morsel from the wayside.

The trees divided the world into black and white. White the snow-fluff around their hooves; black the tree trunks in the snow. Black the silent birds above them; white the morning mist rising from the ground. Black the jagged branches; white the clouds above them. Black Othello, trotting ahead of them; white Maple, Lane and Cordelia following him, huddled together like a single sheep. Black Zora's pretty face; white her immaculate wool. Black the shadows. Black the tracks. Black the scent between the roots. White Maude. White Heather. White even the winter lamb.

Black their pursuer, gliding between the tree trunks a little way away, soundless as a thought.

Only Ritchfield remained grey.

'Next time, we'll do it in the summer,' he muttered.

Motionless, soundless, the forest changed around them. The ground sloped upwards. The air tasted brighter and clearer.

The undergrowth disappeared. The tree trunks got thicker and straighter and edged politely apart.

Not much, but just enough for a classic, if a bit elongated flock formation.

Miss Maple seized the chance and quickly trotted towards the front, right next to Othello.

There was no denying that Othello was a magnificent lead ram. The four-horned ram advanced with determination, not too fast and not too slow, his horns raised, his nostrils flared, his eyes vigilantly darting in all directions.

'Well?' he said then.

'It's not just the vet, is it?' Miss Maple panted as she carefully climbed the hill beside Othello. 'There's something else, isn't there?'

Othello fell silent. Maple was right. All the same, it was easier to run from the vet. They knew the vet. He was terrible, but he wasn't the fastest. He drank schnapps from little bottles and got tangled up in the wires of his own shearing machine. What the black goat and the unshorn ram had described, however . . . and above all what they *hadn't* described . . . It was better to run away from something you knew!

'The humans . . .' said Othello thoughtfully. He wasn't sure how to put it. Or what to say. 'The humans around here, and the goats and the strange sheep . . . they remember something. And they're waiting for something.'

Miss Maple nodded. This morning, as she'd trotted across the goats' meadow at dawn, the goats had done what they always did. They'd looked innocent, gambolled about, stank and found fodder everywhere. All apart from one. One goat was standing a bit apart from the rest, and she didn't let the forest out of her sight.

A sentry. A scout. Grey goat eyes against the dazzling white of the snow.

'Sometimes it's better not to wait too long!' Othello snorted. 'Sometimes it's better to just run away. I think something that humans and goats and sheep are afraid of must be very dangerous indeed,' he said quietly. 'Like fire.' At that moment they heard the howling again, thin and lost between the tree trunks, quiet as a memory. Far, far away.

All of the others had names! All of them! Even the old ram who forgot everything, and the young ram who was afraid of everything. The winter lamb was neither particularly forgetful nor particularly afraid. But the winter lamb had come into the world in the middle of winter, on a cold, dark night about a year ago. He had stolen milk, and comfort and warmth. And come the spring he had only lived through half a winter – not enough to warrant a name. Rules were rules, and rules were stupid. So, now he was right in the middle of his second winter, and nothing! Not a thing! The winter lamb angrily kicked the snow. If he had known where to find names, he would have trotted off to steal one. Something black flitted behind him. For a moment the winter lamb forgot the planned name heist and peered into the forest, shaking. Silent tree trunks, that's all. All the same, something else had just moved. There it was again! Quick and black, from boot to boot. In the middle of two tree trunks, the little goat realised that she'd been spotted. She froze in motion, her foreleg bent delicately, looking cheekily over at the winter lamb.

'Why are you following us?' the winter lamb bleated, still a bit shaken.

'Oh, I'm not following you,' said the goat. 'You're following me!' Then she pushed past him, her horns raised and disappeared amongst the other sheep.

Othello led them along the crest of the hill. A good choice. The sheep could peer far through the tree trunks on both sides and were beginning to get their bearings in the forest: front and back, up and down, thicket and clearing. Sometimes there was an appetising scent beneath the snow, of buds and branches and fallen leaves.

Everything was so new and exciting, so vast and aromatic and cramped that it took a while before Mopple began to wonder about the little black goat at his side. Had she been there before? Was she really there? Mopple tried not to look.

'Listen,' the little black goat said eventually. 'Listen very carefully!'

Mopple didn't even think about listening. He was far too busy trying to work out if he was maybe just imagining the little black goat. After all, he hadn't had a bite to eat for quite some time. His head felt light and his wool shaggy and heavy. Mopple the Whale did what he always did when he didn't know what to do: he chewed.

The goat was chewing too – a long stalk with an interesting-looking seedhead. Hard to believe she'd found that in the forest. Or was he imagining the stalk too?

'We need to talk,' said the goat, with her mouth full. 'About the Garou.'

Mopple remembered all too well what the goat on Sir Ritchfield had said about the Garou.

'No,' he said quickly. 'We don't!'

'You don't believe me!' said the black goat.

Mopple had meant to ignore the imaginary goat. But it was too late for that now.

'No,' he said decisively. 'Have you seen him? With your own eyes?'

'Nobody's seen him,' said the goat. 'At least nobody who's trotted away afterwards to tell the tale.' She thought for a moment. 'I once saw a werefowl. A white one. It looked like any other chicken, but when the geese flocked over the forest in the autumn, it turned into a human, completely white and naked, staggering across the yard gurgling and scratching in the dust. I saw it with my own eyes!'

She looked at Mopple triumphantly.

Zora wouldn't like him talking to goats about werefowls – imaginary or not. 'I don't know,' muttered Mopple. He scrunched his eyes to slits and trotted more quickly behind Lane's woolly rump.

'My name's Aubrey,' said the goat beside him. 'At least sometimes it is.'

Mopple stared resolutely at Lane's tail and didn't say a word.

'If I don't want to be Aubrey, then I'm not Aubrey,' explained Aubrey, undeterred.

'Then I'm Circe. She's got nothing against it. You can be Circe, too, if you want.'

'I'm Mopple the Whale,' said Mopple the Whale. And fell silent.

'Aubrey,' said Aubrey. 'I think we're going to be great friends, Whale.'

Mopple crashed into Lane, who had stopped. There seemed to be a little commotion up ahead.

Ritchfield enjoyed trotting behind his flock, all the woolly backs ahead of him. He liked his flock. Liked watching over them. The old lead ram, well aware of the weight of responsibility in bringing up the rear, kept his horns raised and his eyes peeled.

A wonderful outing. And strangely it seemed to Ritchfield as if they were going backwards instead of forwards. Even that was wonderful because it led to summers full of scents and sounds and joy; there were honourable duels and the sea, and there was Melmoth. The world had become so much quieter since then.

Ritchfield peered expectantly into the forest to see if he could make out Melmoth somewhere. There was definitely something grey moving between the tree trunks back there – but it wasn't Melmoth. Too cumbersome. Too dark. And not elegant enough somehow.

Ritchfield had the best eyes in the flock. He stood for a moment and peered curiously towards where he had seen the movement. Big and round. Something wobbly, but purposeful. Cautious and deft between the trees.

A sheep? Ritchfield wasn't sure.

'How exciting!' bleated Heather. 'I'd never have thought trees could be so exciting!'

'Me neither,' said Zora trotting beside her. Not that she liked the forest. Not at all. It was too confusing. Too cramped. Too strange. But it moved her. Like the sea. Like the starry sky. Like . . .

'How are we going to find Cloud then?' Heather asked.

'We head towards where it feels good,' Zora explained.

'And then?'

'Cloud will head towards where it feels good too,' said Zora. 'We'll find her there.'

'And what if she feels good in several places?' asked Heather. 'What if it doesn't feel good anywhere?'

Zora fell silent and stopped.

Heather ran into Willow, who had also stopped. Willow

maintained a stoic silence. But Lane bleated as she shoved Heather from behind. Heather bleated back indignantly.

The sheep peered curiously ahead.

Othello stood still and upright, looking almost tree-like with his four imposing horns. He stood and scented the air. Scented the air and listened. But by now so many sheep were bleating behind him that he probably couldn't hear very much. Next moment the black ram trotted off, quickly and silently down the hill. The sheep followed him in shock. Othello led them straight into a thicket of hawthorn, brambles and birch saplings. It was cramped and uncomfortable. Branches poked and scratched them from all sides. The lead ram stopped.

Maude scented the air. 'It's . . .'

'Hush!' Othello snorted.

The sheep stood as still as stones.

Something was moving between the tree trunks, a good distance away.

Red.

And black.

And brown.

And a bit of gold. A bell.

And voices.

And the bell again.

Come, sang the bell. *Sheep, lots of sheep, a flock, your flock. All together,* the bell promised, *safe, side by side, warm and complete . . .*

'. . . and why all the secrecy then?' said a man's voice. 'The meetings, the targeted misinformation – and why the light in the tower? And what are the two strangers doing here?'

'They're tourists, Zach,' said Rebecca. 'Winter visitors.'

'They've been here for precisely twenty-one days. Since the first snow. Who in their right mind would stay here for twenty-one days?'

'You,' said Rebecca. 'Me. Mum.' She sighed.

'You've got your sheep and I'm stationed here. That's completely different. Normally tourists stay for two weeks at most. Even without my training I'd be able to tell something shady is going on. And what are they doing in the forest all the time? Foraging for mushrooms?'

Rebecca laughed. 'They're going for walks. What else is there to do around here? The short one, Monsieur . . . I always forget his name; according to Madame Fronsac he's got a lung problem.'

Rebecca could be glimpsed between the trees, wearing her red hat and holding the sheep bell in her hand. Behind her was Zach, unmistakable in his black suit and coat, wearing his sunglasses. Zach always wore sunglasses, even at night. The sheep had known that since the time Zach spent a whole night lying on the shepherd's caravan watching the chateau. But the chateau had done just as it always did: nothing. And Mum had discovered him in the morning and screamed.

'And the tall one? What about the tall one?'

'I don't know, maybe it's his brother. There's bound to be some kind of explanation.'

Rebecca and Zach flickered back and forth between the trees, sometimes red, sometimes black and sometimes brown, sometimes visible, sometimes concealed by the dark tree trunks. At times the bell chimed.

It took a while for the sheep to realise that the two of them were heading straight towards their thicket. The flock looked on in stunned silence as Zach got caught on a branch, stumbled, got up again and straightened the collar of his coat. The sheep liked Zach.

He did interesting things, unlike the other humans. He hid amongst the gorse bushes, blew blue powder over the steps of the shepherd's caravan, photographed the ground and spoke to a clock on his wrist. And he noticed things that most humans didn't: footprints, stones, scents, crumbs on the windowsill. Once he'd searched the feed store for weapons and not closed the door properly afterwards.

And unlike most Europeans, he could speak.

'His brother? Ha!' Zach sounded insulted.

There was a smile in Rebecca's voice. 'Probably not. Maybe they're gay? Or tax inspectors? Whatever. I'm really happy you came with me, Zach. It would have been a bit creepy here on my own, after what happened yesterday.'

Zach's face brightened. 'No need to thank me, Rebecca, I've got a professional interest in the case too.'

'My runaway sheep?' said Rebecca. 'A case?'

For a moment Zach's serious face flashed behind a tree, then he'd disappeared again.

'You shouldn't be so casual about it,' he said. 'There's more to this whole business than there might seem. It's all connected. There's a plan. First the deer, now your sheep. And all the other deer. And the little boy. And the woman and the girl. And of course, the old man dead in front of the mirror with a silver bullet in his head. You don't believe that ridiculous werewolf story, do you?'

'Werewolf story?' said a black tree trunk in Rebecca's voice. 'What werewolf story?'

Rebecca emerged between the trees somewhere else. 'What other deer?' she asked then. 'And what boy? And what old man?'

'I'm not allowed to talk about it,' said Zach. If Zach wasn't allowed to talk about something, then he didn't talk about it.

Rebecca knew that and didn't ask any more.

It was strange seeing their shepherdess stomping towards them like that. She looked smaller amongst all the trees. Small, but spirited. A few sheep's lengths away from their thicket Rebecca stopped and looked around. Looked at them. The sheep tried to look light and fluffy. Light and fluffy and motionless, like the snow.

The little bell chimed.

'If I might say so, that bell isn't exactly ideal for a covert operation,' said Zach.

'Maybe not' – Rebecca grinned – 'but the sheep know the bell. They like the bell. When we're moving around, the black ram has it around his neck. If Cloud hears the bell, she might come.'

Rebecca and Zach were now so close that the sheep could pick up their scent very clearly. Not just as whole humans, but all the details. Rebecca's hair, warm and earthy beneath her red hat, the biscuits in her pocket and the interesting woolly jumper. Zach's cold feet and wet trouser legs, the herbal sweet he was sucking, and his determination. Zach was nothing if not determined.

'I hope we find her,' said Rebecca. Now the shepherdess looked straight over at them. And didn't see them. Or smell them either. And she carried on. It was difficult to fathom. Humans didn't see the things that were there; they saw the things they thought were there. Rebecca could spend hours in the feed store looking for a bucket that was in front of the door. Humans thought too much. Or about the wrong things. Mostly they didn't think about sheep enough.

Somewhere in the forest a twig snapped, and Rebecca gave a start.

'Don't worry,' said Zach. 'You're completely safe. I've got my service weapon on me.'

He tapped his hand on his coat. Rebecca smirked.

'I've got my service weapon with me too,' she said, taking something out of her coat pocket for the briefest of moments.

The sheep were shocked. George's gun! The pistol! It made a hell of a racket and was good for nothing.

'My father used this to keep drug dealers at bay! Not bad, huh?'

That was a flat-out lie. The only thing that old George had kept at bay with that gun had been a crooked, defenceless target.

Rebecca rang the bell again. The sheep really did like the bell. It was comforting like the murmurs of a mother ewe.

'This used to be our base, you know,' said Zach. 'A training base for agents. Camouflaged as a loony bin. Top secret. But then it was all disbanded and the agents left. All apart from me. And I'm left wondering all the time: What's behind it all? Why did they station me here? I really would like to know why they stationed me here all these years!' For a moment, Zach sounded much younger, and a bit lost.

'But I'm very close this time. That's obviously strictly confidential,' he said then, sounding like he always did.

'Of course,' said Rebecca, 'strictly confidential . . .'

For a while the little bell could still be heard, then silence.

The sheep were in a hurry to get out of the prickly thicket, but Maude, of all sheep, who usually favoured comfort, insisted on not moving from the spot. Maude was their warning sheep. She picked up scents the others didn't. So, the sheep continued being stabbed by the hawthorn and waited.

And sure enough, after a little while, something moved again in the forest. Dark this time. Dark and silent. Propped on a crook. Straight towards them. Stomp, stomp, stomp. They recognised the scent before they could properly see the figure between the trees: the smell of far too many goats and some sausage. The sheep held their breath. But the goatherder was looking at the ground, following Zach's and Rebecca's tracks in the snow. He didn't look up. Stomp, stomp, stomp.

Then the coast was clear, and so was the air.

Othello didn't lead them back up the hill, but along a ditch. The sheep moved more quickly and farther apart. Their shepherdess was hot on their heels – she just didn't know it yet. Normally at this time they would all be dozing in the hay barn, and they could imagine Rebecca's surprise when, instead of Cloud, she found a whole flock of runaway sheep. Somehow, they didn't think Rebecca would be particularly happy about it.

Zora zipped along at the outer edge of the flock. Zora liked edges. Every edge was a bit like an abyss, and there was something to be learned from every abyss.

Suddenly something dark brushed her cheek. A crow's shadow. It circled and disappeared. Zora looked around curiously. Next moment she had made a giant leap to the side. Her heart was galloping. Something had leapt out at her from between the trees. Zora was shaking. She wanted to run away, but she had to know what had scared her like that.

Wait. Scent the air. A tiny step.

Nothing.

Another step, neck craned, and ears pricked.

A while ago, when the wind was still busy plucking the final colourful leaves from the trees, Zora had woken up earlier than all the other sheep. The air had felt cool and heavy and strange. Impenetrable. Like the forest. The forest had come onto their meadow.

Zora had got up, curious, reluctant, and trotted to the door of their barn.

And been horrified by what she saw.

On their meadow, not far from the edge of the forest, stood a big, strange animal:

Ears like fluttering butterflies, huge black eyes bulging like dewdrops. A scent so full of ferocity and freedom and fragility that Zora felt dizzy just thinking about it. The animal had stood there for a few moments, black before the milk-white morning sky. Two others like it appeared behind it, frozen too. The three of them looked at Zora, and she stared back, hypnotised, helpless. Then a shudder ran across the strangers' flanks like ripples across a pond. And soundlessly they scattered, way above the fence as if it weren't even there, into the forest. The forest stood black and silent as the bottom edge of the sky slowly turned red.

Deer, said the goats.

Deer were like ghosts, powerful thoughts of flight and vigilance. There were no fences in their world. None that would hold them. None that would protect them. Zora understood why their eyes were so big, their legs so long and their ears so delicate and nervous. Deer had to be faster than the danger. And now one was lying in front of Zora – or rather: something that had once been a deer. A short while ago. Long ago.

'It was the Garou!' said a little black goat beside Zora.

'I think it was a deer!' said Zora.

'It's beautiful,' said the winter lamb.

Strangely, Zora knew what he meant. All of a sudden, the sun shone through the trees, tracing lacy shadow patterns in the snow. The white and the black. The white and the black and the red.

Like a flower in the snow.

6

THE WINTER LAMB MAKES A STAND

'And his eyes glow in the dark like glow-worms. And he's got a long pink tongue that lolls out of his mouth!' said the goat.

This time the sheep listened to her.

'Bullets can't harm him!' bleated the goat.

The sheep nodded intelligently. They wondered if bullets were like pullets? What harm could a pullet do? Peck you to death? The sheep had never come across a particularly vicious pullet. Even full-grown hens didn't pose much of a threat to sheep, let alone humans! Or did she mean the werefowl?

'Silver is the only thing for it!' the goat declared, looking around at them all.

The sheep tried to act like they'd known that all along.

'When he changes – does he have human Things on or not?' asked Miss Maple.

It was an important question. A Four-Legs would soon get tangled up – and then it'd be easy to recognise him.

Three sets of tracks led to the red patch that had once been a deer. Three sets of tracks intertwined like bindweed on a fence. One set delicate, fleeting; one big, elongated; and a red chain of blood droplets scattered here, there and everywhere like poppies in a meadow. The snow was so soft and powdery that it was difficult to glean much more from the tracks.

The patch didn't give away much in terms of scent either. Scents frozen in the cold became brittle and shattered. All that was left was a cold inkling of blood. Now most of the sheep believed some of what the goat was saying. Not everything, but this and that. A wolf slinking through the forest killing deer. Deer and humans, and probably sheep, too, given the chance. A wolf that ceased to be a wolf on the edge of the forest and continued on two legs and lived undetected amongst the humans.

The Garou was all the sheep needed.

'And he hides behind a human?' Lane asked again. It didn't seem to be a particularly good hiding place to her. Humans were upright and thin and constantly in motion.

'Not behind a human,' Aubrey explained. 'In a human.'

'If he's hiding *in* a human, at least he can't be any *bigger* than a human,' said Mopple.

That was something. All sheep were afraid of wolves, but if they were honest, they didn't know exactly what they were afraid of. Wolves were spectres, the horror of countless lamb's fables, breathing hotly down their necks when they were afraid. Wolves existed in stories. It came as a surprise to the sheep that one might suddenly be out there, somewhere in the snow, his muzzle bloody.

'Why is he hiding?' asked the winter lamb.

Aubrey thought for a moment. 'Because the humans are scared of him. And humans are dangerous when they're scared of something. Even the Garou isn't safe from them.'

'We could be scared of him too,' Heather suggested.

'Would we be dangerous then as well?'

'A bit,' said Aubrey. She seemed to like the thought of that.

'I'm scared of him!' Heather led by example.

'Me too,' sighed Mopple, not particularly menacingly. The sheep had huddled together at a safe distance underneath three young firs and were patiently waiting for Miss Maple to finally return from the red patch. Everything here was too fresh. Too . . . open. Like a wound in the snow.

Maple silently circled the red patch. Once. And a second time. She scented the air. Scraped in the snow. Followed the big tracks for a bit. Finally, she trotted over to the young firs too.

'We would only have to follow these tracks,' she said with a strange glint in her eye, 'and we could *see* him!'

The others looked less than enthusiastic.

Maple sighed. 'I know. I'm scared too. But . . .' She looked towards the point where the tracks disappeared between the trees. 'The humans in the stories would do it,' she said quietly.

The other sheep remained stubbornly silent. The humans in the stories did plenty of ridiculous things. Spring cleaning, revenge and diets. No need to run blithely into the jaws of the Garou. That would be just plain . . .

'Mad,' muttered Aubrey. 'I'll do it!'

The little goat jumped out from beneath the firs and before the sheep could bleat a warning, she had disappeared between the tree trunks, small, black, alive – and determined.

'If you want something to happen, then you have to make it happen,' muttered the winter lamb, gnawing thoughtfully on a piece of root.

At that moment something flashed between the trees to the side of them.

'The Garou!' Ramesses bleated in a panic.

Only after a prolonged gallop tearing through the forest, did they realise that it had probably just been a fox. Just? The fox had looked big, sharp and dangerous, self-assured and taunting between the trees. A forest animal. A wild animal. Things were different in the forest, even familiar things. Stranger. Bigger. Unfathomable.

Even if the sheep hadn't really been scared of the fox – at least not with hindsight – running away seemed like a good idea. After all, there was bound to be another beast of prey in the forest. A beast of prey that none of them wanted to meet. Othello led them through a little beech grove at breakneck speed, up a hill and down a hill, past a little wooden hut sitting goat-like on an ancient oak, always straight ahead. Snow fluttered, branches whipped, and birds scattered. Nobody complained. They had the uneasy feeling that something was hot on their trail.

Eventually a stream blocked their way. Not a particularly big stream, but too wide for a sheep to jump, and too steep and sharp and icily whooshing to pick their way across. They didn't like the stream. It penned them in like a fence. But there was no going back – the Garou could be lurking behind any tree boot.

Othello listened for a moment. Maude scented the air. Mopple panted. Ritchfield looked like he'd just forgotten something.

Then they carried on along the stream, their hooves flying and their ears flapping, until they got to a bridge. Well, it wasn't a proper bridge, just a narrow plank, about two hoofs wide. But there was snow on the plank, fresh, fluffy, powdery snow. No deer had crossed it today, no humans – and definitely no wolves.

Othello carefully examined their little bridge. It seemed stable and inspired confidence, but a thin, treacherous layer of ice was lurking beneath the snow. The black ram carefully put his front hoof on the plank, almost slipped off and tried again, more gingerly and precisely this time. He snorted contentedly. Then he was across, scenting the air on all sides again. Zora was next, elegant and casual, as if she were trotting across a summer meadow. Heather followed with sharp, bold steps; Lane and Cordelia moved quickly and cautiously. The whole flock held their breath when Miss Maple stumbled, slipped and saved herself at the last moment, leaping onto the other bank.

Mopple made it to the middle of the bridge and stopped dead.

'I, I . . . I can't go any farther,' Mopple panted, scrunching his eyes shut.

'You can do it,' said Cordelia soothingly. 'It's only a few more steps.'

'I can't see anything,' groaned Mopple.

'Of course you can't see anything. You've got your eyes shut,' said Zora. 'Open your eyes!'

'I can't!' Mopple was shaking and swaying precariously. Something in the forest snapped.

'Come on!' Cordelia, Lane and Zora beckoned.

'Is that sweet-wort?' asked Miss Maple from farther back. 'In the middle of winter! Unbelievable!'

Next moment Mopple had trotted across the plank and was heading towards Maple, his eyes sparkling.

'Sweetwort?' he bleated. 'Really?'

'No,' said Maple. 'Not really.' Mopple's ears drooped.

Sir Ritchfield sailed across the bridge, every inch a lead ram.

Maude hesitated and wavered, but eventually made it across.

The winter lamb stopped dead in the middle of the bridge too.

'Come on!' Lane, Cordelia and Zora beckoned again. 'There's not far to go! You're nearly there!'

'I know,' said the winter lamb, standing completely still, his head raised. He looked at them, his eyes sparkling.

'What is it?' asked Maude.

'I want a name!' bleated the winter lamb. 'Right here. Right now. I'm not going any farther without a name!'

Distant crunching and snapping. Now the sheep were certain of it: there was something moving through the forest behind them. It was quick and loud. And big.

'There's something there!' Ramesses bleated nervously. 'You've got to keep going! We all want to cross the bridge! We don't want to be on the wolf side!'

'I know,' said the winter lamb again, standing still. 'But I want a name!' he repeated.

The sheep looked at one another.

'We . . . erm . . . we haven't got a name,' said Cordelia, at a loss.

'You have!' bleated the winter lamb. His eyes were moist and gleaming. 'You've all got your names! All of you! I'm the only one who hasn't!'

'You can have my name!' bleated Ramesses, panicking at the back. 'Ramesses is a fine name!'

'No! I want my own name!' The winter lamb stamped his foot angrily. The bridge wobbled.

The sheep listened. No doubt about it: the snapping was getting closer.

Othello slowly trotted towards the winter lamb.

'Get off the bridge,' he said quietly. 'Or I'll charge!'

The sheep held their breath. Charging at another sheep on the narrow, icy plank was a bold move. Othello took a few steps back and lowered his horns.

The winter lamb stood firm.

Another twig snapped somewhere. Othello charged.

The winter lamb stood firm.

Othello stopped just shy of the bank, dusting the winter lamb with fine white snow. He didn't want to charge at the winter lamb. He was the weakest amongst them, yet at the same time, in a strange way, he was complete. A born lead ram. Othello liked the winter lamb.

The winter lamb squinted through the snow dust. Behind him his flock was waiting, and in front of him his flock was waiting. And not all that far away, something broke through the undergrowth.

Without a name, and another word, the winter lamb trotted across the plank. He would find his name. Sometime. Someplace.

The rest of the flock made it over the bridge without any problems – and on they went, away from the stream past trees, more and more trees.

Mopple was panting. He could barely remember when he'd last eaten. Trees shimmered by. At least the imaginary goat had disappeared now; instead Maple was imagining sweetwort, and Mopple could hear a distant, lost bleating in his curved horns. He shook his head, but the bleating remained.

'Can you hear that?' he asked Sir Ritchfield, who was trotting along beside him.

'What?' bleated Sir Ritchfield. Mopple sighed.

'I can hear something!' Lane bleated from the back. Soon all the sheep could hear it – apart from Sir Ritchfield: out there, in the middle of the forest, a sheep was bleating. A very lonely sheep.

Cloud!

The sheep bleated back. 'Cloud! Over here! We're over here!'

Cloud bleated more loudly. But she didn't move.

'She's stuck!' said Miss Maple, galloping off in the direction of the bleating.

Othello and the rest of the flock followed.

And sure enough: there was Cloud standing in the middle of a clearing. Unharmed, woolly and, as far as the sheep could tell, in one piece. But she didn't move from the spot. The sheep surrounded her and sniffed her. She smelled quite all right – for a sheep who had been terrified all night. She smelled of forest and snow – and above all of Cloud.

Cloud was shaking.

'Come with us!' said Heather. 'We're going where it feels good! And Rebecca will follow!'

'She can't come with us,' said Miss Maple. 'Her leg's stuck.'

Now the others saw it too: Cloud had a wire snare around her hind leg; it was so tight that some blood from Cloud's ankle was seeping into the snow.

'She can't move!' said Maple.

'But *we* have to go!' bleated Maude. 'The Ga—'

'Not without Cloud,' said Miss Maple sharply.

Cloud looked from one sheep to another and shook even more.

'No flock may leave a sheep,' bleated Sir Ritchfield. 'Unless . . .'

'No unless!' said Othello.

With that, the matter was decided. The sheep huddled around Cloud and waited. Maple hummed deeply and soothingly into

Cloud's ear, just as a mother ewe would. Eventually Cloud stopped shaking.

'So?' asked Maple. 'What happened?'

'I . . . I escaped the vet,' said Cloud, a bit befuddled and a bit proud. 'But then all of a sudden there were trees everywhere, and I didn't know which way to go. And then there were even more trees, and I kept going.'

'Over a stream?' asked Maple.

'No,' said Cloud. 'Just through trees.'

'We crossed a stream,' Heather bleated. 'And Mopple almost didn't make it. And Othello almost charged the winter lamb.'

Cloud looked at her, confused.

'And then what happened?' Maple asked.

'I carried on,' said Cloud. 'Nothing but trees!'

'And then?'

'There were tufts of grass in a clearing somewhere. They didn't taste bad.'

'Where?' Mopple asked quickly.

'I don't know,' said Cloud. 'Behind some trees somewhere.'

Mopple sighed.

'And then?' Maple asked again.

'Then it got dark and I didn't go much farther because I was scared of knocking into something in the dark. Into trees, mostly. And there were noises.'

'What sort of noises?' asked Maple.

Cloud thought for a moment. 'Tree noises,' she said then. 'Snapping and creaking and crunching, and then it snowed. You can't hear that, but sometimes snow slips off the branches, and you can hear that. Snow fell on me at one point.'

'And then?' asked Maple.

'Eventually it got a bit lighter again,' said Cloud. 'And I came into this clearing here because it was even brighter. And then my foot got caught. I tried to break free but couldn't. And then I started bleating. I bleated for a very long time. And then you came.'

'That's all?' asked Mopple with a hint of disappointment. No sweet-wort. No mystery. No Garou. Not even a werefowl. Just a bit of wire.

'That's all?' bleated Cloud indignantly. 'I was on my own amongst all these trees and all these noises that weren't really noises, and all these strange scents, and I couldn't move, and my leg hurt, and the snow . . . That's all!'

'We're just happy that nothing happened to you,' said Lane soothingly.

'And you didn't see anything odd?' Heather insisted.

Cloud thought for a moment. 'Actually, I did see something,' she said then. 'Here in the clearing, early this morning. It was – like a chicken but not a chicken.'

A werefowl? Mopple's ears flapped forwards.

'It moved like a chicken, but its tail was longer, and its head was more colourful, and it was brown and green and blue and much prettier than a chicken. I saw that.' Cloud looked at them all proudly.

That was it. Cloud obviously hadn't encountered the dreaded Garou. Thank goodness! The sheep relaxed a little.

If Cloud had survived a whole night in the forest, alone and trapped, the situation couldn't be that dangerous. Mopple began searching for tufts of grass beneath the snow, Maple examined Cloud's snare, Sir Ritchfield chatted animatedly to a tree, Maude and Cordelia scratched themselves on the tree trunks, the winter lamb was having a think and Heather was looking for the colourful wonder-fowl.

The sun was shining and they were happy to have a complete flock again. Spirits were high until a twig snapped somewhere in the forest. A big twig. And another. Snow crunched. Crunched and crunched.

Something was coming. Towards them. On all fours.

Through the undergrowth.

Something heavy.

Mopple abandoned the grass and Heather forgot all about the werefowl, or whatever it was. Even Ritchfield seemed to sense something wasn't quite right and politely excused himself from the tree boot. Cloud started to shake again. The flock huddled together, and Othello trotted back and forth in front of them like a little four-horned bull.

The sheep waited for whatever might be coming out of the forest, trembling but resolute. At first it looked like a shadow, a bodyless shadow amongst the tree trunks, formless and distorted, as shadows sometimes are. Then a dark figure broke away from the edge of the forest. The sheep were trembling as one, trembling like the surface of the stream when it rains.

Othello lowered his horns.

The unshorn ram glanced at them briefly then trotted past them, his eyes half-closed, and made himself at home between the trunks of two birch trees.

'Carry on, Gris! Well done, Aube!' he muttered contentedly, closing his eyes and dozing off.

'That's a sheep!' bleated Sir Ritchfield in relief. The others couldn't believe their eyes.

And then suddenly something else burst out of the forest, tall and upright, with shaggy hair and glittering eyes.

It was Rebecca. 'Whatever next? Flying pigs?' she said.

The sheep were too relieved to look for the flying pigs. Or to wonder at how quickly Rebecca's state of mind had deteriorated in the short time they'd been away. Flying pigs indeed!

Rebecca's hair was all over the place, her cheeks were red as apples and she didn't even scold them. She silently helped Cloud out of the snare and grabbed Othello by the horns. Nobody else would have been allowed to grab Othello by the horns, not even old George. But Rebecca was allowed. Then they went through the forest again, the shepherdess and Othello leading the way, the flock in tow. Homewards, the sheep assumed. But somehow that didn't seem so bad at all. There was concentrated feed on their meadow, the open sky, the hay barn and the shepherd's caravan. All good things.

'What a wonderful outing!' bleated Sir Ritchfield, and most of the sheep agreed.

But Miss Maple didn't seem best pleased.

'Where did the snare come from?' she asked Willow, who was trotting along beside her.

'And why did the strange ram follow us? And where's Rebecca's hat? And what did the goatherder want? And where's Zach?'

Willow, the second most silent sheep in the flock, remained silent.

7

MISS MAPLE GETS NOWHERE

The sun was high in the sky, the snow was sparkling, and the sheep cast short, fat shadows – especially Mopple the Whale. As yet there was no sign of any flying pigs, or the vet for that matter.

They were surprised at how peaceful their meadow seemed after the skulking silence of the forest – even if the Garou was still prowling around somewhere. Even if Rebecca was screeching inside the caravan. The goats seemed more sensible and the winter grass less dull. They only wished Rebecca would close the caravan window or finally let it rest.

'Sick!' cursed Rebecca. 'It's completely sick! What the hell? What's going on? Can somebody please tell me what on earth's going on?'

Then she stood on the steps of the shepherd's caravan, her face red, holding something that looked like a heap of red rags in her hands. She opened her hands and red rained down.

'There!'

Rebecca stared at the rags in the snow, her eyes sparkling with tears. It looked unsettlingly similar to what the Garou had done to the deer.

Behind Rebecca, Mum stuck her head out of the caravan door, with strangely colourful curly Things in her hair.

'I'm telling you; it wasn't me! Why would I . . . Just think about it! For God's sake, I wasn't even here!'

'Who else would it have been?' Rebecca hissed.

'That . . .' said Mum, lighting a cigarette, '. . . that is the question.'

She pointed the hand holding the smoking cigarette at the snow. 'Pick it up, darling. It might look like a pile of rags, but it's evidence. And I'm not sure it's the right kind of thing to be feeding your sheep, either.'

The sheep looked over at her crossly. The old woman should kindly leave questions of fodder to them. Mopple had the first scrap of fabric in his mouth, and apart from the texture, which was maybe a bit tough, it seemed rather promising.

'Oh, shit!' said Rebecca, hopping off the caravan steps making broad shooing motions. Mopple got away with a second piece of fabric in his mouth, and the shepherdess went about picking the red out of the snow.

Outside the fence, the gardener trudged past and looked over at her curiously. And on seeing all the red, he looked away again.

'There!' The hand holding the smoking cigarette pointed again, over at the chateau, yard and stables this time. 'That's where you should be looking. I'd bet my Chanel handbag on it being one of them!'

'Who?' muttered Rebecca. 'But why? And when? When were you out?'

'Actually . . . let me think.' Mum puffed on her cigarette. 'I got up at eight, had some coffee, then I called two clients and had breakfast after I was done with them . . . I'd say I left the house, you know what I mean, at around nine, and I got back just before you, at around twelve.'

'Three hours!' Rebecca looked up from the red rags in surprise. Mum seldom left the caravan; three hours was a new record.

'What were you doing out there for three hours?'

'I was having a shower in the chateau's guest house,' Mum muttered, enveloping herself in smoke.

'For three hours?'

'First the water was ice-cold. Again. One of those two weird winter visitors must have ridiculously long showers. So, I waited for it to warm up again. And then it just so happened . . .' Mum awkwardly twisted the cigarette in her hand.

Rebecca had finished plucking all of her red rags from the snow and stood up.

'You were . . . working?' She held the red bundle towards Mum, but Mum still had her cigarette in her hand and waved the jumble of fabric away.

'Someone asked. What of it? Why not? Look on it as helping thy neighbour.'

'I quite clearly told you . . .'

The red heap landed on the top step of the shepherd's caravan.

'I have to work, darling. I'm not happy unless I'm working!'

The sheep knew what Mum did for work: humbug. Day after day, nothing but humbug. And Rebecca had implemented a rule, as strict as the daily fence check. Humbug was only to be conducted in the shepherd's caravan. On the telephone. Nowhere else. Especially not somewhere where other people would get wind of it. The sheep would have quite liked to get wind of a bit of humbug every now and then, but Rebecca was not to be messed with as far as humbug was concerned.

'Great, just great!'

'Don't make such a fuss, Becky!' said Mum, flicking her cigarette into the snow.

Rebecca exploded, just like the grey brindle farm cat sometimes did. One moment the cat was peacefully slinking along the fence, rodents and winter birds on her mind, the next moment she was leaping into the air, in every direction at once, hissing, hackles up, eyes glinting and her back arched. At that moment, Rebecca looked quite similar to her, apart from the arched back that is.

'And I've told you a hundred times not to just throw your fag ends on the meadow . . . What do you think will happen if a sheep eats them? Game over!'

Now it was Rebecca's turn to be glared at. None of the sheep would ever have touched one of those stinking butts. Exactly how stupid did the shepherdess think they were? Mopple burped reproachfully, the second piece of material sitting heavily in his stomach.

Rebecca snatched the cigarette butt up from the ground and hurled it into the caravan. Then she slumped onto the steps.

'It's all just a bit much,' she muttered. 'A bit much . . . First Christmas, then the deer and then Cloud, and now this mess . . .' She picked up a handful of tatters from the steps and let them flutter back down onto the heap. 'And you're running around reading people's cards. Do you have any idea what sort of people these are? I mean, I don't! I can't figure them out at all! First, they ask me here, and then the whole time it's as if they've got something against me. Or against the sheep! You should have seen how they looked at me when I unloaded the sheep . . . Paul the goatherder lights something every night on the edge of the forest, God knows why. Eventually they'll burn you at the stake . . .'

'Don't be ridiculous, darling!' Mum sat down beside Rebecca on the caravan steps, astonishingly deftly. 'People are just people, wherever you go. You're just embarrassed, that's all.'

'And why wouldn't I be?! My mother: Mystic Meg! The woman with the third eye! Career, money, love and happiness! Happiness, pah! You run around peddling this humbug and I have to carry the can. I always carry the can . . .'

The sheep shifted closer, all agog. Something was happening in front of the shepherd's caravan. One of Rebecca's fences was wobbling, maybe something would soon appear. Possibly the humbug itself, maybe just the third eye. The sheep were pretty curious about Mum's third eye. But for the time being, only Tess appeared; she trotted out of the caravan at her leisurely old-dog pace and started licking Rebecca's hands, which didn't seem to be carrying a can, or anything else for that matter.

'What about her?' asked Rebecca. 'Was she there when it happened? A fine guard dog she turned out to be!'

Tess wagged her tail.

'I left her with Madame Fronsac,' said Mum. 'The old girl doesn't like being on her own.'

'I need to get out of here!' said Rebecca.

Mum's bony hand patted her back. '*Courage!*' she said. Rebecca fell silent, Mum patted, and Tess wagged her tail.

Three crows flew over the meadow towards the forest with an air of determination.

All of a sudden Rebecca had got back up.

'Who was it, then?' she asked. 'Whose cards did you read?'

Mum grinned. 'Now things are getting interesting, huh? Who would you expect? The Walrus, maybe, or pretty little Hortense. Those are my typical clients, I'd have thought, or at a pinch Yves, the bumpkin. But, who asks me? Mademoiselle Plin! The severe woman with the severe hair!'

'She's a snake in the grass,' muttered Rebecca.

The meadow gate opened and the sheep backed away from the caravan a bit to keep their distance from the visitor. Hortense stopped a few steps away from the caravan and made a respectful gesture, a curtsey almost.

'Bonjour, Madame. I heard . . . Could you read my cards too? Mine and . . . Eric's?'

Mum leaned back a bit and took out a little black book. 'Why not. Let's see: I've got three appointments today already, but tomorrow morning . . . You at ten and Mr Eric at half past, yeah?'

Hortense nodded, breathed '*Salut*, Becca' and was already on her way back, her cheeks rosy and the scent of violets in her hair. The sheep had always wondered where she got all the violets from in the middle of winter.

'You've got . . . appointments.' Rebecca sighed. 'Three!'

'Five!' Mum corrected.

'I need to get out of here!' said Rebecca.

Mum spirited the little black book away into the depths of her coat and sat up. 'Are you mad? There's finally something happening! Today is the first day I don't want to get out of here! I'm telling you, darling, there's an unusually high demand for . . . happiness. For advice. For light in the dark!'

Mum stood up and spread her arms like a bat. 'Becky, I believe you when you say that something's not right. And not because of the police, but because there's such high demand for . . . fortunes around here. And do you know what that indicates?'

Mum paused for dramatic effect.

'Something supernatural!' Rebecca groaned.

The sheep stood in awed silence. Supernatural! Even more natural than natural! Grass was natural, concentrated feed not quite as natural, and plastic wasn't natural at all and was almost inedible. Something supernatural, though, must be a real delicacy!

Mum lowered her bat arms and grabbed Rebecca's chin. 'Don't worry, darling. We'll find out what it is. And who did that.' She jabbed a bony finger towards the red heap. We'll find them too! You wouldn't believe all the things people tell you during a séance! Just let me . . . We just mustn't allow ourselves to be led, like . . . like sheep!'

Like sheep! That hit home!

Maude and Heather started bleating, offended, Mopple looked guilty and Ritchfield shook his head and muttered, 'That's not a sheep!'

'Ritchfield is right,' said Zora suddenly. 'We ought to show them how it's done!'

First the others just chewed, then they understood too. Humans rarely did something of their own accord. They lived in the moment and pursued their little human interests. If something really important was to happen, concentrated feed or the apple harvest or putting an end to the travelling life, the sheep had to take the initiative.

'I could eat some more card!' said Mopple obligingly. But what sort of card? The sheep didn't know. They decided he should eat any card in sight, to see what happened. In the meantime, they could graze or bleat a bit or watch the goats and shake their heads or . . .

'. . . or find the Garou!' Ramesses bleated suddenly. The others looked at him, thunderstruck.

'I mean . . .' stammered Ramesses, 'maybe he's not that . . . and we could . . . or maybe not . . .'

Ramesses scraped in the snow, clearly embarrassed, and the others rolled their eyes, but Miss Maple looked wide-awake.

'He's right!' she said. 'We ought to find out who the wolf is inside!'

'Why?' bleated Heather.

'Why?' bleated the others in chorus.

'So that we can run away in the right direction,' said Miss Maple. 'If we don't know where he is, how are we supposed to know which way is away?'

'If we see him, we can still run away,' said Lane, elegantly turning her neck. Lane was the fastest sheep in the flock.

'Maybe,' said Maple. 'The deer didn't manage it.'

That was true. Deer were so long-legged that even the forest couldn't lead them astray, and yet . . .

'He surprised it,' whispered Lane. 'He must have taken it by surprise!'

Not all of the sheep were sure if they really believed in the Garou, but even those who didn't believe in him very much wanted to run away from him all of a sudden. Preferably now.

'But not through the forest!' said Cloud.

The others nodded. The forest snapped and rustled, it led them round in circles and taunted them. Near was far, and far was near, straight was bent, up was down, and there wasn't any grass either.

'How else are we supposed to get away?' asked Maude, taking a deep breath. 'The forest is everywhere. All around us.'

'The same way we came!' said the winter lamb, his eyes sparkling. 'By car!'

The others bleated in protest. It wasn't a particularly popular mode of transport. It roared and lurched, jumped and stank. It was cramped and dark and terrifying. But it could get them through the forest quickly and safely, away from the Garou. Most of the sheep secretly thought that cars were a bit like dogs: if you once summoned all your courage and didn't run away from them, it usually turned out that their barks were worse than their bites.

With a bit of luck.

A short while later a little sheep expedition was standing at the loose slat in the goat fence again. Maude, Zora and Heather had set out to find the extra-large car that had brought the sheep here.

Maude would pick up its scent. Zora would confront it.

And Heather would convince it to take them away from this place.

Maple looked contentedly after them.

'And in the meantime, we'll search for the Garou!' she said.

The sheep made long faces.

Searching was all well and good, but none of them wanted to actually find the Garou!

Ramesses searched for the Garou amongst the gorse bushes.

Cordelia searched by the shepherd's caravan.

Cloud searched under the caravan.

The caravan door opened, and Rebecca stomped purposefully towards the chateau. The sheep stopped searching and gazed after her.

Then they carried on.

Lane searched along the goat fence.

Othello searched in the hay barn.

Ritchfield discussed matters with the feed trough.

The winter lamb searched between the old oak and the wardrobe.

And Mopple wasn't searching at all. Mopple was chewing. Maple trotted over to the fat ram and cleared her throat. Mopple swallowed.

'So?' asked Maple.

'Nothing!' said Mopple, staring intently at several blades of winter grass that were peeping out of the snow. 'He's not here!'

'Of course he isn't,' said Maple. 'We ought to find the black goat first.'

'Aubrey?'

Maple turned her head. 'How do you know she's called Aubrey?'

'She says she's called Aubrey,' said Mopple. 'At least sometimes she is.'

Maple carried on thinking.

'The black goat is like a clue, I think. Nobody has ever seen the Garou, and yet she knows so much about him. How? If she hasn't seen anything, then she must have heard something! But who told her? Isn't it strange where she's got it all from?'

'The other goats, maybe?' Mopple suggested.

'Maybe,' said Maple. 'Maybe not.'

Miss Maple abandoned the others and trotted off towards the goat fence, making a beeline for a dozing goat. A very dishevelled goat. They had to know more before embarking on their search for the Garou!

'Excuse me,' Maple said to the goat at the fence – not too forcefully and not too politely.

The goat opened her eyes. 'Yes, what can I do for you?'

Her coat was brown, but her eyes were grey and distant like those of a fish.

'I'm looking for a goat,' said Maple. Things were going better than she'd expected.

'I'd say you've found one.'

'A little goat.'

The goat cocked her head. 'There aren't any little goats!'

'A little black goat.'

Her head just kept turning and turning. Maple didn't like how far the goat could turn its head. Like a bird!

The goat's head was suddenly straight again, and dangerously close. She was so dishevelled.

'There aren't any black goats here,' she hissed. 'Not a single one! Black stoats. Black anecdotes, yes.'

The brown goat reeked. Like a stoat. Like a scavenger. Like . . . well, like a goat.

Maple took a step back from the fence and peered towards the goats' meadow: one fox-red goat, one white-brown mottled goat, one white-black mottled goat, one white goat with a black ear, two grey goats and two more brown goats . . . but no black goat.

'She was in the forest with us,' said Maple. 'She's after the Garou! Aren't you worried about her?'

'Garou?' asked the brown goat. 'No such thing in the forest. Just fleas and trees and pleas. Nothing in between. No need to worry.'

'Anybody can go into the forest,' said Maple. 'So, anybody can be in the forest.'

'What doesn't exist doesn't exist in the forest either,' said the goat. 'Little goats, for instance. The forest doesn't change that either. All goats are bigger than they look.' The goat made a face, as if she had just said something very important. Then she trotted away, without so much as giving Maple a second glance.

Maple sighed and started looking for another, more sensible goat, if that was even possible. The white goat with the black ear, Megara, who had helped them get through the fence, was grazing at the back. Miss Maple lay in wait beside a hazel bush and waited for Megara to come closer to the fence on her convoluted grazing route.

When Rebecca returned from the chateau, the sheep's shadows had already started to grow again. She looked livid. *Absolutely* livid. The sheep tried to stand to attention while simultaneously lying low, but the shepherdess wasn't angry with them.

'This place used to be a loony bin!' she explained to the sheep, pointing a blue mitten at the chateau. 'And I'm telling you: it's still a loony bin! They're in for a shock! I'll show them!'

'I could have told you that!' droned from the caravan. 'I could have just asked the cards!'

Then the caravan fell silent for a while, and Rebecca fell silent too, deep in thought.

Finally, she pulled out the talking device.

The talking device started honking, and Rebecca awkwardly honked back in the style of the Europeans. And – unbelievably – as she spoke, she became even more livid. Eventually the talking device was so browbeaten that it stopped honking and finally started speaking.

'. . . Don't have any people,' it crackled.

'I don't care how many people you've got!' Rebecca spat back.

'Now you listen to me, Monsieur. Somebody was in my caravan.'

The talking device crackled.

'Uninvited?' snorted Rebecca. 'I should say so!'

The talking device jabbered.

'No,' said Rebecca. 'Nothing was taken. Vandalised. Do you understand? *Vandalisme!* Of course I don't know who it was – you should be telling me that! Of course I want to report it. *Tout de suite!*'

'No, I can't come to Mauriac!' snorted Rebecca. 'I don't have a car. You'll have to come here . . . *Quoi? Merde!*'

'. . . Black,' Maple explained to the white goat with the black ear, 'and . . . not that big.'

The white goat with the black ear listened attentively. She rubbed her slender horns against the fence thoughtfully. Her ears twirled like butterfly wings.

'In the forest you say?' Maple nodded.

The goat snorted knowingly. 'A figment! The forest is full of them! They grow by the light of the moon.'

'No,' said Maple. 'It was a real goat.'

'Obviously you think that,' said the goat. 'That's what you're supposed to think.'

'It was a real goat,' insisted Miss Maple.

'Figment!' repeated the goat. 'Just like the unshorn sheep! You don't still believe he's real, do you? Nobody gets away unshorn! Nobody!'

'Of course he's real!' said Miss Maple. 'He's standing right there . . .' Then she broke off. There was nobody there. The strange ram hadn't returned from the forest with them, and they hadn't even noticed.

'What do you know about the unshorn ram?' Miss Maple asked.

'Oh,' said the goat. 'He died along with the others back then, but he thinks he's still alive. Classic figment!'

'What others?' asked Maple, but the goat just turned his head to one side and waggled his black ear frenetically.

'You see that? That's all the black you'll find amongst us, you sheep! There was a black goat once, but not any more!'

'And the Garou?' asked Miss Maple. 'Is he some kind of figment too?'

'The Garou?' The goat's eyes went blank. 'I don't know anything about the Garou.'

'But you said it yourself!' bleated Maple. 'Before we went into the forest! "If you meet the Garou," that's what you said.' The white goat with the black ear looked at Maple with respect. 'You're pretty mad for a sheep,' she bleated. 'Keep it up! Mad . . . bad . . . rad!'

Then she turned around and left Maple standing there. Maple was gradually losing her patience.

A very old grey nanny goat started sniggering nearby. Sniggering so much that her whole body was shaking. Maple was afraid she might fall over.

'Exactly!' sniggered the grey nanny goat, shaking even more. She was so scrawny. Maybe she was shivering because of the cold? The old nanny goat turned her head towards Maple, and Maple saw that she had white eyes, white and blind as snow. The blind goat Sir Ritchfield had competed against!

'It's all right,' said Maple soothingly. She felt sorry for the old nanny goat.

'All right!' panted the grey nanny goat. 'All right? Aubrey is not all right. Aubrey isn't a goat! Aubrey is ma–'

At that moment a fox-red goat headbutted the blind old nanny goat. The old goat stopped shaking and started coughing. Coughed and lapsed into silence. The wind whistled.

Maple trotted off to put a good stretch of meadow between her and the goats. She didn't like it one bit. 'Mad' is what the old goat had wanted to say. All goats were mad. But a goat that the other goats thought was mad was either unusually sane – or so mad that Maple couldn't even imagine it in her worst nightmares. But what would a sane goat want with them in the forest – and what about a goat that was completely mad?

8

MOPPLE STRIKES SILVER

Rebecca clapped the book shut and grinned. 'So?' she asked. 'What do you all think?'

The sheep stared at her with blank expressions on their faces. They didn't quite know what to make of the latest meadow read. Their old shepherd, George, had read to them back in Ireland: Pamela novels and half a detective story and once – more's the pity – a book on the diseases of sheep, so they knew a little about literature. It was clear to them that things happened in books that otherwise rarely happened here on their meadow: affairs and balls and duels with guns. But the things usually happened to humans, and they happened either in houses or outside.

This book was different.

Things happened in a wardrobe. There were fur coats in it – human coats with fur, what a ridiculous idea! – and a whole winter forest. How on earth did the forest fit inside the wardrobe? And now to top it all, somebody had turned up who was half goat. A faun. The very thought of it unsettled them. Nobody was only half goat! Nobody!

Something about the book wasn't right.

The sheep peered over at their own wardrobe with newfound suspicion, the wardrobe under the old oak. Was it hiding half goats too? Or – even worse! – whole goats?

They'd quickly accepted it even though they'd never had a wardrobe on their meadow before, never mind such a big one with lustrous golden and faintly stinky brass handles. After all, there were enough other things to marvel at: the deep snow, Zach's wood-banging experiments on the wall of the hay barn, Mum's cabinet of curious scents and the goats, time and time again.

The humans, however, found the wardrobe deeply unsettling. Why was it there, and why was there a sofa and a chest of drawers on the goats' meadow? Mind you, the sheep knew what the sofa had been good for: it had contained an interesting filling of straw and, apart from the apparently unappetising backrest, the goats had scoffed the lot.

But what about the wardrobe and the chest of drawers? The chest of drawers was something like the wardrobe's lamb. It was the same colour, had the same curved legs and was roughly the same shape. All the same, the separation didn't seem to affect either of them: the chest of drawers stood on the goats' meadow without complaint, likewise the wardrobe under the oak, and no matter how closely the sheep watched it, it didn't move a single step closer to the goat fence. The sheep, not able to make head nor tail of it, waggled their ears and blithely grazed around the wardrobe and its secret.

Rebecca, however, was tireless in her desire to find out where the wardrobe had come from, and Mum to find out what might be inside. The sheep, if they were interested at all, were only interested in what was underneath the wardrobe – undiscovered grass that might never have been grazed before? Up to now, none of those questions had been answered, and only recently Mum had tried to tickle it open with a long sparkly hairpin. To no avail.

'I'm going to take another look at it!' declared Lane, trotting purposefully over to the wardrobe. The others went along too.

Lane circled the wardrobe once, and once again to be sure. The wardrobe just stood there and let it happen, big, damp and useless, with its curved feet and cap of snow. It was big, but not *that* big. A few sheep would have fitted inside, or a couple of Two-Legs maybe, but not the oak, and definitely not a second or third tree. How many trees made a forest? At least five, the sheep supposed. That decided it: the book was mad!

Maple looked as if she'd suddenly understood something.

The others cast envious glances her way.

'Out of the wardrobe!' bleated Maple. 'He said he comes out of the wardrobe!'

'Who?' asked Mopple. 'What?'

'The strange ram,' said Miss Maple. 'I don't know what. Nothing good at any rate.'

If you really thought about it, the wardrobe was a bit creepy and very strange, like something from another world. 'Do you think he meant the Garou?' Cloud asked quietly.

'I don't know.' Maple pressed her ear to the wood and listened.

'So?' asked Mopple nervously.

'Nothing,' said Maple. 'But it sounds hollow.'

'In there?' whispered Heather. 'Are you sure?'

Maude nodded. 'In there,' she said. 'Or nowhere.'

Heather and Zora peered uneasily through the half-open barn door. Up to now their expedition had been running pretty smoothly. They had simply walked through the yard gate, in broad, wan daylight and led their pale shadows through a maze of narrow alleyways. Maude had tracked down three small cars, a motorbike, a lawnmower and a huge tyre. But there was still no sign of the extra-large car that had brought them all here.

'Cars don't live in houses,' said Heather.

'Do so!' bleated Maude, huffily holding her magnificent nose in the air.

'Do you hear that?' asked Zora suddenly. The sheep listened.

'Nothing,' said Heather after a while.

'Exactly,' said Zora. 'Nothing. No barking dogs. Anywhere. We've wandered all over the place, here, there and everywhere, and there have been no barking dogs anywhere.'

'That's a good thing!' said Maude.

'It is good,' confirmed Zora. 'But if there aren't any dogs around here . . .'

'. . . where's that howling coming from?' asked Heather.

The three members of the sheep expedition looked at one another.

All of a sudden it seemed vital for them to find the car quickly. Howling with dogs around was bad enough, but howling without any dogs around was not a good sign.

Zora took a deep breath and disappeared into the darkness of the barn, her beautiful horns leading the way.

Something rustled.

'Come on!' bleated Zora from inside. 'It's not that bad at all!'

Heather sneezed shyly. Maude shook her head.

'But you said yourself . . .' bleated Heather.

'I said there was a car inside,' said Maude. 'Not that we ought to go in. I don't want to go inside!'

Heather thought about woolpower, scrunched her eyes shut, jumped forward like a lamb and opened her eyes again.

Maude was standing beside her again.

'But you just said you didn't want to come inside!' bleated Heather.

'Now I do!' said Maude, an embarrassed look on her face. For the first time in her life, Heather really understood something about woolpower: it wasn't just about *you*, it was about the others too. Everything was connected.

Heather looked around.

Cold winter light poured inside through untold gaps in the barn walls. It wasn't even particularly dark in here – more stripy. The dusty floor was stripy, as were the huge field-machines in front of them, and the saws and mowers, as well as the hooks and chains hanging from the barn ceiling. Beside her, Maude looked like a giant moody tabby cat. And Zora? Where was Zora? A draught blew through the barn, and the chains above Heather clinked gently.

'Zora?' bleated Heather. Her voice sounded thin. 'Zora?'

Maude scented the air. 'Back there!' she said, trotting off. Stripes flitted across her fleece.

They found Zora in a corner of the barn, right in front of the extra-large car. She looked pretty pleased with herself.

'Now we just have to convince it!' she said.

'Super!' bleated Maude, relieved.

'Supernaturally!' bleated Heather.

The other two looked at her, mystified.

* * *

There was a man standing in front of the shepherd's caravan, and none of the sheep had heard him coming. Maybe they had all been a bit too busy grazing in an attempt to forget the Garou, the deer and, for good measure, the wardrobe too.

The man knocked, and Rebecca opened the door. '*Bonjour*,' she said, drying her hands on her apron.

Tess remembered her guard dog duties and yapped half-heartedly.

'Hello, Mademoiselle,' said the man. He was extraordinarily tall and broad, wearing a brown overcoat and brown boots and had elegantly curled hair on his top lip. Before the sheep knew what was happening, he was already standing on the top step, pressing a little card into Rebecca's hand.

'May I introduce myself,' he said. 'Dupin. Police.'

Rebecca's thunder face brightened. 'You came!' she said.

'Flock. Rebecca Flock.' The man nodded.

'This is the caravan,' said Rebecca. 'And that's my mother over there. This is where it happened. I don't lock up, so there wasn't a break in. I went out early, at about eight maybe, into the forest looking for one of my sheep. And my mother . . . was having a shower in the chateau's guest house.'

'When was that?' asked Dupin, pulling out a notebook.

'From nine until twelve,' droned from the caravan. 'Three hours?' asked Dupin.

The sheep liked that he was only saying short things. He was like a lake. A very calm lake.

'Three hours,' said Rebecca in a voice that brooked no dissent. 'And when I got back, it was at about twelve as well, I think; I noticed straightaway. Somebody had been in the caravan and destroyed my clothes. With some scissors or something.'

'Just clothes?' asked Dupin.

'Just *red* clothes,' said Rebecca. Dupin glanced up.

'All of them?' he asked.

'All apart from one scarf. They didn't find that one. It was in the laundry. Red is my favourite colour,' said Rebecca. 'It's just plain mean!'

The sheep didn't fully understand why Rebecca was so upset. She had a brown hat (a very attractive one at that, vaguely reminiscent of a cottage loaf) and blue and green jumpers and trousers, as well as the beloved woolly jumper. If they were honest, they'd never really liked all the red. It tickled their eyes. It put them on edge.

'Did you find your sheep, Mademoiselle?'

'I did! In a snare!' Rebecca frowned.

'And did you find anything else?'

'More sheep!' Rebecca laughed.

Dupin stroked the frosty hair on his upper lip. 'Can you remember where you found the sheep?'

'No,' said Rebecca. 'It was just a stroke of luck.' She laughed again and looked conspiratorially over at the sheep. 'In a clearing somewhere, near the path. You can't even imagine what a stroke of luck it was!'

'I think I can,' said Dupin. He got a bar of whole-nut chocolate out of his pocket and offered Rebecca some. The tall policeman was beginning to grow on the sheep.

Rebecca shook her head.

'You . . . you're not here because of my clothes, are you?'

'No,' said Dupin. 'But maybe we could – how do you say it in your language? – kill two birds with one stone.' The sheep's ears twitched. Killing one bird with a stone was bad enough, but two seemed positively barbaric.

The shepherdess looked very pale.

'You think whoever did that to the deer was also in my caravan?'

Dupin pointed inside the caravan. 'May I? You will already have heard things about the situation here, Mademoiselle. Unbelievable things.'

'No,' said Rebecca stepping aside slightly so that Dupin could get through the door. 'No, actually, I haven't.'

The caravan door shut behind them.

The sheep retreated sulkily to the hay barn. Nobody had thought to offer *them* any chocolate. And while Rebecca was busy mourning her red clothes, here they were busily sleuthing out in the snow.

'If only we could ask the goat!' Maple scraped impatiently in the snow. 'We have to think about what she told us back in the forest. Do you remember what she told us?'

Mopple the Whale raised his curved horns proudly. He was the memory sheep. Of course he remembered!

'The Garou is a wolf who can turn into a human,' he began. 'Or a human who can turn into a wolf. Whatever the case may be!'

The sheep tried to imagine it. They had never seen a human turn into anything – not even a poodle. The whole thing seemed a bit far-fetched to them, yet still . . .

'In order to transform, he had to take off his clothes and cover himself with an ointment. Nothing happens without the ointment. He transforms, but his eyes don't. His eyes are always wolf eyes. That's what Aubrey said, anyway.'

That wasn't particularly encouraging either. The reality was that most creature's eyes looked pretty similar. Tess's eyes looked like Mum's eyes, and George had once even said that all of their eyes looked like the eyes of an octopus that lived at the bottom of the sea. It was clear to the sheep that eyes wouldn't be much help. The scent, maybe? There were a few humans around here who had a strong scent: Yves and the goatherder and sometimes the gardener too. But what did a wolf smell like exactly?

'He hunts deer and humans and goats and sheep,' continued Mopple. 'He hunts everything.'

That was without a doubt the most unpleasant part of the whole story.

'He can't cross flowing water . . .' Mopple looked at the others. 'I can cross flowing water!' he said proudly.

'Just about,' said Maple. 'But that doesn't help us either. We can't sit at the stream waiting for somebody not to cross it.'

'He's afraid of silver – and holy water!'

Neither of them had ever seen water with holes in it – or did it mean bubbles maybe? But silver they knew. It was bright and cold and shiny, it shimmered like the sky on a grey day, crackled, reflected the light and had a delicate metallic scent. Rebecca wrapped most of her sandwiches in it.

'That's a start!' Maple looked satisfied. 'Let's look for a piece of silver, and then we'll watch to see who's scared of it!' The others liked the idea of looking for a bread-scented piece of silver paper too – maybe they would even find one with some bread still in it? They trotted purposefully back towards the shepherd's caravan.

Rebecca was normally very tidy when it came to her silver paper, but a little while ago a piece had eluded her. Fluttering like a tin butterfly, it had hung around between the wheels of the shepherd's caravan for a while and had then disappeared beneath snow and still more snow. The sheep rooted around determinedly – a good opportunity to graze a bit while investigating!

Snow, damp earth, winter grass, more snow, wet, cold stone, an unappetisingly sodden cigarette end that Rebecca must have missed, a mouldy branch, more winter grass, dirty ice, a forgotten apple core. A muddy biscuit.

They were beginning to enjoy this detective lark.

More snow, better grass and – right next to the wheels of the caravan – metal. But the wrong kind of metal: a rusty screw from the hub. And then suddenly: butter. Just a whiff, more like a memory of butter. But it was there nonetheless. Mopple carried on rooting, until something crackled beneath his nose. A decent piece of silver! Mopple plucked it carefully out of the snow.

What now?

The winter lamb, who up to now had been hanging around a little way from the others under the old oak, came by and looked curiously.

'What are you lot up to?' he asked.

'Mmmh,' said Mopple, the paper in his mouth.

'That's silver,' Miss Maple explained.

'Why isn't he eating it?' asked the winter lamb.

'Mmmh,' said Mopple.

'It doesn't taste very good,' said Maple, 'but it helps fend off the Garou!'

'Maybe each of us ought to eat a little piece of it,' said the winter lamb bravely. 'Even though it doesn't taste very good.'

'No,' said Maple. 'We'll put it somewhere where everybody can see it and then we'll watch to see who's afraid of it!'

'Nobody'll be afraid of it,' said the winter lamb. 'Not even the little humans.'

But he came along anyway as the sheep started to look for a good position for the paper. Near the fence in any case, where it would be seen by as many humans as possible. Somewhere where the wind wouldn't carry it off!

With some difficulty, the sheep managed to skewer the silver onto the branch of a bare hazel bush near the yard gate and goat fence. The little piece of paper flickered and crackled in the wind, and the first goats came closer, curiously.

'Bold!' said the first, a brown-white mottled goat.

'Avant-garde!' confirmed a second, a red goat with the air of a connoisseur.

'No bread and butter!' said the third.

'We're just imagining it all anyway,' said the goat with only one horn, shaking her head.

The sheep didn't respond. More goats flocked closer.

'How boring!' bleated a goat from the second row.

'We want Ritchfield!' Megara called down from the sofa. 'We want Ritchfield!' the other goats sang in chorus. Luckily Ritchfield was engrossed in a conversation with the feed trough and didn't realise what was going on. The goats bleated for Ritchfield for a while, then they started to arrange themselves by colour; first Megara, then two grey goats, the mottled goat, the red goat and finally the brown goats. 'Maybe we're just imagining them *all*!' Miss Maple muttered to herself.

The goatherder trudged across the yard, without a trace of fear of the paper. The goats gathered themselves a bit. As soon as he had disappeared around the corner, they lined up along the fence again and tested to see who could stick their tongue out the farthest. They could all stick their tongues out pretty far.

Eventually, Cloud couldn't take it any more.

'Your herder stinks!' she said to the goats.

The other sheep were flabbergasted. They had never seen

Cloud start an argument before, but since that night in the forest, she seemed a bit more irritable to them and – they hardly dared think it – less strong-wooled.

'Who says so? Show yourself! Where are you?' bleated a brown goat.

'Where? Where? Where? Where? Where? Wolf!' sang the other goats.

Cloud thought for a moment.

'Our shepherdess!' she said then, fluffing herself up. It wasn't true, but she was trying to impress the goats.

'Your shepherdess!' said the goat. 'Your shepherdess can't smell a thing!'

That was true.

'Can too!' bleated Cloud.

'And she can't speak either!' bleated the brown-white mottled goat.

Cloud looked at the goat incredulously. 'Of course she can speak – your herder can't speak!'

'He can too!' said the mottled goat.

'No, he can't!' bleated Cloud,

'Yes, he can!' bleated the goat.

'No, he can't!'

Maple started to consider different locations for the werewolf silver.

'Yes, he can!' bleated the goat.

'No, he can't!' bleated Cloud.

'No, he can't,' said the goat.

Cloud fell silent, puzzled.

'You're supposed to say "yes, he can,"' explained the goat. 'It gets boring otherwise!'

Cloud didn't say another word, but Miss Maple looked wide-awake.

'You can all understand what the goatherder says?'

'Of course,' said the goat.

'And *the things* he says!' said another goat shaking her head chidingly.

'And you understand the other humans as well?'

The goats stretched their goats' beards forwards. 'We understand what everybody says. It's just your shepherdess and the old bat we don't understand!'

The shadows of the tree trunks were getting longer and longer, and the forest was full of sounds. Little sounds. The wind shook forgotten leaves. Snow crunched. Small animals rustled in search of a hiding place. Birds landed on branches, making a sound that could be sensed rather than heard, a dry, brittle bounce in the air.

A little goat stood soundlessly waiting in the darkness of a fir, so black that only her eyes could be seen, flickering, slightly bulging goat's eyes.

Deep in the snow.

Aubrey was shivering. She had followed the Garou's tracks, uphill and downhill, straight ahead and zigzag, in loops and circles and wavy lines, without rhyme or reason. The Garou was obviously in high spirits. If she didn't know better, she would have taken him for a gambolling nanny-goat. But she knew better. Far better. Once, at the stream, the Garou had almost given her the slip. Aubrey searched upstream, and Aubrey searched downstream, and eventually she was back on track again. The Garou was clever, but not as clever as her.

On the other side of the firs was an old, dilapidated wooden hut. The Garou's tracks led inside – but they didn't come outside again. Other tracks, yes, but not the Garou's.

Aubrey scented the air. Nothing. Just a bit of frozen wood perhaps.

A fox darted past. Aubrey glared after it.

Then she warily ventured closer to the hut. The black on the other side of the half-open door enticed her, murmuring sweet threats. Aubrey turned around. Behind her, standing in the darkness of the firs where she had just been standing was another little black goat. The goat that always followed her. The goat that nobody else could see. Aubrey was happy she was there.

'Come on!' she said, before pressing her sharp horns against the wood of the hut door. Suddenly she was standing inside. The air here was older, mustier – and even colder. Lots of broken wood was lying on the ground. And dead rats. No: not dead – sleeping rats! Everything was broken – apart from a table in the middle of the room. There were some boots underneath the table. Very different boots. There was something on the table. With one bound, Aubrey was up there – and landed on something soft. She gasped in surprise – a half-open feed sack! Bread and mangelwurzels. Of all things, a feed sack was what she had least expected. Beside the feed sack was a glass with powder in it. A bitter scent, like medicine, wafted around the glass.

A rustling made Aubrey look up. The little black goat had followed her into the hut and was looking at the fodder. Aubrey was about to start eating, but the other goat shook her head mutely. No!

Aubrey kicked the glass off the table, and it shattered mid-air making a cold, thin sound, almost a scream. Powder dusted everything like bitter snow, and Aubrey held her breath as best she could.

'That should do it,' said Aubrey when the dust had settled. She felt dizzy.

'I hardly think so,' said the little black goat from below.

'You'll see,' responded Aubrey. 'That was his ointment. His wolf ointment!'

'But it wasn't an ointment,' said the goat.

'It doesn't matter!' answered Aubrey, waggling her tail proudly.

Suddenly there was an opening at the back of the hut where there hadn't been an opening before, and in the opening stood . . . *something* – looking right at her.

9

AMALTÉE TAKES LIBERTIES

The sheep's shadows were longer and thinner, even Mopple's, and the mood was sombre. Even Miss Maple had to admit that their investigations weren't going particularly smoothly. Nobody seemed to be afraid of the silver paper. Neither of the two winter visitors who had left together for one of their many walks, one of them tall, the other short; not Eric busy with goat's cheese in the tower as usual; or timid Madame Fronsac. And the gardener, who was secretly their prime suspect, had walked along the fence without the slightest sign of fear, a little fir tree in tow. The fir tree ended up by the chateau wall, on a heap with some other fir trees.

A little fat cloud edged in front of the sun, and the shadows disappeared.

'Tomorrow is spring,' said Sir Ritchfield, in high spirits. The others did not share his optimism.

The caravan door creaked open again, and Dupin stepped outside. Rebecca stood with him on the top step and passed him his brown hat. She looked pale.

'*Au revoir*!' said Rebecca.

Dupin put his hat on. 'Be a little afraid of ghosts, Mademoiselle, that's unfortunately all I can advise as far as things with the investigation currently stand.'

'*Au revoir*,' repeated Rebecca.

Dupin bowed, which looked slightly ridiculous – maybe just because he was so tall – then turned around and walked back towards the chateau.

Mum and Rebecca stared after him.

'More deer like that,' muttered Rebecca. 'And probably not just deer, otherwise the police wouldn't send an inspector over here, would they? But he didn't say any more than that.'

'So, you were alone in the forest?' said Mum.

'No.' Rebecca shook her head. 'I just wanted him to leave Zach in peace. They're sure to be looking for a lunatic. Something like this could only have been done by a lunatic. And if they find out about Zach . . . even if he's got an alibi, they'd probably take him away somewhere.'

'What if it was Zach?' asked Mum. 'You didn't come back together, did you?'

Rebecca sighed. 'We met Yves. Well, not really met. More like saw him from a distance, with an axe over his shoulder. And Zach wanted to . . . shadow him, he said. Keep him under surveillance. That's Zach, there's no talking to him. He put on my hat – as a disguise. And suddenly, I was on my own in the forest, without a hat. I was a bit cross, to be honest.'

'What if it was him?' repeated Mum.

'There is absolutely no way it was Zach,' said Rebecca. 'Zach has lived here for years.'

Mum huffed scornfully. 'Whoever it was has probably lived here for years. This isn't exactly the kind of place where strangers blend in. And do you know what? If I'd lived here for years, I'd have gone mad too.'

Mum threw her arms theatrically into the air, then looked at a little sparkling clock on her wrist. 'Is that the time already? I've got to get ready! Time flies!' She disappeared into the depths of the caravan, banging and clattering. The sheep were left a bit baffled at the thought of time flying. First pigs, now time! What was next?

'And shall I tell you something else?' she shouted from the depths of the caravan. 'There is no way on this earth that that was a policeman!'

'Nonsense,' said Rebecca. 'You and your conspiracy theories!'

And then, without another word, she shut the caravan door.

The negotiations hadn't been going particularly well up to now. They had tried flattery, pleading, threats, even a little kick to the bumper. But the big car remained stubbornly silent.

'It just doesn't want to!' said Maude. 'I can scent that it doesn't want to!' Maude wanted to go back to the meadow.

The sheep weren't naive. They knew that cars weren't alive in the same way as sheep or dogs or humans. But sometimes they moved and sometimes they didn't. There had to be something that made them move. But what?

Heather thought about woolpower and fluffed herself up a bit. 'Come on! We've just got to promise him the right things!'

The sheep looked at one another: were mangelwurzels, concentrated feed and overnight stays in the hay barn not the right kind of things?

'And you can drive about on our meadow as much as you like!' bleated Heather.

Zora and Maude looked dismayed. Now Heather was taking things a step too far!

Luckily the car didn't show any interest, even now.

'Strange,' said Zora. 'It ought to be happy about an outing. I mean it must be bored all on its own here in the barn.'

'It's definitely bored,' said Maude. Maude was bored too.

'Maybe it likes stories,' said Heather suddenly.

They decided to tell the car a story. A story with cars in it. Sheep liked stories with sheep in them – unfortunately they were few and far between, and usually the sheep were just in the background. They could imagine cars liking stories with cars in them. Only the sheep didn't know any stories with cars in them. But maybe they could adapt one of the romantic Pamela stories that had been told on the meadow in George's time?

'In a remote manor . . .' Heather began.

'Barn!' bleated Zora.

'In a remote barn, there lived a poor, but noble family of cars. They were all fine cars, but the youngest car was the finest of all. It, err, was a particularly fine colour . . .'

'White!' suggested Maude. '. . . and was wild and free.'

'. . . and liked taking friendly flocks of sheep for rides!' bleated Zora.

The story ought to be a bit educational too.

'Exactly!' bleated Maude.

'Exactly!' bleated Heather.

They looked expectantly at the car, but if it had got the hint, it didn't let on.

'The young car lived happily and peacefully until one day a

mysterious stranger arrived in the village . . .'

'Barn!' bleated Zora.

Suddenly Mum was standing on the caravan steps again, wearing dark flowing clothes and holding a cigarette in her hand. And – no doubt about it – there was her third eye, right in the middle of her forehead! It was slightly smaller than the other two and twinkled when it caught the light. Mum's face glittered and sparkled, her cheeks were red, as was her mouth, and the first two eyes were black-rimmed like the eyes of a Kerry Hill sheep that the flock had once met at a sheep competition in Ireland. The Kerry Hill sheep had won. The wind blew back Mum's clothes, and for the first time, the sheep saw how gaunt she was beneath the many layers of baggy clothing. Gaunt and frail. Then the wind blew in another direction and Mum looked big and imposing again.

Rebecca coughed inside the caravan. 'That stinks!' she said.

'Joss sticks,' said Mum, unfazed.

Now the sheep could smell it too, even out here on the meadow. One of Mum's unfathomable scents, no doubt. As if something were burning. Something from a far-off land.

'I can't bear it!' groaned Rebecca. 'In such a confined space!'

'Speaking of which,' said Mum, flicking her cigarette butt onto the meadow in an unobserved moment, 'my clients need a bit of . . . privacy.'

'You want me to make myself scarce!' said Rebecca. 'From *my own* caravan!'

'Oh, come on, let's not get all dramatic about it,' said Mum. 'Go for a walk! You like going for walks!'

'Great!' said Rebecca. 'There's a violent nutcase on the loose and I'm supposed to go for a walk so that you can perform your hocus-pocus in here.'

But she already had her brown bread hat and her red scarf on, and a green anorak in her hand. 'I've got to feed the sheep anyway.'

Mum's big red mouth smiled.

'That hocus-pocus is our best chance of finding out what's going on around here. Otherwise, nobody talks to us. There's some kind of secret, and I'm going to . . .'

She broke off and looked towards the chateau. A man was standing at the meadow gate. A man with broad shoulders and dark hair. A man who left his shirt collar unbuttoned even in winter, revealing dark chest hair. Yves.

'*Him?*' hissed Rebecca. 'In my caravan? He just wants to have a nose around.'

Mum shrugged. 'A client is a client. Fortunes don't discriminate.'

'Maybe fortunes don't,' said Rebecca, 'but I do!'

She grabbed the feed bucket and stomped silently past Yves, who grinned at her toothily. Then he looked up at Mum, who was still standing in the door of the caravan, smoking and dark and flowing, and his smile vanished. For a moment it almost looked like he was scared. Then he grinned again, stepped into the darkness of the caravan and the door creaked shut behind him.

'Come with me!' he said. 'The world is our oyster!' And they rode . . .'

'Drove!' bleated Zora.

'. . . drove off into the sunset together.'

Zora, Maude and Heather looked expectantly at the car. Admittedly the middle part had got a bit muddled because they had never seen a car carry another car in its strong arms – arms? –

and female cars dressed as male cars was quite difficult to imagine too. If they were honest, they couldn't really even imagine female humans dressed as men. 'You must be able to smell it! You must be able to smell it.' Maude had bleated when George had first read the story to them back then on the steps of the shepherd's caravan.

But it had turned out to be quite an ordinary story, with green meadows and shiny paved roads and a duel – 'accident!' Zora had bleated – and a lot of sun, and sheep in the background of course.

And sure enough: the car's eyes suddenly lit up.

'It's playing along!' bleated Heather, relieved. If you really thought about it, it had been an extraordinarily good story.

'Somebody's coming!' bleated Maude.

Now the others heard it too: footsteps in the barn. Coming towards them.

'It had to be now, didn't it?' muttered Heather.

The sheep hid behind the car and peered through under its belly. Two yellow gumboots made their way along the alley between the machines and finally stopped at the extra-large car.

And stood there. And stood there.

Then the gumboots were on the move again – straight towards them! The sheep looked around for better hiding places. Behind them was the barn wall, to the left a big saw blocked the way, and on the right the gumboots were coming round the side of the big car.

'In there!' bleated Zora, leaping forwards, from a bale of straw onto a tool bench and from there into the empty hindquarters of the car. Heather and Maude followed. Inside, it smelled exactly the same as it had smelled before, of old nerves and even older straw.

Something clacked. Then silence.

'Wool!' bleated Heather.

She was right. A decent-sized tuft of white wool had snagged on the side of the car.

'Ritchfield!' said Heather, sniffing. 'No! Willow! Or Maple? Mopple?'

Maude, the sheep with the best sense of smell in the flock stuck her nose into the wool.

'So?' asked Zora. 'Who is it?' Zora secretly hoped that it was Mopple's wool.

'I don't know,' said Maude after a while. 'Nobody. Nobody we know!'

The extra-large car shuddered and slowly started moving.

Rebecca had shovelled new straw into the hay barn and new hay into the rack. She had poured a decent amount of concentrated feed into the trough for them and checked the fence. The sheep looked nervous. They knew what was coming next: the count. Rebecca would find out that Maude, Heather and Zora were missing. But just as she pointed her finger to count, the caravan door opened again and Yves stepped outside. Rebecca waited until he had disappeared from the meadow, then she relaxed her counting finger and strolled towards the caravan in a markedly casual way.

'Tea?' asked Mum.

Rebecca nodded. 'So – did you find anything out?' The sheep edged closer, curiously.

Mum lit a cigarette. 'Actually . . . I didn't really understand him. And he probably didn't understand me either.'

'I could have told you that,' said Rebecca. 'Did he at least pay?'

'He, erm, he hasn't got any money, he'll . . . erm . . . pay in kind,' said Mum, blowing smoke into the air. 'Let's just wait and see!'

And sure enough: a few minutes later Yves was back on the meadow and he was dragging a little, but seemingly heavy box towards the shepherd's caravan. He placed the box on the caravan steps and grinned at Rebecca. Rebecca grinned back icily.

The sheep scented the air: Was there something edible in the box? But they could only smell metal and plastic and a bit of glass.

'A television!' said Rebecca, impressed, once Yves had disappeared from the meadow for the second time. 'Did you see something good in his cards?'

'Not really.' Mum looked guilty. 'To be quite honest, his cards were pretty dreadful. I can't remember ever seeing such dreadful cards. A big change – that was the best thing I could read from the cards. But maybe he didn't understand me.'

'You don't really believe it, do you?' asked Rebecca. 'That the cards reveal the future? I mean: How is that even possible?'

Mum puffed on her cigarette. 'If I didn't believe in it at all, I wouldn't be any good at it. And if I believed in it too much, I wouldn't be any good at it either. You need to find a happy medium to be a happy medium. Ha!'

The sheep were thoroughly confused: fortune-telling didn't seem to be about fortune at all. It was about all of the different things that might happen, good or bad. Rebecca had asked her map 'where to?' and the card map could more or less be relied upon to respond. Mum asked her cards 'what?' and the cards responded with things. Not things that had happened, but things that might happen. Mum's cards were like a map for the future!

'That's the kind of card you need to eat!' Cordelia whispered to Mopple.

Mopple nodded dutifully.

Then the next human stood expectantly at the fence and Rebecca disappeared towards the chateau, her scarf wafting in the breeze, to secretly read a book behind the sheep's backs in the chateau library. The sheep had known what she was up to for a while.

The next human was the gardener. The gardener of all people! The gardener was their natural enemy. He guarded the apple orchard and the blackberry bushes, the pea plants and the vegetable garden. He guarded all the tasty things. The goats even claimed he had a house where it was always summer, and apparently, he secretly grew lettuce there.

The sheep watched with a sense of unease as he walked across the meadow. Everything about him was pale, and nothing about him was bright. To the sheep he seemed like a mangelwurzel growing in the ground – an unappetising, pale mangelwurzel, and he looked at the ground too much. They were happy when he had finally disappeared into the shepherd's caravan with Mum and her third eye.

The sheep tried to relax. Othello had a play-duel with Sir Ritchfield, Lane scratched herself on a post, Cloud worked on her woolpower, and Mopple ate. The winter lamb tried out names: Linton, Hannibal and Summerfield – but none of them suited him.

Eventually Hortense came through the yard gate with the two children. Hortense was often out and about with the two children, even though they weren't her own young.

The children played in the no-man's-land between the yard gate and the meadow. At first, they played hide-and-seek and then, when they were bored of that because there were only two hiding places between the fence and the yard gate, a bush and a fountain, they played Zach. They sneaked around, examining the ground and speaking to their wrists.

Hortense was shivering. Looking to the left and right, as if she were waiting for somebody.

Neither Hortense nor the children were afraid of the silver. The children started throwing snowballs at each other.

It was a bit unfair because the older boy was a much better shot.

Hortense, shivering even more, leaned against the fence and secretly peered towards the shepherd's caravan. A big dark shadow appeared in the yard gate and watched her shivering for a while: Dupin.

The older of the two little humans honked and threw a snowball, but the younger one didn't honk back; instead, he started watching the sheep, a little wide-eyed. He went down on all fours, rooted in the snow and ripped up some grass. At times he even bleated — thinly and badly and unprofessionally. The older boy seemed to like it. He was already on all fours as well, sticking his nose into the snow like his little brother.

'I think they're grazing,' said Cordelia approvingly. The sheep looked favourably at the little humans, recognising their obvious gesture of goodwool. It was always nice to see humans doing something sensible for a change.

'Why aren't they eating the grass?' asked Mopple. The most important part of grazing seemed to have eluded the children.

'They're learning,' said Cordelia. 'Hortense ought to show them how it's done.'

But Hortense just carried on pointlessly standing there, shivering. When Dupin leaned on the fence next to her, she gave a start. Dupin did one of his ridiculous little bows and started honking. Hortense honked back.

'What are they saying?' asked Ramesses.

'We need a goat!' bleated Miss Maple anxiously. 'Now!'

Mopple didn't want any part in it, but Ritchfield and the winter lamb accompanied Maple to the goat fence again.

The shaggy brown goat, the mottled goat, and a young grey goat looked at them with curiosity.

Maple took a deep breath.

'They're wanting again!' the mottled goat said to the brown goat.

The brown goat nodded earnestly.

'Do you all understand what the humans at the fence are saying?' asked Maple.

'Of course!' bleated the three goats in chorus.

'So,' asked the winter lamb truculently, 'what are they saying then?'

'We can't understand it from here,' said the brown goat. 'They're too far away!'

Maple scraped impatiently in the snow.

'I want to know what they're saying!' she said finally.

The goats cast meaningful glances at one another, shook their heads and made long goat-beards.

'I'll do it!' a young grey goat said all of a sudden and had already slipped through the fence.

'Mad!' muttered the mottled goat, and the brown goat nodded in agreement.

Maple, the winter lamb and the grey goat trotted briskly across the meadow towards the two humans. Ritchfield stayed at the goat fence showering the goats with compliments. The goats giggled.

'I'm called Amaltée,' said the young grey goat as she trotted along. 'What about you?'

The winter lamb didn't respond.

'So?' asked Maple once they had ventured just a stone's throw from Dupin.

Amaltée put her head on one side and listened.

'He says she smells like a midday autumn apple, warm and ripe and it's driving him crazy . . . She's saying she wants his strong horn. Her back is only for him . . . He says he'll win every duel for her . . . She doesn't want to wait; she wants him right now. In the pig pen.'

'Really?' asked the winter lamb, fascinated. In winter?

Neither of the humans looked particularly frisky.

'No.' Amaltée stuck out her bottom lip. 'They were talking about the weather. Saying that there's going to be more snow. Even the silliest old goose knows that there's going to be more snow. That's boring. It's bad enough that it's been said once.'

Maple gasped for air, exasperated. 'If you're not going to tell us what they're saying . . .'

'I'm telling you what they should have said. Poetic freedom. All translators take liberties.'

Maple had no desire to ask what poetic freedom was. Probably just another mad goat thing. The winter lamb didn't know exactly what poetic freedom was either – he was suddenly dizzy with joy all the same. Poetic freedom was *important*. It was like a place. The place where things were how they wanted and ought to be. Names, for instance. And the goats knew where to find it!

'They're speaking about the goatherder,' said Amaltée. 'About the fact that he won't speak to the police, that he's not himself any more after everything he's had to deal with.'

The sheep knew what the goatherder was dealing with, day after day: goats. No wonder he was lost for words.

Amaltée put her head on one side. 'But if he's not himself any more – who is he?'

'The tall human wants to know where she sleeps,' she continued. 'In the chateau, she says. He'd like to know which way her window faces.' The goat sniggered. 'I've never seen a window with a face!'

She had a faraway look in her eye.

'Carry on!' bleated Miss Maple nervously.

'Her window faces the meadow,' said the goat. 'Can you see a window with a face from your meadow? You can't on ours! She's lying! . . . He's asking if she saw anything unusual through her meadow window . . . She's not saying anything. He's not saying anything either. She's still not saying anything.'

'Yes, yes,' said Miss Maple. 'We can hear that too.'

'I can't hear it,' said the goat.

Finally, Hortense said something. Very quietly.

'Not recently, she says,' continued the goat. 'But before.'

Hortense carried on talking, quickly and quietly. 'Two winters ago, she saw . . .'

The goat fell silent.

'Yes?' asked Miss Maple impatiently.

'Nothing,' said the goat. 'Nothing at all.'

'But they're talking!' bleated Maple.

'I can't hear anything,' muttered Amaltée, trotting away, back to the goat fence.

Hortense made a sweeping gesture across the whole sheep

meadow, shuddering, and talked and talked, until the younger boy, who had long since given up on his inexperienced grazing attempts, ran over to her again and brought her a stick with a clear little icicle on it. Hortense stopped talking, crouched down and hugged him.

Madame Fronsac came out of the yard gate and waited a way off until Dupin had said goodbye to Hortense. Then, without so much as a word, the two women walked towards the shepherd's caravan. The sheep supposed that Hortense was something like Madame Fronsac's translator-goat. That showed just how important this was to Madame Fronsac.

When Mum opened the caravan door to let the gardener out – and Hortense and the Walrus in, it wasn't only aromatic clouds of smoke that escaped the caravan. The sheep also saw a paper thing that briefly fluttered through the air and then got stuck in the cold snow.

The sheep sprang into action. Unlike the map, this piece of card wasn't patterned. It was smaller, harder and shinier, and had a picture on it.

'A human falling from a tree!' bleated Sir Ritchfield confidently. Ritchfield still had the best eyes in the flock; there was no doubting that. Next moment the card had disappeared into Mopple's mouth. Mopple chewed dutifully, swallowed and chewed again just to be sure.

The sheep eagerly awaited what would happen next.

10

THE WINTER LAMB FINDS HIS NAME

The fox was coming along after her. He was big now, so big that he could look down on her, and his eyes glowed green through the forest, and blurred. Sometimes he ran on all fours, sometimes on two legs, but always after her.

Aubrey doubled back; the fox ran through the tree trunks. He had just devoured her ghost-kid – again! Then her shadow, and now he would devour her.

Aubrey knew something about the whole thing wasn't quite right. She had never seen tree trunks that bent like grass and grabbed at her with their twig fingers. Maybe she had finally gone mad; maybe it was down to the wolf powder that had drifted into her nose in the hut.

Then again . . . then again, there was definitely somebody after her.

Aubrey slowed down and stumbled. The ground in front of her was rippling like the surface of a disturbed puddle. She glanced back and saw hands and the flash of a knife and red, but it wasn't fox red. The forest was so quiet.

Then she heard something. Roaring and rattling. Aubrey summoned all of her courage and shook the fog from her head. The ground smoothed out again and Aubrey galloped off.

She reached the road just as the car drove past, a big transporter. The tailgate at the back had just come loose and clattered to the ground, slowing the car down.

In that moment Aubrey had an idea. An idea that felt mad in a pleasant kind of a way. Aubrey galloped behind the car as fast as her legs would carry her.

'It's too cold!' said Sir Ritchfield. 'Cold isn't good for your head.'

'Too little fodder,' groaned Mopple the Whale. 'Too little fodder can send you mad.'

'It's the goats' fault,' said Cloud emphatically.

A cold wind blew, the birds sat fat and stubborn in the branches, and all things cast long, lean shadows. The sheep had gathered beneath the old oak and were staring up into the branches in shock.

'Come down!' they bleated. 'Sheep don't climb trees!'

Exactly, thought the winter lamb. 'If I climb a tree, I won't be a sheep anymore!'

The winter lamb didn't want to be a sheep anymore. He silently carried on climbing up the old oak's boot, his hooves spread cautiously.

It actually wasn't particularly difficult. The boot of the oak tree sloped to one side, almost horizontally, a comfortable, broad path skywards. Any determined sheep would have made it up there.

But sheep don't climb trees.

Goats do. When the winter lamb was bigger, he wanted to be a goat.

'You'll never be big though,' the other sheep had said, and the winter lamb was indeed smaller than all the others and had shorter legs. He had tiny, pointy horns and still didn't have a name.

'Come down!' came the bleats from below.

Quite far below by now. The winter lamb didn't listen.

Poetic freedom was a goat place!

The old oak's boot was getting narrower and steeper, leaning and slanting more. Above him, on a branch as thin as a hair, sat a red squirrel with a puzzled look on its face. The winter lamb hesitated. What now? Maybe he wasn't a sheep anymore, but he wasn't a squirrel either. A few steps ahead of him the oak's boot split into two, and at the fork, a thin branch was growing straight out of the boot. A branch with a little reddish bud.

The winter lamb inched forward. One step. Another step. The squirrel fled to a higher branch. One step. The trunk swayed. Two, three. The winter lamb stretched his neck and chowed down.

'He's eating something!' came bleats from below.

The winter lamb languorously chewed the impending summer that slumbered in the bud, sweet yet bitter; he chewed and chewed.

He had conquered the winter.

Heathcliff, thought the winter lamb. *I'm called Heathcliff!*

He struck up a chorus of triumphant bleating, as goatily as he could muster, which rang out across the meadow, reaching as far as the chateau, and even into the forest.

Then he went quiet all of a sudden, completely quiet, and stared wide-eyed into the forest.

Stared and stared.

A gust of wind shook the branches of the old oak. Snow and

a few dead leaves drifted down onto the sheep and the winter lamb fell, not like a leaf, more like a stone, crashing through dry branches, landing on the frozen ground with a surprisingly hearty thud.

The sheep were speechless. The red squirrel chattered high up in the branches.

The winter lamb lay there motionless and looked rather strange. Not like a sheep, more like a heap of shaggy, fuzzy wool.

Then he moved, gingerly, first his hind legs, then his forelegs, until he was standing upright again, shaking, tiny and bandy as ever.

The other sheep settled down. Sheep don't climb trees, and if they do, they fall back down again. That's what they'd said all along.

Miss Maple trotted closer to the winter lamb, curiously. 'You saw something, didn't you? You saw something in the forest!'

'A human,' said the winter lamb. 'A human up in the trees!'

'There's Aubrey!' bleated Heather.

The sheep stared out of the car onto the road that was rolling beneath them at a dizzying speed. No doubt about it: there was Aubrey – small, black and determined. Galloping like the wind.

They had just got used to the car ride a little. As long as you didn't think forwards and didn't think back, and definitely not about the flock grazing unsuspectingly somewhere, it wasn't so bad. With a bit of imagination, you could make yourself believe you were in a particularly dark and draughty corner of the hay barn. Then the car's flat tailgate crashed down, and the grinding and clanking made any hay barn illusions vanish in an instant. But the car had slowed down.

And now Aubrey was racing along after them.

'I think she wants to come too!' said Heather.

The sheep looked on as Aubrey inched closer to the car, foaming at the mouth, a crazy glint in her eye. Soon she was so close that Maude could even pick up her scent against the wind.

It was exciting.

'Jump!' bleated the sheep. 'Jump, Aubrey!'

Aubrey jumped and because at that very moment, the car had slowed down even more she was suddenly standing beside the sheep on the load bed and even looked a bit surprised herself.

Something in the forest snapped.

Zora looked at Aubrey, who was standing beside her in the straw, her legs shaking.

'Was that the Garou?' she asked.

But Aubrey didn't respond. She looked on as her black ghost-kid galloped through the snow behind them – the fox must have spat her out again – and finally escaped into the back of the car in a single crazy leap too.

'It was the fox!' she said then, and shuddered.

Rebecca returned from the chateau when the afternoon was already beginning to turn grey and dull, and scowled at the mysteriously glowing caravan window.

'She can suit herself!' she said.

The shepherdess stomped up the hill to the edge of the forest and pulled out the talking device. There, right near the fence where a beautiful beech stretched out its fingers towards the meadow, was a spot where the talking device did its best talking.

The sheep followed her curiously, but Rebecca was honking away in European again.

'Bon jaw!' she honked, and '*vétérinaire*!'

The sheep didn't like it one bit. Jaws were rarely a good thing. And the word *vétérinaire* sounded suspiciously familiar.

Rebecca honked and honked.

'Fodder!' bleated Mopple, to see what would happen. Soon all of the sheep were bleating for fodder.

Rebecca glanced up from her talking device.

'The vet's sick,' she explained to the sheep. 'Just what I needed!'

The sheep tried not to look too relieved. Mopple made an apple-orchard face. Cordelia kicked out a bit in high spirits.

Rebecca listened into her talking device again.

'I'm trying to find another one,' she whispered to the sheep. 'We've got to get out of here! Pronto. And we need the vet to find a new place for you guys.'

The high spirits evaporated.

'No new vet!' bleated Ramesses.

'No new vet!' bleated the rest of the flock with fervour.

Over and over again.

Cloud was the first to stop bleating: there was something in the air. She scented: the meadow still smelled like the meadow, earth beneath grass beneath snow, vastness and wind.

The goats still smelled like the goats – more's the pity. The chateau smelled like the chateau, stone and smoke, secret fodder stocks, mould in the depths. The forest smelled like the forest.

The forest smelled like the forest? Not completely.

The forest smelled like the forest with something inside it. Like the forest and a lavender bush. The lavender bush was wandering between the trees, heading their way.

Cloud was too sensible and strong-wooled a sheep to be afraid of a lavender bush, but something wasn't quite right.

It wasn't the right time of year for lavender, especially not wandering lavender. Now the other sheep fell silent too. Lavender and herbs, mint, skin and hair. Leather boots. And . . . fur.

One of Rebecca's woollen mittens fell in the snow. Rebecca was so busy with the talking device she didn't even notice.

The crunch of snow. A twig snapping. Rebecca leaned on the fence, her back to the forest, listening into her talking device.

A dark figure had appeared between the trees. A furry creature was slowly making its way towards Rebecca's back. Slowly, with a slight limp. The sheep stared, entranced. Nobody even thought about running away.

A black-gloved hand landed on the boot of the beautiful beech. A hairy arm slowly reached for Rebecca's neck.

The arm seemed to be getting longer, longer and thinner like a growing branch. All of the sheep were holding their breath. The hand reached Rebecca's shoulder and tapped.

Rebecca squeaked and dropped the talking device. '*Pardon, Mademoiselle*,' said the Jackdaw.

Then he climbed over the fence – not particularly gracefully, but not clumsily either.

The sheep stared at him in disbelief: the Jackdaw was wearing one of the legendary fur coats from the book. It was the most peculiar thing the sheep had ever seen, shaped like a human coat, with a collar and buttons and sleeves, but furry like an animal.

Rebecca stared at the Jackdaw, then she bent down to get the talking device. But the Jackdaw was quicker. He picked the talking device out of the snow. And the mitten.

'*Pardon*,' said the Jackdaw again. 'I just wanted to ask you to stop scaring my people.'

Rebecca took a deep breath. 'Your people are scaring me,' she said quietly. 'And so are you.'

She took the talking device and mitten from his hand. 'I'm sorry,' said the Jackdaw. 'But please understand this: you and I are enlightened people, people of the twentieth century. My people on the other hand . . .' He paused for a moment, playing with a little shiny thing between his fingers.

'This is a very old village. A secluded village. A village with history. Nothing you say is going to change that. Please forgive them their superstitions. They can be like children, but they don't mean any harm.'

'Superstitions?' said Rebecca. 'I'd call it vandalism!'

The Jackdaw stepped quickly towards her, and for a brief moment it looked like he was going to pounce on her. But then he just grabbed her hand and put something silver in it.

'Oh,' said Rebecca.

'My card. Should you have any further problems, please don't speak to the staff. Call me direct. Any time. And I mean any time. You are my guest, and you should feel comfortable here.'

Rebecca burst out laughing briefly. 'I've never seen a card like it. For a minute I thought you were giving me a charm or something. To ward off evil spirits.' She stared at the card. '*Chirurgie esthétique?*'

'It's a card and a mirror,' said the Jackdaw. 'My clients like that kind of thing. *Au revoir.*'

'Do you think there will be any further problems?'

'*Au revoir*, Mademoiselle.'

'Rebecca,' said Rebecca.

'Pascal.'

The Jackdaw bowed, then turned and walked across the

meadow towards the chateau. He walked right through the middle of them, without spooking a single sheep. Carefully. Gently. With a hint of a limp that made the sheep feel safe with him.

Like a snake charmer, thought Othello. Othello knew the world, the zoo and the circus. As well as charming overweight, giant refrigerated snakes, the snake charmer in the circus had charmed crocodiles too. He had walked between their open jaws and none of them had ever snapped. None of them had even considered snapping; that's how carefully the snake charmer moved. This caution was the caution of the hunter. It was the opposite of fear.

At that moment the caravan door opened and Tess darted out. First, she sniffed a circuit around the caravan and scratched her ear like mad. Then she discovered the Jackdaw in the middle of the meadow and ran up to him with a dutiful if not particularly enthusiastic growl.

The Jackdaw froze and slowly raised his furry arms. He didn't smell of lavender any more, but of fear.

Tess, intoxicated by her success, bounded triumphantly around him, until Rebecca called her off.

The Jackdaw lowered his arms but still didn't move.

'You're scared of dogs,' said Rebecca, who had come running.

The Jackdaw laughed nervously.

'My father kept dogs. Monsters! If you'd known them, you'd be scared too!'

'That's why there are no dogs here,' said Rebecca.

'Could you take him away, please?' asked the Jackdaw.

'Her,' said Rebecca. 'She's a girl.'

Then she grabbed Tess by her collar and led her back to the shepherd's caravan.

The Jackdaw rushed off the meadow, looking more like a frightened rodent than a snake charmer.

'They exist then,' muttered Cordelia. 'Fur coats!'

It gave the sheep the creeps. Maybe there was something in the story with the wardrobe after all.

It went dark all of a sudden. Clouds hung in front of the moon, and the sheep couldn't see their shadows any more.

Rebecca went into the caravan, and Madame Fronsac came out and loped towards the chateau, dragging her feet, her eyes lowered.

But what about Hortense?

The caravan window was open, and Miss Maple trotted closer, curiously. An inexpressible scent wafted out of the window. Joss sticks and violet perfume and Madame Fronsac's sadness.

'Tea?' Rebecca asked inside the caravan. Something clattered and liquid gurgled.

'*Merci*,' said Hortense and fell silent. She was probably drinking her tea.

'What now?' asked Rebecca after a while. 'She wants to tell us something!' droned Mum.

'Because nobody else is going to tell you,' said Hortense.

'Okay,' said Rebecca.

Hortense took a deep breath, so deep that you could even hear it outside the caravan.

'Becca, the deer you found . . . There are often deer like that. It's been happening for years. Always in the winter. Always in the snow.'

'Are you cold?' asked Rebecca.

Hortense didn't make a sound, but Rebecca shut the caravan window anyway.

Miss Maple sighed, then pressed her forehead determinedly against the wooden side of the caravan. Like that you could understand what was being said inside even if the window was shut. The side of the caravan was cold. Cold as ice.

'... Only ever deer and sometimes a hare and a wild boar once. The wild boar scared everyone – such a big, strong animal, yet still ... But people got used to it. And then ... there used to be sheep here, you know,' said Hortense. 'Three years ago, there were still sheep here. Pretty sheep.'

'And then what happened?' whispered Rebecca.

'And then, there weren't any sheep anymore. The whole flock in one night. All like the deer! Here on the meadow! *Mon Dieu*, Becca, when I woke up and looked out of the window in the morning! *Mon Dieu!* And nobody saw or heard a thing. *Personne!* I told the inspector about it today, and I realised how important it is for you, and that I had to tell you too. Had to. No matter what Mademoiselle Plin ...'

Hortense fell silent, and Rebecca remained silent too.

Maple, her cold forehead pressed against the side of the caravan, was shaking. Sheep! Red and dead like the deer!

'And not just sheep, huh?' said Rebecca. 'Zach implied as much.'

Hortense laughed warily. 'How can you believe anything Zach says? Zach's crazy.'

'Maybe, but I don't think he just makes stuff up. I think he's pretty clever in his own way. Did you know he learned all of his English from films?'

'Spy films,' said Hortense haughtily.

'There were people, weren't there?' said Mum in a deep voice. Her second, or maybe third voice, Miss Maple supposed.

'Three,' said Hortense quietly.

Maple pressed her forehead more firmly against the wood.

'First a boy in the forest. *Un petit garçon.* Then obviously the police came. They didn't find anything. *Rien!* They just made him angry. And then a mother and daughter. They weren't in the forest. He *snatched* them!'

'Who were they?' breathed Rebecca. 'People from here?'

Hortense was silent.

'No,' she said then, a bit too late, a bit too shrilly. 'Not from here . . . from . . . a neighbouring village.'

'And then what happened?' asked Rebecca.

'The police didn't find anything again. And then . . . nothing else happened. Nothing for two years. Not even a deer. And now . . . now you've found a deer again, and people are waiting. *Voilà!*'

'Nothing for two years?' muttered Rebecca. 'Odd.'

'Not that odd,' said Hortense. 'Two years with no snow. It always happens in the snow.'

'But now it's snowed. And there's sheep again. And a dead deer . . . no wonder the police came so quickly. More tea?'

Liquid gurgled.

Hortense sighed. 'They won't find anything, Becca! They never find anything!'

'Why did she ask me here?' whispered Rebecca. 'I'd really like to know why she asked me here.'

'Mademoiselle Plin?' Hortense laughed quietly. 'She's a cold person, only interested in money.'

'But she's not exactly earning a fortune from me and my sheep.'

'She's the estate manager. The *patron* has debts. She even

makes Eric pay rent, for a couple of empty rooms in the tower where he stores his cheese.'

Hortense sighed deeply. Rebecca noisily slurped her tea.

Then silence. A long silence.

Maple removed her forehead from the side of the caravan and listened. It was as if she'd heard a noise out here. On the other side of the shepherd's caravan. She scented the air, but the air was cold and empty. Maple shuddered and pressed her forehead to the side of the caravan again. The voices inside had got louder.

'But it's not that simple!' said Hortense indignantly. 'The deer weren't shot, you know. How can a human catch a deer, just like that?'

'Maybe with a snare?'

'Not a snare!' said Hortense with conviction. 'Becca, I don't know much either. I'm just the nanny, and who talks about such things in front of children? But I know that it's not that simple.'

Maple removed her head from the wood again. This time she was sure: a sound – a sound on the other side of the caravan. Like something scraping in the snow. Miss Maple looked around for the other sheep: nothing. The meadow was dark – and empty.

Maple took a deep breath, then she craned her neck and peered around the corner. There stood Othello, his head pressed against the side of the caravan too. One of his front hooves was scraping in the snow. Over and over. Maple was sure that Othello wasn't aware of his front hoof.

Ahead, at the other end of the caravan, a door quietly clicked, and Hortense's footsteps retreated.

'A werewolf!' cried Mum inside the caravan. 'I might have guessed! Maybe we can take a photo of it!'

'I thought you couldn't take photographs of werewolves,' said Rebecca irritably.

'Don't be ridiculous!' Mum boomed. 'That's vampires!' The caravan door slammed shut.

Othello stepped back from the caravan and turned his head towards Maple. They looked at each other and knew that they wouldn't tell their flock about the dead sheep in the snow. It was better not to. Not yet. Then they silently trotted back to the hay barn, where warmth and the other sheep awaited them.

Ritchfield was still standing outside in the darkness, peering towards the chateau. He had the best eyes in the flock. And ever since the world around him had become quieter, he enjoyed looking at things even more. Little colourful moving images full of life – and sometimes, out of the corner of his eye, Melmoth. He was on his way to him; Ritchfield was sure of it.

For now, the ram was interested in the chateau's windows. During the day they were dull and dark, but at night they glowed like eyes and started telling stories.

The bigger of the two human boys for instance was gazing spellbound at a flickering box, and the small human boy was draped in a white sheet, wandering through the room like a ghost, obviously having a whale of a time. As usual Mademoiselle Plin slinked from window to window. The Jackdaw was talking into a talking device.

Two storeys down, a window suddenly lit up, and Hortense was standing there, surprised, in the middle of the room. The Walrus waddled towards her, and the two of them talked with lots of arm-shaking and pointing and throwing of hands in the air, until Hortense wrapped her coat around herself and fled.

Ritchfield sighed contentedly. He liked the little humans behind the little windows. And up there, on the third storey of the chateau, in a window that was only dimly lit, stood someone else, barely more than a shadow. Was he really looking down at Ritchfield? Despite his good eyes, Ritchfield wasn't quite sure. He'd seen enough for today and trotted back to the hay barn, past the old oak where Yves had stationed himself in the shadow of the boot, as he did most evenings, to enjoy the illuminated windows just like Ritchfield.

Especially Rebecca's.

11

AUBREY HAS A DRINK

'He's not really a problem,' said Lane. 'Not in the winter.'
The others nodded.

In summer it would have been a completely different scenario. The stench! The flies! Curious fox eyes in the darkness. But in winter . . .

The sheep stood beneath the old oak in an unusually rosy dawn gazing at Yves, who was lying on his stomach with his legs spread wide and had almost completely lost his scent to the cold. Red sky in the morning, shepherd's warning, indeed! 'If they find him,' Ramesses said, 'humans with caps and sheepdogs will turn up again. And they'll want to find out why he's dead.'

The sheep knew why Yves was dead. There was a red patch in the middle of his back that still had a scent, and the bang the sheep had heard in the middle of the night belonged to the patch. The bang of a gun! But it would take a while for the humans to join the dots. And then . . .

'They'll take Rebecca away!' bleated Cloud suddenly. They knew that from the many hours they'd spent in front of the shepherd's caravan listening to detective stories. Rebecca had taken her gun when she went for a walk in the forest yesterday. She found broad-shouldered Yves 'slimy' and suspected him of stealing a piece of her red underwear from the washing line in the autumn. Now that red Things were in short supply, she had probably just pulled the trigger. To be on the safe side. The sheep understood Rebecca's thinking. But the humans with caps wouldn't understand.

'They mustn't find him!' bleated Cordelia. 'He's got to go!'

Othello lowered his horns and tried to roll Yves a bit, but Yves was unwieldy and already a bit stiff, and fought back with the cold bloody-mindedness of the dead. The sheep looked at one another, at a loss. You really couldn't miss the dead human, a big heap of darkness on the morning pink-white of the snow.

'If only he were *under* the snow,' said Lane. 'Under the snow wouldn't be so bad.'

'We could scrape a hole and push him into it,' said Ramesses. 'Maybe.'

The sheep scratched in the snow a bit, but the snow was frozen solid, and Yves was simply too big.

'Or we could wait for new snow to come from above!' Miss Maple looked mischievously round at them all. Not a bad idea! New snow from above seemed like a particularly elegant solution to the problem.

'And when's new snow going to come from above?' asked Mopple nervously. Rebecca had to stay here!

'Soon,' said Cloud, scenting the cold air. 'Lots of snow! I can smell it already!'

Now she mentioned it the others could smell it too!

'Soon isn't soon enough,' bleated Lane.

She was right. The first lights were appearing in the chateau and somebody could look out of the window at any moment and wonder what the strange dark lump under the old oak was.

The yard gate creaked open and the goatherder stepped through, a big sack over his shoulder. Probably a feed sack! Under different circumstances the sheep would have been very interested in that sack, but today they just hoped the goatherder would disappear behind the yard wall with it as quickly and shortsightedly as possible.

The goatherder didn't disappear. He shuffled to the right along the fence towards the goats' meadow, looking at the ground. A crow landed in the upper branches of the old oak. Snow dusted down. The goatherder carried on purposefully along the fence. The first goats had spotted him and were gambolling across the meadow towards him.

The crow squawked in triumph. The goatherder looked over at the sheep. His eyes were so blue that they could see them even from that distance.

The sheep stood guiltily around Yves, their ears drooping. The crow squawked more loudly.

The goatherder turned and shuffled farther along the fence. He tipped the contents of the sack over the goat fence – mangelwurzels and carrots! – then he examined his goats as they ate. Thoroughly. He didn't quite seem satisfied with what he saw, and his eyes wandered farther across the meadow. Back and forth, up and down.

'He's looking for Aubrey,' said Miss Maple.

But the goatherder didn't find her. Finally, he went back to the gate. The gate creaked shut.

The sheep looked at one another.

'He must be very short-sighted,' said Mopple. 'More short-sighted than me! Or he's not interested in Yves.'

'No,' said Miss Maple. 'He can't see through us. As long as we stand in front of Yves, he can't be seen from the chateau either!'

The sheep decided to stand around Yves for as long as it took for the promised snow to completely cover him.

A second crow landed in the branches of the old oak. Then a third.

They tried to make the best of the situation and grazed a bit. But the shady patch under the tree was cold and draughty and didn't have much to offer in terms of tasty morsels. It was light now and fat grey clouds were jostling in the sky.

The wind picked up.

Rebecca's window woke up. The sheep looked gloomily over at the shepherd's caravan, where Rebecca and Mum were sitting in the warm eating bread and honey for breakfast, while they were outside suffering the consequences of her trigger-happy escapades. The first snowflakes drifted over the meadow. Yves had completely lost his scent now.

Meanwhile the crown of the old oak was full of crows. They were pecking and squawking and making the sheep nervous. Ritchfield was the only one who liked the crows. A light fluff started to build on Yves – not enough by a long shot, but promising. The sheep stood there resolutely waiting. A few crows dropped down from the treetop to the meadow. They craned their necks, stalking around curiously between the sheep's legs and peering at the dead human with their beady black crow eyes.

'This isn't going to work!' Othello snorted. 'As soon as they start hopping about on him, the snow isn't going to be any help at all!'

Othello started zigzagging between the sheep, chasing the crows. It wasn't easy; the crows were clever. They darted through under the sheep's bellies, fluttered onto the sheep's backs and seemed to find it hilarious when Othello came within an inch of mowing down Ramesses. Ramesses started bleating hysterically. Lane, Cloud, Mopple and Cordelia bleated to keep him company.

'Stop it!' snarled Othello. 'If you keep making all that racket . . .'

He didn't get any further.

All of a sudden, the air around them was white. White and biting. The chateau and the shepherd's caravan disappeared. Everything disappeared.

Ritchfield stood in the middle of nothingness; he was in shock. He'd just . . . But now! Where was everything? And why was it so white? Ritchfield liked white. White as a butterfly, white as milk, white as a lamb, white as a flock . . . Where was his flock? Somewhere! Ritchfield peered intently through the white. And then he saw it – grey! Finally! Quite a way away to start with, and at first, he thought he was just imagining it, but then it got bigger and more graceful, bigger and clearer and greyer and greyer. Horns. Ritchfield felt warm and calm. He could hear things he hadn't heard in a long while: the wind whistling, the snowflakes crackling. Hooves in the snow.

Melmoth stood a little way away looking over at Ritchfield. Ritchfield just stood there, young and happy; he felt complete. He wanted to trot over to his twin like he used to. Not yet! Melmoth raised his horns and looked at him with a solemn expression on his face. Ritchfield raised his horns a bit higher too and . . .

'There's Ritchfield!' somebody bleated.

The old lead ram blinked snow out of his eyes and when he was finished, Melmoth had disappeared. Ritchfield wasn't all that worried about it. Melmoth would come back. Melmoth would *always* come back. All of a sudden, the sun was shining again.

You had to give it to them: Yves was now completely hidden. The sheep had difficulty finding one another in the snow again. Gradually more or less all of the remaining sheep gathered on the leeward side of the haybarn, where the snow wasn't quite as deep, and looked around. Everything had disappeared, everything: the fence, the feed trough, even the goats – wonders never ceased! The shepherd's caravan: a white, fluffy toadstool. The stream: an icy snake-trail burbling through the nothingness. The whole thing was completely over the top.

They were a bit angry with Miss Maple, whose suggestion had got them into all of this snow. And they were angry with Yves – why couldn't he just keep his hands off Rebecca's underwear? They were angry with Rebecca too.

Morale was low.

Ice glittered in the sun. The sheep watched sullenly as the goats gradually appeared out of the snow again, hopping and skipping, their eyes and fur gleaming, as if nothing had happened at all. And why not? They didn't have a trigger-happy shepherdess that they had to protect from the police.

And then, something else moved in the snow, something on their side of the meadow, unsettlingly close. The snow bulged and broke, and a head appeared, the head of the unshorn ram. Now that you couldn't see that he was unshorn because of all the snow, he actually looked like a pretty normal sheep. For the first time they noticed how brown the strange ram's eyes were – and how alert.

'Tourbe!' he bleated in high spirits. 'Aube! Gris! Marcassin!'

The unshorn ram waded through the snow past the sheep, towards the meadow fence, without so much as glancing in their direction. Yet the sheep got the impression he was happy to be back. And they were happy too, albeit very, very tentatively.

Zora, Maude, Heather and Aubrey had spent the night at a bus stop. A shelter had protected them from the wind and all the snow, but no bus had come as yet. Now it was light again – extraordinarily light, because of the new snow.

Aubrey stuck her head out of the little hut at regular intervals and scented the air.

'That way!' she bleated confidently, looking either up the road or down the road or straight on and once even up in the air. The others remained sceptical. Not even Maude could pick up the scent of where they had come from underneath all of the snow.

The sheep squinted nervously outside. They wanted to go back. They *had* to go back. But which way was back?

As they stared indecisively out into the white, an old woman turned up on the road wearing a woolly scarf round her head and carrying a plastic bag in her hand. She walked very slowly and gingerly, and because she was walking so slowly the sheep only noticed her once she was already quite close. There was nothing left for them to do but retreat into the shadows of the bus shelter and hope that the woman would pass by like some kind of hypnotised snail.

But in all the excitement, Heather's hind hoof hit the tin wall of the shelter, and metal clanged. The woman turned her head towards them. Her eyes were glass-rimmed and as big as an owl's. The woman honked at them, then she shuffled on, painfully slowly.

'She says we'd be better off on foot,' said Aubrey. 'The buses won't run in this weather. Or at all for that matter.'

Easier said than done. All the same: they had to get back, as quickly as they could! The others had to know what they'd heard in the house in the forest yesterday, before it was too late.

After Aubrey had boldly leapt into the car with them, they'd rolled on a while, more and more slowly. Then, with a sigh, the car had ground to a halt.

The sheep peered uneasily outside. They were in the middle of the forest. The extra-large car wasn't just over-zealous, it was stupid to boot! A door clacked and footsteps came closer. The sheep huddled together in the darkest corner, but the human wearing the gumboots just flipped the loose tailgate back up again. What sort of human? The sheep couldn't make out anything more than a green anorak with a hood. Then they carried on, hoping that the car had enough sense to find its way back to the chateau somehow.

But when the car stopped for the second time there were still trees outside. Trees and a house.

Footsteps retreated, and Aubrey, who had completely recovered during the short journey and was already starting to get on the sheep's nerves with her random little jumps, opened a latch on the tailgate with her muzzle. The flap flapped down, and Aubrey jumped out.

'Come on!' she bleated. 'The human's gone!'

Nobody wanted to stay in the dimwitted car for a moment longer, but as soon as they were out in the open, a big black dog bounded up to them snarling, and there was nothing left for them to do but flee headlong into the dark doorway of the house. The dog was still barking a bit outside, but he didn't follow them. Inside, everything was quite dark and confusing and full of tables and chairs. There were bottles on the wall and lots of mugs hanging from the ceiling.

The human wearing the yellow gumboots was already at the other end of the room and threw back her hood. Severely scraped back hair appeared; a few rebelliously frizzy strands had broken free: Mademoiselle Plin. She impatiently pulled a chair out and sat at a table. The two winter visitors were already sitting at the table, one tall, the other short. The two winter visitors were the only other humans in the room, and they were both drinking beer.

Mademoiselle Plin honked away animatedly.

'What are they saying?' said Aubrey. 'Don't you want to know what they're saying too?' And she had already scurried out of the niche near the door, heading straight through the middle of the room towards the humans, and hidden under one of the neighbouring tables.

Aubrey was enjoying being in a house again. The meadow and the forest and the goat shed were all well and good, but she had been reared in a house and felt most comfortable in the half-dark amongst useless furniture. The little goat happily sniffed the tabletop above her: the familiar smell of beer. The humans next to her were talking.

'. . . took the lorry,' said Plin. 'Yves is always running around in it. It won't attract any attention around here.'

The shorter of the two winter visitors sighed. His feet scraped across the wooden floor impatiently.

'It's still risky. Why's it so damned important, Madame?'

'Mademoiselle!' hissed Plin. 'Important? It's crucial! I looked at Pascal's calendar this morning – don't worry, he doesn't know I've still got the key – and tomorrow is marked with an *X*. And we all know what *X* means! I thought we'd agreed that it would happen in two weeks' time, when I'm on holiday.'

'The boss is a very busy man,' said the short man. 'And unpredictable too.'

'I don't care, I want him to wait until I'm away!'

'Just go on holiday a bit earlier,' said the short man. His voice didn't sound small at all, more like the rumbling of an ill-tempered watchdog.

'I can't move my holiday now; how suspicious would that look? I never change my plans. Pascal would smell a rat.'

'That, Madame, is your problem!'

'Mademoiselle!'

'At your age!' the short man muttered.

'It goes against the agreement,' said Plin bitterly. 'I kept to my side of the bargain, lodgings for you both – and the sheep, it was pretty difficult getting sheep here again after all that business. I had to wax lyrical, and now . . .'

'You got your money, didn't you?'

'It's not about that,' said Plin.

The tall man hadn't said a word up to now, but his foot had been tirelessly tapping on wood. Tap. Tap. Tap. Now the foot suddenly stopped tapping.

'It's always about money,' said the tall man, his voice flat. 'Don't be so difficult, Madame!'

'Difficult? That's just how it is!' Mademoiselle Plin smoothed her hair with her hand.

'Isn't it too early?' she asked then. 'Doesn't it need more prep?'

'We got one deer,' said the short man. 'They found that straightaway, and maybe we'll take another one down tomorrow morning, and then the sheep are for it, and as far as I can see, people are already wetting themselves. The police were there groping around in the dark. The little shepherdess has caught wind of everything. They all believe the lunatic is on the loose again. What more could we want?'

'Three,' said Plin sharply. 'Three deer.'

'One,' said the short man. 'Wouldn't have imagined it'd be so difficult to catch the beasts and prep them. We've got snares all over the place. Well, at least the sheep'll be easier.'

'The goatherder found some more deer in the forest,' said Plin obstinately.

'Well,' said the short man with feigned indifference, 'they're not ours.' He surreptitiously gave the tall man the evil eye. The tall man didn't look.

'But what's worrying us a bit is the old bag,' said the short man. 'One outsider, fine, but two makes it a bit . . .'

He fell silent. Another human had entered the room, a man with narrow eyes, wearing an apron. He didn't come through the front door, but from the side, from inside the house, and he was carrying a tray.

Mademoiselle Plin laughed an unpleasant laugh. 'Don't worry, he's deaf as a post! See!'

Next moment she'd swept the tall man's beer off the table, and glass shattered, clashing onto the hard wooden floor. The sheep gave a start in their niche, but the narrow-eyed human didn't even look up from his tray. The tall walker looked angrily at his glass and said, 'Well done!'

Aubrey tasted some of the beer on the floor.

'The old battle-axe is completely harmless,' said Plin, pointedly loudly. 'I had her read my cards today. Completely nuts, she believes everything you tell her, as long as it's a bit mystical. She'll be the first to cry "werewolf."'

'I want another beer!' said the tall man.

At that moment Aubrey, looking for a little puddle of beer, stretched her neck a little too far forward and brushed Mademoiselle Plin's knee. Plin screeched and slapped the short winter visitor across the face. Next moment the tall man had a knife in his hand. Aubrey ran straight through the room and out of the door, the sheep following behind.

Then the four of them had run from the black dog until they got to the bus stop. Aubrey had sung goat songs and smelled funny. But later, in the middle of the night, she had told the sheep what she had heard under the table. And now they had to get back to the meadow to warn the flock about the walkers' plans.

'I think it's that way!' said Zora suddenly, stepping decisively out of the bus shelter and struggling up the road through the deep snow. Heather, Maude and Aubrey trotted along behind her.

Rebecca came out of the shepherd's caravan, or rather: to begin with, she didn't come out of the shepherd's caravan because there was too much snow in front of the door. Then the door swung open with a jolt and Rebecca, who had been pushing against it from the inside, tumbled down the steps and landed in the snow.

The sheep readied themselves for a fit of temper, but Rebecca laughed, brushed the snow from her coat and straightened her brown bread hat. She cleared a path to the feed store, found the trough again, shovelled it clear and tipped a rather generous portion of concentrated feed into it. She hummed and skipped and tried to throw a snowball at Mopple. He was an easy target, but she missed all the same. For someone with Yves on their conscience, she was in a remarkably good mood.

'Everything looks different in the morning, doesn't it?' she said to the sheep. 'You haven't got it easy in this weather either. Don't worry, I'll look after you.'

As if! *They* were the ones looking after Rebecca, with snow and silver and everything else.

'Do you want some hay?' Rebecca asked.

The sheep bleated. Of course they wanted hay.

'Mum and I have been invited to dinner this evening,' Rebecca explained to the sheep as she scooped hay into the rack. 'At the chateau. By Pascal.' She grinned at the sheep. 'Posh, huh?'

Heathcliff was having a think. About whether it was worth making his way towards the feed trough or whether he'd be pushed off anyway until the last grain had disappeared from the trough. Since the fall from the oak, Heathcliff was thinking very carefully about the choices he made.

Everything hurt, especially his ribs, his back and everything in between. It hurt between his ears, his foreleg hurt and his left hind foot too. Every step hurt and every movement, of course. The very thought of pushing between the other sheep like he used to made him black out for a moment.

Not now. He didn't need any hay. He had managed with less milk than any other lamb; he could live on muddy winter grass for as long as he wanted.

Heathcliff kicked out defiantly behind him and waited for the pain to subside, an unconcerned look on his face. The others mustn't notice a thing.

Nobody must notice a thing. He was a sheep just like all the others, not weaker, not slower. Not somebody who would fall behind if the flock were running from a predator. He wasn't easy prey.

On the way back from the hay rack Rebecca spotted the silver – and gave a start.

The sheep gave a start too. Rebecca – the Garou?

'Well, will you look at that,' said Rebecca. 'And I'm always so careful.'

She stomped over to the hazel bush and plucked the paper from the branch. At first the sheep were just relieved. The shepherdess didn't seem to be afraid of the silver paper! But then! With the tips of her fingers, Rebecca carried the silver to the bin attached to the fence – on the side facing away from the meadow. The lid of the bin banged shut and the shepherdess wiped her hands on her coat in satisfaction.

'It doesn't bear thinking about what would have happened if you'd eaten that,' she said to the sheep.

The sheep looked at Rebecca in frustration. Of course they wouldn't have eaten the werewolf silver – how stupid did she think they were, exactly? But how was it supposed to give away the Garou in the depths of the bin?

They looked reproachfully at the shepherd's caravan, where the shepherdess – still in high spirits – slipped into some other shoes, threw the red scarf over her shoulder and then stomped off towards the meadow gate.

'You don't think I've forgotten the business with the clothes, do you?' she asked. 'Of course I haven't!'

The sheep could hardly believe it. While they'd been hiding Yves and hunting down the Garou, their shepherdess had nothing but clothes on her mind!

'We've got to get the silver out of the bin!' Mopple bleated. He liked the silver. He had found it and was rather proud of the fact. Aside from that, he'd wanted to take a peek in the bin for a while now. If he remembered correctly, Hortense had just recently thrown half an apple in there that the younger little human had dropped in the snow.

As soon as Rebecca had disappeared through the yard gate, the flock trotted to the fence. It was a tricky situation. The bin was tantalisingly close, but attached to the outside of the fence, and it had a heavy metal lid. The sheep tried to lean over the fence like the goats did – with limited success. 'That won't work,' said Othello. 'One of us will have to go outside.' He thought for a moment.

'I'll do it,' he said then.

First Othello tried jumping over the fence, but it was impossible to get a good run-up in the deep snow.

'I'll go across the goats' meadow,' he said finally.

'And if the goats don't want you to?' bleated Heather.

'I don't care if the goats want me to or not!' said Othello, already on his way to the goat fence.

Luckily the goats were engrossed in one of their peculiar rituals again and far too busy to want anything at all. They were standing around the chest of drawers, in a kind of circle, and didn't even notice Othello, who had slipped through the loose slat in the fence. Every now and then one of them bleated. Whatever they were doing seemed important. Then, all of a sudden, most of the goats retreated from the chest of drawers – except two. The two of them reared up on their hind legs and clashed their horns together.

Othello contorted himself through the loose wire and stood on the edge of the forest. Now he had to go round the outside of the goats' meadow.

The sheep watched uneasily as their lead ram turned into a small black dot at the other end of the goats' meadow. But then Othello started to grow again, and eventually he was standing full-sized with his flock once more – only on the wrong side of the fence. Or the right side. Whatever the case may be.

Othello effortlessly pushed up the lid, stood up on his hind legs and rooted in the bin, his forelegs leaning against the fence. Soon he appeared again, the silver paper in his mouth. He passed it to Maple through the fence.

'So?' asked Mopple the Whale. 'Is there anything else in there? I mean, anything interesting?!'

'No,' said Othello. 'Nothing interesting.'

Then he was already making his way back along the goat fence.

The sheep carried the paper triumphantly back to the hazel bush and speared it on the same branch – a warning to all the werewolves out there.

Just as they had finished, the gate creaked open and Paul the goatherder stepped out, wrapped up warm and carrying a rope in his hand. The goats craned their necks expectantly, but this time the goatherder wasn't concerned with them; instead he made a beeline for the forest. The sheep were scared he would catch Othello on the goats' meadow – but Othello was nowhere to be seen.

12

MAUDE CAN'T SMELL A THING

O thello hesitated.
He'd only trotted a few steps into the forest to avoid being spotted by the goatherder, but now he heard a voice. Angry, muffled and nervous. And belonging to the voice were some tracks; they led through the snow not far from Othello before disappearing into a dip. The tracks beckoned Othello. He wanted to stay with his flock and protect them from the Garou, but these tracks were important. Someone had circled the meadow like Othello, under the cover of the forest. Othello snorted. Nobody prowled around his meadow. Nobody!

The black ram looked back at his flock again. They were safe. For now. A feeling, more still, a kind of memory. Something the little goat had said about the moon . . . Othello snorted and disappeared between the tree trunks, following the tracks. Not wolf tracks, that was for sure. Simple, clumsy human footprints.

Unlike the other sheep, Othello might have actually seen a wolf once – maybe. In the zoo, a long time ago. He wasn't sure though. Othello had been very young – his four pointy little horns had only just started growing – and was blacker and more curious than a raven. That's why he wasn't like the rest of the zoo-flock, who had fled to the other end of the pen when the scent had wafted up the path. The scent followed a humming vehicle with two humans at the front and a cage at the back. And in the cage stood a creature, the very sight of which made Othello's hackles rise. Every single strand of his fleece stood on end. The creature was big and beautiful, a bit like a dog, but also very different. Long-legged and agile, and grey as a ghost. It had looked at Othello with its grey, burning spirit-eyes, and Othello had realised that the wolf's hackles were up, too, from the heat and sheer glee; and that they had known each other for a very long time . . .

Othello stopped dead in his tracks.

At the bottom of the dip, partially concealed by a bare bramble, a man was kneeling in the snow. One of the men who was always going for walks. The taller of the two. This time he wasn't walking; he was angrily honking in European. In front of him lay a dead deer, twisted strangely, its head in a snare, silent. The man had very white hands (or maybe they were gloves?), and one of the hands was holding a knife, the other a pot. The man stabbed the deer in the neck. He'd done that a few times already. Nothing happened. He honked away irritably. Every now and then the tall man glanced over his shoulder. Othello could see why he was so nervous: just up there a path led past the dip, and anyone coming along the path would see them. The tall man and the deer that didn't want to bleed. It was a stupid location. Any respectable predator would have dragged its prey away, at least into the next thicket.

Eventually the tall man let go of the deer. He heaped snow on it and rushed off, going deeper into the forest, leaving clumsy human footprints in his wake.

Othello lingered in the shadow of a fallen tree trunk, surprised. That wasn't how he'd imagined the Garou.

A bang made the black ram jump. He wanted to run but didn't know where to and what from. Then he saw the branch that had split under the weight of the snow and crashed to the ground. A branch as thick as Othello's head was wide.

The lead ram listened to the creaking of the trees, the moaning of the ice-cold wood and the heavy silence of the snow. He realised that there were branches like that all over the forest, groaning under snow. And some of them would break.

The forest was a dangerous place in the winter.

Zora, Maude, Heather and Aubrey were at a crossroads. Up to now they had followed the road, and because they had passed an angular sign with a deer painted on it, they were fairly sure they were on the right path. They had noticed the sign on the way in the car. But now, there were three possible routes and lots of pointy signs pointing in every possible direction. Signs with symbols. White and yellow, blue and brown.

Maude self-importantly scented the air every which way, but there was nothing there, just snow and forest, forest and snow. Zora peered through the treetops looking for the sun; Heather was in favour of just guessing. Aubrey put her head on one side and carried on looking up at the signs.

'So many signs,' she said. 'I'm sure they're here for a reason.'

'What sort of reason?' bleated Heather. 'There's no reason for the trees to be here!'

'There is,' said Aubrey. 'The trees are here because we're in the forest!'

That was true. The sheep looked a bit more closely at the colourful metal Things. Most of them were pointy on one side and flat and square on the other. There were symbols on all of them, the symbols stories are made of, but on one of them there was a picture too.

'Look at that!' bleated Aubrey. 'That's the tower!'

She was right. The tower on the picture was much squatter and fatter than the chateau's tower, but they both had the same jagged points.

'So what?' said Maude, scenting the sign. 'It doesn't smell like the tower!'

'That's the nose,' said Heather, looking at the pointy side of the sign. 'That screw there is the eye, and the tower means it's looking at the tower!'

It was a bold theory, but it was all they had. The sheep turned right and followed the brown sign's nose, deeper into the forest.

Heather was cold, and she didn't even dare bleat about it. The cold wasn't a very popular topic amongst sheep. It was said that if you were strong-wooled enough, the cold wasn't a problem. So much for the theory. Things were different in practice.

Maude was depressed because, despite her superior sense of smell, she could scent nothing but forest and snow. How was she supposed to know that she still had a good nose if she couldn't smell anything?

Aubrey was zigzagging. Zora was thinking.

'So?' she eventually asked Aubrey. Aubrey stopped zigzagging. 'So what?'

'Have you seen the Garou?' asked Zora.

'Mostly no,' said the little goat. 'Bits of him.'

'Bits?' snorted Maude. 'Which bits?'

'Hands,' said Aubrey.

'Do wolves have hands?' asked Heather.

'This one does,' said Aubrey. 'Two. He needs them to coat himself in werewolf ointment. Only the ointment's a powder.' She kicked her hind legs out dramatically and powdery snow sprayed up.

'How do you know all of this?' asked Zora. 'The thing about the ointment, I mean, and the bullets and the silver and the moon and all the other things about the Garou?'

'The herder told me,' said Aubrey. 'It's all he talks about.'

'The goatherder talks to you?' asked Zora.

'The goatherder *only* talks to me,' said Aubrey proudly. 'He hasn't spoken to the others for a long while.'

'Why not?' asked Heather.

'Because the others are stupid,' said Aubrey. 'Stupid and mad isn't the same, you know? The herder gets that.'

Aubrey fell silent for a moment.

'They used to all be mad,' she said then. 'The whole chateau. And now only a few of them are mad. Secretly mad, that is.'

'Who says so?' asked Zora.

'The herder,' said Aubrey. 'All of us used to live together up until recently.'

'Who do you mean – all of you?' asked Heather. 'Well – me and him,' said Aubrey.

'Really?' asked Heather. 'On the meadow?'

They tried to imagine the goatherder grazing and jumping and ripping up grass, but they couldn't.

'Not on the meadow,' said Aubrey. 'In a house made of stone and wood and fire.'

'Why on earth?' bleated Heather. But Aubrey didn't want to say why.

The sheep would have spent far longer wondering at Othello's disappearance had it not been for Eric appearing on their meadow – Eric, the human who had mauled a musical instrument in front of Hortense's window that autumn. The sheep eyed him sceptically. Someone who spent day after day dealing with goat's cheese couldn't be right in the head.

Unlike the other humans, Eric noticed the silver paper. He stood still and briefly watched it playing in the sun and the wind, glistening and crackling. The sheep held their breath, but it didn't look like Eric was particularly scared. He smiled. Then he ran his hand through his light hair, carried on to the shepherd's caravan and knocked politely. The door opened and Mum stood on the steps, swathed in flowing blue robes, a sparkling band round her forehead just above her third eye. Her lips were pink and her eyes were black, as if she'd had a fight with someone. Old George had once had a fight with someone, for fun, and his eyes had looked a bit like that afterwards.

Mum's appearance from the caravan would have been rather more impressive if at that very moment Tess hadn't bounded out of the caravan and done a little doggy dance around Eric. Tess liked Eric. And Eric liked Tess. He crouched down and scratched Tess behind the ears, under her chin, on her belly and her sides. Tess rolled in the snow making gurgling sounds of delight, while Mum just stood there looking a bit surplus to requirements with her arms spread dramatically.

Finally, Eric remembered Mum, brushed the snow from his trousers and passed her a package. The sheep scented the air excitedly, but there was only goat's cheese beneath the paper. Even Mopple couldn't get excited about goat's cheese. Mum smiled and pointed inside the caravan with her red fingernails; Eric smiled, too, and the two of them disappeared, Tess in tow.

The sheep grazed and tried not to think about Yves, who was lying rather unappetisingly on the grass beneath the snow. Oddly enough, Mopple was the only one not grazing. He was standing at the fence beside the unshorn stranger, eyeing the chateau with concern.

'It can't be that difficult to find a big car!' he said. 'They ought to be back by now!'

'Tourbe!' confirmed the stranger. 'Gris. Tache. Marcassin!'

They both sighed. Today Mopple understood where the strange ram was coming from.

Hortense walked out of the chateau with a spring in her step, wearing rather a lot of violet perfume, and slipped inside the caravan with Mum and Eric. A little later she appeared again, arm in arm with Eric. The two of them walked silently across the meadow, blond and golden, and disappeared silently between the chateau's outbuildings.

Rebecca came back at about midday. Her red scarf fluttering proudly in the wind.

'So,' she said to the sheep. 'It's lunchtime now, then we'll . . .'

The shepherdess fell silent and stared at the hazel bush. 'Well, I never,' she said. 'Didn't I just . . . I could have sworn I . . .'

Rebecca stomped over to the hazel bush, plucked the silver paper from the branches and carried it over to the rubbish bin again.

'Funny,' she said.

The sheep didn't find the situation very funny at all.

Rebecca plunged the werewolf silver into the rubbish bin for the second time, then she went back to the caravan and knocked.

All three of Mum's eyes peered out of the door. 'Have they gone?' asked Rebecca.

Mum nodded and pulled out a packet of cigarettes. 'Want one?'

Mum's cigarettes were longer and thinner than Rebecca's, and normally Rebecca pulled a face when she saw them. But not today.

The two women perched on the steps with their strange smoking sticks in their mouths, and all of a sudden, they looked alike.

'The vet is nowhere to be found,' said Rebecca. 'Yesterday his receptionist told me he's ill, and today nobody's budging an inch. I don't need him personally; the immunisations can wait. I just want to know where I can find new quarters for the sheep.'

'Yesterday?' asked Mum. 'Yesterday!' said Rebecca.

'Funny that. I thought I saw him talking to Mademoiselle Plin yesterday morning, before . . . well, before the séance.'

'Funny,' said Rebecca disinterestedly. Both the women blew smoke into the air.

'So?' asked Rebecca finally. 'Did you find out anything important with all your sorcery?'

'Maybe!' Mum puffed contentedly on her stick. Rebecca looked curious but didn't say a word.

'I know where the wardrobe came from!' Mum blurted out.

'Well,' said Rebecca, 'not exactly our most pressing concern.'

Mum fell silent and eyed her red fingernails critically.

'Where did it come from?' asked Rebecca finally.

'Where did it come from?' bleated the sheep. They were interested too. If they knew where the wardrobe came from, maybe they could convince it to scurry back there on its little feet, taking its creepy inner life of forests and fur coats and half-goats with it, and they would gain some new pasture into the bargain.

'From the chateau!' said Mum.

'Everybody knows it comes from the chateau,' said Rebecca. 'Where else do you get oak wardrobes like that with carvings and metal fittings and lion's feet?'

'If you know everything already you needn't ask,' said Mum tapping ash into the snow. 'But it's not a bad story.'

The sheep edged closer, even the strange ram, who supposedly couldn't understand a word.

'Go on, then!' said Rebecca.

'Did you know that this used to be a psychiatric hospital?' asked Mum.

'Yes,' said Rebecca.

It wasn't a good start. Mum took a puff on her cigarette, a bit crossly, and fell silent.

'Why didn't you tell me that?' she asked finally.

'I didn't want to fuel your imagination even more. And, well, it's in the past, isn't it? Now it's just a chateau again.'

'Well, this story is from the time when it was still an asylum,' said Mum. 'Which, by the way, isn't that long ago. Five years or so. The snob's father was a psychiatrist . . .'

'He's not a snob!' said Rebecca.

'If that's not a snob, I don't know what is! I've never seen a man wearing fur before . . . look, never mind. In any case, it was the kind of institution where people didn't have to feel bad about dropping off their old folks, with a chateau and grounds, and each patient had their own room. Fancy. Only there wasn't anything in the rooms! Nothing at all, no table, no chair, nothing, just metal beds. And at some point, a patient complained that he didn't know what furniture looked like anymore, and that he had the right to a desk. And then the doctor ordered furniture to be brought out onto the meadow: the wardrobe and the sofa and the chest of drawers, the finest furniture, so that all of the patients could see them when they looked out of their windows on the third floor. He said it was therapeutic. Therapeutic! Can you imagine how the people must have felt when they saw the goats on the sofa? He was a sadist, if you ask me.'

'That's a good story,' said Rebecca approvingly, stubbing her cigarette out in the snow and putting it neatly into her pocket. 'Who told you that one?'

'Eric. Or rather: Hortense, but Eric told her. Hortense wasn't here back then, but Eric helped to carry the furniture out onto the meadow. Apparently, they had a really vicious billy goat back then.' Mum had stubbed out her cigarette too and wasn't quite sure where she should put the butt.

'Something's not quite right with Eric!' Rebecca sighed. 'What's not quite right now?'

'Well, I laid out his cards and he wasn't interested at all. No emotion. Nothing. As if it weren't his life at all.'

'He just doesn't believe in it! Hortense dragged him along because she's head over heels for him, that's all.'

'Who else could she be head over heels for around here? Poor thing.' Mum had gouged a hole in the snow with her foot, and surreptitiously dropped her cigarette butt into it.

'Madame Fronsac asked me if I can contact the dead,' she said abruptly.

'And?' asked Rebecca. 'Can you?'

'Don't be ridiculous,' said Mum, secretly covering up the hole in the snow.

Rebecca fell silent. Mum had her eye on the packet of cigarettes again.

'The television doesn't work,' she moaned then.

Rebecca chuckled. 'I could have told you that.'

'Oh, I don't think it's broken,' said Mum with dignity, straightening her headband. 'People aren't that brazen. But the aerial needs to go on the roof, and if I understood Yves's gobbledygook yesterday, he was going to do it this morning. But he didn't turn up. You're right. He's a slime ball. I had a bad feeling about him straightaway.'

'You and your feelings,' said Rebecca getting up from the steps. She looked over towards the goats' meadow, where three goats were standing on the sofa, staging a bleating spectacular.

'Weird that the furniture's still here, isn't it? I'd have cleared it away ages ago.'

Mum nodded. 'That's what I said, and Hortense translated it, and Eric stared at me aghast as if . . . as if he was still scared of the old man.'

'Maybe he comes back once or twice a year and throws his weight about,' said Rebecca.

'He can't throw his weight about anymore,' said Mum. 'He's dead. But nobody around here will tell me how he died.'

Mum looked impatiently over at the chateau.

'You can make contact with him!' suggested Rebecca. 'In the meantime, I'll give Yves a call. I think Madame Fronsac gave me his number once, for repairs and stuff. I'll ask him if he'll put the aerial on the roof for us. I'd like to watch a film. That'd be something! A werewolf film so that you know what to take a photo of. What do you think?'

She poked her talking device with her pointy index finger and the talking device squeaked indignantly.

'You ought to take this a bit more seriously. Let's have something to eat, shall we?' said Mum and got up as well, surprisingly gracefully. 'I'll cook!'

Rebecca pulled a not particularly enthusiastic face but nodded and followed Mum into the depths of the caravan. As soon as she had closed the door behind her, a talking device started ringing beneath the snow at the foot of the old oak.

The sheep watched as unusually black smoke billowed out of the caravan, first just out of the little, grimy chimney, then out of the window and finally the door as well. Rebecca and Mum sought refuge on the caravan steps, coughing. Tess rubbed her muzzle in the snow.

'Pasta sauce!' ranted Rebecca. 'Pasta sauce! How could you go wrong?'

'I'm not used to your cooker,' said Mum.

'You've been here for three weeks already, and you're still not used to my cooker . . .' muttered Rebecca. 'Don't light up again! How can you smoke now? I'd stopped, you know, and then you turn up! Have you at least found something out about my clothes, with your fortune-telling sorcery?'

'Not yet. But that was probably Yves too! I've got this funny feeling. I wouldn't put anything past him!'

Rebecca laughed. 'No, this time it wasn't Yves for a change. The guy's completely colour-blind – he wouldn't be able to tell which things were red. I noticed it when we were apple-picking in the autumn. I kept saying to him: not the green ones, and he carried on . . . it drove me mad!'

'I could read the cards this afternoon . . .' said Mum rather meekly.

'Bloody cards! Let's try something different. I've still got a red scarf left.' Rebecca grinned grimly. 'And you can make yourself useful too! I want you to make yourself scarce this afternoon. Go and have a shower! And take Tess with you!'

And sure enough: that afternoon Mum, in a surprising show of obedience, went for a shower, Tess on the lead.

Rebecca watched the two of them leave. Shortly afterwards she hung her last red scarf on a hook outside the caravan.

'To air it,' she said, winking at the sheep. The sheep were standing around trying to look like they were relaxed and all there. Up to now they had narrowly escaped being counted!

The red scarf flickered in the wind like a flame.

Rebecca put her brown bread hat on again, wrapped a blue scarf around her neck this time and made a lot of fuss about locking up the caravan. Then she was off again and disappeared through the yard gate. The sheep watched her leave.

A few minutes later Rebecca appeared again, through a little gateway in the side of the courtyard wall. From a distance the sheep almost didn't recognise her without a single scrap of red on her. Rebecca crept cautiously along the wall, then under the cover of the fruit trees, towards the edge of the forest – and disappeared inside. But the sheep could still pick out her scent. Rebecca's scent skulked closer to the meadow again, under the cover of the forest, and finally settled near the beautiful beech.

The sheep looked at one another, waggled their ears and started to graze again.

Monsieur Fronsac went halfway across the yard, hit himself in the face with the palm of his hand and turned back around again. A door in the wall opened and the gardener came out, holding a bundle of branches. Madame Fronsac walked across the yard and glanced fleetingly over at the sheep. A fox darted along the meadow fence. It was still too early for lambs, but the sheep didn't let it out of their sight. Madame Fronsac walked across the yard for a second time. Then a third. She glanced to the left and to the right and up at the chateau.

She wiped her big hands, red with cold, on her apron, rushed over to the meadow gate and went through it towards the shepherd's caravan. The sheep were starting to wonder what was going on. After more furtive glances in all directions, the Walrus had stolen the scarf and disappeared behind the caravan, where she couldn't be seen from the chateau. But Rebecca, crouching somewhere near the beautiful beech probably had an excellent view of the Walrus.

Then several things happened at once.

Hortense stepped into the yard holding the little boy's hand, the Walrus pulled out a potato knife and Rebecca burst out of the forest like a diminutive but determined wild boar.

This time it wasn't because he was hungry. Mopple had eaten more than his fair share of concentrated feed at the trough earlier. Maybe it was the cold? Or the snow? All that white all over the place really could discombobulate a sheep.

Mopple just carried on grazing, his head deep in the snow, trying to ignore the gorse bush as best he could.

'Psst!' hissed the gorse bush. 'Over here! Over here, Mopple the Whale!'

Mopple didn't look over. A European gorse bush that knew his name? He didn't like it. First imaginary goats and now talking gorse bushes. What was next? He saw himself embroiled in an animated discussion with a clump of brag-wort. Mopple sighed. It was about time for winter to be over.

The gorse bush started to kick snow at him, and Mopple was getting cross.

'Stop it!' he said to the bush.

'I'll only stop if you come with me!' the gorse bush whispered.

Now Mopple was certain he was imagining the whole thing.

'If you go, I'll come with you!' he said to the gorse bush daringly.

'Excellent!' said the gorse bush. Three young goats poked their pointy heads out of the branches: one grey goat, one red goat and a brown mottled goat.

'I'm Amaltée,' said the grey goat.

'I'm Circe,' said the red goat.

'And I'm Calliope,' said the brown mottled goat. Mopple sat on his haunches in surprise.

'Do you lot really want to do something about the Garou?' asked Calliope. 'Because a bit of sparkle isn't going to cut it!'

Mopple nodded bravely.

'Then come with us!' whispered Circe.

The three goats turned around and trotted back to the loose slat in the goat fence, their tails wagging behind them. Mopple hesitated for a moment, then he thought about Zora and the other expedition members, who might be in trouble. Mopple *wanted* to do something about the Garou.

There seemed to be a commotion at the caravan and Mopple squeezed his way through the gap, unnoticed, and trotted resolutely after the three goats.

* * *

The Walrus was bawling and shaking and gulping, Rebecca was hissing '*Pourquoi? Pourquoi?*' Hortense was crying, 'Becca! Becca!' and the sheep were aghast.

Rebecca had caught the Walrus. Red-handed. In the act. There was no doubt about it.

The rescued scarf and the knife were now lying in the snow, and everyone was upset.

'I'd like to know why!' Rebecca hissed, too furious to use her laborious European. 'I've never done a thing to her – never! If she doesn't tell me why, I'm calling the police!'

'Becca!' said Hortense reproachfully, but then she talked to the Walrus.

The Walrus was shaking so much that to begin with she couldn't say anything at all – not even in European.

Eventually she started honking away, sobbing and snivelling, and the only thing the sheep understood was the word 'Garou.'

'She was trying to help you,' said Hortense.

'Ha!' said Rebecca. 'Does she think red doesn't suit me, or what?'

'Red is the wrong colour,' said Hortense, looking at the ground. 'Nobody wears red around here.'

Hortense took a deep breath. She glanced over at the younger little human, who was standing at the fence looking wide-eyed at the shepherd's caravan, then she moved closer to Rebecca.

'*Écoute*, Becca,' she said quietly. 'Red is the wrong colour because it attracts the Garou. You can choose to believe it or not believe it, but here it is. The little boy in the forest had a red jacket on, and the woman had a red skirt and the girl was wearing a red hat. And she did it because she knew you wouldn't believe her – because she didn't want to find you in the snow. And *le petit*, that was her little grandson. He was visiting her. And she gave him the jacket. *Voilà!*'

Rebecca's arms drooped, she stared at Hortense and the Walrus, and didn't say a word. The Walrus dabbed the tears from her eyes with her apron. Now she'd started honking, there was no stopping her.

She grabbed one of Rebecca's limp hands and honked and honked.

'What's she saying now?' muttered Rebecca.

'Becca!' Hortense looked at her wide-eyed.

'I want to know,' said Rebecca in a strangely flat voice. 'She says that you shouldn't have dinner with the *patron* this evening,' said Hortense. '*Voilà!* And now enough of this nonsense. I have to see to the children.'

The Walrus insistently honked away at Rebecca for quite some time, stroking her hand. Then she hugged the shepherdess, who went stiff as a board, and rushed back to the chateau.

Rebecca picked the red scarf out of the snow and looked at it critically for a long time.

'Nonsense,' she muttered then. 'Nonsense!'

The sheep didn't think it was nonsense. They'd seen the deer in the snow. There was no doubt about it: the Garou liked red.

To and fro, to and fro, to and fro. Mopple couldn't keep his eyes off the goats' madly wagging tails. What they could be happy about in this no-man's-land between the forest and the chateau wall was a mystery to Mopple. They had silently stolen from the meadow and were now silently trotting along the wall, the goats thronging ahead, Mopple behind. Mopple didn't like the silence. Everything was far too quiet: the snow and the bricks, the path, the gorse and the brown brambles and even Mopple's stomach.

Mopple peered down, on the lookout for possible grass on the wayside. When he looked up again, the goats had disappeared. Mopple bleated in alarm, and a grey goat head appeared round a corner of the wall again.

'Don't bleat,' said Amaltée. 'Come on!'

Mopple thought about Zora's clever black head and resolutely turned the corner. The goats had stopped in front of a weather-bleached wooden door. Circe pressed her pointy little horns against the wood and the door creaked open a crack.

Mopple slipped through with them, resigned to his fate.

Walls, nothing but walls. A hodgepodge of walls and alleys and nooks and crannies. And everywhere smelled suspiciously of humans, and even pigs.

Mopple realised he was shaking like a suckling lamb.

'Don't worry,' Circe whispered to him. 'We've got a plan! Every goat has a plan. We've got three plans. Plan B and plan F, and if all else fails, plan Z.'

Mopple was just about to get the hiccups again. Amaltée was listening, Circe was looking and Calliope was scenting the air. All three goats were thinking.

'What are we looking for?' bleated Mopple nervously. 'Bernie,' said the three goats in chorus. 'We're looking for Bernie!'

13

THE MOST SILENT SHEEP IN THE FLOCK IS AN INSPIRATION

'That's how she knew nobody was in the caravan,' said Rebecca.

'Because you took Tess over to her!'

'And then she left poor old Tess on her own anyway!' said Mum.

Rebecca was smoking. Mum was flicking through her cards, repeatedly. Tess was sitting with them, wagging her tail every time she heard her name.

'I don't get it,' said Mum eventually. 'The Hanged Man is missing.'

'Part of me's happy about it,' said Rebecca. 'I mean, it's a sad story, but at least it wasn't destructiveness for the sake of it. She did it because she likes me!'

'The Hanged Man is missing,' said Mum stubbornly. 'What am I supposed to do without the Hanged Man?'

Rebecca shrugged. 'You manage just fine without Justice!'

'That's different,' Mum snapped. 'Completely different! The Hanged Man stands for self-sacrifice and insight. How am I supposed to read the cards properly without self-sacrifice and insight?'

The sheep were sheltering from the wind by the shepherd's caravan, trying to ignore Rebecca. She had been in their bad books since the shepherdess had put their silver in the bin for the second time.

'I think Mopple ate the wrong card,' said Cordelia, shivering. 'Now Yves is under the oak, and for what? What good is that?'

'Mopple ought to eat another type of card!' bleated Cloud.

'Where is Mopple?' asked Ramesses.

The sheep looked around. Mopple was nowhere to be seen!

They huddled closer together. It stuck out a mile that there were fewer of them. First Zora, Heather and Maude, the warning sheep. Then Othello. Now Mopple. They seemed thinner – like they'd been shorn. Up to now, all of their plans against the Garou hadn't made them feel safer; there were just fewer sheep on the meadow. This time nobody wanted to venture away from the meadow to get the paper.

'Marcassin!' The unshorn ram had trotted closer, not so close that he was touching them, but close enough that they could smell him. Nobody minded. One more sheep was one more sheep, and it felt warm and good.

'What on earth should I wear tonight?' said Mum, staring at the cards.

Rebecca took a deep breath.

'I've got an idea,' she said then. 'I'll make sure the aerial gets put on the roof, and you can stay at home tonight.'

'I'm an embarrassment to you,' said Mum.

'I don't want the sheep to be left alone,' said Rebecca, looking at the ground. 'Not after everything that's happened. But I'd like to go. I've never been inside the chateau properly; I've only been down in the kitchen and in the library.'

'I'll ask the cards,' said Mum.

Rebecca angrily flicked her cigarette into the snow. For a moment the sheep forgot to ignore her and were astonished.

'You always have to ask the stupid cards! Why?! What on earth do you imagine is in those cards that isn't out here in the world?'

'Nothing,' said Mum. 'But sometimes they help us to see things.'

Miss Maple looked curiously.

Mopple the Whale had had enough of goats, both real and imaginary. He had been hissed at by a ginger tabby and grunted at by a stinking pig, he'd almost sunk into a heap of manure and nearly got stuck between two fat barrels. Mopple had even seen the extra-large car sleeping in a corner. But there was still no sign of Zora, Heather and Maude.

'I want to go back!' bleated Mopple, but the goats seemed to be even deafer than Sir Ritchfield all of a sudden. Finally, they stood still, in the cover of a log pile.

'He's not here!' Calliope sighed.

'Definitely not here,' Amaltée confirmed. 'You know what that means,' said Circe.

The other two nodded. 'We'll have to go *around*!'

Mopple didn't like the way they said 'around.'

'Why?' he asked. 'Around where?'

'Around that!' said the three goats, looking up. Really far up. Mopple put his head back too.

'Around the chateau?' he asked quietly.

Circe nodded. She carefully slipped out of the shadows of the log pile, towards the chateau. Followed by Amaltée. Then Calliope. Then – very reluctantly – Mopple.

They walked along the moat that surrounded the chateau, past stark, bare trees and a swan made of stone. It smelled of water down in the moat. Mopple risked a peep and was horrified by what he saw: three goats and a ram were trotting along down there too. A rather rotund ram. Mopple would have liked to know where he found so much food with all this snow. The goats looked thinner and more adventurous. The fat ram looked back up at Mopple, clearly frightened. He felt sorry for him. In the moat with three goats – poor lamb! At least Mopple was up here in the fresh air, he could smell the wind and see in all directions. Emboldened, the fat ram trotted on.

Then, they had stepped out of the shadows of the chateau and were standing on a kind of stone plateau. And behind that . . .

'What's that?' croaked Mopple.

'That?' said the goats in chorus. 'That's the maze!'

'A bit to the left,' said Rebecca.

'A bit to the right,' said Mum.

Zach was standing on the caravan roof shifting metal antlers back and forth. The sheep stood and watched.

All apart from Miss Maple. As a lamb, Maple had stolen maple syrup from George's slice of bread, and now she was in the process of stealing one of Mum's cards from the caravan steps. These cards might not be the same as the cardboard map, but they helped you to see, that's what Mum had said – and Miss Maple wanted to see: the truth and even the Garou if need be. There was something that looked a bit like the chateau on the first card she sniffed out. Humans flying through the air. Not particularly appetising, but Maple had no time to be picky, and chowed down, chewed, chewed again and swallowed. It was tough and dry. And a bit bitter. She couldn't understand why Mopple liked eating card.

She took a few steps away from the caravan and looked around. Could she see better already? She could see Zach, Mum and Rebecca, her flock and the unshorn ram, the goats on the other side of the fence, the forest and the chateau. Nothing new there. Mum's cards were just as useless as the stalk-eyed contraption. Maple suddenly had a funny feeling that she didn't need to see at all. That she'd already seen whatever it was she needed to see – she just hadn't understood it yet. The clue to the Garou was somewhere in her head, within touching distance.

Maple closed her eyes and peered again. This time she didn't see a chateau or a meadow. Just the sea. Then a river. No, it wasn't really a river. A moment on the country lanes, the sky stormy and dark, with the sun in front of it, the wet asphalt glistening like a river. They weren't on the country lanes anymore because the woman with the scraped-back hair had asked them here. But why? Maple saw a spider struggling to rid its web of a stray birch leaf, and the meadow in an oblique, yellowish light, moments before the sun disappeared behind the chateau. Even once the sun was hiding behind the chateau, you could tell it was still there by the bright glow around the edges. You must be able to tell the Garou was still there in his human hiding place too. But where were the edges of a human being? Maple didn't know and kept looking. The deer in the forest. The look on the little goat's face before she followed the Garou's tracks. Why was the little goat so determined to find the Garou? The other goats didn't seem bothered about him. Zach in the forest. Hortense with the little humans on the meadow. The goatherder here and the goatherder in the forest. Yves beneath the old oak. What was the point of it? It had to serve some kind of purpose! All of a sudden, Miss Maple was certain that Rebecca didn't have Yves on her conscience. Otherwise, she wouldn't have spent so long looking for him earlier. So, it had been somebody else – and this somebody must have had a reason. Maybe Yves beneath the old oak served a purpose after all! But what was it?

Maple opened her eyes.

'That's it!' said Mum and Rebecca in chorus. The little metal antlers looked ridiculous on the caravan.

'This way!' said Circe.

'This way!' said Amaltée.

'This way!' bleated Calliope.

The three goats were looking in three different directions, and Mopple the Whale was looking back and forth between them.

'Isn't there another way?' groaned Mopple. They had entered a labyrinth of evergreen hedges, and behind every corner was the straight edge of another hedge. Hedge after hedge after hedge. Nothing but the clipped edges of hedges, every way he turned. It was unnatural.

'Yes,' said Amaltée. 'But this is more interesting! This way!'

'Why are we here? What's this all about? What do you want?' Mopple had had quite enough of hedges with straight edges.

Suddenly, all three goats looked at her reproachfully.

'We are goats,' said Circe, smirking.

'We are not wanting.'

'But we're also not just going to stand around while the Garou is on the prowl,' said Amaltée.

'No matter what the old goats say!'

'The old goats say a lot!'

The three goats rolled their eyes.

'What do the old goats say?' Mopple wanted to know.

'That the Garou has never got a goat. That the Garou leaves goats in peace.'

'Then what are we doing here?' asked Mopple again.

'*You lot* are wanting,' explained Amaltée.

'You lot are wanting to do something about the Garou,' said Calliope.

'*We* know where the Garou is hiding,' said Circe.

'Maybe,' said Calliope.

'At least we know who might know where the Garou is hiding!' corrected Amaltée.

'This way!' said Circe.

'This way!' bleated Calliope.

'I want to go back,' panted Mopple.

'This is the maze,' said Circe quietly. 'There's no way back. Backwards is also forwards. This way!'

'I think we know something we don't know,' Miss Maple explained.

The other sheep eyed her with concern. It had been commendable to eat one of Mum's cards, but it didn't seem to be doing her much good.

They had retreated behind the hay barn to investigate together, and Maple was ranting.

'I think we know something about the Garou,' Maple started again. 'Something the little goat didn't tell us. Something we saw – or something we nearly saw. What do we know about the Garou?'

The sheep strained to think. Silver and bullets and glowing eyes and wolf ointment – all goaty madness. All apart from the deer. The deer had been very real, very red and very dead.

'He must be very fat!' Ramesses blurted out. 'Deer are big and heavy, and if he's eaten lots of deer . . .'

They looked at one another. Very fat! Then Madame Fronsac was the only possible hiding place!

Maple looked dreamily down at the shepherd's caravan for a moment, where Rebecca, Mum and Zach were shaking hands.

'No!' she said then, deep in thought. 'No, that's not right!'

'Why?' bleated the winter lamb.

'Because he doesn't eat the deer!' said Miss Maple. 'And that in itself is . . . interesting.'

Maple was reminded of the children playing sheep by the yard gate. Sheep ripped up grass and ate grass. The children had ripped up the grass, but not eaten it. Because they weren't really sheep. Because they were just pretending to be sheep.

'Wolves eat deer,' she said. 'And humans. And,' she sighed, but it had to be said, 'sheep. But the Garou didn't eat the deer – he just . . . scattered it about. Like the children with the grass. The children didn't know what to do with the grass because they're not sheep. And the Garou didn't eat the deer because he's not a real wolf. He's a pretend wolf. A wolf that someone's made up!'

The sheep chewed. They might have a bit of experience with imaginary goats. But imaginary wolves . . .

'So, what does he eat then?' asked Cordelia.

Lane shuddered. 'Maybe he eats his human. From the inside!'

Circe wanted to go left, Amaltée and Calliope wanted to go right, and obviously none of them had admitted to wanting anything at all. Mopple did want something, namely to get out of there, but nobody was interested in him.

'Megara would go right too!' bleated Calliope, trying to convince Circe. 'So would Xantippe and Arachne and Io!'

'And Aubrey!' bleated Mopple. Anything to keep moving! All three goats looked at him keenly.

'Oh,' bleated Calliope. 'You mustn't take any notice of what Aubrey does.'

'Aubrey's not a goat!' said Amaltée. 'Not really.'

'Why not?' asked Mopple.

'She did something,' said Amaltée.

'Terrible. Terrible,' Circe and Calliope muttered.

'What is she then?' asked Mopple.

The three goats put their heads together and whispered. 'She's not a human either,' muttered Calliope.

Circe turned her head and looked over her red back at Mopple. 'We don't know what Aubrey is.'

'The herder reared her with a bottle,' said Calliope. 'Spoiled her.'

'Careless. Careless,' Circe and Amaltée muttered.

'And she sucked up all sorts of human foolishness with the milk.'

'Pity. Pity,' Circe and Amaltée muttered. The goats sniggered.

'This way!' muttered Circe, turning left round the corner.

The others followed.

Finally, the blasted maze was behind them.

At last! thought Mopple. Then he thought: *The Garou!*

Next moment, he knew he must have been mistaken, since the Garou was one and these animals were two. They were sitting on plinths to the left and right of a gateway and were roaring soundlessly into the afternoon air.

Mopple and the goats took a few steps back. Beasts of prey, that was for sure, with long, curved claws and too many sharp teeth in their mouths, crouching, stony, ready to pounce.

'This way!' Circe decisively bleated, stepping towards the gateway.

'And you're sure they're not going to do anything?' asked Mopple.

'Surely not,' said Amaltée.

'What's sure, anyway?' said Circe.

'The one-horned billy goat hits the bull's-eye!' said Calliope.

The other two goats looked at her as if she'd just said something very wise.

'Stone is a Thing, stays a Thing, is always a Thing,' muttered Circe, but Mopple could see their hackles rising under the gaze of the stone beasts of prey.

The red goat kicked out behind her briefly, then she galloped through the gateway. Followed by the grey goat. Then the mottled goat. The two beasts of prey could now give Mopple their full and undivided attention.

Mopple scrunched up his eyes, thought about Zora's beautiful horns and galloped forth.

It was surprisingly pretty on the other side of the stone beasts of prey. An invitingly open area that would surely provide good pasture in the summer, surrounded by bushes and young birch trees, and a little white house on the other side, with a few outbuildings. The only thing that interrupted the peaceful scene was two distant brown patches on the white of the snow: the two men who were always going for walks were making their way across the snow towards the chateau.

Mopple and the goats hid in a gorse bush and waited.

The men were talking, in a not particularly friendly manner. It was strange that two humans who liked each other so little spent so much time together. Maybe they were scared of going into the forest alone. Or maybe they did like each other after all, because all of a sudden, they both laughed. Laughed and laughed and laughed until the tall human had to blow his nose into a colourful cloth.

'What did they say?' asked Mopple, once the two snorting walkers had passed.

Amaltée cocked her head. '"This time it doesn't have to look like an accident," is what the short one said. Is that funny?'

'I don't know,' said Mopple. 'What now?'

'This is where Eric lives and makes goat's cheese,' Calliope explained proudly.

'He used to make sheep's cheese too,' Circe added comfortingly. 'And if we're lucky, Bernie's here too.'

'Who's Bernie?'

The three goats shuddered. 'Bernie is mad!'

Mopple and the goats raced up to the white house and in doing so didn't see the black ram following the two men at a distance.

'How does Aubrey know so much about the Garou if she's never seen him? If nobody's seen him?'

Maple was still standing behind the hay barn, thinking. Everything had got too complicated for the other sheep and they had scattered, grazing. Only the most silent sheep in the flock was still standing beside her, listening thoughtfully.

'And how does Mum know about the werewolf? And Madame Fronsac?'

The most silent sheep in the flock didn't know.

'Not from Aubrey at any rate,' said Maple. 'So, it must be the other way around: Aubrey heard the story from a human. A human story! The Garou is a made-up wolf! That's why he can live inside a human. He lives in their heads!'

The most silent sheep in the flock looked at her enquiringly.

Maple nodded. 'The question is: Who told the human story? And how did the wolf get out of the story?'

All of a sudden, she scented an important clue. Clear and bright like a path. The most silent sheep in the flock was a surprising source of inspiration.

'Do you know what that means?' she bleated excitedly. 'It means that the human doesn't really turn into a wolf. He only thinks he turns into a wolf. And that means that somebody who's seen the Garou could recognise the human! But nobody has seen the Garou . . .'

The most silent sheep in the flock snorted. Maple sensed a kind of gentle dissent.

'You're right,' she said. 'Someone has!'

She looked over to the gorse bushes, where the unshorn ram was standing enjoying the sunshine.

'And then we inherited. And we travelled to Europe. Only something wasn't quite right with Europe. Then I ate the map made of card and now we're here!' Mopple the Whale looked proudly over at the goats. He had decided to make a bit of conversation, to distract himself from all the open doors – and from the question of what might be lurking behind them. Around the pretty white house there were a good many less pretty sheds and huts and stables, and the goats trotted between them scenting the air searchingly in every doorway.

'But we want to get away from here. By car. Because of the wolf! Zora's gone looking for the car, and then . . .'

The three goats looked at him a bit pityingly.

'Who still believes in wolves in this day and age?' The goats pulled enlightened faces.

'Wolves are made up by the herders,' explained Amaltée.

'So that they can better oppress us,' bleated Circe.

'Because goats aren't that easy to oppress.'

The three goats rebelliously craned their necks. 'Cassandra in turn claims that herders are made up by wolves,' added Calliope.

'What does Cassandra know?!' bleated Circe and Amaltée.

The three goats trotted on, embroiled in a heated debate about herders and wolves. Mopple followed.

They came to a half-open stable door. Inside, it was light and smelled strange: sour and milky and slightly goaty.

'Look!' said Circe. 'That's interesting!'

Mopple didn't want to look, but obviously he looked anyway. Inside stood Eric, busy with goat's cheese, dunking it in liquid and then lifting it out again. The goat's cheeses glistened in a cold white light, like moons.

'Goat's cheese,' said Amaltée with a mixture of derision and pride.

Mopple didn't have eyes for the goat's cheese. 'The dog!' he breathed.

And what a dog! Mopple had never seen a dog like it. It was so big. So grey and shaggy. It had such long legs. The dog dozed contentedly a little way from the door and its feet chased creatures through the snow in its dreams – rotund white rams, Mopple supposed.

'It can't pick up our scent,' whispered Amaltée. 'The stench of cheese in here is too strong.'

'There used to be lots of them,' whispered Circe. 'A whole pack. So that the patients didn't run away!'

'Oh,' said Mopple. 'Oh.'

14

ZORA, MAUDE AND HEATHER FIND THEMSELVES

'Faster!' bleated Zora.

'I can't go any farther!' groaned Heather.

Maude didn't say a thing, barely stopping to scent the air. That showed just how tired she was.

And – through some kind of miracle – Aubrey hadn't hopped for a while.

They had followed the tower sign's nose and carried on along the road until Aubrey had claimed she could see something between the trees in the distance – maybe the chateau, but definitely a building, and Maude had claimed she could smell goats. Zora and Heather hadn't seen or smelled anything, but they had decided to investigate all the same.

But then the building had disappeared again, Maude hadn't been able to smell anything any more, and a heavy snow shower covered all their tracks. Since then, they had been criss-crossing their way through the forest, and they were too tired to even be afraid.

'Tracks!' Aubrey suddenly bleated excitedly.

There really were! Up ahead somebody had walked through the forest. Several clear tracks led through the snow up a hill.

Maude scented the tracks thoroughly. Finally, there was something to scent!

'A goat!' she said. 'And three sheep! Sheep . . .' She drank the air in. 'Sheep from our flock!'

Heather bleated triumphantly. If more members of the flock were on the move in the forest, soon they could merge into one big flock, and then everything would only be half as bad!

'Who?' bleated Heather excitedly. She really hoped that Othello was amongst the sheep – or at a pinch Sir Ritchfield.

Maude sniffed again.

'Zora!' she said. 'Heather! And . . . a strange sheep!'

'That's us!' Zora sighed. 'The strange sheep is you!'

'It's not me!' bleated Maude indignantly.

They carried on, Zora up ahead, then Heather and Aubrey, and Maude a little way away, offended, because Zora had called her a strange sheep.

Zora sensed a kick. She looked around: nothing, just Heather behind her, too tired to trot and definitely too tired to kick. There it was again! A kick in her stomach. Next moment Zora knew where the kick was coming from: it was coming from inside her! A good, strong kick. The first one. Zora was proud of her lamb.

She stood and thought for a moment. Her lamb was trying to tell her something. Zora looked around. The snow was beginning to soak up its nocturnal blue once again, the forest stood blackly, and the cold was gathering in the shadows. Her lamb was right. They had to eat something before darkness fell.

They needed rest and somewhere sheltered from the wind to stay the night.

'It works! It works!' Mum cheered from the shepherd's caravan. 'And the picture's not bad either! Maybe Yves isn't that bad after all!'

'Well,' said Rebecca then: 'I'm beginning to wonder where he is. It's weird that I haven't seen him since yesterday.'

'Oh,' said Mum. 'He's got his ladies: one here, one over in the village; that's what I've heard. He'll be around here somewhere.'

Rebecca laughed. 'I've got to give it to you – you really could hear the grass grow! Nobody tells me stuff like that. And you barely understand them! How on earth do you get it all out of people?'

The sheep made envious faces. Hearing the grass grow! It must be a truly beautiful sound, fresh and green and young, like a whisper! Even more beautiful than any story, if not quite as beautiful as bleating. Lane, Cloud and Cordelia retreated to a quiet corner of the meadow to listen to the grass grow. But no matter how hard they listened, the grass didn't grow. Instead, music blared out of the shepherd's caravan – and honking voices.

'The sound's not bad, is it?' said Mum. 'I'm going to have a lovely cosy night in front of the box!'

'But you don't understand a word of it,' said Rebecca.

'Maybe not the films,' said Mum. 'But the adverts! Everyone understands the adverts! Desires, dreams, pictures – that's the best education for me, I'm telling you!'

Then she poked her head out of the door and her tone changed. 'Oh dear, the snob!'

Rebecca looked up. The Jackdaw was standing by the fence

waving to her, then he opened the gate and walked across the meadow towards her. Rebecca waved back.

Mum closed the caravan door behind her.

'Tell him I'm not here!' she hissed through the closed door.

'He's seen you already.' Rebecca sighed.

'I don't care!'

The shepherdess looked angry for a moment, then, as the Jackdaw got closer, she painted a smile on her face.

The sheep retreated from the caravan a bit. They could forget about being read to now.

The Jackdaw stopped a few steps away from the caravan and bowed elegantly.

'Sorry to disturb you, Mademoiselle . . .'

'Rebecca,' said Rebecca.

'Rebecca,' said the Jackdaw. 'I just wanted to ask if you could come half an hour earlier this evening . . . it's the cook's day off tomorrow.'

'Of course,' said Rebecca. 'Only, unfortunately, my mother can't make it.'

She smiled.

'Oh,' said the Jackdaw, looking far from pleased. 'What a shame! Well, never mind . . .'

'Are you really a cosmetic surgeon?' Rebecca asked as he turned to leave. 'Does that mean you do nose jobs for rich women? And . . . boob jobs as well?'

The Jackdaw smiled again. 'Noses are our bread and butter, I'm afraid.' The sheep cast meaningful glances at one another. 'It's more interesting to completely remodel whole faces though. Faces maimed in accidents – or faces disfigured from birth. That's what I specialise in. Believe you me – I keep my distance from rich women's breasts. *Au revoir*, Mademoiselle!'

'Rebecca!' said Rebecca. '*Au revoir*!' She smiled at the Jackdaw, and then, as soon as he'd turned his back to her, she jumped up and disappeared into the caravan with her book.

'Bad!' bleated Willow, the second most silent sheep in the flock, indulging in an unusual fit of loquacity, and the sheep got the feeling she didn't just mean the abrupt end of story-time.

'It's not really her fault,' said Cloud. 'She's a bit like a lamb. Curious. Distracted by every butterfly, and she forgets the important things. Like stories.'

Cloud was an experienced mother ewe. She knew about these things.

'Butterflies?' bleated Sir Ritchfield enthusiastically. Ritchfield was a bit like a lamb too. He liked butterflies. The sheep lowered their heads. There was no guarantee that Sir Ritchfield would ever see a butterfly again.

'Can you smell him?' Amaltée whispered reverently.

The three goats had retreated behind a barrel of rainwater and were scenting the air.

'Yes!' Mopple groaned. The pungent stench of goat surrounded the pretty house and its little flock of stables, huts and sheds. A different smell to all the other goats that Mopple had scented up to now: Older. Ripe. Mature.

'He really is here,' said Circe quietly. For the first time, she looked worried – and meek.

Mopple scented the air again.

'It's coming from back there,' he said. There, a bit removed from the other buildings, stood a little ramshackle wooden hut – and it stank. The hut had something sinister about it.

'I'll wait here,' said Mopple, edging deeper into the shadows behind the barrel.

'Absolutely no way!' said Amaltée.

'Do you think we brought you along for the fun of it?' asked Circe.

'No!' bleated Amaltée.

'Not that it hasn't been fun,' Calliope reassured him. 'But you're here to memorise something.'

'And tell the other wanting woolly ones all about it,' said Circe.

'They'll believe you!' bleated Amaltée. 'You're their memory sheep!'

Mopple sighed, thought about Zora's sure-hoovedness and trotted after the goats, resigned to his fate.

Then they were standing in front of a half-open door; the stench was almost unbearable, and the goats hesitated.

'What now?' bleated Mopple.

'Hush!' the goats hissed. 'Or he'll hear us!'

'How are you going to ask him anything without him hearing you?' Mopple whispered back.

'I don't know yet,' whispered Amaltée. 'I don't know why the door's open either. The door should be shut.'

'That's good,' said Mopple. 'We can just go in and ask him.'

'And he can just get out,' said Circe.

Mopple thought for a moment. It was starting to get dark, and he definitely didn't want to run into the wolfhound from before in the dark.

'I'll look!' he said. Mopple held his breath and poked his head through the doorway; it took a while for his eyes to adjust to the darkness. Mopple pulled his head out again.

'I know why the door's open,' he said then. 'Take a look for yourselves!'

Three goats poked their heads through the door and looked, Circe on top, who was long and lanky; Calliope in the middle and Amaltée on the bottom, the smallest of the three. Yellow straw on the ground and a wonderful, rich scent, so thick you could almost see it, like smoke or fog, or a veil of secrets and cobwebs. And behind the veil there stood a sleeping billy goat, his goat-beard touching the ground. He must have lived so many lives! And his horns . . .

The goats pulled their heads out again.

'He can't fit through the door!' whispered Calliope. 'His horns won't fit through the door! Just don't wake him up whatever you do!'

'You can't ask him if he's asleep!' Mopple was gradually getting impatient. It was hay barn time and he wanted to go into the hay barn!

'The fat ram's right, kids,' said a voice all of a sudden, so quietly and softly that it took a moment for Mopple and the goats to work out where it had come from. They peered round the corner again. Bernie had woken up and was looking at them with young, sparkling eyes.

'Why don't you come in?' he said. 'We could eat a bit of hay together – fresh hay – and the ladies can ask me some questions. I like questions! And I like dazzlingly beautiful she-goats even more!'

The three goats giggled bashfully.

Mopple didn't need to be asked twice. He already had his hoof over the threshold and was making his way towards the hay.

The goats instantly stopped giggling.

'Don't!' Amaltée bleated in a panic. 'Bernie charges at anything that comes through the door. Anything! Even the wind! And the sun!'

Mopple's hoof froze mid-air.

'Unfortunately, the lady's right about that, fat ram,' said Bernie cheerfully. 'Shame, it really is very good hay.'

Mopple took a step back from the open door.

'Mad,' whispered Circe reverently. 'Completely mad.'

'Now don't just run away because of something so trifling,' said Bernie in the half-dark of the shed. 'I assume the ladies can ask their questions from out there. It's just a pity about the hay!' He was the friendliest goat Mopple had ever met.

Circe bobbed nervously on the spot.

'Well, ask him, then!' Mopple wanted to go home.

'It's a question about something that happened many, many years ago,' Amaltée whispered.

'At least five,' said Calliope.

The three young goats shuddered at the thought of the vast space of time.

'You were still on the meadow,' said Circe. 'On your own on a meadow because you charged everything even then.'

'That's what Cassandra says!' said Amaltée.

'Ah, the meadow!' Bernie sighed. 'And the she-goats! Ah, their beautiful horns, their tangy fur, their feathery lashes! Do you think the fence could have kept me from the ladies, from their fragrant backs! Pah!' Bernie's front hooves wove mysterious patterns in the straw.

The goats' eyes gleamed with wonder.

'Cassandra also says that a goat once gave birth in the winter.'

'Outside.'

'In the snow.'

'But the birth went wrong, and the kid was dead, and the mother goat bled and bled.'

'A white kid,' said Amaltée.

'A white mother goat,' said Calliope.

'And then the Garou came, the young Garou, still an inexperienced hunter, and chased the mother goat through the snow,' said Circe.

'He couldn't help it,' said Calliope.

'And there was red everywhere,' said Amaltée, shuddering.

'And then you came!'

'Over the fence as if it weren't even there!'

'And chased the Garou away!'

'According to Cassandra.'

'Cassandra was there.'

'Cassandra remembers.'

'But Cassandra was already blind then and didn't see the Garou,' said Amaltée.

'But you, oh handsome-horned one, you saw the Garou many, many winters ago,' fawned Circe.

'Who, far-grazed one?' the three goats whispered in chorus. 'Who was the Garou?'

'Ah,' whispered Bernie. 'Ladies, ladies! Don't be so impetuous now! Youth is a strange flea.'

Bernie looked up, out of the door, through Mopple and the goats, into the far distance.

'I remember . . .' he said dreamily. 'I remember so much. The shapes of the clouds on that day, beautiful wispy shapes like reeds in the wind, and all the lights. Back then the chateau had more eyes than it does today. I remember Calypso was in heat, in the middle of winter, what a delight, and she was all I could think about. But I can't remember the Garou's face.'

The goats' ears drooped. 'Oh!' They sighed.

'He looked like a human,' said Bernie. 'Just like a human. Two-Legs! Who can tell them apart with all their false coats?'

Bernie fell silent and the clear, sharp howl of a dog cut through the twilight silence. The wolfhound! The wolfhound had tracked them down! The goats spun around and ran away in three different directions: plan B, plan F and plan Z. Mopple didn't have a plan, and he didn't know which of the three he should follow. He had the feeling that the wolfhound wouldn't come into Bernie's shed . . .

The moment's hesitation was too much. A drooling dark mass had already appeared between the sheds and was darting towards Mopple. If he ran, he didn't stand a chance. Mopple took a deep breath, as much as his round body would hold, and plunged into the resinous darkness of Bernie's shed.

Othello stopped. The wind hissed, too biting and cold for him to be able to scent anything properly, and too loud and howling. Othello was still certain that somebody was standing around the corner.

Othello waited a moment to gather himself. It had been a long, tumultuous day. First, he had followed the walker on his walk. The walker didn't walk; he bounded in great leaps through the snow, criss-crossing to the stream. Then he climbed into the water, with his tall, dark boots and waded upstream for a while. At first it seemed to Othello like a particularly stupid way of moving forwards, but then he got it: the walker was trying to obliterate his scent – and his tracks in the snow. As Othello followed the wading man along the bank, it became increasingly apparent that he wasn't as stupid as he looked. Not by a long shot. The tall man moved sparingly and precisely, with an elegance that surprised Othello. When the tall man scrambled out of the water, he didn't climb onto the bank, but onto a tree root and from there up an oak, crouching up on a thick branch to take off his dark boots, wrap them in a bag and put them in a hole in the boot. He pulled some other boots out of the hole in the boot, boots that looked very similar, but seemed smaller to Othello. Then the man climbed from the oak onto a beech, onto another oak and finally, almost soundlessly, dropped back into the snow, at a point where there were already tracks, bigger and smaller ones, up and down. Deep in the forest a branch cracked again, and Othello understood how brave the man had to be to climb trees in this weather.

Then the man walked along deceptively innocently until he met the shorter walker. The short man asked him something. The tall man honked awkwardly.

The short man hissed in annoyance.

The tall man hissed back.

They honked away at each other for a while, then they carried on walking, side by side, looking like they always did. Othello had followed them. It wasn't that easy; for humans the two of them seemed to be unusually alert and tense. Once they almost spotted Othello in the shadow of the trees. He didn't really understand what was going on, but he knew that the two men were dangerous.

Maple would understand – Othello just had to see it and remember it.

He followed the walkers, who weren't really out for a walk,

along wide tracks through the forest, along the edge of a little lake, past a pretty white house, across a meadow and through a stone gate with two animals sitting either side of it. The men laughed.

Othello eyed the animals cautiously. *They're lions*, he thought, but obviously they weren't really lions. Real lions had a scent like thunder and fur scorched by heat. These were covered in snow. Othello slipped through the gate.

As soon as the two humans had walked around the chateau, they wrapped their coat of innocence around themselves a bit more tightly, every movement a lie.

Othello had lived next to an old jackal in the zoo who used to pretend to limp until the zoo sparrows started blithely hopping around in his enclosure pecking away at his meat. And when they got too close, he pounced. The little birds forgot every single time. The men here were play-acting as well. It was obvious that they were hunting something too. And not just deer.

The black ram followed the two of them until they disappeared inside one of the bigger outbuildings. There was a little fire burning inside and the aroma of food. Madame Fronsac opened the door to the two men and greeted them, amicably honking across each other. Othello had seen enough. He knew roughly where the meadow was and he wanted to go back and watch over his flock. He had to watch over them.

But now somebody was lying in wait for him behind the corner of a wall. Othello had spent the whole day scurrying after the two men; he'd had enough of hide-and-seek. The black ram lowered his four sharp horns and galloped in a wide arc around the corner.

* * *

'Othello,' Mopple screeched.

'Mopple,' bleated Othello, stopping just in time.

Mopple went weak at the knees with relief. He had sensed someone round the corner too and had closed his eyes and hoped for something harmless. The fat tabby cat maybe, or Madame Fronsac at most. But Othello was even better. He wasn't harmless. He was the lead ram and he would protect him. Mopple could use a bit of support.

'What are you doing here?' asked Othello.

'The goats . . . The billy goat . . . I don't know any more . . .' Mopple was a nervous wreck.

At first, Bernie hadn't moved at all, and the wolfhound had stood in the doorway slobbering, his eyes gleaming and his hackles raised. Mopple had just stood there trembling.

'He won't come in,' said Bernie finally, a hint of regret in his voice.

Outside a whistle could be heard, and the wolfhound whimpered. Then it was only darkness that rushed through the doorway.

The old billy goat turned his head back and forth and craned his neck.

'I . . . I thought I might try a bit of hay,' said Mopple, his voice weak.

Bernie took a few steps back and got ready to charge.

'Why?' croaked Mopple.

'I don't know,' said Bernie, his voice gentle. 'It's just how it is.'

He lowered his enormous, broadly curved horns, and charged towards Mopple, so slowly that Mopple could make out every single strand of his goaty beard. Mopple had retreated as far as he could. There was a hard impact, horn on wood. The shed shook.

Mopple reeled. He waited for the pain, but the pain didn't come.

'Now open your eyes,' said Bernie, his voice friendly. Mopple blinked, then he scrunched his eyes shut again. Bernie's ancient goaty face was hovering in the darkness in front of him, barely a nose away. Mopple kept his eyes closed and waited for something terrible to happen, but nothing did. Mopple opened his eyes again. It took a while for him to realise why nothing was happening: Bernie had got his huge horns stuck and was now wedged between the shed wall and the fodder rack.

'Oh!' said Mopple, strangely moved.

'These things happen,' said Bernie nonchalantly. 'No need to worry! It gives us the chance to have a little chat.'

Bernie looked at Mopple expectantly. Mopple couldn't think of anything to say. 'You're a sheep, aren't you?' asked Bernie. Mopple nodded.

'And there are other sheep? And you're all wanting, is that right?'

Mopple nodded again.

'There's something you ought to know about the Garou,' said Bernie, giving his horns a jerk that made the shed shake. 'The old chap had a weakness for dangerous animals. He had his dogs, and he had me, and then . . . it's not outside the realms of possibility that he reared the Garou too. You've got to ask yourselves where the old chap would have hidden the Garou! In somebody who wouldn't leave, I'd say. In somebody who will always stay here.'

'Who is the old chap?' asked Mopple. He imagined a horned human with an enormous goaty beard.

Bernie jerked his head back and forth. The fodder rack shook.

'The old chap is no more,' said Bernie. 'The old chap was. But he left traps behind. Mind traps. Snares and snap traps. Loonier than all of his lunatics! He used to feed me sugar, that's how mad he was. Best you go before I free myself!'

Mopple didn't have to be told twice. He clumsily pushed past Bernie and slipped out of the door. Then he just stood there for a while and breathed. The air was so sweet! The sky so clear! And life was so beautiful!

From then on, all he did was run: from the pretty little house, from the wolfhound scent and the stench of goat, from the darkness of the forest and the voices of the humans, on and on, through frozen snow that stung his ankles. Somehow Mopple had found his way back to the chateau, around the chateau, to the corner behind which someone had been lurking.

'Let's go back now,' said Othello. 'Right now.'

But before they could start towards the yard gate, they heard footsteps – and voices.

Mopple and Othello positioned themselves round the corner again, both on the same side this time.

'. . . And what a pity that your mum can't come,' said the Jackdaw.

'Oh,' said Rebecca. 'She goes to bed really early. Can't be helped. She sleeps like a log.'

'I'll send a nice bottle of wine over,' said the chateau owner.

'Oh no!' said Rebecca quickly. 'I . . . I don't think that's a very good idea. Wine's . . .'

'. . . a problem?' asked the chateau owner.

'Not good for her health,' said Rebecca firmly. 'Aren't you at all worried?' she asked then.

'About your mum?' asked the chateau owner with a grin.

'About the deer situation!' said Rebecca. 'It's not natural!'

'Well, you know, we have so many deer,' said the Jackdaw.

'And, strictly speaking, it's not exactly unnatural.'

'Isn't it?' asked Rebecca. 'Why not?'

'Well, the first living creatures were single-cell organisms. Single-cell organisms don't age – they divide, over and over. Single-cell organisms are immortal.' The Jackdaw paused for dramatic effect. He was clearly enjoying himself. 'But obviously single-cell organisms die – when they get eaten by other single-cell organisms. Evolution feeds on its children. The first death was a violent death – violent death is the most natural death of all.'

Rebecca didn't say a word, but Othello and Mopple, who knew their shepherdess well, could hear her thinking, *great!* in that voice of hers that meant it wasn't great at all.

'But of course, I'm co-operating with the police so that this can all be cleared up as quickly as possible,' the Jackdaw reassured her. Something about the way he said *police* piqued Othello's curiosity. He cautiously peered around the corner.

Rebecca and the Jackdaw were standing in the light of a lamp. Rebecca was smiling. Her lips were very red. The Jackdaw had his back to Othello. He was standing too close to Rebecca. Far too close for Othello's liking.

'He's lying!' said Mopple.

Othello nodded. The Jackdaw didn't want to help the police. Not one bit. The very thought of the police made the Jackdaw nervous.

Othello slipped out of the shadow of the wall, after Rebecca and the Jackdaw.

'Wait!' bleated Mopple. 'I thought we were going back?'

Othello turned around. 'She's our shepherdess,' he said. 'And he's lying.'

Mopple thought for a moment. Should he go through the

dark outbuildings on his own again? No way! Better to be with Othello! No matter where he was going. Mopple tried not to think about the *where* too much, and trotted along behind the lead ram.

'Is that a wolf howling at the moon?' Rebecca asked at the chateau door. 'On your family crest?'

The Jackdaw chuckled. 'My family doesn't have a crest. My father bought the chateau. For his clinic. More's the pity, I sometimes think. Although, it is an impressive building. No, if anything, that's Eric's crest!'

'Eric's?' said Rebecca.

The Jackdaw nodded. 'His father sold the chateau to my father and just kept the hermitage.'

'I didn't know that,' said Rebecca. 'And what's written underneath?'

'"*La lune n'est pas trop loin.*" The moon isn't very far away. My father . . .'

The Jackdaw fell silent.

'Your father?' asked Rebecca.

'Oh,' said the Jackdaw. 'I only just realised that my father always used to interpret it differently: 'Lunacy isn't very far away.' And how right he was! I hope you like fish?'

'Mhm, fish,' said the shepherdess. 'My favourite!' Rebecca was lying too.

15

SIR RITCHFIELD IS SEEING THINGS

'Noses are his bread and butter!' said Ramesses, shuddering. 'And he invited her over for something to eat,' said Cloud. The sheep scowled at the chateau where Rebecca and the Jackdaw had disappeared between the outbuildings.

A shepherdess without a nose just wouldn't be the same. They were just about to retire to the hay barn when Monsieur Fronsac rushed onto the meadow with a bottle in his hand. He knocked on the door of the shepherd's caravan, honked, passed the bottle through the crack and then rushed off again towards the chateau. Tess slipped out of the door and rolled in the snow.

A short while later a purring sound approached the meadow. A flat, metallic purr, as if it were being made by a giant mechanical cat.

'A car,' said Lane.

The sheep peered at the road where cars were normally found, but there was nothing there. Just darkness.

And then a car did appear after all. A dark car crept cautiously onto the yard, its eyes closed. It shuddered and fell silent. Two dark men got out of it, along with a woman wearing a white hat. The hat glowed blue in the darkness. The shorter of the two men (he wasn't particularly short either) had something cutting about him – the way he moved and even when he was standing still. The car was scared of him. The other two humans were perhaps a bit scared of him too.

The humans walked to the gate that led directly to the tower, and the car rolled away from the chateau, relieved, its dark eyes fixed on the road.

Everything happened unusually quietly and gently and only lasted a few moments, but it gave the sheep a strange sense of unease all the same. They were certain that what they had just witnessed was some kind of stalking. But who was doing the stalking? And who was being stalked?

They were finally getting comfortable in the hay barn when Sir Ritchfield's alarmed bleating called them back onto the meadow.

Ritchfield was standing in the snow, completely beside himself.

'Rebecca!' he bleated. 'Rebecca's behind the windows!

No shepherd may leave the flock!'

'Unless he comes back,' said Cloud soothingly. 'Or she.' The sheep thought for a moment. The old lead ram might get a bit muddled sometimes, but he still had the best eyes in the flock. And Rebecca was important.

'Can you really see Rebecca?' Lane asked.

Ritchfield looked at her enquiringly.

'REBECCA?' Lane yelled.

Ritchfield nodded anxiously.

'She . . .'

Ritchfield had a sneezing fit.

'She's standing . . .'

Ritchfield wheezed and coughed.

'She's going . . .'

The old lead ram panted and sneezed. Then he raised his horns and peered over at the illuminated windows, wearing his proud lead-ram expression. The sheep looked at him in awe.

'So?' asked Miss Maple.

'So what?' snorted Sir Ritchfield impatiently.

'What's she doing?'

Ritchfield thought for a moment. 'Nothing,' he said then.

'Nothing?' the sheep bleated. That didn't seem like very much.

'She's standing there doing nothing,' said Ritchfield decisively. 'And the Jackdaw's not doing anything either,' he added. 'He's wearing a red ribbon around his neck. But no bell.' He didn't want anybody thinking he couldn't see enough detail.

Another searching look at the chateau. 'And now . . .' Ritchfield bleated in shock. 'He just bit her hand.'

The sheep looked at one another. Their worst suspicions were confirmed!

'She ought to run away!' bleated Ramesses. 'Is she running away?'

'No,' said Sir Ritchfield. 'But she's red in the face. They're walking again, to the next window, and . . .' Sir Ritchfield bleated again in surprise.

'There's Othello! In another window!' His flock looked at him sceptically. 'And there's Mopple!'

'Mopple?' asked Cordelia. 'In the chateau?'

'He's eating some flowers,' said Ritchfield.

The sheep cast meaningful glances at one another. There were no flowers in the winter. The truth was out! Ritchfield was delirious!

'And fruit,' said Sir Ritchfield. 'On a table.'

'And summer grass, right?' bleated Heather.

'No,' said Ritchfield. 'No summer grass. But there's a piece of material. And Othello's standing beside a wild boar.' Ritchfield sighed. He was in the process of losing the last remaining vestiges of his lead ram credibility, but . . . oh, how sweet the air smelled! Like a day from his youth, a clear, cold, fine day . . .

'What about Rebecca?' Miss Maple asked.

'George is in the shepherd's caravan!' Sir Ritchfield responded, lost in thought.

From outside, the chateau looked bigger than the hay barn. Much bigger. But inside, it was smaller. Room after room after room, each of them small and secretive. It didn't make any sense. Why such a big thing if there was then so little space inside, between all the nooks and walls and Things?

Before, the sheep had sometimes been a bit envious of the inhabitants of the chateau. Now Othello was wondering why the chateau inhabitants didn't drive the sheep out and move into the hay barn, where you could see the sky through the window and breathe in snowflakes. Not that he'd allow himself to be driven out that easily.

Mopple was doing less thinking than Othello. He was trying to make the best of the chateau situation and was tasting anything that looked partway edible. When you were eating, you weren't afraid. Or not quite as afraid as you would be otherwise. They had followed Rebecca and the Jackdaw deep into the bowels of the chateau, across slippery tiles, echoing stone floors and deep, velvety rugs, and the Things were getting stranger and stranger. Summer warmth and flowers and fruits in the winter, little trapped fires that hissed fiercely, and now a wall full of human faces.

'Art?' asked Rebecca hesitantly.

'More like the opposite,' said the Jackdaw.

'Nature.

Freedom. The end of civilisation.'

'So, art then!' said Rebecca.

'Not made by human hand in any case. Not really. They're all death masks.'

At the other end of the room Rebecca nervously took a step back.

'Death masks?'

'We say "masks," but actually here we can see the very moment when any mask slips. Do you see how beautiful the faces are once all the thoughts have disappeared from them? As if being human were an illness, and now they're healthy and whole again. Complete release. If I'm thinking about how to model a face, I often come here.'

'They're beautiful,' said Rebecca quietly. 'Do you do that often? Whole faces, I mean?'

'Now and then,' said the Jackdaw. 'It's always something very special. A new face is a new life. This way!'

Rebecca and the Jackdaw slowly walked on, but Mopple and Othello stood looking at the wall of faces for a moment.

'He makes faces,' said Othello. It was almost more than a

sheep could fathom. 'I wonder if he had anything to do with Mum's third eye?'

Mopple was chewing on some flowers he'd found in a floor vase, completely baffled by it all.

It was dark. Too dark. Maple was sure she wasn't in the hay barn anymore. The wind was blowing. It smelled of fir trees and more snow.

Maple bleated quietly and uneasily. It was dark.

And silent. She was alone.

And then suddenly, Maple could see something. Something very bright came out of the forest, through the fence, as if it weren't there at all, straight towards Maple. A glow. A sheep. It looked like the unshorn stranger, but without the moss. Dazzlingly white and pale as moonlight.

Maple knew it was the moon-sheep.

She stopped chewing – she'd been chewing up to now – and stood up straight. You didn't meet the moon-sheep every day.

'Hello!' said the moon-sheep. She was very big.

Maple was relieved that the moon-sheep was talking to her. The strange ram hadn't spoken to her when she'd asked him about the Garou earlier on.

Since the glowing moon-sheep had been standing beside her, she could see everything again. She was standing in the middle of the meadow, between the chateau and the forest. All the lights were on in the chateau, and a human was looking down on her from every window. All eyes on her fleece, too many eyes. Maple quickly looked away. Where the shepherd's caravan usually stood, there was a big stone, and the hay barn had disappeared completely. But Yves had emerged from the snow again and was lying spreadeagled under the old oak, unmissable.

'A sacrifice,' said the moon-sheep. 'For insight. You mustn't ignore it!'

Next to the old oak, the wardrobe awoke and flapped its doors open and shut like an insect does its jaws.

Sheep lay scattered all over the meadow, sleeping sheep, all separate; Ritchfield, Maude and Cloud, but also lambs and sheep Miss Maple didn't know.

Maple wanted to ask the moon-sheep what had happened to the hay barn, but instead she asked: 'What's that?'

Only then did she realise what she meant. The sounds.

The cracking and crunching and dragging.

'Oh,' said the moon-sheep. 'That's him.'

'Who?' asked Miss Maple.

'The Garouuuu!' squealed Mopple. The last flower fell out of his mouth, partially chewed.

'That's a hippo.' Othello sighed.

'And back there? With the huge jaws?'

'A crocodile.'

'Crococo . . . ? Is it dangerous?'

'Very,' said Othello. 'It waits under the surface of the water, somewhere where it's so hot that there aren't any cloud-sheep, and when you come for a drink, it grabs your head and drags you underwater until you drown.'

'Really?' asked Mopple, cautiously taking a few steps back and bumping into a water buffalo. The water buffalo didn't seem to mind.

'Really,' said Othello. 'At least that's what the Cameroon sheep in the zoo told me. But this one isn't real. Nothing here is real. And there's no water either.'

'The grass here is red,' said Mopple. 'And very short. And it's not very tasty.'

'That's a rug,' said Othello.

'And there's no sky,' said Mopple, looking up.

That was true.

Maple looked up at the sky. It seemed very empty without the moon-sheep.

'What are you doing here?' she asked.

'I'm shedding,' said the moon-sheep. 'I'm shedding light.'

Maple understood. The moon-sheep was shedding light on something in particular. The creature that had just stepped out of the wardrobe, maybe. The creature making the cracking, crunching and dragging sounds. Maple could see that it had too many faces – and too many legs.

'Is that . . . ?' asked Maple.

The moon-sheep nodded. 'He's actually after me. But he'll never catch me. I'm too bright and too light.'

With that she galloped away, but her light remained. Maple wasn't bright and light.

She looked over at the wardrobe, where all of the Garou's many noses were sniffing.

'Hey!' whispered Mopple. Rebecca and the Jackdaw had settled down in one of the many rooms and were sitting on plush Things and drinking rank fermented liquid.

'How tragic,' said Rebecca.

'Zach was the only patient who didn't move on when the clinic closed,' said the Jackdaw. 'Strange. But he is an excellent bookkeeper.'

'I think he's very clever,' said Rebecca. 'In his own way.'

'Very,' said the Jackdaw. 'If only he didn't live his whole life in a James Bond film.'

'Hey!' whispered Mopple again.

'What?' asked Othello.

'Water!' said Mopple, scenting the air and trotting off.

The room with the water in it was even smaller than most of the others and unpleasantly dark, with a floor as slippery as ice and as warm as a living thing. First, they looked at the floor and couldn't find the water. Finally, Mopple spotted it in a deep white bowl that was growing out of the wall.

Water! The two rams instantly felt better.

Mopple had just stuck his head into the bowl to try a bit of the water when it suddenly got much brighter. Something moved in the doorway.

The sheep made it behind a weird plastic curtain just in time and watched as the Jackdaw stepped into the room, fumbled around with his trousers, and . . . the sheep couldn't believe their eyes. Water rushed. The Jackdaw sniffed the air and grimaced. Then he grabbed a colourful can and sprayed mist in the air. Mist that smelled like somebody had tried to make a meadow out of plastic.

Mopple and Othello wrinkled their noses.

The Garou's progress wasn't particularly quick, but he was moving towards them, nonetheless. Maple could run away but the slumbering sheep around her couldn't. She had to wake them up!

Maple bleated loudly in alarm. Not a single sheep moved. Maple bleated even more loudly. This time the Garou raised all of his heads and smiled at her with all of his teeth. Suddenly the light was disappearing, as if someone were sucking it up. Maple realised that she would soon be standing in the dark again and she had to do something quickly. She galloped over to Cloud, who was closest to her, and nudged her with her nose, bleating and bleating.

But Cloud wouldn't wake up.

Ever since the incident with the water, the Jackdaw had been in Mopple and Othello's bad books. He could have done a wee anywhere, in any of the many superfluous corners of the chateau, but he had chosen to do a wee in the only water source they'd come across. It was . . . sickening.

The Jackdaw talked a lot about Things. Wooden Things with feet that didn't run, stone Things standing on the wooden Things, fabric Things on the walls and sparkly Things hanging from the ceiling. All the Things seemed to be frightfully old, and Rebecca said 'ooh' and 'ah,' and once she stifled a yawn. But not well enough.

Then the Jackdaw pushed open a door that he'd been ignoring up to now.

The room behind the door was once again smaller than the sheep would have liked. The walls seemed to be covered in shiny, bright fabrics, and one of the old Things with feet was standing in the middle of the room again.

'Now we're going into the most private part of the chateau,' said the Jackdaw. 'Here on this sofa is where my mother found my father and the chambermaid in a compromising situation. Back there on the rug, Indian silk, late eighteenth century is where she tried to slit her wrists afterwards. Obviously, they saved her. Even the rug was unharmed. The same can't be said for the chambermaid, however . . .'

He suddenly turned to Rebecca, who was standing in the doorway listening and looked a bit pale.

'Do you find it interesting?'

Rebecca smiled warily. 'Well. Yes and no. It's obviously very private. But . . .'

'Yes, or no?' asked the Jackdaw.

'Yes!' said Rebecca, and they both smiled.

Othello had the feeling that the Jackdaw was talking about all of these old Things and past events so that the shepherdess missed something else. Something that was happening right now.

'What's happening?' Othello whispered to Mopple. 'What's happening?'

At first Mopple looked at him in surprise. Then he let go of the curtain material that wasn't nearly as juicy as it looked, despite the appetising green colour, and listened. Othello listened too. The chateau was silent, but cutlery was clattering somewhere. A child's voice was singing somewhere. Footsteps were going up some stairs somewhere. They stopped. Carried on. Footsteps behind walls. Then a door slammed.

The door slammed so loudly that Rebecca heard it too.

'What's behind there?' she asked.

'The tower,' said the Jackdaw.

'Can that be viewed too?' asked Rebecca.

'No,' said the Jackdaw unusually curtly.

Rebecca frowned.

'There's nothing interesting to see,' said the Jackdaw. 'Nothing but cheese.'

'Cheese?'

'The cheese is excellent though. Eric's cheese. Have you tried it? The temperature and humidity are ideal for the ripening process. Like a cave.' The Jackdaw chuckled. 'The old baron would never have dreamed that his son would be making cheese. But after all of the problems he's had, he should just be happy he's back on his feet.'

'Problems?' asked Rebecca.

'Drugs,' said the Jackdaw. He opened another door and led Rebecca away from the tower room.

'Where does that lead?' Rebecca asked, pointing to a door.

'Oh,' said the Jackdaw. 'Those are the back stairs up to the third floor. The patients used to be on the third floor, and my father used those stairs to secretly observe them.'

'Unusual methods,' said Rebecca.

The Jackdaw laughed bitterly. 'You could say that! My father was obsessed with studying the nature of insanity.'

Rebecca looked curiously at the door to the back stairs.

'These days the third floor is closed off,' said the Jackdaw firmly. 'This, incidentally, is the oldest part of the chateau, early sixteenth century, look at the wonderful oak parquet.'

'What a strange mirror,' said Rebecca.

'Yes,' said the Jackdaw slowly. 'It really is a strange mirror. My father brought it back from his travels in the East, and twenty years later he shot himself in front of it. With a silver bullet. I'm sure you can imagine the gossip. Some said there wasn't enough left for a gold bullet. Other people said . . . something else.'

Maple was standing in the dark again, but she could still sense Cloud's aromatic woolliness under her nostrils. Cloud, whom she had to rescue from the Garou. Cloud, who wouldn't wake up.

In her desperation, Miss Maple gave Cloud a powerful kick in the stomach.

Cloud bleated in panic.

It caused bedlam and lots of jostling.

Suddenly there were sheep bleating all over the place. Maple was so relieved that her flock was awake again. 'She kicked me in the stomach!' bleated Cloud, outraged. 'When I was asleep! Why did she kick me in the stomach?'

'Why did you kick her in the stomach?' asked Ritchfield sternly. 'No sheep . . .'

'I had to warn her!' bleated Maple happily. 'I've got to warn you all. I think we ought to stay away from the moon-sheep, but Yves is significant after all, and the Garou . . .'

Then she fell silent. She realised that she had met the moon-sheep on the meadow of dreams, and she understood why: her flock mustn't be asleep when the Garou came. She had to tell them the story she'd overheard last night at the shepherd's caravan. The story of the other flock of sheep. The dead flock in the snow. Now! Right now!

It wouldn't be easy.

And kicking Cloud in the stomach had been a very bad start, indeed.

Mopple looked at Othello. 'What's a mirror?'

'I don't know,' said Othello.

Othello wanted to know. He slipped out of the safety of the shadows behind the old wooden Thing, across silent rugs, over to the door and peered into the room. Inside stood two Jackdaws and two Rebeccas. In his surprise, Othello forgot to hide and just stood open-mouthed in the doorway. Two shepherdesses! Was that a good thing or a bad thing? Othello saw double quantities of hay and concentrated feed, but also double vigilance and double the annoyance about nibbled T-shirts. Would two Rebeccas call two vets? Would they simultaneously read aloud from different books?

'A silver bullet?' whispered the two Rebeccas with one voice.

'I hope I haven't shocked you,' said the Jackdaw.

The two Rebeccas shrugged. 'They found my father on a sheep meadow. With a spade in his chest. Parents can be a real pain.'

The Jackdaw nodded earnestly. Then he smiled all of a sudden. A real smile. The first real thing Othello had ever seen him do.

One of the Rebeccas looked at him and smiled back.

'Dinner?' asked the Jackdaw. Something in his voice had melted.

The Rebeccas nodded.

The Jackdaw led the way to a door on the other side of the room. The Rebeccas used the brief moment alone to examine each other. They tugged at their hair, stroked their eyebrows and made their mouths pointy.

Then one of the two Rebeccas raised her eyes and saw Othello. Othello darted under a hanging fabric Thing.

'What is it?' asked the Jackdaw.

'A . . . a sheep! I think . . . no . . . I *did* just see a sheep! One of mine! There in the doorway!'

'You read too many children's stories, Rebecca,' said the Jackdaw.

'I . . . it was clear as day! I'm absolutely certain of it! I'm going back! I have to count them! My God, I haven't counted them since yesterday morning!'

Footsteps quickly approached Othello's curtain. 'Impossible,' said the Jackdaw. 'Rebecca, how would a sheep get in here? This is an old place. A place with history – no wonder you're seeing things. Sensitive people see things here.'

The footsteps trailed off.

'But sheep?' Rebecca asked doubtfully. 'It was so real! I've never experienced anything like that before!'

The footsteps could be heard again, but this time they were getting quieter.

'What sort of history?' asked Rebecca.

The Jackdaw sighed. 'A long history.' But he didn't elaborate.

Othello peered carefully out of his hiding place again and saw Mopple, who had also ventured out from behind the fat wooden Thing and was now standing in the middle of the room – round, white and clearly visible. He was trying to bite into a fabric Thing. It was lying on a wooden Thing, and there was a stone Thing standing on it. The fabric Thing was tough and Mopple tugged at it. The more Mopple tugged, the closer the stone Thing got to the edge of the wooden Thing.

Othello galloped forth, across soundless rugs.

Mopple saw Othello coming, and, with a final energetic tug, he tried to bite off a piece of the fabric. The stone Thing leapt from the wooden Thing and smashed noisily on the stone floor – the only piece of stone floor in sight. The fabric Thing leapt after it and wrapped itself around Mopple the Whale, obviously keen on revenge.

Mopple twisted and turned, snorting and kicking until he had managed to shake off the fabric. The Jackdaw's head appeared in the doorway. His face turned from blank disbelief to something like anger – he was obviously not very happy to see two sheep and a broken stone Thing.

Mopple and Othello gazed back at him guiltily.

'What was that?' asked Rebecca.

'Nothing,' said the Jackdaw. 'Just the wind . . .'

Othello and Mopple didn't hear any more than that. They ran, across stone and wood and velvet and silk, past lots of old Things – like the wind.

Once the initial outrage had subsided, the flock huddled around Maple.

'You dreamed it all,' bleated Cloud. 'No wonder you were scared!'

The others hummed soothingly.

Maple didn't say a word. Had she really dreamed it all? The moon-sheep – sure. The moon-sheep never came down from the sky. But the Garou? And the dead flock of sheep Hortense had spoken about? Maple would have dearly loved for that flock to just be a dream.

'What about the strange ram?' asked Miss Maple. 'What about his sheep? Where are they?'

'He's 'round the bend!' bleated Ramesses. 'He's been on his own for too long, and now he's 'round the bend!'

The others bleated in agreement.

'But why?' asked Miss Maple. 'Why is a sheep on his own? What has to happen for a sheep to be on his own?'

Something terrible, that was for sure.

'You've got to believe me!' bleated Maple indignantly. 'You've got to believe me, whether you want to or not!'

'Of course we want to!' said Cloud earnestly.

Then the sheep started to get scared, as a flock at first, then each sheep individually.

Mopple and Othello were standing between the crocodile and the wild boar again.

And just a few steps away was Madame Fronsac, tickling the hippo with a frond of feathers. The two rams took shallow breaths and tried to look like the other animals there. Immobile. Glass-eyed. Thing-like.

As Madame Fronsac tickled and the dust danced around the hippo, Othello got a terrible feeling in his horns. The feeling that the animals were real after all – just dead. The only thing that was fake about them was their eyes. Why? Why did someone want dead animals in the chateau? Othello imagined the Jackdaw walking through the rows doling out glass eyes. Nature! Freedom! Ha! The Jackdaw had been less than thrilled to have two sheep trotting through his chateau sampling the fabric Things. Yet he hadn't let on to Rebecca. Why not? Because he didn't want her to go outside and count them. He wanted Rebecca to stay here. Why? What was happening outside that he didn't want Rebecca to see?

Madame Fronsac seemed to be satisfied with the hippo. She opened a glass door – a delicious cloud of real, snowy air enveloped the two rams – and fanned her dust outside.

Outside was . . . outside! The world! The real world with real living animals. They wanted to go outside!

Just then they heard the howling again, clear and lonely and cold as the stars. Madame Fronsac dropped her feathers, folded her hands in front of her chest and muttered something to herself. Then, with a sigh, she picked up her feathers again and started tickling the crocodile. The crocodile didn't move, its glass eyes fixed. In an unusual show of daring, Mopple rushed past Madame Fronsac, out of the door. Madame Fronsac didn't even notice him, but she noticed the draught, shivered, and pulled the glass door closed right in front of Othello's eyes.

Othello almost kicked the antelope behind him in the face,

such was his frustration, but at that moment he saw something unexpected. Two feet. Human feet. Behind a curtain. At first Othello thought that this strange flock might also have a dead human amongst its number, but then he saw a hand appear behind the curtain and push it aside a little. A face with sunglasses was watching Madame Fronsac as, on hands and knees, she tried to tickle the crocodile's stomach. Othello was flabbergasted.

It was Othello's turn after the crocodile and unlike the other animals, he objected.

Othello sneezed.

Madame Fronsac froze.

Looked left.

And right.

Othello edged sideways.

The Walrus turned to him again and was surprised to find her tuft of feathers waving into space. Then she moved closer.

Othello bleated indignantly.

The frond of feathers dropped to the ground, its handle clattering on the glassy wood. The woman screamed. Then she composed herself and walked towards Othello, her arms outstretched.

Othello made a run for it.

Madame Fronsac waddled after him.

Deep in the snow, the hay barn was dark and aromatic and especially comfortable. It was so still, as if the world outside had disappeared – the chateau, the goats and the forest – and tonight that was a beautiful thought.

They had hatched plans to escape and promptly scrapped them all. Everything had a catch.

Now they were standing in the dark at a complete loss.

And there was the howling again. The sheep trotted to the hay barn door and looked uneasily into the night.

'Do you think that's *him*?' asked Ramesses.

'I don't know,' said Maple. 'But we heard it before Rebecca found the deer in the forest. And it was there again before we found the other deer in the forest at dawn. Do you remember?'

Luckily, most of the sheep had long forgotten the terrible howling and shook their heads.

And then they heard another sound, not as creepy, but even stranger, very strange and very familiar at the same time. Tess, the old sheepdog, was sitting in the middle of the meadow, her muzzle stretched up to the stars, and she was howling, too, using her fine, familiar sheepdog voice. Tess and the Garou were howling together! Tess, whom they'd known her whole life!

And then, all of a sudden, Tess wasn't howling any more, but whimpering, and finally she curled up underneath the caravan steps and her scent got colder and colder, and less and less like Tess. The sheep knew that death had come to their meadow, and warily retreated from the door of the hay barn.

But the Garou was still howling and even he sounded sadder than before.

Zora stood in the forest, a bit apart from Maude, Heather and Aubrey, listening to the Garou howling. She missed the sea. Zora wanted to show her lamb the sea. It was important for a sheep to see the sea.

It was their second night away from the flock and this time they spent it under the protective branches of a large fir. Even Aubrey, who had slept like a log in the bus shelter yesterday – a snoring log – was restless today. Zora, Maude and Heather were wide-awake and stared wide-eyed into the darkness.

And then Zora had a mad plan. She knew it was mad straightaway – she'd been spending far too much time with that goat! But it was a plan, nonetheless.

'Let's get going!' she bleated. 'Right now! We're going to head towards where the howling's coming from!'

'You mean away from!' corrected Heather. 'Away from the howling, you mean!'

'No,' said Zora. 'Don't you get it? We heard the howling from the meadow. That means that the howling isn't that far away from the meadow. If we follow the howling, it might lead us home!'

Aubrey liked the plan – obviously! That confirmed Zora's worst fears.

The others were too tired to really protest.

They left the safety of the old fir tree and got going again, Zora leading the way.

And when the howling stopped, they carried on.

Othello galloped through room after room after room, past fires and windows, around pillars, zigzagging between all manner of old Things. At one point he jumped over a little stone horse.

At first Othello wasn't all that worried – Madame Fronsac was old and clumsy. But she knew the chateau and tailed Othello with surprising determination and agility. Othello's breathing was quickening. The floors were too slippery. He ran through a long corridor with lots of doors, Madame Fronsac on his tail.

The doors were all closed, every last one. Othello galloped round a corner. More closed doors and then an open door. Without a second thought, Othello leapt through, and the door shut behind him. Othello spun around. There stood Zach, complete with sunglasses, smiling at him. Outside, Madame Fronsac sailed past. Zach opened two more doors, one for himself and one for Othello, nodded at the ram and disappeared.

Othello trotted on, in search of the sky.

He didn't manage to find the sky, but he found . . . a sheep. In one of the many rooms that Othello scented inside in search of the sky, in the half-dark of a doorframe, stood a black ram, silent and menacing. A rival defending his territory. Othello's heart was thudding. Of all the strange chateau Things, this lonely sheep that lived in the darkness on the other side of the door seemed to be the strangest and most terrible of all. How did he get here? What did he eat and drink? Where was his flock? Who had shut him in here? And why was he standing there in the doorframe, motionless, like a stranger?

Othello snorted. His opposite didn't make a sound. Othello warily stepped closer, and the strange sheep stepped out of the shadow of the doorframe, too, into the light, soundless as a ghost.

Othello just stood there, stunned. He knew the ram, had known him a long time. He was the sheep of windless days, the sheep from the depths of puddles, ponds and water troughs. Othello bleated enquiringly, guardedly. The sheep from the depths remained silent. Little wonder. He was the most silent sheep he'd ever met, even more silent than the most silent sheep in the flock. Othello had always thought that this sheep belonged to him like his shadow. He had never banked on meeting him face to face, horn to horn, and especially not here, in the stone world of the humans.

The black ram moved his head back and forth, and saw that

the sheep from the depths was trapped in an oval shape. It must be something like a puddle. A clear, smooth puddle that had crept around the room and was now sitting on the wall like a spider. Most unnatural behaviour. Othello looked more closely: there was a fire in the hard puddle too. It was burning just as brightly as the other fire here in the room, but it was cold. Cold and silent. In the depths of puddles there was light, but no warmth.

A gust of wind rippled through velvety curtains. The heavy fabric shuffled across the stone floor like cat's paws, gently and casually, but with a suspicion of hidden claws. The sound unsettled Othello. He looked over at the windows. When Othello turned back, the sheep from the depths wasn't alone anymore. A little ghost had appeared behind him.

Othello whipped around hoping that the sheep from the depths would do the same. He didn't want his eyes boring into the back of his head when he turned to face the ghost. The ghost was very small indeed, about as tall as Othello; he smelled young and alive, not ghostly at all. The little spirit gathered his white sheet up from the floor, padded closer on bare human feet and started talking.

Othello didn't understand very much of the little ghost's honks. A young chateau human, that much was certain. He waved at Othello and started opening doors for him. The door to the next room, the door to a long corridor that had lots of doors leading off it and where it smelled much fresher. Mademoiselle Plin was stuck to one of the doors. She had her ear pressed to the wood and her face was completely still, as still as the faces on the Jackdaw's wall. But her hands were clawing into the fabric of her skirt, her knuckles white.

'I'm the owner of the chateau,' said a voice behind the door.

'You're the beautiful shepherdess. How could I not fall in love with you? It's what my people expect of me.'

'If you always do what your people expect, you'll soon end up running through the woods on a killing spree. *That* is what your people expect of you,' said Rebecca.

The little human took a step back so that Mademoiselle Plin didn't spot him, opened another door and then another, an important one. The door to the sky.

Othello stepped outside, into the clear cold night, and let the little ghost's fingers shyly stroke his fleece. It felt strange.

16

RAMESSES ACTS THE LEAD RAM

Lane sneezed. Ritchfield scraped his hooves. Cordelia scented the air; Ramesses was chewing nervously. Cloud was rifling through the straw. The winter lamb stood in the shadow beneath the hay rack, slightly apart from the others, wide-awake and very still. The most silent sheep in the flock cast a long shadow. Too much moonlight streamed through the empty window frame above their heads, tracing a pale square around Miss Maple.

None of the sheep were asleep anymore. It was too silent outside. Far too silent. Even Ritchfield could hear the silence. The silence had crept through cracks and gaps and woken them up, one after the other. The hay barn seemed to have very thin walls all of a sudden.

Then, as if they'd been expecting it, a sound crept around the hay barn: crunching and dragging and breathing. A sound just like the one in Maple's dream.

'Do you think it's the . . .' said Cordelia under her breath.

Lane, Cloud and Ramesses nodded.

'First they lured Rebecca away, and now . . .' whispered Lane.

The crunching was gradually getting closer to the door of the hay barn.

'Let's charge at him!' whispered Ramesses. 'Right now! Everyone to the door!'

The sheep huddled together behind the door with a sense of quiet determination, every last one of them, even Willow and the most silent sheep in the flock. Even the winter lamb.

Before Ramesses knew what was happening, the flock was surrounding him, ready to charge.

'Really?' he whispered. 'Do you think so? What if . . ? When?'

'Now!' bleated Cloud, daringly shaking her fleece.

Sir Ritchfield didn't really know what all the commotion was about, but he knew enough about flock life to huddle together with the others and make a run for it with them. When they all did something, it was good! Something touching his flank let him know that Melmoth was by his side, strong and magnificent and grey, his horns lowered, ready to charge. Ritchfield lowered his horns too. Something inside him sang.

Cloud stopped abruptly in front of him and Ritchfield was pushed onto her woolly back by the sheep behind him. It was rather embarrassing. All of the sheep were bleating so loudly that he could hear them quite well. Behind him they were bleating 'Charge!' and 'All together!' and 'Hay!' and whatever other rallying phrases occurred to them, but in front of him they were bleating 'Oh!' and 'Ah!' and 'I see!'

Then they all fell silent and didn't say anything at all. The strange sheep stood in the door of the hay barn. In the moonlight he looked even bigger, even more unshorn and stone-like – and very wise indeed.

'Aube!' he bleated amicably, then trotted past them and dozed off in a cosy corner of the hay barn. Normally the strong scent of the strange ram would have got on their nerves, but today there was something calming about it. It was a bit like the moon-sheep was protecting them. The sheep retreated from the door, let out a sigh of relief and relaxed – until the sound of crunching and cracking drifted around the hay barn once more.

'Charge!' bleated Ramesses again. The others huddled together at the hay barn entrance in their tried-and-tested way. The strange ram had opened his eyes again and was looking at them with a sense of mild amusement.

'Woolpower!' bleated Cloud. The others bleated 'Hay!' and 'Flock!' and 'Fodder!' and 'Grass!' and 'Lambs!' and other good things.

The winter lamb bleated 'George!'

Ritchfield bleated 'Summer!'

In the first row, Miss Maple bleated 'Stop!'

'Are you all still awake?' Othello asked, standing in the door of the hay barn, black and drenched in moonlight, ice in his fleece and a glint in his eye.

Later, once the moon had already got a little fuller, the sheep were still standing in the straw, wide-awake, marvelling mutely at what Othello had told them. Cracking branches and walkers who weren't really out for a walk, two Rebeccas, animals with glass eyes, the sheep from the depths, a barefoot ghost and the Jackdaw doing a wee in the water.

'He's mad,' Cloud muttered with a shudder.

'He's the Garou,' bleated Lane. 'It's got to be him!'

'The Garou! The Garou!' bleated the sheep. Lane was right. Weeing in water – that was just the same as mauling deer and not eating them. Sick and wrong.

'He's got lots of faces,' said Othello. 'He makes faces!'

He saw the Jackdaw standing in front of the wall of faces again, the faces he found so beautiful. But the Jackdaw was wrong: a new face wasn't a new life at all. A new face was just a new place to hide.

'The Garou! The Garou!' the sheep carried on bleating, partly because they were creeped out, partly out of relief that they finally knew what the Garou looked like. And that he had a slight limp.

'He's not the Garou!' said Miss Maple. 'He can't be the Garou!'

'The Garou!' the sheep carried on stubbornly bleating. Whenever they had understood something, Miss Maple always came along and confused things again.

'He can't be the Garou!' Maple repeated mulishly.

'Why not?' bleated Ramesses irritably.

'Because of the silver! He gave Rebecca a card made of silver; don't you remember? If he's the Garou, why did he give her silver? If he were the Garou, he would be afraid of it.'

'Maybe the silver thing isn't true,' said Lane. 'Maybe the little goat's round the bend!'

'The little goat's round the bend!' Ramesses, Cloud and Cordelia bleated in chorus.

'But Mopple remembered it!' said Maple.

The bleating stopped. Goats aside – if Mopple remembered something, then it was true. And for some reason, the fact that Mopple hadn't come back made the things he had remembered even more important.

'If the Jackdaw isn't the Garou, then he's something else!' said Othello. 'He's afraid of the police. He didn't want any sheep in the chateau.'

Several sheep bleated indignantly.

'Yet he didn't drive us off. He didn't want Rebecca to see us and bring us back to the meadow. He wanted Rebecca to *not* see something. Something important. Something that happened. Did something happen?'

The sheep thought for a moment.

'The car!' bleated Cordelia. 'The car happened!'

'And Tess . . .' Lane murmured quietly.

They told Othello about the mysterious car and the creepy man who had arrived at the tower in the dark. The man nobody saw coming. Apart from them.

'Are there really flowers in the chateau?' asked Cordelia.

Othello nodded. 'Flowers and fire. And far too many old Things standing around all over the place. It's no place for a sheep.'

'Do you think we ought to free the sheep from the depths?' asked Ramesses, still feeling a bit bold after his brief foray into lead-ram life.

'You can't free the sheep from the depths,' said Othello. 'You can only meet him. I think he lives underwater.'

'Like a crocodile?' asked the winter lamb who had been paying keen attention.

Othello nodded. 'A bit.'

'And he's a black ram like you?' asked Lane.

Othello nodded.

Cloud cleared her throat. It wasn't easy to contradict such an experienced lead ram. Othello knew the world and the zoo, and even crocodiles. And yet . . .

'I think the sheep from the depths is white,' she said gingerly, 'and really woolly.' Cloud had never given it much thought before, but as far as she could remember, she had only ever seen a really woolly sheep in the water. She would have noticed a black, four-horned ram like Othello.

'No,' said Othello. 'Surely not!'

'I . . . I think the sheep from the depths is small and shaggy like me!' bleated the winter lamb. 'I'm called Heathcliff,' he added. 'And I think the sheep from the depths is called Heathcliff too!'

The sheep rolled their eyes. The sheep from the depths – such a bedraggled little thing? What a ridiculous idea!

'The sheep from the depths is pretty and white!' bleated Cordelia.

Suddenly all the sheep knew something about the sheep from the depths and were frantically bleating over one another.

Othello fell silent, surprised. Melmoth the grey had shown him the sheep from the depths long ago, something that most sheep didn't take any notice of, and Othello had always been a bit proud of him being a black four-horned sheep just like him. But now it didn't seem as though it was quite that simple.

Outside on the meadow something made a plopping sound. It didn't sound like the Garou, more like a rotten plum falling from a tree. The sheep peered bravely outside. The meadow looked unnaturally bright in the moonlight, and Mum was sitting on her behind in the snow in front of the caravan.

'Upsy-daisy!' she said.

The sheep looked around for daisies, but were left bitterly disappointed.

She tried to stand up, but didn't manage it and giggled like a goat.

'Well, let's have a look,' she said, pulling something from her pocket. At first the sheep couldn't see what it was because they were too far away.

'The Magician!' said Mum. 'What a snob! I can't stand him! One day I'll replace him with the Devil! Seventy-five percent, I'd like to see anyone else manage that, and it's all down to the Devils!'

Mum seemed to be busy with her cards again. The sheep knew what was going on: humbug. Humbug outside the caravan! They could finally watch!

'The Devil is to blame!' whispered Cordelia. 'I think we ought to eat the Devil!'

The others nodded.

'Three,' said Lane. 'Three Devils! They can't all be to blame for everything!'

'But each one must be to blame for part of it!' said Cloud.

'The Fool!' said Mum down near the caravan, placing a second card in the snow. 'Just walking off the cliff like that! What does he think he is – a bird? Do you think I didn't think about it sometimes, George? A sip from the right bottle, and they'd be on their own, ha! But I always had enough love tying me to life. Love ties you to life, whether you want it or not . . . and I didn't always want . . . don't imagine for a moment I always wanted . . . and you didn't have her, that's . . . you ought to have had her . . . that's what you deserved!'

Mum sobbed.

She felt around in her clothes for a tissue, found one and blew her nose.

Then she looked up. Rebecca was standing silently in front of her with her arms crossed.

'Just like your father,' said Mum, smiling again.

'I don't believe it,' said Rebecca. 'I . . . Get out of the snow! How long have you been sitting there? Holy cow!'

The holey cow was a very special cow that Rebecca invoked on special occasions. The sheep had never seen it, just like the flying pigs, and they hardly dared imagine what a cow with holes in it might look like but presumed it must drink holey water.

Rebecca heaved Mum out of the snow. It was a struggle. Mum staggered to the left and to the right and didn't seem to be taking the situation particularly seriously.

Finally, Rebecca somehow managed to haul Mum up the steps, quietly singing as she went.

'I'll make some tea!' said Rebecca. 'Where's Tess?'

'God knows!' Mum drawled from out of the caravan.

'Nonsense!' said Rebecca, going down the steps again, blowing the high-pitched, enticing bird whistle that Tess particularly liked. But Tess didn't come.

'Tess?' Rebecca called. 'Tess Tess Tess!'

She shined a light over the meadow towards the yard, towards the wardrobe and towards the hay barn, and then, finally she shined a light underneath the caravan.

'There you are!' said Rebecca. 'Tess, come on girl!' Then she didn't say anything at all for quite a long time. Rebecca pulled Tess out from underneath the caravan, laid her in her lap and stroked her black and white fur, which was black and blue in the moonlight. She stroked Tess for a long time.

Then she stood up and carried her sheepdog up the steps. 'I need the number!' she said. 'Where's the bloody number?!' It sounded like a scream.

'That inspector! I'm going to call him! I'm calling him

right now! She was fit as a fiddle this morning. Fit as a fiddle! Somebody's poisoned her! I just know it! Somebody's gone and poisoned her!' said Rebecca, her voice choked.

The caravan door slammed shut.

The sheep were standing in the entrance to the hay barn. They hadn't really started to miss Tess yet. At night there was no Tess. Tess was only there during the day, with her folded ears and bright dog voice and so much joy in her body, especially in the tip of her tail. The most wonderful thing about Tess was that there was always a bit of George with her. When Tess watched over them, the sheep could see him, a hazy figure at the edge of the meadow, with his shepherd hat and crook, and a smile they could feel.

Tomorrow morning, they would miss Tess terribly.

'Was she really poisoned?' asked Cordelia.

'And by whom?' asked Lane.

'The Garou!' bleated Ramesses shrilly.

'Nonsense,' said Cloud. 'Wolves bite. They don't use poison.'

'Maybe they do!' said Maple suddenly. 'Maybe the Garou is afraid of dogs! Maybe he poisoned Tess so that there's nobody to watch over us any more!'

It was an unsettling thought. Not all of the sheep dared to think it through to its final conclusion, but some did.

'We know who's afraid of dogs!' said Lane slowly.

'The Jackdaw! The Jackdaw!' bleated Cordelia and Cloud in chorus.

'Yes,' said Maple. 'But the Jackdaw isn't afraid of silver.'

Maple thought about the silver in the Jackdaw's gloved hands, and then she suddenly remembered Rebecca's stroking hands.

Hands.

Hands were the problem.

Humans believed that they thought more than other creatures. That was a fallacy. Sheep thought incessantly; deep, woolly, sheepy thoughts. But humans had hands to grasp their thoughts, hold them, shape them, drag them from the cloudy world of thoughts onto the meadow of life, to write them down and pass them on, from head to head, and hand to hand. The Garou was a thought that someone had shaped. But why? And to what end?

'What if there is no Garou?'

Lots of sheep's eyes gazed at Maple, who was standing in her patch of light again, looking a bit like the moon-sheep.

'No Garou?'

Maple stepped towards her flock, out of the light into the shadows.

'Do you all remember what Othello told us about the walker? About the deer he was trying to make bleed? And in such a stupid place where somebody would definitely find it! Maybe he wanted it to be found. Maybe he wanted people to believe that there's a Garou! At first, I thought the Garou was a human pretending to be a wolf. But now I think a human is pretending to be the Garou.'

The sheep thought for a moment.

'If you're the wolf, you don't have to be afraid of the wolf anymore, do you?' said Heathcliff quietly.

Maple started trotting back and forth, deep in concentration, as probably only the cleverest sheep in Europe, maybe even the world, could.

'The men want it to look like there's a Garou. Why? Because the Garou can't be caught – especially not by the police! They create a story and then make it look like it's real. The men are trying to pin something on the Garou! But what – or whom?'

'Yves?' asked Cloud.

'Maybe,' said Miss Maple.

Mopple didn't know how he'd ended up in the forest. He had been standing outside in front of the chateau, and a stone animal had scared him, flickering animatedly in the moonlight. And now? Trees, far too many of them. Trees and distant howling. And something was lying amongst the trees, breathing.

It took a moment for Mopple to realise that the deer was just sleeping, slender and whole and bathed in moonlight. Yet, something wasn't right. No sheep would sleep like that, outstretched and helpless on the ground, and a wild forest animal like a deer definitely wouldn't.

Something rustled amongst the trees, and Mopple spun around.

'Zora?' he asked.

A warm feeling spread in Mopple's chest. Zora really was standing there, with her beautiful horns and her black face and her big, wide eyes. Maybe she'd come into the forest looking for him!

Mopple was just about to happily trot out from his thicket when Zora spun around, tripped, picked herself up again and bolted away.

At the same moment, something big burst out of the undergrowth somewhere behind Mopple and bounded through the forest after Zora.

Zora was running.

Had she really just seen Mopple? Fat and round and friendly Mopple, who was so short-sighted that he couldn't see the stars at night? Mopple the Whale in the woods?

Then Zora didn't think back anymore, just ahead, at lightning speed.

At first it didn't hurt at all. Her hoof just suddenly gave way when she spun around and was at a strange angle, but after just a few leaps, Zora realised that there was something wrong with her leg. With every step she took, it gave way a little under her weight, and she had a sharp pain deep in her hoof. Everything was very loud, then very quiet. The trees drew more closely around her, whispering and blurring in front of her eyes. Zora could hear something galloping straight towards her, and it took a while for her to realise that it was her own heart galloping away.

Zora got stuck on a root, stumbled and fell. She heaved herself up and tried to limp on aimlessly through the undergrowth, on and on, anything to get away from the bottomless shadows beneath the trees, the velvety, barely audible footsteps and the long, lurking silences in between. She would get tangled up again, she would fall again, and – hopefully – she would pick herself back up again.

Then, Zora could hear another heartbeat beneath the hammering of her own, quiet as a thought, but distinct. Calm. Constant. Unwavering, like a sheep confidently careering along the brink of the abyss, towards life.

Wait, said the heartbeat. Breathe. Scent the air. There are two of us.

Zora breathed. Not far away from her, a twig snapped. Zora waited. Took another deep breath. There were two of them. That's why she had to get away. She had to get away for both of them. The panic streamed out of her hooves, seeping into the cold forest floor. The pain vanished too. The wolf was after her, the Garou, and Zora would need more than just four panicked legs to get away from him. She would need her nose, her eyes and ears, her head, her heart and if need be, her horns too. Because there were two of them. Zora listened. The snapping had stopped. The Garou was standing somewhere nearby, and he was listening too – for a sheep crashing through the undergrowth, out of its mind with fear. Zora warily took a few steps back, deeper into the shadows. She scented the air. Why wasn't the Garou scenting the air? All he had to do was follow the trail of her unmistakably panicked scent.

Zora fearlessly lowered her elegant horns and waited.

Only when the first rays of wan morning light fell on the sheep did they realise that they must have been asleep after all, huddled closely together in a deep and sound sleep, the unshorn ram in their midst.

'The sun!' said the unshorn ram, trotting over to an early golden patch of sun in the straw. It was the first time he'd ever said anything that made sense. The sheep could understand him. The sun had made it through the night and was warming the world like a mother ewe. It happened every day, and yet it was still nothing short of a miracle. Especially in the winter.

As they so often did, they huddled together in front of the hay barn to watch the sun-sheep take its first tentative steps across the sky.

Rebecca was already awake – or, judging by how pale she was, she was still awake – and was leaning on the caravan door smoking.

Morning mist hung over the little stream, and the meadow looked beautiful. As soon as Rebecca had finished her cigarette, she went to the feed store and duly dished out concentrated feed. The sheep could hardly believe their luck.

'I'll look after you,' said Rebecca quietly. 'This time, I'll look after you!'

She was just about to extend her index finger again to count the sheep, when someone cleared their throat beside her. Rebecca and the sheep gave a start. They had been so busy feeding and being fed that they hadn't even noticed the human who had appeared beside Rebecca in the morning mist.

'Good morning, Mademoiselle,' said Dupin. 'I came straightaway. I'm very sorry for your loss.'

'Do you want to see her?' asked Rebecca.

'I would like to take her with me, if I may,' said Dupin. 'I'll take her to the vet, and he can hopefully tell me the cause of death. I'm afraid our forensics team isn't interested in a dog. The case is too old – and my colleagues say – too cold. They don't want to turn out for an animal again.'

Rebecca sighed. 'Okay,' she said then.

'What I would like to know is: Was she with you the whole time? Who would have had the opportunity to give her something?' asked Dupin.

Rebecca nodded. 'I've been asking myself the same thing. The thing is: Mum left her with Madame Fronsac while she went for a shower. We use the chateau's guesthouse, where the tourists stay in the summer. And Madame Fronsac's normally in the kitchen, and there's a lobby in front of the kitchen where Tess stays, and she's always quite happy there. Was – she was happy. But anyone can get in the lobby, anyone. And I know that Madame Fronsac wasn't with her the whole time. And all because of the stupid thing with the clothes. I'm so sorry.'

Rebecca's eyes sparkled damply.

'And she would have taken food from a stranger?'

'Oh, yes.' Rebecca sighed.

'I'll see what I can do,' said Dupin.

He pulled out a bar of whole-nut chocolate and offered some to Rebecca. This time, Rebecca broke off a large chunk.

'I'm also here because I've had an idea,' he said. 'Two ideas, to be precise.'

Rebecca nodded and chewed.

The tall inspector turned his face to the sun and squinted. 'I have a friend,' he said. 'A very clever woman.' Rebecca stopped chewing.

'She's an art critic who owns a gallery in Mauriac. You should take a look if you're ever in the area, Mademoiselle; it really is very good.'

Rebecca carried on chewing.

'Yesterday she paid me a surprise visit. It wasn't a huge surprise, but surprising enough, and the photos from here were out on the table. Crime scene photos. From now and before. And she came in and the first thing she said was "*magnifique.*" *Magnifique!* I was obviously surprised, but then I realised that she hadn't seen crime scenes at all, just pictures. And she found them very beautiful. All apart from one. The deer that you found, Mademoiselle, she thought that was "*null.*" And she was certain that it was a fake. Not by the same artist.'

Rebecca swallowed the final piece of chocolate and nodded.

'I've had a few thoughts since then. For a start, I believe that your deer isn't by the same "artist." It's a copy. There were a few other things that made me wonder too: the place where it was found – so exposed on the edge of the forest. Highly unusual. And this deer was caught in a snare. The original deer weren't, I can say that with relative certainty. As far as we know, the original deer were all mauled to death.'

'Mauled?' asked Rebecca. 'The deer? My God!'

'And then my friend asked, 'Where does the artist exhibit?' and I said 'nowhere,' and as I said it, I knew that it was true. The original wasn't putting on a show. The crime scenes were protected. Secluded. Places that an animal would choose. Apart from the flock of sheep. I assume you've heard about the flock of sheep?'

Rebecca nodded.

'But,' Dupin pulled out the bar of chocolate again, 'I get the feeling the forger is putting on a show.'

'Brrrr,' said Rebecca.

'I don't want to scare you,' said Dupin. 'I'm telling you this, Mademoiselle, because I think that you and your animals are very attractive victims – for the original as well as the faker, and now, after the dog . . . I think you need to know that there's a kind of forger. Danger on two fronts.'

Rebecca nodded, pale faced. 'Okay.'

Lane shook her head. 'Sometimes you listen to them and don't understand a single word of it. Not a single word!'

'Hmm,' said Miss Maple. 'I think he's also found out that somebody's playing the Garou. And not just that: he's saying there are two Garous, a real one and a fake one. And I think he's right.'

Dupin smiled and kissed Rebecca's hand.

'I have a plan I'd like to run by you, Mademoiselle!'

A talking device rang out shrilly across the meadow. The inspector and the shepherdess looked at each other expectantly.

'Is that yours?' asked Dupin.

17

HEATHER SCARES A TABBY CAT

'It's all your fault!' bleated Heather.

'No, it's not!' muttered Maude. 'It's the goat's fault!'

'But I didn't do anything!' bleated Aubrey.

'It's always the goats' fault,' said Maude, adamant. Since they had lost Zora in the nocturnal forest because Maude had stood scenting the air for too long, the remaining members of the sheep expedition weren't on particularly good terms. They trotted in the direction of the howling for a little while longer, then in another, for a change – and because nobody really wanted to run into the mysterious howler. They had all spent the night under a beech tree together and eaten tough forest grass, then in the morning, they'd sunbathed in a clearing for a bit. Now that Zora wasn't with them any more, things were going steadily downhill as far as discipline was concerned.

'On the contrary!' bleated Aubrey. 'Goats are never at fault. We have a scape goat, it's always his fault, but nobody knows who he is.'

'Nonsense!' said Maude.

'Pssst!' hissed Heather.

The two sheep and the goat retreated into the shadows of a tree boot overgrown with ivy and peered down the hill, where two dark dots were carving their way through the white expanse.

The walkers!

'We should get out of here!' whispered Heather.

'We should follow them!' said Aubrey.

'Why?' the two sheep looked at the goat in astonishment. 'Well, they live in the chateau, don't they? And at some point, they'll want to go back there.'

'To have a shower.' Heather nodded. 'Mum says they spend all their time in the shower!'

Having a shower was a peculiar process whereby natural scents were replaced by artificial ones. They'd never seen exactly how it worked, but one thing was for sure: you couldn't have a shower in the forest.

'Exactly!' said Aubrey. 'Let's follow them and they'll take us home!'

It wasn't such a crazy plan. Better than the howling plan. Except . . .

'What if they spot us?' asked Maude.

The little goat put her head on one side and her tongue lolled out of her mouth.

'That!' she said then. Heather gulped.

The three of them very warily followed the two winter visitors. It was snowing. Nothing stirred in the forest.

The two men walked in silence for a while, then the taller of the two had to stop to blow his nose.

'Hopefully he'll be done soon,' he said. Aubrey's ears pricked up. 'I can't tell you how fed up I am! I mean, there's nothing here! Not even an ice-cream parlour! Just that weird tavern in the forest!'

The short man laughed mockingly. 'You miss the women, that's all. But don't worry. Today the boss is going under the knife, and tomorrow, all being well, he can get out of here and then we'll strike. The sooner the better. I hear there's one of those shoots at the weekend. People are coming from all over. Perfect! Now, don't you tell me you're not up for a shoot. All those dead animals. What do you reckon?'

'He'll look different, won't he?'

'That's the whole point,' said the short man. 'Prettier. Not like the mugshots. Without a hole in his gob.'

'But . . . if he looks different . . . I mean, how are we going to know he's the boss?'

'Oh, we'll know, believe you me! The boss is the one holding the purse strings!'

The short man sped up a bit. 'Come on!'

'And do you think the bitch is going to make things difficult?'

The short man shook his head. 'She won't make things difficult! She's more desperate to get rid of the doc than we are! Women!'

'Women!' grumbled the tall man. It sounded a bit wistful.

Yves's talking device had long since stopped ringing, but Dupin was still digging. He carefully uncovered a leg first, then an arm, then a head.

He reminded the sheep a bit of the two little humans when they built snow creatures. The same absorption in the task. Their eyes lit up in the same way.

The sheep had nervously retreated to the other side of the meadow. They knew now that Rebecca didn't have Yves on her conscience after all – but would Dupin understand that as well?

'Do you recognise him?' Dupin asked Rebecca, who was standing a few feet away, pale as snow.

'Yves. He was a sort of dogsbody here. A servant is probably what he'd have been called in the past. Yves is the only one who would wear that awful shirt.'

Dupin nodded. 'I remember questioning him. He wasn't particularly bright. I mean: Did you know him well? Is there a reason for him to be out here on the meadow? Was he repairing something?'

'He . . . he was supposed to be putting an aerial on the roof, but he never showed up.'

'When was that?'

'Yesterday morning. Do you think it was the . . . ?'

Dupin shook his head. 'Too clean. I don't mean him; I mean the wound. A single gunshot, nothing more. Barely any blood. No, that would really surprise me. But do you know what wouldn't surprise me?'

Rebecca didn't really look like she wanted to know. Dupin sighed. 'Let's see. It's best I turn him over.'

'Shouldn't we call the police . . . ?' said Rebecca.

Dupin glared at her.

'Mademoiselle, I *am* the police! And please don't ask me to wait until my forensics colleagues have wrecked this beautiful crime scene. Do you know how long it will take for my colleagues to get here? Hours with all this snow! The roads are blocked. And what will they tell me then? That these fibres here come from your sheep? Pah! I don't need them to tell me that!'

Dupin slipped thin gloves on and, in an extraordinarily delicate manner, turned the dead man over.

'Oh,' said Rebecca, strangely affected.

'Hmm,' said Dupin. He positioned himself under the old oak, where Yves must have been standing before he fell, and looked in all directions: to the right – the oak's boot. To the left – the goats' meadow. Behind him – the forest, and even up into the oak, where two days previously Heathcliff had triumphantly bleated and where the first crow was now sitting, like a strange black fruit. Finally, he looked ahead, straight over at Rebecca's caravan.

'He . . . he was watching me, wasn't he?' Rebecca welled up. 'A peeping Tom!'

Dupin gently touched her shoulder. The sheep hadn't thought the tall and broad Dupin capable of such a gentle gesture.

'Please try not to worry, Mademoiselle,' said Dupin. 'At least we now know why he was here. Would you perhaps like to go inside for a while?'

Rebecca shook her head. 'Far from it. My mother's sleeping off a hangover in there!'

'I see.' Dupin unbuttoned Yves's stiff shirt and made a sound of contentment.

'Aha! Look, this is the exit wound. That means he was shot at close range. And the bullet can't be far away. Sometimes they even get caught in clothing . . .'

Dupin patted down Yves's shirt.

'Aha!' he said again, pulling a shiny little box out of Yves's breast pocket.

'Stuck in his cigarette case! I've never seen anything like it . . . It's like something out of a film! Except of course, the bullet came from the wrong side! That really is very unusual!'

Dupin grinned at Rebecca, his cheeks red, and looked decidedly chipper all of a sudden.

'Let's have a look,' he muttered then. 'Let's . . .'

He held something small up to his face and squinted with one eye.

'You can't buy ammunition like this, that's for sure. This bullet has been handmade, and the metal' – he weighed the little thing in his hand – 'it wouldn't surprise me if it's silver!' The sheep pricked up their ears. Yves was killed by some silver! A bullet! A little silver ball! Nothing to do with pullets after all! And that meant . . .

Rebecca covered her mouth with her hand. 'Do you think he was . . . ?' she whispered.

'Now that's a completely different question,' murmured Dupin.

'The Garou!' bleated Ramesses.

The sheep looked expectantly at Miss Maple.

'Maybe . . .' she murmured.

'Maybe . . .' murmured Dupin as well.

'Maybe?' asked Rebecca.

'Maybe somebody's looking out for you, Mademoiselle.'

'Well, great!' said Rebecca.

'Speaking of which,' said Dupin. 'That's actually why I'm here. *He* can wait a while, I think.'

Dupin kicked a bit of snow over the dead man again.

Rebecca looked at him in shock.

'Unconventional?' asked Dupin. '*Oui*, Mademoiselle. But at least he'll stay fresh. I'd like to ask a few people some questions before it's common knowledge that he's dead. And speaking of unconventional . . . please wait a moment, not here, maybe – down there near the fence? I'll get my car quickly; it's parked over on the other side. I'd like to show you something, okay?'

'Okay.' Rebecca nodded.

Dupin's car had strangely long legs and an unusually broad forehead. It purred effortlessly through the snow, past a few of its sleeping contemporaries, straight towards the meadow gate.

Dupin got out and waved Rebecca over. Then Rebecca stared through the pane of glass at the back of the car and Dupin looked at her expectantly.

'I know it's probably a bit difficult, so soon after . . .' said Dupin. 'But here's what I thought: If we assume we're dealing with a wolf, how would we react? Wolves used to be a problem around here. And problems have solutions. And this – well, this is the best solution I know of.'

'Where's the front, and where's the back?' asked Rebecca.

The inspector smiled. 'Good question! A truly criminological question. And as is so often the case, it can only be answered once you see things in motion.'

Dupin opened the boot and put something in his mouth. A high thin sound rang out, a sound that went right through the sheep, to the ends of their fleeces. Something white and woolly whirled out of the boot like a little snowstorm.

'I think it's a sheep!' bleated Sir Ritchfield excitedly. The others looked sceptically down at the meadow gate. The creature *was* woolly. Yet – something wasn't right. Something wasn't right at all. The way it moved. It was far too quiet for a sheep. Too quiet and too quick.

'He looks like a . . .' said Rebecca.

'*Exactement*,' said Dupin. 'And that's an advantage. Oh, a four-legged wolf will soon scent him out, no doubt about it. But what if we're dealing with a two-legged wolf? Then we might be able to take him by surprise!'

Gradually the sheep caught a distant scent.

'Not a sheep!' said Cloud with certainty. 'A . . .'

Cloud scented the air again and again, in disbelief.

The other sheep could smell it now too. But they couldn't quite believe their noses.

'A sheepdog?' asked Rebecca.

'A Komondor,' said Dupin. 'An old Hungarian breed of sheepdog. Not for herding the sheep as such. More a livestock guard dog. Oh, he can herd them, too, of course. But above all he'll guard them. Day and night.'

'I don't know that much about dogs,' said Rebecca. 'I'm new to the job.'

Dupin passed the dog whistle to Rebecca, smiling. 'But he knows a lot about sheep. I got him from a friend of mine who used to be a shepherd in the Pyrenees up until a few months ago. The dog's been sulking ever since, and it didn't take much to convince him to let us borrow him. I think he'll be happy to have a flock again. His name is Vidocq.'

'Vidocq?' said Rebecca.

'I just christened him that,' explained Dupin. 'He likes that name. His shepherd just calls him 'Dog.''

'And you're sure he won't do them any harm?' asked Rebecca.

'He's very well trained,' said Dupin. 'He would rather bite his own tail than touch a single strand of a sheep's fleece.'

Vidocq had run back and forth to the yard a few times, zigzagging in fluid, fleeting movements. It looked as if he wanted to go in every direction at once. Then he saw the sheep, calmed down, and sat and watched.

The sheep looked back at him sceptically.

Rebecca blew the dog whistle. The sheep sighed, but nothing else happened.

'He's headstrong,' admitted Dupin.

'I'm headstrong too,' said Rebecca, blowing the whistle again. 'And as for them . . .' she nodded towards the sheep, 'you can't even imagine how headstrong they can be!'

Finally, Vidocq tore his eyes from the sheep and trotted reluctantly over to Rebecca. She crouched down and reached out her hand. Vidocq sniffed it. Rebecca laughed quietly, then her hand disappeared into Vidocq's thick, white mop. All of a sudden, there were tears streaming down her cheeks.

Vidocq hesitantly wagged his tail. 'He likes you,' said Dupin.

'What are you expecting to gain from all of this?' asked Rebecca. 'I mean, as a police officer?'

'A whole load of aggravation,' said Dupin. 'I'd like to see things in motion, understand where the front and back are, so to speak. If somebody really did poison your dog, then it might mean that dogs represent a problem for the perpetrator. Well – let's create a few problems for him!'

'What if they poison him too?' asked Rebecca.

'Oh,' said Dupin. 'He won't take food from strangers. He'll eat your food as soon as he realises that you belong to the sheep! That's it!'

Vidocq barked as if in confirmation. Not excitable barking, just a few deep, demanding sounds. It sounded more intelligible than the Europeans' honking.

'I'd like you to closely observe any changes caused by Vidocq,' said Dupin. 'Who takes an interest in him. Who's scared of him. Who likes him. Who doesn't like him. Who he doesn't like.'

Vidocq barked again.

'I think he wants to get to know them,' said Dupin, opening the meadow gate.

Vidocq darted towards the sheep, a happy ball of snow.

'I hope he doesn't drive them mad!' the sheep heard Rebecca say before they got to know Vidocq.

It took a while for the sheep to realise that they were running, all together, up the hill, along the edge of the forest, towards the chateau, back to Rebecca, past the goat fence where several very interested goats were standing, and back towards the forest. Snow was flying and ears were flapping. Vidocq was everywhere and nowhere.

Hill, edge of the forest, chateau, Rebecca, goat fence, hill. Edge of the forest, chateau, Rebecca, goat fence.

By now, a fair few goats were standing at the goat fence.

'That's Vidocq!' Heathcliff bleated to them as he galloped past. 'He's driving us mad!'

The goats made envious faces.

Heather, Maude and Aubrey were standing on the edge of the forest staring after the two men in frustration.

'It didn't work.' Heather sighed.

'It's the goat's fault,' muttered Maude.

The two men were undoubtedly making their way towards a chateau – but it was the wrong chateau! The tower was on the wrong side, the windows weren't right and above all, there was no meadow.

Maude scented the air. 'It smells like the right chateau,' she said.

Aubrey started sniggering. 'The chateau is right!' she bleated. 'We're wrong! We just have to go around the chateau, and everything will be right: meadow and herd and herder. We're there! Wahey! Wahey!'

'Hay! Hay! Hay!' Heather and Maude struck up a little bleat of triumph too. They followed Aubrey over a bare white surface, then along the chateau wall and through the chateau's outbuildings, just like old times. A tabby cat frightened Heather, but Heather frightened the tabby cat even more.

Suddenly Maude began nervously scenting the air. 'Back there!' she bleated then. 'A chicken!'

'Who cares about a chicken? We're back!' bleated Heather enthusiastically.

Actually, it was more like half a chicken that the snow had sucked all of the blood out of. And another chicken. And another. A live black chicken darted past the sheep in a panic and disappeared between the buildings.

'What . . .' said Heather and fell silent.

Aubrey didn't seem to hear her. She was staring at the half-open door of the chicken shed, spellbound. There were even more dead chickens inside. Lots more. Amongst them, white feathers in its red fur, sat the fox, smiling as only a fox can.

The fox was all Aubrey could see. The fox was all she could hear. The fox was all she could smell. The world disappeared.

There had been a fox once before. Red death in the snow. The fox had been the first thing she'd seen in this world: a flowing shadow with eyes of light. Somewhere a goat bleated – a goat Aubrey would never know. The fox was bigger and faster and more cunning than her. He was the end, and Aubrey was curious. When she had stood up for the first time, she had seen him, seen him circling, and her first wobbly step in this life had been towards him.

Aubrey was shaking just as she had shaken back then, with cold and rage. When death circled, you had to stand up. You had to see the circle, with clear, yellow goat eyes, and then once you had understood it, you had to leave it behind. No matter what it took.

Back then, just as today.

The fox wasn't a danger to her anymore.

The wolf was though . . .

The little sheep expedition carried on in complete silence, past the guesthouse to the yard gate.

'He didn't even want to eat them,' murmured Heather. 'He *couldn't* possibly eat them all. So, why?'

'He's a fox. He can't help it.' Aubrey barely seemed to be listening. 'We're nearly there!'

The sheep stood between the hay barn and the feed store, still a bit breathless from being herded, and tried to ruminate on the latest events: Dupin, Yves, the silver bullet and the new sheepdog. Vidocq was sitting by the shepherd's caravan, his tongue lolling pinkly out of his mouth, being stroked by Rebecca. Although you could barely make out the tip of his nose beneath his mop, you could tell he was happy. 'The Garou has to be killed by a silver bullet,' said Lane suddenly.

'And Yves *was* killed by a silver bullet,' bleated Ramesses. 'Clear as day! If he hadn't been the Garou, he wouldn't have died. It was so small! Silver's actually pretty harmless, you know? Mopple carried some in his mouth.'

All of a sudden, most of the sheep were of the opinion that Yves was the Garou, even the most silent sheep in the flock, who was clearly nodding her head for all to see. A good result! The sheep were happy to have got rid of the Garou so easily. Yves, who was still lying dead beneath the old oak, latterly on his back, was the best possible Garou of all!

'I don't know,' Miss Maple muttered into the general enthusiasm. 'Something's not right!'

The other sheep looked crossly at Maple. Whenever they had solved the case, Miss Maple always came along and said that something wasn't right! Maple wasn't a detective sheep at all – more like the opposite: a sheep that just kept finding out what wasn't true!

'There's Heather!' bleated Heathcliff suddenly. 'Heather and Maude and the goat! Down by the yard gate.'

'No sheep may leave the flock!' bleated Ritchfield sternly. All the same, he went along when the sheep trotted over to the fence to welcome the homecomers.

'Where's Zora?' asked Cordelia.

'We . . . we lost her,' bleated Heather, too relieved to really be worried.

'It's the scape goat's fault!' Maude explained.

Aubrey didn't say a word, she just gambolled wildly across the meadow bleating 'Wahey!'

Her excitement was infectious and soon all of the sheep were bleating for hay. It started snowing again.

Mopple's heart was thudding. Thudding like . . . He didn't know. Something quick, anyway. Too quick. It wasn't normal. The snow fell slowly, soft and fluffy. He liked the way the snow was falling. The thudding in his chest should follow the snow's example. Thud, thud, thud, light as the wind.

The snow lay cold around his feet, smooth and blank, like . . . whatever, it seemed odd to him. The snow around him shouldn't be so smooth. It was wrong. The snow should tell him which way he'd come from. Had he even come from somewhere? He couldn't remember. Something inside him felt empty. He lowered his head and snorted into the snow. The snow had fallen from the sky. Had he fallen from the sky too? The thought of it made him . . . sad, maybe.

He wanted to go back. He desperately wanted to go back.

Something was coming towards him. Not from above. From the side. A crunching. Crunch, crunch, crunch.

Thudthudthudthudthud. His heart was galloping away again, faster than the snowflakes. Then he saw it. Striding through the snow, big, dark and two-legged, leaving tracks behind. It definitely hadn't fallen from the sky. It stopped not far away and turned its head back and forth. He didn't like the way it was turning its head. Its eyes were colder than the snow. But the snow was Mopple's ally, dancing and whirling around the dark creature, going in its face so that its eyes couldn't look in his direction for long. The wind hissed, and then, finally, drove the creature away.

Crunch. Crunch. Crunch. Thud thud thud. Thud. Thud.

The snow carried on falling, and then at some point it stopped, just like that.

He warily moved past the trees, heading towards the light. Soon there were no more trees, but there was a fence instead. Somebody was standing behind it.

Another creature. White and fluffy like snow. He liked this creature better.

'Hello, Mopple,' said the creature.

'Hello,' said Mopple the Whale.

18

CORDELIA MEETS THE DEVIL

Mopple had returned from the forest.
And Mopple had not returned from the forest.

Mopple looked like Mopple. He was friendly like Mopple and greedy like Mopple. He smelled like Mopple and moved like Mopple.

But Mopple the Whale was the sheep with the best memory in the flock.

Their memory sheep.

Once he'd memorised something, he never forgot it.

The sheep who had come out of the forest had forgotten everything.

Everything.

Ireland. George. Europe. The meadow and the chateau. Sir Ritchfield. Miss Maple. Heather. Zora. Even his own name.

As the sun headed for the chateau and the men in caps finally came to take Yves away, the sheep stood around the fat ram, as if to warm him up. Maybe a few of their memories would jump across to Mopple – like fleas. Mopple actually seemed quite contented. He was grazing happily, chewing and swallowing, squinting into the sun every now and then, and allowing himself to become embroiled in long, one-sided conversations with Sir Ritchfield. Every once in a while, he seemed to pause and listen as if he were looking for a sound – the sound of a falling apple, the sheep supposed.

They watched with relief as Yves disappeared feet-first through the meadow gate, neatly wrapped in plastic, like a piece of goat's cheese.

Now there was nothing standing in the way of a nice, relaxing graze!

Hortense came by to hug Rebecca and envelop her in violet perfume.

'Oh, Becca,' she said. '*C'est terrible!* You must be in shock! And your poor dog! And the poor deer! It's all so terrible!'

'She was old,' said Rebecca quietly. 'What deer?'

'Paul found them this morning,' said Hortense. 'The goatherder. Two in one night. We've never had two in one night before.'

'Maybe they're not both from last night?' asked Rebecca.

'*Si*,' said Hortense. 'They were both *on* the snow!'

'Oh,' murmured Rebecca. She looked pale.

'I . . . I think you should relax a bit,' said Hortense, placing her little white hand on Rebecca's arm. 'Let's go to the kitchen and have a hot chocolate, yes?'

Rebecca looked like she could do with a hot chocolate. But she shook her head.

'I don't really want to go anywhere,' she said. 'The sheep . . .'

'But surely your *maman* can look after them for a bit.'

Rebecca thought for a moment. 'I'll wake her up,' she said then.

She briefly gave Vidocq a scratch behind the ears – or where she thought his ears might be – then she went up the caravan steps.

Vidocq and Hortense eyed each other sceptically. It was snowing and Maple was thinking.

Snow.

Snow fell from above and separated things. The grass from the light. The cold from the warmth. The living from the dead.

'We need another silver!' Maple bleated suddenly.

'But Yves . . .' said Ramesses.

'What do we need another silver for?' asked Heather. 'Do you think there are more wolves?'

More wolves? The sheep looked shocked. One wolf was bad enough.

Maple put her head on one side, as if she were trying to listen to the snow or maybe even the grass beneath the snow. But the snow didn't make a peep.

'Yves wasn't the Garou,' she said slowly.

'But the silver got him!' bleated Cordelia.

'Yves was under the snow,' said Miss Maple. 'And the deer Hortense was talking about were on the snow.'

The sheep imagined it: Yves, stiff and scentless, trying to reach out his hairy hands through the snow towards the deer. Impossible. Snow was like a fence in time.

'Maybe – maybe it was the other man?' said Lane hesitantly. 'The walker? The one who's just playing the Garou?' They all so desperately wanted Yves to be the Garou!

Maple shook her head. 'I don't think so. Do you remember what Othello said? The walker isn't playing the Garou particularly well. And two deer in one night – that's not easy! I don't think the walker would have managed that. Aside from that, Yves was colour-blind, do you remember?' Rebecca said.

'What's colour-blind?' asked Heathcliff.

'It's when you can see everything, just not the colours, probably. And I think colours are very important to the Garou. Seeing is very important.'

Maple could see it now. The white and the red. The white and the red and the black. Flowers in the snow. That's why the silver was a danger to him. Because it glittered and gleamed. The Garou wanted to see. He hunted with his eyes. He hunted for his eyes – not for his stomach. She thought about Hortense's window, facing the meadow. She was sure that the Garou must have a window like that. A window he could stand at and see from. Seeing was half the hunt.

'The Garou lives in the chateau,' she said.

The sheep looked over at the chateau in shock; it was already stretching its shadow fingers out towards the meadow. The Garou! So close!

'I think it's important to find out who shot Yves,' Maple continued. 'I think Yves was mistaken for the Garou. That means somebody is hunting the Garou. We must find out who it is. Maybe we can help him to get it right next time.'

Rebecca came out of the shepherd's caravan. Vidocq had to promise her he'd look after the sheep, then she linked arms with Hortense and the two women disappeared through the yard gate together.

Vidocq watched them leave, then he stood up, had a stretch and trotted up the hill to the fence. From there, he spent a long time looking longingly into the forest.

Finally, the coast was clear.

The sheep were just about to go looking for another silver when three goats suddenly appeared at the fence. One of them cleared her throat. It sounded like a bleat. Maybe it was a bleat?

The sheep didn't look at them.

The second goat gave a little cough.

'We . . .' said the first goat.

'. . . are wanting . . .' said the second goat. The other two looked at her crossly.

'. . . would . . .' the second goat hastily corrected herself, '. . . like to be driven.'

'Mad,' added the first goat.

The sheep looked at the three goats incredulously.

'By your dog,' explained the third goat.

All three goats looked at the ground.

'If it's not too much bother,' muttered the second goat.

'Even if it's a lot of bother,' bleated the third goat.

'We don't have time,' said Heather sharply. 'We need a silver. And we've got to find out who murdered Yves.'

'Yves?' asked the first goat. 'Who's interested in Yves? Is it important?'

The sheep made important faces.

'But that's no problem at all,' said the third goat. 'We can find that out for you! It'll be really quick! And then . . . he can drive us mad, yeah?'

'Maybe,' said Lane, a serious look on her face. 'If he has time. We'll put in a good word for you!'

The goat delegation trotted back to their meadow, bleating as they went, and soon all of the goats were standing in a circle around the chest of drawers again. They were making mysterious faces and meaningfully swaying their heads back and forth. Then there was a duel, the black-eared goat versus a brown goat. The black-eared goat won.

The sheep were astonished.

After a while the young grey goat, Amaltée, slipped through the fence, onto the sheep meadow.

'Madame Fronsac!' she declared.

The sheep looked at her, full of respect.

'How on earth did you find out so quickly?' asked Cordelia.

'We had a vote. Three were for the *patron*, two for the herder because he fed us too few mangelwurzels yesterday, one for Yves himself, I voted for the gardener because he's got such bad breath, and Circe voted for Monsieur Fronsac because he doesn't do anything. And Megara voted for Madame Fronsac. It's indisputable.'

'You can't just decide like that . . .' Maude looked mistrustingly at Amaltée. Something wasn't right here.

'Why not?' said Amaltée. 'Somebody has to.'

'Smart,' said Maude.

'But that's not how it works,' bleated Cordelia. 'Out there is the big, wide world . . . you can't just take a vote on it; it's too big.'

'Of course, you can,' said Amaltée, undeterred. 'What would the world be without goats and their votes?'

'And only Megara voted for Madame Fronsac?' asked Maple. 'And yet . . .'

'Megara gets the most votes,' Amaltée explained. 'Each goat gets as many votes as she likes. That way it's fair. Whoever knows the biggest number is the cleverest. The cleverest goat decides.'

'And then what?'

'Then they decided it under the tree with their horns. That's what we always do. We call it "democracy." Simple, huh? And if he happens to have a bit of time . . .'

Amaltée looked longingly over at Vidocq, who was happily rolling in the snow at the edge of the forest.

'We'll have a word,' Lane promised, a serious look on her face.

'Maybe it's not that stupid,' said Miss Maple once the goat had gone.

'Democracy?' asked Cloud sceptically.

'Driving them mad?' asked Cordelia. '

No,' said Maple. 'Madame Fronsac.'

'She's not particularly clever,' said Heather.

'But she has a reason to be hunting the Garou,' said Maple. 'Do you remember the boy Hortense spoke about? The boy the Garou got? That was her young human. She had every reason to be after the Garou. And if she thought Yves was the Garou . . .'

The most silent sheep in the flock snorted sceptically into the snow.

'I know,' Maple admitted. 'She's clumsy and nervy. I can't imagine her skulking around with a gun at night either. Or hitting her target for that matter.'

Maple imagined Yves beside the old oak and the darkness behind him. She couldn't see Madame Fronsac in that darkness. She couldn't see anything in it. But then . . .

'There were more humans, weren't there?' she said. 'A woman and a girl. Who did the woman and the girl belong to?'

Zora was limping along the road. She was happy that there was a road again. If only it were the right road. She felt cold and miserable and too nervous to eat. But she had escaped the Garou, deep in the forest, all on her own. Now that it was over, she wished she'd got a better look at him. But all she could remember was a flowing shadow. A Two-Legs? Zora wasn't even sure.

The road led up a hill, and when Zora had reached the highest point, she could see something between the trees, big and grey and very tall. The tower! The chateau's tower! Zora had made it!

Next moment she heard something. A car was coming up the hill behind her, making its way towards the chateau. Zora limped into a thicket of fir saplings and waited for the car to drive past. But the car didn't drive past. It stopped on the road, and a human got out. Something about his scent made Zora shudder. She peered out of her thicket of firs and recognised the vet, who was a few steps away from his car and was now nervously pacing.

Why did it have to be the vet?! Zora melted farther into the darkness of the firs.

The vet paced back and forth, smoking and muttering. Finally, he stood still, pulled a talking device out of his jacket and jabbed at it.

While the vet honked into his talking device, Zora slipped out of her hiding place towards home, giving the vet and the car a wide berth.

When Rebecca returned from the chateau, Mum was sitting on the caravan steps smoking and looking rumpled.

'Hello,' said Rebecca, stopping in front of the caravan.

'Hello,' said Mum rather contritely. 'Has something happened?'

Rebecca took a deep breath. 'You could say that! Pass me one!'

Mum gave her one of her long thin cigarettes and Rebecca started to explain everything. About Tess and Yves and Dupin and the deer, and Tess over and over again.

Mum wasn't particularly affected by Yves's death – 'his cards were bad,' she said – but she sniffed and sobbed over Tess.

'It's all my fault!' she howled. 'Me and the bloody booze!'

Rebecca didn't disagree.

Mum, who had probably been hoping she'd disagree, stopped sniffing and frowned at Rebecca.

'There's something else, isn't there?'

'What else could there be?' asked Rebecca.

'Something,' said Mum. 'There's something else!'

'Why can't life just be simple?' said Rebecca. 'Just for a change. It was a nice evening yesterday, you know. At first . . . at first, he was really rather snobby, but then it was really lovely. Romantic almost. And then he suddenly got all unsettled and weird and short with me, and I realised he was trying to get rid of me. It . . . it didn't fit the mood at all. It just didn't make sense. And he sent you a bottle even though I said not to, and then I find Tess, and today Hortense tells me about the deer! And do you remember how scared he was of Tess? And according to everything he told me, he had quite a screwed-up childhood. I know it's not always about someone's childhood, but still. I think . . .'

Rebecca didn't want to say what she thought.

'You should tell the police,' said Mum.

'Dupin?' Rebecca laughed bitterly. 'Sure, he's nice and friendly and everything, and he brought us Vidocq, but he's using us as bait for his Garou. You should have seen him with Yves today. He was delighted to have a new clue. He'd be just as happy to pull us out of the snow. No, we have to get out of here!'

'Don't worry, darling,' said Mum. 'Where there's darkness, there's also light.'

Well, she couldn't be more wrong there. Where there was darkness, there wasn't any light at all!

'The vet just called me,' said Rebecca. 'He wants to meet me. Alone. In the forest. Well, not really in the forest, but at this rest area up by the road. He doesn't want to come into the yard. Said it's important. Sounds odd, doesn't it? But I think I'm going to go anyway. He says he's found somewhere for the sheep!'

'I'm coming with you,' said Mum.

'No,' said Rebecca. 'You stay here and look after the sheep. I've told him you'll know where I'm going. I mean he'd have to be really stupid to try anything . . . They'd catch him straightaway.'

'And you're sure it really was the vet?' asked Mum.

Rebecca nodded. 'He's waiting. I'm off.'

'Wouldn't you rather consult the cards first . . .'

'No. If I'm not back in half an hour, call the police!'

The sheep, Vidocq and Mum watched as Rebecca disappeared into the forest, the brown bread hat on her head. Then Mum went back inside the caravan, Vidocq bounded to the edge of the forest, and the sheep resumed their search for silver. The silver in the rubbish bin was a lost cause, lurking somewhere in the depths of the bin after Rebecca had stuffed two jars and a screwed-up old newspaper on top. But maybe there were more pieces of silver bread paper around the caravan?

The sheep rooted and grazed away until Ramesses spotted something in the snow near the front of the caravan: not silver but one of Mum's cards.

A group of sheep stared curiously at the card in the snow.

'Is that the Devil?' asked Cordelia.

'I don't think so,' said Cloud.

That friendly gentleman with horns and sheep's hooves couldn't possibly be the Devil! The sheep were surprised at how attractive even humans could be when they had horns. They felt sorry that Rebecca didn't have any horns, then they left the card in peace and carried on looking for a silver.

The gardener came across the yard again, another fir tree in tow. This fir tree ended up on the heap with the others.

'I know where we can get a silver!' said Lane.

Some time ago, the humans had started to get very interested in fir trees. They had taken little firs into their homes, even Rebecca had taken a very small fir into the caravan. But just a few days later they'd had enough of the trees and started to pile them up in a dry, brittle heap where the wind cackled and mice scurried – and sometimes metal flashed there too, like the sun at the bottom of a pond.

None of the sheep wanted to leave the meadow on their own anymore, but finally Lane, Maple and Cloud said they were prepared to search the fir trees for sparkling silver together. They had just got to the gap in the goat fence when, all of a sudden, Vidocq was sitting in front of them, like a little white mountain, and let out a deep 'woof!'

Nothing more. Just a single woof.

The sheep were impressed.

'Wolves are a sheepdog invention,' said Mopple suddenly. 'So that we're easier to herd.'

The others looked at one another: Mopple had remembered something – but it was nonsense!

'We need to distract Vidocq!' bleated Heather. 'Otherwise, he won't let them go!'

And that's how it came to pass that a troop of conspicuously untended sheep was soon galloping back and forth in front of the sheepdog, who observed the situation for a while, then gave another 'woof!' and ran after the sheep while Lane, Maple and Cloud stole from the meadow.

They came back with a little sparkly silver star and were just about to skewer it on the hazel branch, when Maple shook her head.

'If Rebecca finds it, she'll throw it away again. The silver has to be put somewhere where Rebecca can't get it.'

'But where we can?' asked Heather.

'But where we can!' Miss Maple confirmed.

It wasn't that simple. With their hands and their two ridiculously long legs, humans could reach practically anything.

'That's not a sheep!' muttered Sir Ritchfield, shaking his head at Vidocq, who was still conscientiously carrying out his sheepdog duties.

'I know where!' bleated Miss Maple suddenly.

A while later, a little silver star was nestled in Ritchfield's imposing horns, protecting them all from the Garou.

'Zora!' said Mopple suddenly.

The sheep looked at him, and then they looked towards the edge of the forest, where Zora was silently peering through the fence. They were so relieved Zora was back that they didn't even notice the two walkers suddenly appear at the bottom edge of the meadow. But Aubrey, who had already grown tired of the goats' meadow and was busy searching the sheep trough for concentrated feed leftovers, did.

'These things happen!' said the short walker, shaking his head and leaning on the fence. Aubrey pricked her ears. She liked it when things happened.

The two of them looked up at the old oak, the snow beneath it dirty and trampled.

'I wonder who it was,' said the short man. 'Interesting, huh? Normally we know who did it.'

The two of them sniggered.

'With a silver bullet, that's what the old biddy says.'

The tall man huffed. 'How does she know that?' The short man shrugged.

'Didn't make a bad job of it anyway. Clean and simple. Best way.'

The short man sighed. 'And if it really was a silver bullet – brilliant! Simple, but genius. What do you think? We could have saved ourselves all the bloodshed.'

'The old biddy says a lot of things,' muttered the tall man.

The short man wasn't listening. 'You seem to be enjoying yourself. Another two deer! *Merde*. I'm telling you; you're taking it too far! Every time is a risk, how many times do I have to tell you? The first one near the sheep's meadow and another one, that would have been sufficient for our purposes. Just act a bit professional for once! Dammit, we're not being paid per kill.'

The tall man broke little splinters of wood off the meadow fence and threw them onto the ground. 'But I'm telling you, it wasn't me. If I've told you once, I've told you a hundred times.'

'Oh, stop it. Who else is it supposed to have been? The Garou? Haha! I know what you're like. And I don't have a problem with it as long as it doesn't affect the job.'

'But it wasn't me!' the tall man had pricked himself on a splinter and watched impassively as a few drops of blood rolled into the snow. 'And do you know what: if it wasn't me – then it was somebody else. And I know how difficult it is. And I don't like it one bit! And I'm beginning to wonder: What if he really exists? After all, I'm always out and about in the forest.'

The short man passed the tall man a tissue for his finger.

'Come off it, Garou – a wild dog or a lunatic. And I'll tell you something: if that nutter from before is still on the loose, it's the best thing that could have happened to us.'

The men fell silent.

Up on the hill, the sheep had surrounded Zora and were enjoying being a complete flock again.

'Look at them!' said the tall man. 'Have you ever taken the time to watch sheep? They spend the whole day eating. Nothing but eating! What do you think they're going to do if we bump off a few of them?'

Suddenly the tall man had a piece of metal in his hand. Aubrey scented the air: old heat and sweat, and something else, just a whiff: fear.

The short man sighed. 'The whole point is to make sure that they really believe in their stupid Garou. Then we can just pin the doctor on the Garou too, and nobody will connect it with the boss. And voilà: everyone believes in the Garou. Dammit, *you* believe in the Garou! The sheep are next, along with the doctor, as planned, end of. And do you know what: I'll get hold of a few silver bullets. No mess. That'd make a nice change for us.'

'I don't mean for the job. I mean just for a laugh!'

The tall walker stood stubbornly at the fence, pointing his metal Thing at the meadow. It was so still. Midday was the quietest time of day. Vidocq had left the sheep alone and was asleep under the shepherd's caravan. The yard gate yawned. The chateau was silent.

'Come off it!' said the short man not particularly forcefully, but obviously sickened by the idea.

'Just one or two,' whinged the tall man. 'With my amazing silencer, nobody will notice a thing. Just think how surprised they'll be!'

The metal Thing's pointy muzzle looked from sheep to sheep. Aubrey didn't like it. One or two what? And who would be surprised? The herder had a metal Thing like that as well, big and heavy and old. It was cleaned and looked after and stroked, but it spent most of its time asleep. The metal Thing was waiting for something, the right time, silently waiting.

'Paff!' said the tall man. 'Paff! Paff! Paff!'

'Leave it!' said the short man. 'I'm hungry. Let's go and see what the old biddy's cooking today. She can cook, you have to give her that.'

'Paff!' said the tall man.

'Someone might see you. You'll probably miss anyway!' said the short walker.

'Paff!' said the tall man.

'It's been a while, hasn't it? Too much blade work! I'm forever telling you!'

The metal Thing turned and pointed at Aubrey.

'What about that one?' asked the tall man. 'At least we can see it properly!'

'Pah! If you shoot that, I won't speak to you for three days. See the black one at the back, right at the top of the hill? Now that would be a challenge!'

The metal Thing looked uncertainly towards Othello.

Then it sneezed.

'And then we followed the howling,' Zora explained, 'and then the others were gone and I saw Mopple and the Garou, and then I got away.'

Zora stretched her beautiful black horns proudly into the air.

'Why did you follow the howling?' asked Cordelia, shuddering.

'Because we had to get back!' said Zora. 'We had to get back to warn you!'

'About what?' bleated Ramesses nervously.

'Well, about the . . .' Zora paused and cast a withering glance at Maude and Heather.

'Haven't you told them?'

'It's the goat's fault!' bleated Maude.

Heather waggled her ears awkwardly. 'We . . . we wanted to! We just . . .'

'We're next!' bleated Zora. 'Like the deer! Mademoiselle Plin lured Rebecca here so that the two winter visitors could . . .' She broke off. 'They're down there! Down by the fence!'

All of a sudden, all hell broke loose; there were sheep galloping all over the place. But only for a moment. Then they disappeared! Three behind the old oak, five behind the shepherd's caravan, a whole troop behind the hay barn and two sheep behind the feed store. The last sheep still zigzagging across the meadow was Mopple the Whale, but eventually, after a lot of anxious bleating from the others, he found a place behind the hay barn. Aubrey was flabbergasted.

'Did you see that?' asked the tall man.

The short man remained silent. The metal Thing turned slowly towards Aubrey. Aubrey chewed nervously.

'Oh, for God's sake!' said the tall man, then, and the metal Thing crept back into the warmth of his coat. 'Do you know what I need? A nice warm bath!'

'You and your bloody baths,' said the short man.

The two men plunged their hands into their coat pockets and plodded towards the chateau. Without so much as another word.

19

MOPPLE REACHES FOR THE MOON

A short while after the sheep foes had withdrawn from the meadow fence with their gun, Mum appeared on the caravan steps again, chain-smoking and looking nervously over at the forest. Twice she took her talking device out of her pocket. And twice she put it away again.

Vidocq was looking out from under the caravan too.

Then he started gently wagging his tail.

Rebecca had appeared at the edge of the forest, her cheeks red, so red that the lack of a red hat wasn't noticeable anymore. She made a beeline for the shepherd's caravan.

Mum flicked her fifth cigarette into the snow with relief.

'So?' she asked when Rebecca got to the caravan.

'He wants to help us,' said Rebecca. 'Dupin took Tess to him this afternoon for a post-mortem – and somebody really did poison her! I knew it!'

'Swines!' said Mum.

'Apparently someone advised him not to get involved. He didn't say who. But he said he'll help us anyway. He had to take the sheep away last time and he said he never wants to see anything like that ever again. He knows of a yard with a free stable, a horse sanctuary, and all being well we can go the day after tomorrow. We just have to organise transport. And obviously we shouldn't shout it from the rooftops. I'm so happy! You know what: I will have one!'

The sheep were relieved too. It seemed that Mopple had eaten the right card after all! The sheep surrounded the fat ram and gave him a friendly nibble, and although he couldn't remember his act of heroism, a look of contentment spread across his face.

Only . . .

'The day after tomorrow is further away than tomorrow,' said Cloud. 'Anything could happen before then.'

To start with, the right things happened. Rebecca extended her index finger to count them.

'All there!' said Rebecca, putting down the feed bucket. 'Thank God. I had this stupid feeling, but they're all there! That's something!'

Rebecca smeared some stinky ointment on Zora's lame foot, and all the sheep were grazing happily. All except one.

Heathcliff was standing a bit apart from the others, scowling over at the feed trough. His head felt much better, and his ribs didn't hurt every time he breathed, but his throat and hooves burned from the inside like stinging nettles: small, sharp, stabbing pains with every false move. Every move he made felt like a false move. The only thing that felt good was his name. Heathcliff! The name Heathcliff felt magnificent, like a warm, glowing feeling of completeness inside. He thought about how good the goats must feel. Full of names, round and healthy.

Heathcliff trotted over to the goat fence and stared longingly through the slats.

Suddenly, the little black goat was standing beside him, on the sheep's side, and she was leaning her head against the fence too.

Heathcliff sighed.

'I'd like to be a goat,' he said.

'Me too,' said Aubrey.

'But you *are* a goat!' said Heathcliff.

Aubrey shook her head. 'It's not that simple; the herder is my mother. You absorb it with your mother's milk, or, in my case, you don't. If you don't, it's complicated.'

Heathcliff thought about everything he'd absorbed from the milk he'd had as a lamb. All sorts of things, that's for sure. He'd stumbled from mother ewe to mother ewe, filching milk wherever he could. And then George had come and bottle-fed him. What had been in the bottle? Human milk? Sheep milk? Heathcliff had the feeling that it might have been goat's milk in the bottle.

'I had goat's milk when I was a lamb,' he said then.

'Really?' Aubrey looked at him enviously.

'Maybe we can both be goats,' said Heathcliff tentatively.

'Why not,' said Aubrey. 'I think we've got the knack for it!'

After the counting, Rebecca had gone off to the chateau again, and she came back a short while later in a very bad temper.

'Nowhere to be found!' she said to Mum. 'No phone, nothing! As if the ground's swallowed him up! Maybe . . . maybe he's got a patient!'

'Here?' asked Mum. 'I thought his practise was in Paris.'

'It is,' said Rebecca. 'Only . . . I saw a man in the chateau yesterday. I was on the way to the loo and I looked out of the window, and right below me, there was a man smoking on a balcony facing the courtyard. And his face . . . I've never seen anything like it. One side was . . . almost gone, I'd say. Nothing but a hole. And all red and raw. It made me go cold. And he was just standing there smoking, like he didn't have a care in the world. I . . . I was quite relieved he couldn't see me from down there.'

'There, you see,' said Mum. 'The snob's working.'

'Still,' said Rebecca. 'He could have called. He could have said something, couldn't he?'

'What do you want from him?' asked Mum. 'After everything you've told me, I'd keep my distance!'

'I think I wanted to give him a chance,' said Rebecca. 'To explain himself. Or something.'

'You must have it bad,' said Mum. 'Now shut the door. You're letting the cold in!'

She pulled the caravan door shut behind her.

Rebecca wrangled with a tin can, and after a lot of swearing and words of encouragement, she managed to finally get it open and tip the contents into a bowl.

The sheep craned their necks, but the food was for Vidocq, who was lying under the caravan, looking sad.

To some extent, the sheep could understand why: he looked like a sheep, but he wasn't a sheep. Rebecca was his new shepherdess, but he barely knew her. The big sheepdog was pretty alone. Rebecca seemed to understand too. She gently stroked his shaggy fringe, and Vidocq wagged his tail wearily. Then the shepherdess and the sheepdog sat together in front of the caravan, their hearts heavy.

'Oh, life!' Rebecca sighed, and Vidocq's tail tapped the wooden caravan steps in agreement. Just as the general malaise was about to spread to the sheep as well, Rebecca jumped up from the steps and crawled under the caravan herself.

'I've got it!' she cried. 'I've got it, I've got it! Fetch! Fetch!' Rebecca pulled a mature piece of wood out from under the caravan, and Vidocq suddenly jumped up like an enormous overexcited snowball.

The sheep couldn't fully comprehend all the excitement. A stick. So what? There were lots of sticks in the forest!

Rebecca held the stick above her head and waved it back and forth. Vidocq whirled around her, opening his mouth to reveal his pink tongue. Then the stick flew through the air, and Vidocq flew after it. He caught the stick mid-air, raced across the meadow in a wide arc, herding a few sheep as he went and then hurtled towards Rebecca, who was absolutely beside herself with excitement.

'Well done! Good boy! Who's a good boy, then? Bring me the stick! Where's the stick?'

The sheep couldn't believe their ears. They'd been grazing here day after day, model sheep in the most challenging of circumstances, and even found time to protect Rebecca from the Garou on the side. Not a single word! And now their shepherdess was waxing lyrical because the dog was carrying a stick across the meadow.

Vidocq laid the stick at Rebecca's feet, she picked it up and the stick flew through the air again. With Vidocq in pursuit, the stick didn't stand a chance.

It went on like that for quite a while.

The sheep looked at one another, waggling their ears and rolling their eyes. All apart from Zora.

'Will you look at that!' she said. 'Look how he's chasing that stick! He can't help it!'

It was true: Vidocq was chasing the stick like one possessed. And yet he was barely interested in it once he had it in his mouth. He was only interested in the action.

'He's hunting!' said Cordelia, shuddering.

And then the stick hit Mopple on the head, Mopple the Whale, who was grazing unsuspectingly on the hill. Mopple's eyes opened wide and he fell over – onto the stick. Next moment Vidocq had ploughed into Mopple. Mopple was bleating in a panic, but couldn't get up because Vidocq was sitting on him rooting around for the stick, and Vidocq couldn't find the stick under Mopple and so wouldn't move from the spot.

'Oh shit!' said Rebecca, running up the hill to separate Vidocq and Mopple. That was the end of fetch for now.

Rebecca and Vidocq went back to the shepherd's caravan and looked sad again.

Mopple just stood there doing nothing for a long while, his eyes wide and fixed. He wasn't even chewing, and that was very unusual for Mopple.

Finally, he blinked.

His memory was back, *all* of it. Just like that. Mopple sank into it like it was water. He'd been dipped in water once, back home in Ireland, because of some kind of dubious parasite, and suddenly, he remembered it vividly: the cold and a floating feeling. The cold and the confined space. The cold and the fear.

Mopple gasped for air. There was Ireland and the sea and George and the butcher. Sweetwort and hay and Rebecca, Europe and the tasty map made of card. A lot of concentrated feed. The story of the Garou, and the goats and Bernie and the wolfhound. The Jackdaw, flowers and crocodiles. Fresh, cold night air, moonlight, and howling. Far too many trees and a very bad feeling all of a sudden. A lurking feeling. Being stalked. Then a deer sleeping in the snow – as if it were dead. And then – through some kind of miracle – Zora, and then something moving behind Mopple – a Two-Legs, but maybe not a human. The Two-Legs was chasing Zora, and Mopple was frozen in terror.

He had stayed with the sleeping deer. The deer might not have been a flock, but it was better than nobody at all. Only once the forest had started to turn grey and pink in the morning light, did he hear something: the mysterious Two-Legs came back.

Mopple wanted to run away. Out of the forest. There and then. That wasn't possible. But there was something else you could do to get yourself out of difficult situations.

Mopple the Whale slumped into the snow and played dead. No thrashing around, no bleating. Just dead. The Two-Legs didn't take any notice of him. Maybe he couldn't see Mopple in the nocturnal snow. He crouched over the deer and waited. And waited. Time passed. Mopple carried on playing dead. The Two-Legs laid his hand on the deer, and the white hand and the grey flank rose and fell together in the thin morning light. Mopple didn't like it. He didn't know much about deer, but he knew they were wild. Free. They weren't fed or shorn and didn't get any concentrated feed or calcium tablets. They didn't want hands on them. Laying a hand on a wild animal like that, when it was asleep and defenceless – that was cruel. The deer became increasingly unsettled under the weight of the strange hand, and finally woke with a start.

Then a knife flashed in the moonlight, and the deer screamed, almost soundlessly, and leapt up. Leapt through the forest on three legs, staggering clumsily with panicked, ineffectual movements. The Garou went after it on his two healthy legs. Moments later, Mopple heard another one of the choked screams, and then nothing.

Mopple lay in the snow for quite a while, then he gingerly stood up. The forest was quieter than before. He wanted to forget the white hand on the wild fur, and then, miraculously, he really did forget it. The hand and everything else along with it, as fat snowflakes floated down from the sky. And then, all of a sudden, it was light and daytime and Mopple felt like he'd fallen from the sky too.

'So?' asked Heather excitedly. 'Who is it?'

Mopple thought for a moment. 'I don't know,' he said then. 'I didn't recognise him.'

'It's not the Walrus,' he said after a while. 'Is it really a wolf?' asked Heathcliff.

'I don't know. It looked like a human, but the way he moved . . . like a human that's forgotten it's a human. Or is trying to forget.'

'And you really don't know what he looked like?' asked Miss Maple. 'Not at all?'

Mopple waggled his ears awkwardly. 'It was dark. I was lying in the snow. I only saw him from behind. He had a hat on. But . . . but maybe he smelled a bit of goat. But then again, maybe not.'

'What if the Garou doesn't live inside a human,' Ramesses bleated. 'But in a goat?'

It was a terrible thought. They all knew the horror story about the wolf in sheep's clothing. A wolf in goat's clothing was even easier to imagine, bleating and sniffing and lurking and blabbering.

'Or in a sheep!' bleated Heather, eyeing the strange ram with suspicion, as he stood with his eyes shut enjoying the evening sun. 'A sheep would attract other sheep, and then . . .'

The sheep were just about to break into bleats of hysterics, but Ritchfield managed to maintain order, the silver star in his horns. The old lead ram stood beside the strange ram and reared up to his full lead-ram height.

'I'm quite sure that's a sheep!' he declared to anyone who would listen, and they felt a bit silly. They bleated amiably, and a bit awkwardly, to the strange ram and grazed closer to him than ever before.

'Marcassin!' bleated the unshorn ram, his spirits high.

Suddenly, Maple stopped grazing.

There was a clue. Right in front of her. Somewhere. She didn't really believe that the strange ram was the Garou. But Heather had just said something true, all the same. A sheep attracted other sheep – and what about lots of sheep together – what did they attract?

Miss Maple looked around. There were so many sheep in the snow. It was so white!

And then she remembered the big spider that had built its web between the gorse bushes in the autumn. One day an oak leaf had got caught in the web and Miss Maple had watched the spider diligently and delicately remove it. It had taken a while for Miss Maple to realise why, but finally she got it: the leaf would have given the web away to the flies – so it had to go.

'It's a trap!' she bleated loudly. 'We're a trap! And Yves was a leaf!'

The others looked at her blankly.

'Yves was far too big to be a leaf,' said Cloud reassuringly.

'And he wasn't flat enough,' explained Heather.

'And he didn't grow on a tree,' said Mopple.

It was beyond obvious, but Maple stubbornly shook her head.

'I'm not saying he was an actual leaf. But he was like a leaf. That's why he had to die!'

'Have something to eat!' said Cloud, concerned. Maple couldn't think about eating. She stood there ruminating – on grass and thoughts.

'A spider doesn't build its web to catch leaves. It's trying to catch flies, but sometimes it catches a leaf, and then it has to be removed so that it doesn't scare off the flies. And we're a web for the Garou! Do you remember the werewolf hunter? What better place for him to lie in wait than here on the meadow? The forest is big and confusing, but the meadow is easy to watch. And everybody knows that the Garou showed an interest in sheep once before. And then Yves came, like an oak leaf, and watched Rebecca every night. And the werewolf hunter wanted rid of him so that the real Garou could come, and that's why he shot him. So that the Garou would have the confidence to come for us! He must be desperate to catch the Garou. And that means he's almost as dangerous as the Garou himself!'

The sheep looked around in alarm for the huge spider's web that Yves must have got tangled up in but couldn't see anything.

Heather couldn't take it any more.

'So, where's the web?' she bleated.

'We're the web,' said Maple. 'But who's the spider?'

While the other sheep kept a lookout for the spider's web – as well as the gigantic spider that built it – Aubrey edged towards Sir Ritchfield, who was still grazing beside the unshorn ram in solidarity and had missed most of the commotion.

Only once Aubrey was right under his grazing nose did the old lead ram look up and glare at her.

'Where's the other black goat?' he asked sternly. 'No goat may leave the flock!'

Aubrey looked long and hard at the old lead ram.

'You can see her?' she asked then. And – after a while: 'There's two of you as well!'

'Sometimes,' admitted Sir Ritchfield. 'Actually always. He visits me quite regularly nowadays. He's called Melmoth.'

'We're called Aubrey,' said Aubrey. 'All two of us!'

'Lovely,' said Sir Ritchfield, but he probably just meant the sun casting its final fat rays on his grey fleece.

The sun had long since disappeared behind the chateau and the sheep were already thinking about returning to the hay barn, when the gate creaked and Zach stepped onto the meadow, his sunglasses perched on his nose and a box in his hands. He was holding the box out in front of him with both arms and was walking painstakingly slowly towards the shepherd's caravan, like a snail.

'Rebecca!' he cried in hushed tones once he'd finally arrived at the caravan steps. 'Rebecca!'

Rebecca flung open the door and looked a bit disappointed on realising it was Zach, but only for a moment.

'I've got a favour to ask of you, Rebecca,' said Zach, and the sheep could hear that his otherwise calm voice was shaky. 'It's quite a delicate matter.'

Rebecca nodded. 'Come in, Zach.'

Zach violently shook his head. In doing so he kept the rest of his body and the box strangely still. 'Sorry, but I have reason to believe that your caravan is bugged.'

Bugs? Yuck! Rebecca was always so keen on cleanliness when it came to the sheep, yet when it came to herself . . . The sheep decided to keep their distance from Rebecca and her bugs in the future.

Rebecca pulled her scarf more tightly around her shoulders. 'My God, Zach, it's bitter out there. Come in!'

But Zach just stood there in his sunglasses, coat and thin black spy shoes, and didn't move an inch.

Rebecca sighed. 'Okay, then. We can go into the hay barn, at least it's sheltered from the wind. The barn won't be bugged, I'm guessing.'

The sheep looked down their noses. Of course it wouldn't be. Rebecca should take note.

Zach put his head on one side and seemed to be thinking about the likelihood of bugs in the hay barn. Then he nodded happily.

'I'll go now. You follow in ten minutes.'

'Zach . . .' said Rebecca, but Zach was already on his way with his box, still strangely gingerly, as if he were on ice, and disappeared into the hay barn.

A few minutes later, the caravan door opened again, and a figure beneath coat, scarf, bread hat and mittens, only recognisable as Rebecca by her scent, trudged after Zach.

If Rebecca was going into the hay barn, so were the sheep. They couldn't help it. Rebecca in the hay barn meant fresh hay in the rack and fresh yellow crispy straw on the ground. And even though the sheep knew that this time Rebecca was only there to meet Zach, they could already smell the hay: sun, dust and summers gone by.

Rebecca led the way – the sheep in tow.

Zach was already standing in a corner, his nose red with cold, motionless. He had taken the top off the little box and was holding it at arm's length. Fodder? The sheep peered curiously at the box, but they didn't dare go near Zach.

'I managed to retrieve them from the forest.' Rebecca glanced into the box. 'Pine cones?'

Zach laughed bitterly. 'Ingenious camouflage, huh? No, Rebecca, they're boob traps. Highly explosive. Russian.'

'Ah,' said Rebecca not very enthusiastically. 'And what do you want me to do with them?'

Zach glanced furtively towards the door of the hay barn. 'I'm being followed, Rebecca. They're not safe with me anymore. But here . . . can . . . can I leave them here? Just for a day or two, until I can pass them to my contact.'

Rebecca nodded impatiently. 'Okay, Zach. Just leave them here.'

Zach very, very carefully put the box down on the ground, and very, very carefully put the lid back on. Then he quickly went up to Rebecca and held her hands. 'I'm so grateful, Rebecca. I'm . . . I'm really sorry to put you in a difficult position like this, but I've got to stop the Russians from . . . I'll never forget what you've done.'

A single tear rolled out from underneath Zach's sunglasses and sparkled in the wan light of the hay barn.

'It's all right, Zach,' said Rebecca, embarrassed. 'Now let's have some tea, yeah?'

Zach shook his head. 'I've got to go. Counter-espionage!'

They both turned to leave.

'Aren't you worried the sheep will set off the boob traps?' Rebecca asked in the doorway.

'Oh, no,' said Zach. 'Animals have instincts. They'll smell how dangerous the stuff is straightaway. The slightest vibration and the traps will spring and everything'll go flying! Believe me, they won't touch the stuff.'

Mopple's nose, which was just about to investigate the box, froze.

The sheep stood silently around the box for a long time, trying to pick up a scent.

They couldn't smell how dangerous the stuff was. Not even Maude. The box smelled like a damp box with pine cones in it. That was it. Bugs? Russians? Boob traps? There must be something wrong with their instincts!

They didn't like having a box full of boob traps in the hay barn. What were they even for? First boob jobs and now boob traps! They didn't want to go flying like the birds and the cloud-sheep, not to mention pigs and time. They liked watching the cloud-sheep from below, and they liked to think that the sheep in the sky were happy and free. But being up there themselves, away from all the grass?

That thought was even less appealing.

The sheep decided to wait outside on the meadow for a bit. Maybe the highly explosive boob traps would spring of their own accord and hop out of there like little goats.

Outside they spotted the Jackdaw standing at the caravan door, his arms hanging limply, smelling of lavender and looking indecisive. Indecisive and absolutely exhausted.

Finally, he decided to knock on the door after all. The door opened hesitantly, and for a moment the sheep saw Rebecca, a slim silhouette in front of the cosy reddish light of the caravan interior.

'Can I have a word?' asked the Jackdaw. 'Just a quick one. I know what you must be thinking . . .'

'Not here,' said Rebecca after a moment's consideration. 'My mother's asleep.'

'Exactly!' came a shout from inside the caravan.

'I'll come outside quickly.'

Rebecca slipped out of the door and then the two of them walked up and down along the chateau wall, up and down, talking in hushed tones. When the Jackdaw brought Rebecca back to the caravan, the light on her face seemed softer to the sheep. Softer and more alive. Rebecca's voice was as soft as the fleece on a lamb's tummy too.

'Thanks, Pascal!' she said. 'Thanks for telling me all of that!'

The Jackdaw was silent for a moment.

'I didn't want you getting the wrong idea,' he said then. He laughed quietly. 'It really couldn't be further from the truth.'

Rebecca stood on the top step for much longer than was actually necessary.

'Look,' she said. 'The moon's out. And it's red. Does that mean anything?'

'The weather's changing,' said the Jackdaw, his voice velvety. 'Maybe it'll thaw soon.'

The two of them fell silent and stood there, without saying another word.

The sheep looked up at the moon with renewed interest, hanging up in the sky like an almost whole oatcake.

'Do you remember what the little goat said about the moon?' asked Zora. 'About the moon and the Garou?'

The others nodded. The wolf needed moonlight to crawl out of its human form. Without moonlight the Garou couldn't change.

A little later, the sheep had a perfect plan: Mopple would eat the moon and in doing so free them from the scourge of the werewolf forever! Sure, they'd miss the moon, but it was for a good cause. A very good cause.

'I think it tastes like an apple,' bleated Heather excitedly. 'A really big one.'

'It's bound to taste like a biscuit,' said Cordelia. 'A biscuit that someone's dipped in clear honey.'

Mopple didn't need any more encouragement. He was off to bite into the moon, and Heather went with him to help. Down by the gate, perching their hooves on the edge of the feed trough would be the best bet.

Mopple found a comfortable position and stretched. 'Stretch your neck!' bleated Heather. 'Farther!'

'Almost got it!' groaned Mopple, stretching farther than he'd ever stretched in his life, so much so that he almost wasn't fat any more. 'Nearly there! So close!'

Then snow crunched. Mopple lost his balance and fell into the feed trough. The Jackdaw walked across the meadow, back towards the chateau. Mopple and Heather watched until he'd limped off the meadow in his strange snake-charmer way.

When the Jackdaw opened the meadow gate, something fluttered out of his pocket. Something that sparkled and shimmered like mad, even in the darkness.

Mopple and Heather looked at each other.

'Did you see that?' asked Heather.

Mopple nodded. 'That's a silver.'

'Like the piece he gave Rebecca!' said Heather.

Mopple and Heather abandoned the moon, which had turned out to be a rather too ambitious undertaking, and instead decided to skewer the new silver on Sir Ritchfield.

Unlike the other silver paper, the little card was easy to corral and catch. It just laid flat against the ground and didn't move. It was trickier to pick up though.

Mopple tried with his teeth. Heather tried with her lips.

Finally, Mopple managed to scrape the card up from the ground with his hooves, and Heather carefully picked it up between her teeth. Next moment she'd spat it out.

'What is it?' asked Mopple.

'That's not a silver!' Heather bleated indignantly.

That evening umpteen sheep trotted over to the little shiny card in the snow. They sniffed it and scented it. Mopple even nibbled it. They all came to the same conclusion. The thing looked like silver and played with the light like silver, but it didn't smell like silver, didn't crackle like silver, and above all didn't taste cold and metallic like silver. It tasted like paper: mealy, bland and woody. The Jackdaw's silver was fake!

20

CASSANDRA SPEAKS

The sheep spent a long time standing around the deceptive card, thinking.

'It looks like silver, but isn't silver,' muttered Miss Maple. 'Why?'

'Maybe he hasn't got any real silver?' asked Cloud.

'He's got a car,' said Heather. 'He could buy some real silver.'

The sheep didn't know exactly what 'buying' was, but they had a rough idea: you drove along the road in a car and if you saw something you liked, you just stopped and took it. The sheep themselves had seen a lot of enticing things on their travels (once they even saw a big sack of mangelwurzels), but it wasn't much good to them since they didn't have a car. It was different for the Jackdaw – with his big car he could pick up as many mangelwurzels and pieces of silver as he wanted.

Behind them, the caravan window tilted open and some of Mum's mysterious aromas escaped outside, as did Rebecca's cheerful voice.

'. . . not easy,' said Rebecca. 'But everything's all right. Well, maybe not all right; moonlighting isn't exactly all right, but it's not that, well, you know. And I do kind of get it, he told me everything. His father left him nothing but debt, and the chateau is a bottomless pit. I'm really glad he told me.'

'If it's even true,' said Mum. 'I could get the cards . . .'

'Why wouldn't it be true?' asked Rebecca.

'Well,' said Mum, 'if he's a psychopath, then it's not going to be true, is it?'

The caravan window slammed shut.

The sheep looked over at the chateau, just standing there as it always did, no sign of a bottomless pit. The Jackdaw was leading Rebecca around by the nose again. But at least she still had a nose!

The sky was getting darker, and the moon paler, brighter and fuller. Another night, or maybe two, and it would be completely round. The sheep could feel the moonlight running through their fleeces like water, making them tingle all over. Was this what moonlighting felt like? It seemed all right to the sheep.

Maple thought about how the Jackdaw had pressed a shimmering card of fake silver into Rebecca's hand at the edge of the forest, and about the werewolf-hunter who was shooting the wrong people with real silver.

'It's a trick,' she bleated suddenly.

'What is?' asked Maude.

'The Jackdaw!' bleated Maple. 'He knows the forest. His father was killed by a silver bullet. He thinks there are too many deer. He's scared of the police. He was scared of Tess – and then Tess was poisoned. He's got windows in the chateau, all the windows, and he can look down at the meadow to his heart's content. And he's giving out fake silver so that nobody gets wise to him! So that the werewolf-hunter doesn't realise and try with real silver!'

The sheep didn't say a word, clearly impressed. Miss Maple really was the cleverest sheep in the flock!

'What now?' asked Cloud.

'We leave!' said Ramesses.

'By car?' asked Lane.

'Anything but that!' said Zora.

'Through the forest?' asked Cordelia doubtfully.

'Through the maze?' asked Heather. Mopple had told them about the maze, and they'd been a bit baffled by it. They couldn't imagine Mopple simply walking through maize without making any attempt to eat it. There must be more to it. They were stuck here until the day after tomorrow at any rate, right under the Garou's nose!

'If we can't disappear – then we'll have to make the Garou disappear!' bleated Ramesses bravely.

The others looked at him aghast.

'I mean . . . someone ought to . . .' Ramesses looked at them all, a bit shocked. The others liked the idea of making the Garou disappear. On the other hoof . . . it had been so difficult making Yves disappear – and at least Yves had just lain there, cold and stiff. The Jackdaw was running around with a wolf inside him, and none of the sheep would have dared even go near him.

'We could lure him to a pit,' said Zora. 'Then he might fall in!'

But the sheep didn't have a pit big enough for the Jackdaw. The biggest pit they had seen was in the open meadow behind the caravan, and not even Heathcliff would fit in it. And anyway, pits didn't seem to work on him; Rebecca had said the chateau was a bottomless pit and he hadn't fallen in yet.

'Maybe Mopple ought to eat another card!' said Lane. 'The right card.'

Looking back, the card thing had worked every time.

Maple thought about her own, less encouraging experience with Mum's cards, first of all the taste, mealy and hard and bitter at the same time, and then about the picture, the tower and the humans going flying, and was just about to shake her head when she realised something.

Mum was right! The cards really did help you to see things.

'We might not have a pit!' she said. 'But we've got the *opposite* of a pit! Follow me!'

The sheep followed Maple into the hay barn – it was time anyway – and into the corner where Zach's box was.

Contrary to expectation, the boob traps hadn't moved an inch.

'Boob traps!' declared Miss Maple. 'Do you remember what Zach said about these boob traps?'

'Instincts!' muttered Maude.

'Russians!' bleated Heather.

'The slightest vibration and they'll spring and everything'll go flying!' said Mopple.

Maple nodded. 'Exactly. Everything – even the Garou!' The sheep imagined the Jackdaw: first menacing, limping and wolfish, and then flying helplessly through the air. And all because of these little boob traps! It was a nice thought.

The sheep were happy. To mark the occasion, Mopple ripped an extra-large portion of hay from the rack, Cloud fluffed herself up and looked even woollier than usual, Ritchfield started a duel with one of the hay barn posts, and the whole hay barn was shaking. Maude, Cloud and Lane were bleating in chorus, the most silent sheep in the flock's eyes were sparkling, Heather was singing 'Wa-hay! Up, up and away!' and Heathcliff was jumping for joy like a giddy goat, despite the pain.

'There are still a few issues,' Maple admitted.

The sheep stopped singing, jumping and bleating. Cloud's wool seemed to deflate a little. Only Ritchfield carried on crashing into the post, shaking the hay barn.

'What sort of issues?' asked Heather.

'Well,' said Maple. 'The boob traps are in here in the box, and the Jackdaw is somewhere out there. We have to take them to him. And we need a vibration!'

The sheep didn't really know what a vibration was. When something shook, that much was clear. But how much did it have to shake? As much as Madame Fronsac's double chin? Or like Heather's tail when she was in a good mood? Or like Megara's ear?

Othello looked over at Ritchfield and the post. 'That's a vibration!' he said.

The sheep looked expectantly at Maple.

'Yes,' she said hesitantly. 'Only we want the Jackdaw to go flying, not Ritchfield. Ritchfield needs to stay here!'

'Ritchfield needs to stay here!' bleated Ramesses, Lane, Maude and Cordelia.

Sir Ritchfield realised they were talking about him, abandoned the post and lowered his head bashfully.

'We need a vibration with no sheep involved!' Miss Maple explained.

The sheep fell silent and thought for a moment. It wasn't that simple. Most of the things in their lives involved sheep. 'When something falls from a tree!' bleated Heathcliff suddenly. 'That's a vibration!'

Miss Maple stood there for a while without saying a word, her eyes closed.

And just as the others were convinced that the cleverest sheep in the flock had fallen asleep, she opened her eyes looking fresh as a daisy. And more determined than ever.

'I've got a plan!' she said.

'Does the plan have a catch?' asked Heather suspiciously.

The sheep looked enquiringly at Miss Maple – the counting-lock plan hadn't exactly been a roaring success.

'No,' said Miss Maple. 'No catch, but a goat. At least one.'

'What can a goat do about a wolf?' asked Maude.

'Stink to high heaven,' said Zora drily.

Maple gingerly settled down, chewing on a blade of straw, and started speaking. The others listened. It was a complicated plan involving Lane, Heathcliff, a boob trap, limping, running, climbing – and a goat. At least one.

They didn't understand it in its entirety.

'But why would the Jackdaw be under the old oak?' asked Heather.

'Because he's chasing Lane!' said Miss Maple.

'Chasing me?' asked Lane.

'Chasing you!' said Maple.

'Why is he chasing Lane?' asked Heathcliff.

'Because she's the fastest,' said Maple. 'She can get away from him more easily if need be! And because she'll be limping!'

'I don't limp!' bleated Lane indignantly.

'You'll pretend,' said Miss Maple. 'No wolf can resist a limping sheep. It'll be like Vidocq with the stick. The Garou will just have to chase her! And then all you have to do is lure him under the old oak.'

'And then the boob trap will fall from the oak, and he'll go flying?' asked Ramesses.

Maple nodded.

'Wa-hay!' bleated the sheep.

Then they fell silent.

'And how are we going to get the boob trap up the tree?' asked Othello.

'Heathcliff will climb up with the boob trap,' Miss Maple explained. 'And when the Jackdaw is standing under the oak, he'll drop it!'

'Hay! Hay! Wa-huh-hay!' bleated the sheep.

'And how do we get to the boob traps – through the lid and without any vibrations?' asked Zora.

Miss Maple sighed. 'I'm afraid that's what we need the goat for!'

Some time and fraught negotiations later, the sheep watched uneasily as three goats slipped through the loose slat in the fence and trotted across their meadow in single file – three young goats with long, straight, pointy horns. Amaltée, Circe and Calliope, taking far too many liberties with Mopple for Zora's liking.

They actually only needed one goat, but the goats had explained one goat was no goat, and two goats were only half a goat. The truth was that after the sheep had promised them that Vidocq would drive them mad, three pointy-horned goats wanted to remove the lid from the boob-trap box. Contrary to what they had agreed, Calliope nibbled a few buds from the hazel bush. The other two sniggered.

Then the goats went into the hay barn and snorted in feigned wonderment.

'A window!' bleated Amaltée. 'Chic!'

'And straw!' said Circe, eating a few blades.

'Back there!' growled Othello.

The goats stepped curiously closer to the box and craned their necks.

'What now?' bleated Circe cheekily.

'The box has a lid,' explained Mopple the Whale, who had memorised everything. 'The lid needs to go. You lower your heads as if you're having a duel, and put your pointy horns in the gap between the box and the lid, then carefully move your head up, and the lid is gone! But it mustn't shake! Nothing can shake, otherwise . . .'

'No dog, no driving us mad!' the goats bleated obediently.

'Exactly!' said Othello. 'The grey goat is first!'

Amaltée couldn't get her horns in the gap.

Circe got her horns in the gap, but then got them stuck and could only be separated from the box after a whole lot of hassle. Calliope lowered her head, found the gap with her horns, moved her head carefully upwards, and wa-hay – the lid lifted up and fell into the straw next to the box.

The sheep took a few steps back and held their breath, half expecting the boob traps would spring out of the box like fat fleas. But the only thing that was springing – or rather, hopping – was the goats.

'Pine cones!' smirked the goats. 'Pine cones! Pine cones!'

The sheep made embarrassed faces.

'They look like pine cones,' Mopple explained. 'But they're boob traps. Russian. Don't you have any instincts at all?'

'You don't have to believe everything you're told,' said Calliope.

The mottled goat craned her neck and whispered something into Mopple's ear.

'She says we're all Indy-vi-jewels,' bleated Mopple, offended. 'Especially me!'

'No, we're not!' bleated the sheep in chorus. 'We're sheep!' added Maude with dignity.

It was about time they got rid of the goats again.

Afterwards the sheep trotted over to the old oak in the dark, so that they could better imagine everything. The broad, horizontal branch here, the boob trap there, Lane over here, the Jackdaw over there.

So far, so good.

Heathcliff looked at the old oak for a long time. It looked particularly old in the moonlight, extremely high and a bit hostile.

'I'm not climbing the old oak,' he said suddenly. 'Never again!'

They tried pleading, threats and sweet talk, but Heathcliff stood firm, and none of the other sheep could imagine climbing a tree.

'I could ask one of the other goats,' said Heathcliff finally. 'Aubrey, for instance. I'll go and get her.'

There was a light wind that would carry the floating Garou far away. A good sign! While the sheep enjoyed the anticipation of a Garou-free life wafting around their noses with the wind, another dark, quiet car skulked along the road towards the chateau and shuddered to a halt. Three humans came out of the door to the tower, a man and a woman supporting another man whose face was wrapped in white ribbons that didn't have the effect of making him look any less dangerous. The sheep watched with a certain sense of relief as the car whisked the three of them away and the light in the tower went out.

Heathcliff hesitantly trotted over to the goat fence. During the day he really wanted to be a goat, but at night he far preferred the company of other sheep.

He passed the unshorn stranger who was asleep under a gorse bush.

'Aube!' bleated the strange ram encouragingly, and Heathcliff trotted a little more decisively towards the fence. There was no goat as far as the eye could see, never mind a black one. But wait! The old blind nanny goat was sitting back there on the chest of drawers, chewing the cud. Chewing and chewing and chewing.

'I'm looking for Aubrey,' bleated Heathcliff. His voice sounded thin and ragged in the moonlight.

'Wrong!' bleated the nanny goat. 'Nobody looks for Aubrey.'

'I do!' bleated Heathcliff bravely.

'And?' coughed the nanny goat. 'Has she told you the story of the fox? The fox she got away from?'

Heathcliff nodded. It had been the first lesson in goat-craft. Then it occurred to him that the blind goat couldn't see him nodding.

'And how did she manage to get away, hmm? Did she tell you that?'

'She left the circle,' muttered Heathcliff.

The old goat made a noise. A laugh? It sounded like a cough and dry leaves.

'She got away from him, the crafty little thing, you have to give her that, but not because she left the circle. She *altered* the circle. And how do you alter a circle, hmmm, little one?'

Heathcliff had no idea. He probably would have nibbled away at it, little by little.

'You find it a new focus,' coughed the goat. Spittle and cud dribbled out of her mouth. 'A pretty, little, black focus. A motionless focus. A twin kid maybe, a weak, defenceless little sibling!'

Heathcliff stood and stared at the nanny goat in disbelief.

Suddenly, a second goat stepped out from behind the chest of drawers, the goat with only one horn. 'We're just imagining it all!' she explained to Heathcliff, making a superior face and winking.

Heathcliff turned his back on them and walked away, slowly and cautiously, so that it didn't even cross their minds to follow him.

But the voice of the blind nanny goat easily caught up with him.

'What lengths do you think she'd go to, little ram, to get away from the wolf?'

Like the whispers of the wind. Heathcliff could just about convince himself that it was just the whispers of the wind.

Somebody poked him in the side.

Heathcliff gave a start.

'Hello, Heathcliff!' said Aubrey, and trotted back to the old oak beside him.

The little goat listened very carefully to Maple's detailed instructions, and once she had understood everything, she leapt into the air.

'That's an absolutely wonderful, mad con-trap-tion you've found there!' she said. 'Don't worry! I'll climb the tree for you! And we'll get the Garou, Garou, Garou to shoo, shoo, shoo! Wa-huh-hoo!'

The sheep were happy that they were still going to be able to get the boob trap up into the oak, even if it was with the help of a goat, but they didn't want Aubrey to carry it across the meadow as well – Aubrey couldn't go ten paces without hopping, skipping and shaking.

Eventually Heathcliff said he would carefully carry the boob trap from the hay barn to the oak – Heathcliff who, since his fall, was very sensitive to vibrations.

That was it then: soon the Garou would float away over the forest. Now they just had to practise.

21

LANE IS NO LONGER THE FASTEST SHEEP IN THE FLOCK

The next day was a big day. You could scent it in the air. Big and strange. The sun wasn't shining. The sky was like the mottled fur of a wolfhound: dark, restless and ruffled. There was tension in the air; crows circled above the forest. A black hen had strayed onto the meadow and was running back and forth between the sheep with a look of panic in her eyes.

The sheep were up and about early, practising.

Lane was Lane, and Mopple was the Garou. The others were bleating words of advice.

Lane had to learn to run away from the Garou.

Mopple had to try to catch Lane.

Up until now they hadn't been particularly successful on either count. Mopple trotted half-heartedly towards Lane. She limped a few steps, and when she saw that Mopple wasn't following her, she stopped again.

The black hen startled Mopple.

'No, no, no!' Othello sighed. 'You're the Garou! You have to hunt her! How is she supposed to run away properly if you don't hunt her properly?'

'Hunt?' Mopple peered longingly down at his feet where, beneath a layer of snow, the winter grass was waiting to be grazed.

'Hunt her, catch her and eat her,' explained Othello.

Mopple looked at Othello with disgust. 'I don't want to eat her,' he said.

'You do! You're the wolf!'

'I don't.' Mopple stood firm.

'You want to eat her like grass!'

'Like grass?' asked Mopple with interest.

'Imagine that she's not Lane; she's a tuft of grass!'

'Summer grass?'

'Summer grass and sweet-wort mixed together! But with eyes to see you with and legs to run away with. And it doesn't want to be eaten.'

'That's not going to do it any good,' said Mopple decisively. 'If it's summer grass, I'll get it! I'll wait in the shadows, completely still, like a bush, like a stone, breathing silently. I'll wait and watch like a bird, with sharp, blank eyes. I'll only have eyes for the grass and ears for the grass, and think only of the grass, and then the moment will come, the right moment, and off I'll go . . .'

Before the sheep knew what was happening, Mopple had darted under the old oak and was biting Lane's backside.

Lane bleated in pain and surprise, then kicked Mopple.

Mopple pulled.

Lane made a run for it.

The goats smirked.

And the Jackdaw stood over at the meadow fence and looked

over at them with mild interest.

The sheep stood around as if they'd been caught doing something they shouldn't.

The Jackdaw opened the meadow gate. He looked different. Greener. Wearing a green hat and a green coat. And green boots. For a moment the sheep stood frozen in terror, then they fled to the remotest corner of the meadow as inconspicuously as possible and from there, they watched the Jackdaw knock on the caravan door.

He was hiding something behind his back.

Vidocq woofed from under the caravan, and the Jackdaw took a few steps back, surprised.

Rebecca poked her head out of the door and smiled.

'I've got a surprise for you!' said the Jackdaw, pulling out a long package from behind his back. 'Two, actually!'

'Ooooh!' squealed Rebecca. 'Come in!'

'I'd better not,' said the Jackdaw, glancing nervously at the door.

'Okay,' said Rebecca. 'I'll come out. Just a minute!'

The sheep stood around on the meadow and didn't know what to do. This hadn't been the plan. The Jackdaw wasn't supposed to surprise Rebecca; he was supposed to chase Lane over to the old oak, foaming at the mouth. And then he was supposed to go flying.

'It's gorgeous,' said Rebecca, once she'd finally opened the Jackdaw's package after much oohing and aahing, and something red had appeared. 'Thank you, Pascal!'

'It's the least I could do after the unpleasant incident with your clothes.'

'And the wool is so soft,' said Rebecca.

'Cashmere,' the Jackdaw corrected her. 'Cashmere is from goats. Softer than any wool!'

'Pah!' Cloud scorned up on the hill.

The sheep looked down at the Jackdaw and the red goat Thing with hostility.

'It's got to go!' muttered Heather. It wasn't clear if she meant the Jackdaw or the goat coat.

'It's a lovely surprise, anyway!' said Rebecca down at the caravan. 'I'm going to put it straight on!'

'Oh,' said the Jackdaw. 'That's the first part. Why don't we go for a walk?'

'Now?' asked Rebecca.

'Now!' said the Jackdaw.

'Now!' bleated Maple agitatedly. 'Don't you get it? It's happening right now! He's luring her away from Vidocq! They'll go into the forest and – bam! White and red!' Maple could see it clear as day – too clearly.

'We've got to follow them!' she bleated. 'With Lane and the goat and the boob trap! We've got to get him before he gets her!'

'We can't take the tree with us!' Maude objected.

'Oh, come on! We'll use another tree!' Maple snorted impatiently. 'The forest is teeming with trees! We just have to find the right one, and Lane will have to lure him there, and Mopple will have to memorise everything! Quick! They're going! Now!'

A short while later, a determined little sheep expedition was trotting into the forest following Rebecca's and the Jackdaw's tracks. Maude led the way with her good nose. Maude's job was to scent out the humans – and any danger. Next was Lane, the bait sheep. Aubrey, who would climb a tree. Heathcliff gingerly carrying the boob trap in his mouth. Othello, the lead ram, to defend them if necessary. And bringing up the rear, shaking and quietly protesting, was Mopple the Whale. Mopple was their memory sheep again. He had memorised every detail of Maple's plan and he would help them find their way out of the forest once they had completed their mission. Mopple's sense of direction had been particularly good ever since he'd eaten the map.

The unshorn ram stood at the meadow fence for a long time, watching the sheep expedition. He consulted with Pâquerette, Gris and above all with Aube. Finally, they came to a decision. The strange ram left the meadow and trotted into the forest after the other sheep.

Shortly after the sheep expedition had disappeared, the goatherder appeared through the yard gate. The goats bleated, but the herder didn't have a feed sack with him this time. Just his gnarled crook. He stood at the edge of the meadow and took lots of deep breaths, as if he were scenting the air. Scenting and waiting. Then he clasped his crook and off he went – into the forest.

On the other side of the chateau the two walkers were getting ready for a walk, guns in their pockets and silver bullets in their guns. It promised to be a very special walk indeed.

Following Rebecca and the Jackdaw wasn't particularly difficult. They walked slowly side by side, and Rebecca blazed red between the tree trunks. They kept off the paths. The Jackdaw knew the forest well. The sheep trotted and paused, peered and scented, and looked for a tree that Aubrey could climb. So far, it wasn't looking good.

Unease was in the air, and the birds were too quiet. There were dogs barking somewhere.

'Have you ever been on a shoot before?' asked the Jackdaw.

The sheep didn't hear Rebecca say anything. But maybe she just answered very quietly.

'It's actually pretty simple,' explained the Jackdaw. 'There are the guns and the beaters. The beaters walk in a line, with or without dogs, hitting trees and making noise to flush the game towards the guns. The guns stand on the other side and wait.'

'And how do the guns know what to shoot at?' asked Rebecca. 'I mean: How do they make sure they don't shoot the beaters?'

'Oh, it does happen sometimes.' The Jackdaw laughed quietly. 'No, but seriously, it's quite safe. The beaters all wear signal colours: yellow, orange, red. If you see any of those colours, you don't shoot. Speaking of which . . .'

The Jackdaw did something with his hat and the sheep saw an orange patch flash between the trees.

Rebecca sniggered. 'Chic! But I still think the whole thing's a bit risky.'

'It's safe,' said the Jackdaw. 'Completely safe. This way.'

Rebecca and the Jackdaw came to a path now, in a gully, following a little stream. There was bank to the left and right, and trees loomed over the gully like warning fingers. The sheep watched them go. Nothing and nobody could have made them step hoof on that path.

A tunnel. A trap. An ambush. The view was obstructed – and there was no escape route.

So, the sheep trotted through the undergrowth along the bank, peering down at the path below, where orange and red kept flashing between the leaning tree trunks.

'I could climb one of those trunks!' said Aubrey suddenly.

Moments later the sheep had a plan.

'What about Rebecca?' asked Othello. 'She mustn't go flying!'

The sheep looked at one another. They could only hope the Jackdaw would run faster than Rebecca. Much faster. But not as fast as Lane.

'They're taking the narrow pass!' said the short walker. 'That was more by luck than judgement!'

The tall walker grunted.

'Well, we're definitely due a bit of luck after trudging through all this snow!' muttered the short walker. 'Come on!'

A fox! thought Rebecca.

She had stopped to tie the laces of her old worn-out walking boots. They didn't match the fine cashmere coat at all, but they were warm.

And then she saw him, almost at eye level, red in the undergrowth. A pointy muzzle, already greying, and deep, yellow fox eyes. Rebecca didn't care for foxes on the meadow – but here in the forest he was truly beautiful.

Rebecca glanced at Pascal, who was walking along the path in front of her, engrossed in a monologue about hunting before the invention of guns, probably unaware that she'd stopped. Rebecca had heard enough about hunting for one day.

She turned around and walked warily towards the fox. The fox looked at her, and then, as if abiding by a secret rule, he turned around and ran away, deeper into the bushes by the path. But she could still see him.

Only as Rebecca stepped into the bushes, too, did the fox disappear, as if by magic.

Rebecca sighed and turned back to the path.

But there was no sign of Pascal.

Pascal was chasing the sheep – he didn't even know why he was doing it. Probably because sheep don't belong in the forest. Because it was limping and looked helpless. And because he wanted to impress Rebecca. She would be amazed if he turned up with one of her sheep! Maybe she would finally believe that he had nothing to do with the death of her dog.

But suddenly the sheep foundered, stumbled and fell. Next moment it was up again, but it wasn't running anymore. It was twisting and thrashing about. Pascal's mouth went incredibly dry. His heart was racing. Something moved above him. Something wasn't right. The sheep struggled desperately, but it couldn't free its foot. He tried to make a soothing sound, but all that seemed to come out of his mouth was a guttural growl.

From above, the Jackdaw looked odd, an orange glowing dot with an uneven green rim.

'Now!' Heathcliff bleated.

Aubrey carefully opened her mouth and dropped the boob trap.

The boob trap fell and fell, finally landing in the snow right in front of the Jackdaw.

Plop!

Up on the bank Maude, Othello, Heathcliff and Mopple held their breath and waited, but nothing went flying. Not the snow, not the Jackdaw, not even the boob trap itself. The Jackdaw brushed snow from his green coat and was just about to take a step towards Lane, who hadn't run away as planned. She was struggling manically on the ground, her foot in a snare, when something else flew through the air. Aubrey.

She landed on the Jackdaw's shoulders, and the Jackdaw slumped in the snow like a sack of fodder.

Aubrey picked herself up and bleated triumphantly. Then she went quiet and listened. She thought she'd heard a metal Thing sneeze as she'd jumped.

'A gun!' bleated Maude up on the bank, and Aubrey heard rustling and galloping. The sheep ran, just like they'd run from the gun back then on the meadow. Aubrey wondered whether she should run away too.

'Did you see that?' asked the tall walker. 'From above. Just like that! What the hell was it?'

'A sheep, I think,' said the short man.

'A goat,' the tall man corrected him. 'Let's shoot it!'

'With silver bullets? Are you mad? Did you at least get him?'

'He . . . he fell over just as I pulled the trigger. I think he's still moving,' the tall man admitted. 'But not for much longer!'

He took aim again.

Now the goat was making a run for it too. It had something in its mouth.

'Great!' grumbled the short man. 'Do it!'

'Freeze!' said a voice behind them.

An ice-cold voice. Icy, calm and cutting.

It sounded a bit like the boss.

'Drop your weapons!' said the voice. 'Hands behind your heads!'

Before the two of them could give it a second thought, their guns were lying in the snow. That worried the tall man. Being down there, wet and cold, wasn't good for the guns.

They warily turned around, their hands on the backs of their heads. Never in their lives had they ever had to put their hands behind their heads like that. 'Hands up!' sure, but they'd only seen 'hands behind your heads' in films.

'The clown!' said the tall man.

They'd seen the guy a few times before, always lurking and buzzing around with his ridiculous sunglasses perched on his nose. 'Our bookkeeper,' the old biddy had said, with a strange laugh that was almost sad. Bookkeeper! As if! The guy was standing impassively in the snow, wearing his weird black suit. He was holding something in his coat pocket. The muzzle of which was presumably pointing straight at them. Probably at me, thought the tall man pessimistically.

'Do him in,' said the short man to the tall man. 'You like using a knife!'

'Okay,' said the tall man, but he didn't move an inch. He didn't really know why. Maybe because the guy wasn't scared. Not a jot. It wasn't normal. There were always a few nerves when you were doing a job like that.

'Clever.' The mouth beneath the sunglasses smiled coldly. 'Believe me, it's better this way. And now get moving. Keep your hands behind your heads.'

'Who sent you?' asked the short man.

The weird guy laughed quietly. 'It's better you don't know! Off you go! Back to the chateau!'

'I'm sure we can come to . . .' said the short man.

'Quiet!' the guy wearing the sunglasses ordered. 'Not another word. Move it!'

The tall man and the short man got moving. What else could they do? The guy was obviously a professional.

*　*　*

Lane was completely alone, stuck in the treacherous snare. It was terrible. She was a sheep, the fastest sheep in the flock. She had to run, run like the wind. As long as you were running, you were safe. As long as you were running, something inside of you was calm and free. But Lane couldn't run. She wasn't the fastest sheep in the flock anymore. She was trapped.

And maybe soon she wouldn't be a sheep anymore either.

The Garou stirred in the snow again. Lane froze, too terrified to struggle. The Garou gingerly sat up. He looked around, looked at Lane, without showing a great deal of interest in her, without showing any interest in anything at all, and absent-mindedly felt his head and shoulders. Some blood was running out of his nose. The sight of the blood frightened Lane. The Garou touched his nose and got a bit of blood on his hand. He stared at his hand for a long time, then he tried to stand up, clumsily, as if his legs weren't his own. Like a lamb, Lane thought.

The Garou finally stood up and looked down at Lane for a long time. Lane stood completely still. The Garou looked around in the snow for something – but he wasn't looking for Lane.

Then the Jackdaw went back the way he came, wary and wobbly, without so much as another glance at Lane.

Lane stood there and watched him go. Stood and stood, too frightened to bleat.

She stood and scented the air and breathed.

And time passed.

Although it was barely afternoon yet, the forest was beginning to swallow the light.

Suddenly, Lane felt like she wasn't alone anymore. Behind her, not far away in the middle of the narrow pass, stood the goatherder.

Even here in the forest you could see that his eyes were blue.

22

OTHELLO LISTENS

The goatherder walked slowly towards Lane, so slowly that Lane was barely afraid. Only once he was close enough to touch her, did her heart skip a beat. And another. Trot. Gallop. Lane just stood there shaking, but her heart was bounding through the snow. Faster and faster. Lane was the fastest sheep in the flock. Her heart knew that.

The goatherder crouched down and looked at her – not with empty, dazed eyes like the Jackdaw earlier, but intently. Too intently. Lane pulled away as best she could with her leg in the snare. The goatherder didn't move, but Lane could sense that things were happening all the same. Things inside of him. Things like thoughts, only more palpable, more physical. Lane noticed his pupils constrict; his scent changed, from just unwashed to sour and finally an intense bitterness. Anger . . . and sadness.

A voice fluttered through the forest like a lost bird.

At first Lane couldn't make out any words, just a thin lament in a familiar pitch.

Then the voice ventured on.

'Pascal!' called Rebecca. 'Pascal?'

Lane looked over at the goatherder. He was still crouched in front of her, full of thoughts, and didn't hear a thing. Lane was happy he couldn't hear the voice.

'Pascal? Pascaaaal!'

This time the goatherder reacted too. He didn't move, but he was listening. Then, all of a sudden, he was really close to Lane and grabbed her. Lane thrashed her legs. She was thrashing and kicking, when she suddenly realised that all of her legs were thrashing – all *four* legs.

The goatherder carefully lowered her into the snow, and Lane made a run for it. She ran like the wind.

The goatherder stood up again and followed the voice deeper into the forest.

After the initial panic, they felt ridiculous. And a bit embarrassed that they had just left Lane behind in the snare like that. After all, the walker's gun hadn't been pointing at them, but – rather sensibly – at the Garou. Still, a gun was a gun, and it didn't always get what it was pointing at – they knew that from George's target practise on the old Irish meadow. It was best to run somewhere where you couldn't see the gun. If you couldn't see the gun, then the gun couldn't see you either.

But where were they now? And where were the noises coming from? Something wasn't right.

Othello stopped. Maude scented the air. Mopple panted and Heathcliff looked defiantly in all directions.

The snow wasn't smooth anymore; it was full of tracks. Tracks of humans, tracks of forest animals, tracks that looked like something had been dragged across the snow. The forest wasn't quiet anymore. Rustling in the undergrowth, distant voices and the barking of guns farther away. Lots of guns.

The sheep huddled more closely together and carried on warily trotting back and forth, to and fro, here, there and everywhere. It was difficult deciding on one direction. Everywhere they turned something wasn't right. The air. The shadows. The space between the tree trunks.

It wasn't long before they saw the first dead animals. Hares and deer, and every now and then, a brightly coloured wonderfowl. The animals lay outstretched in the snow, some with their eyes wide open, some with their tongues lolling out, still fleeing in death. One deer looked like it had curled up in the snow to sleep.

Othello snorted nervously and lowered his horns. Maude scented the air, her nostrils flared. Mopple was trembling. Heathcliff didn't say a word.

Then, suddenly, the noise found its way and roared towards them like a field machine, banging and screaming and crunching and beating and rustling.

The sheep ran away from the noise towards where the forest was still quiet. Quiet and menacing.

Up a hill. Down a hill. Between pale birch trunks, then beneath young firs. Thicket. Brambles and – finally – a clearing. In front of them, at the other end of the clearing, a hare was fleeing from the noise, and then, he suddenly wasn't fleeing anymore; he arced through the air and just lay there.

Othello baulked, and the four sheep retreated into the forest, wide-eyed.

The noise was getting closer. The sheep stood and peered out at the clearing again, where the afternoon sun was frolicking with the shadows, wild and free. Othello was just about to risk a step out of the forest again, but Maude bleated in alarm. Othello froze. A few paces away from the sheep, a deer burst through the undergrowth; it leapt out of the forest into the clearing, running, and then it wasn't running anymore. The bang still echoed as the deer lay motionless. Othello led them deeper into the forest. The clearing was too treacherous. Its sunny silence too tempting.

Yellow and orange amongst the trees. Everywhere.

There was no sense in running into a clearing that had dead deer lying in it. Better to face the terrible noise. Othello lowered his horns. His hooves scraped in the snow. His breath danced in the frozen air.

Maude, Mopple and Heathcliff looked at him in disbelief.

Othello was completely calm and clear; he took a deep breath and . . .

'Don't do it!' said a voice. 'Do something else!'

Othello whirled around, but nobody was there, just a big stone.

'What you have to do, is just *not* run,' said the voice. 'Not in this direction and not in the other direction. Stand and wait in the right place. That's what I told Tourbe and Farouche and Aube, and I'll tell you lot too.'

The stone edged closer. Now the sheep noticed sheep's ears, sheep's eyes and a sheep's nose. The unshorn stranger! And he didn't seem particularly scared of all the noise.

'Come on!' said the unshorn ram, trotting clumsily towards a bramble thicket. 'Hurry up!'

* * *

Lane was running. Unimpeded. Using all four legs. Like the wind. If you were running, you were safe. Things only got difficult when you stopped running.

Still – the forest had got unusually loud. Lane had changed direction multiple times, but now she knew where all the noise was coming from, and was running in the opposite direction. She wasn't particularly worried. The racket was slow. She was fast.

Hadn't she just galloped past a little black goat?

No! She couldn't have!

Lane heard snow crunching behind her, and then the crunching got quieter. Shame! Running together was better than running alone; Lane knew that. She couldn't just stop; her legs didn't want to, but she slowed down. The goat caught up.

'Hmf!' groaned the goat. 'Hmf! Hmfhmfhmpf!'

Lane didn't understand a word.

It was probably because the goat had something in her mouth: the Garou's glowing orange hat. Lane shuddered and sped up again.

'Hhmf!' she heard, coming from behind her.

The goat was trying to tell her something, but she couldn't because of the Thing in her mouth. Why didn't she just drop the Thing? Things were bad!

'Hmfhait!' bleated the goat. It seemed important.

Lane decided to wait somewhere suitable for the goat and listen to what she had to say. Over there, for instance, between the trees, where it was lighter. A clearing? Clearings were good!

Lane sped up even more.

'Hmmmmmfhaaa!' she heard, quieter already and farther away, but strangely insistent. Something about the goat noise finally made Lane get her legs under control and wait for the goat. The clearing wasn't far off, and sunlight swept its soothing fingers through the forest.

Aubrey stopped beside her and dropped the wolf hat, puffing and panting.

'So?' said Lane impatiently. 'There's a clearing over there! Let's at least go . . .'

'No!' Aubrey panted.

'We'll be able to see farther,' explained Lane. 'And it's brighter!'

'Listen . . .' panted Aubrey, '. . . to me! Now!'

Lane spun around twice, then turned towards the clearing again. She wasn't going to let a little goat boss her around that easily. Goats were mad, especially this one. But hadn't she just jumped on the Garou from above? The Garou hadn't done anything to Lane because Aubrey had landed on him just in time. Lane forced herself to calm down and waited impatiently for what the goat had to say.

'We . . . need . . . the . . . hat . . . !' panted Aubrey.

Mad! thought Lane. The hat hadn't even suited the Jackdaw, and it looked downright ridiculous in Aubrey's mouth, nothing more than a glowing lump. Lane was about to run off again, but then she didn't.

'Why?' asked Lane.

'Quiet!' ordered the goat.

Lane was quiet, but the forest wasn't. Screams and bangs and then – a shot! Lane spun round. A gun! Where was the gun?

'Back there!' whispered Aubrey. 'We run away from the noise, and they're waiting in the quiet.'

Lane looked over towards the clearing, where it looked so warm and peaceful, and shuddered.

'What should we do?' she whispered. 'Where should we run?'

'Across the clearing,' said Aubrey. 'With the hat. They won't shoot at us if they see the hat. The Jackdaw said so. The hat will protect us. The colour will protect us.'

'Do you believe that?' asked Lane, looking sceptically at the colourful scrap of cloth.

'No,' said Aubrey. 'But the humans and the metal Things believe it. That'll do! We just have to stick together so that the hat can protect us both.'

Lane took a deep breath and nodded.

He'd hit the hare bang on. Top-notch shot, even Jacques would say so, the arrogant sod! But now it was quiet again. That was the annoying thing about these shoots. Standing and waiting and freezing your arse off. The beaters had a better deal; at least they got to move around. Still: thinking about it, he wouldn't want to be on the other side, despite all the high-vis clothing. He'd heard the stories . . .

There!

Something finally moved on the edge of the forest. He drew his gun. Took aim. Quiet now! Very quiet!

He saw the fluorescent colour at the very last moment. He lowered his weapon. Sweat was beading on his forehead. Damn, that was a close one! He'd just been thinking about the stories, and now . . . But something wasn't quite right. The colour was too low down, flapping up and down, and moving far too quickly.

With his mouth agape and his weapon lowered, the gun watched as a sheep and a black goat with a safety hat in its mouth darted across the clearing and disappeared into the forest on the other side.

Then he closed his mouth.

* * *

'Hush, Marcassin! Quiet, Pâquerette!' urged the unshorn ram.

At least Othello, Maude, Mopple and Heathcliff were standing as still as stones, surrounded by thorny brambles and dense undergrowth. The noise was now so close that it seemed like the whole forest was full of it, and the roaring sent shivers down their spines. It was hard to imagine their thicket not being flattened, and them along with it.

Othello lowered his horns again. Mopple was standing completely still, in a kind of frozen stupor, and Heathcliff just looked wide-eyed. But Maude couldn't stand it any more and was just about to make a run for it when the unshorn ram turned his head and looked at her intently.

'Stay, Gris!' he said. 'We survived the bad winter, and we'll survive this too.'

Maude didn't really know what to make of it, but the urge to run had passed. Right in front of them, the noise seemed to split, to shatter into lots of pieces, and, three humans wearing ridiculous brightly coloured waistcoats wandered through the thicket. They banged sticks against tree trunks and yelled. Then they went past, one to the left of them and two to the right, and once again they were just surrounded by the forest, still and weary.

The sheep stood there aghast and let their flanks slowly settle. Heathcliff looked at the unshorn ram, shyly and respectfully, then he took a few steps towards him, even though the strange ram smelled so strangely mossy and damp.

'What's your name?' he asked.

The strange ram swung his head back and forth. 'I . . . I'm called . . . I'm . . . I don't know. I've forgotten, I think.'

'How could you forget that?' Heathcliff was astonished.

The strange ram cocked his head on one side and thought. 'It . . . it just wasn't that important. It was important to not forget the others . . . Gris and Pâquerette and Aube . . .'

Heathcliff looked up at the strange ram who had forgotten his own name to protect the others' names. It was something you couldn't learn from a goat – and yet it was important.

'We'll find a new name for you,' he said then. 'I know where to find one! You'll see.'

The rest of the sheep were standing on the edge of the meadow, grazing and listening, scenting the air and digesting, but they didn't let the sky above the forest out of their sight. At first the sky was bright blue, then it got darker, then it got paler, then it even went reddish. But nobody went flying. Not the Jackdaw – or the Garou, or whoever he was. And not anybody else for that matter. A big bird flapped and then fell to the ground like a stone. The opposite of flying, you could say. Distant shots whispered across the meadow and the sheep were worried. Even the goats were acting quiet, putting their heads together in a huddle.

Then, there was a rustle at the edge of the forest, and Lane and Aubrey stepped out from amongst the trees. Aubrey had somehow managed to skewer a glowing orange hat on her horns. Lane looked exhausted and particularly long-legged. They both slipped through the wire in the goat fence, and while Aubrey stayed on the goat meadow with her hat and was enviously surrounded by the other goats, Lane trotted on, through the slat and back to the sheep meadow.

'So?' asked Miss Maple. 'Did you get the Jackdaw?'

Lane shook her head. 'No. Aubrey dropped the boob trap, but it didn't spring, so Aubrey did, and the Jackdaw fell in the snow. But then he got up again. And then I was on my own all of a sudden, and the goatherder set me free.'

'The goatherder?' asked Maple.

'The goatherder!' said Lane. 'I ran, and it was loud and quiet, and the most dangerous place was where it was quiet. And sunny. But the hat protected us.'

The sheep didn't say a word. It all seemed a bit . . . mad.

'What about the others?' asked Miss Maple.

'I don't know,' said Lane quietly. 'Gone. I can't remember.'

But she did remember something; she remembered all the shots she'd heard, and shuddered.

Later Othello, Maude, Heathcliff and Mopple came out of the forest, too, and to everyone's surprise, so did the unshorn stranger who didn't seem as strange any more – but just as unshorn.

'He saved us!' bleated Heathcliff. 'From men in waistcoats. All of us!'

The sheep were amazed. The unshorn ram was being sniffed from all sides. He stood there happily, silently chewing.

'I always knew he was a sheep!' Sir Ritchfield said – and he was right.

Heather and Heathcliff played hide-and-seek around the unshorn ram, Cloud complimented him on his woolpower, and, strangely enough, Maude didn't think he smelled that bad, just rather tangy and appetising like sheep-wort.

Later, when the chateau shadows were creeping slowly, but relentlessly, towards the meadow again, like a slug, the strange ram looked over towards the apple orchard and the edge of the forest, and an odd look crossed his face.

'Something's wrong,' he said, distressed. 'Tache, Pâquerette, Gris. They're not growing. The lambs aren't growing, and their horns aren't growing. Not even their wool is growing.' He turned his head thoughtfully. 'My wool is growing.'

The unshorn ram said goodbye to Farouche, Grignotte, Boiterie, Sourde, Tache, Pâquerette, Gris, Marcassin, Pré-de-Puce and finally to Aube.

Then he sighed and trotted over to the other sheep to graze in the afternoon light. It was a beautiful moment, and the sheep felt more complete than they had in a long time.

Only when more and more cars containing loud men in green and orange flooded into the yard for the hunt banquet, and Mum came out of the shepherd's caravan, unusually pale and with no sign of her sparkly third eye, did it occur to the sheep that somebody was missing after all.

Rebecca.

Rebecca was the only one who hadn't returned from the forest.

Zach sat in the barn holding the tape in his hands, trying to get to grips with his disappointment. After all, it wasn't just about results, it was about doing the right thing. And Zach had done the right thing – albeit with the wrong people. The two men hammering on the locked hayloft door above him weren't Russian double agents. Just run-of-the-mill contract killers who had been hired for a hit on the *patron* for run-of-the-mill money.

Zach yawned. The two killers hadn't given away the patient's identity, even under Zach's stepped-up interrogation methods. Psychological interrogation methods, that was what seemed to strike them the most. He hadn't touched so much as a hair on their heads. The old man had been right. 'Pain gives them something to hold on to. Give them nothing, and they only have themselves – and that's not usually very much, Zach.' Zach now had his doubts about whether the old man had really worked for the Secret Service, but he had been well-versed in interrogation methods. There was no doubt about that.

Zach pensively turned the Dictaphone back and forth in his hands. Two killers, a contract, no employer. That meant that the mastermind's reach extended as far as the prisons, and that meant that the truth would never come to light. Organised crime, Zach assumed. The *patron* had probably stuck his nose in things that were a bit too big for him. So what? It wasn't Zach's problem. He would just give the tape and the key to the hayloft to the amateurish police officer and go back to his mission. *The* mission.

Zach sighed and released the safety catch on his service weapon. He had to smile. If the two killers had seen his service weapon, it would have been the final straw. Neon green and neon yellow, an exact replica of a toy gun. Untraceable. They would have understood the technology at the disposal of his employers, and then maybe they'd have sung. On the other hand – regulations were regulations. There were so many regulations. Zach put the Dictaphone and the key to the hayloft in an envelope, wrote a few lines on it and sealed it shut. There.

Back to the chateau. To help out in the kitchen like everyone else. And blend in. At the shoot banquet. What a load of rubbish! Zach was sure there was something behind it, probably Israeli double agents exchanging information. An ideal distraction in any case. He stepped out into the snow and squinted behind his sunglasses. It was so bright. For a moment he thought about whether, on occasions like this, he should start wearing a second pair of sunglasses over the first pair. Then he screwed up his eyes and plodded off towards the chateau.

* * *

The fox crept out of the hollow tree boot, where he'd been waiting out the shoot, and licked his fur. The shoot itself hadn't been a problem, at least not for a fox as old and slick as him.

The problems came later.

The forest and everything in it had become stiller, more elusive, more distant, scarcer. The surviving rabbits were now deep underground in their warrens, quivering, and it would be days before the forest mice were playing care-free beneath the fir boughs again.

It was a bad time for the fox after the shoot. It was a bad time for all predators.

The fox decided to go looking for the human that was different to all the others. When the deer were too timid and skittish, he had other ways of catching prey.

There were trees above her.

All well and good – she was in the forest after all.

Was she in the forest?

Rebecca squinted. Something wasn't quite right with the trees. Something about the way they were moving, maybe.

The way they weren't moving! The trees above her were so still.

And – green!

Green leaves.

Summer trees.

Then Rebecca spotted the fauns. Three dancing fauns with horns and hooves and ivy in their hair. The middle faun reminded Rebecca of something. Somebody. Pascal? Frank? Next moment Rebecca realised that the faun reminded her of Othello. She smiled.

Smiling hurt.

It's just a dream, thought Rebecca, but deep down she knew it wasn't a dream. The fauns were too still for it to be a dream.

Everything was too still.

Rebecca rolled onto her side.

There was no forest to the side or on the floor. The floor was shiny wood, the walls were white with some scratches that looked as if they'd been made by claws.

When Rebecca saw the tall French windows, she knew she was lying on a metal bed.

A metal bed on the third floor.

She rolled onto her stomach, closed her eyes and passed out.

23

HEATHCLIFF GAZES AT THE MOON

'That's it!' said Mum. 'I'm calling the police!'
She wasn't smoking this time.

She had gone across the meadow to the chateau and come back later, quieter somehow, smaller and even thinner. As if she'd been condensed. Like a Mum concentrate that had to be diluted with water before you could drink it. But Mum had no intention of diluting herself.

'It looks like the snob came back from the forest on his own,' she said to nobody in particular. 'I can't talk to him. They're saying he's had an accident. Something heavy fell on his head. He claims it was a sheep. The others think it was a branch. I think somebody clobbered him and made off with Rebecca. Or it was him and he's just pretending. At any rate, nobody saw her, not a single one of all those ridiculous forest men. That's what they're saying anyway.'

Mum was shaking.

The sheep listened attentively. They knew that a goat had

fallen on the Jackdaw's head, or on his neck to be precise, not on his head. But they didn't know where Rebecca was either.

They weren't thinking about fodder right now, but soon they would be. Who would give them their concentrated feed today if Rebecca didn't come back? Who would give them concentrated feed full stop?

Mum?

It didn't look like it.

Mum went inside the caravan and talked so loudly with the talking device that the sheep could even understand some of it through the closed door. Not the words, but the general mood. It wasn't good.

A little while later the new, concentrated version of Mum came out, in gumboots this time, and wearing gloves. The sheep could tell she had been crying.

'They're coming!' she said. 'And I'll feed you! I'm going to go mad if I don't do something useful!'

Mum wasn't very experienced when it came to doing something useful, and that made her an exceptional giver of fodder. She sloshed the bucket back and forth far too forcefully and in doing so spread extra fodder on the meadow, and she tipped an unbelievable eight buckets into the trough. Then she scooped hay out of the feed store, just like that, and a little haystack appeared on their meadow – not in the rack where it belonged, but in the middle of the snow. The haystack looked surreal – like something out of a story.

'Hay! Hay! Wa-huh-hay!' the sheep bleated.

But for some reason it didn't feel right. It was too early for the haystack. The story wasn't over yet.

* * *

Cold. Cold and empty.

Rebecca lay on the metal bed wrapped in her red coat, trying not to think. She had stood up and walked around the room. She had screamed for a while. 'Help!' and 'Pascal!' and sometimes just 'Aaaaagh!' and – most disturbingly of all – 'Mum!'

And then she'd stopped screaming. Not out of conviction. Not through exhaustion. Just because. She had the uneasy feeling that too many people had screamed and howled here before her, uninterrupted and unheard by anyone, apart from the painted fauns on the ceiling. The room was big and empty, and screams echoed.

The windows couldn't be opened or – she'd tried – smashed, at least not with a bare fist. And there was nothing to smash them with.

Well, there was one thing. It made her think.

It was such a simple thing.

There was a bottle of water in the middle of the room on the reflective parquet. A fresh, full plastic bottle of water. Evian. *L'evian. Live young.* She definitely wanted to live, young or otherwise, and she understood, better than she'd ever understood anything in her life, that that bottle of water was life. Two litres of life.

The bottle was both heartening and disheartening at the same time.

Somebody didn't want her to die of thirst.

But that somebody wanted her to stay there.

How long could you survive with one bottle of water? Two days? A week?

And a third question flitted around the bottle, fleeting as a flash of light. Whenever she looked at it, it disappeared. Yet still.

Yet still. A plastic bottle. Not glass. Maybe it was a coincidence. They sometimes used plastic as well as glass in Europe.

She couldn't smash a plastic bottle. A plastic bottle wouldn't produce any sharp shards that she could cut someone with. Or herself. What was she thinking? Why would she want to cut herself?

Rebecca decided that these weren't her thoughts. They were thoughts from the past. Thoughts that had been thought far too often in this room.

Outside, it started to snow.

Two big black police dogs sniffed earnestly at Rebecca's beloved woolly jumper in the yard.

'Don't expect too much in this weather,' Dupin said to Mum at the fence, putting his hands back in his coat pockets. 'But it's worth a try. We now know which route she probably took. And we're trying to draft in reinforcements.'

'She was trying to get away,' said Mum, staring into space. 'And now she's gone.'

'Get away?'

'The vet had found somewhere new for us to stay,' said Mum. 'We're moving tomorrow.'

'Did she tell anybody else about it?' asked Dupin.

Mum shook her head. 'The snob maybe. She had a soft spot for the snob.'

Dupin smiled.

'What is there to grin about?' asked Mum.

'Just a thought,' said Dupin. 'Maybe somebody's trying to stop her from going tomorrow. That would be better than . . .'

'Better than what?' asked Mum.

'Better than the alternative,' said Dupin. 'We'll do what we can.'

'And what can you do?' asked Mum.

'The same as you,' said Dupin. 'Guess. But we don't use cards.'

The sheepdogs had finished sniffing and off they went into the forest, pulling their humans on leads behind them. The sheep looked at the dogs with newfound respect.

'Is their sense of smell really *that* good?' asked Maude. 'So good that they can scent out a single Rebecca from a whole forest? I could barely smell a thing in the forest!'

The sheep were just standing around, too stuffed to graze, all apart from Mopple, seemingly surplus to requirements. Something strange had happened. Since they'd stuffed them-selves with all that fodder, they missed Rebecca more, not less. They missed Tess. They missed George. They even missed Vidocq, who was sitting at the edge of the forest watching the sheepdogs, not showing any interest in the sheep for the moment.

Rebecca looked down at the dogs and the police and could have screamed. If only she weren't so hoarse already. Should she take a sip from the bottle? Not yet!

Rebecca tried to think. There must be a way out somewhere. If not here in this space, then in her head at least. Her head was just a space too.

But then she didn't think after all – she told herself stories. Pascal had caught the murdering psychopath and locked her up for her own safety, while he did battle with the lunatic in the corridors of the chateau. Meh. How long would that take? Mademoiselle Plin was jealous and had locked her in here so that she could declare her undying love to Pascal by the open fire downstairs.

There was something odd about her. Something about her eyes when she looked at Pascal. She was welcome to him! Him and his sick chateau too! Rebecca suddenly realised that she wouldn't put it past Mademoiselle Plin to let someone starve to death.

Then she remembered his father. The mad doctor and his furniture. What if he was still alive and took private patients every now and then, to continue his research? Maybe he was watching her now? No, no. Not good. Not a good story. Next! But hadn't Pascal said that there were back stairs, secret passageways to the third floor? Maybe she could find them and escape!

She started tapping the walls, walls that were peppered with dents and scratches and claw marks. Walls that many hands before her had tapped. For years.

Rebecca stopped thinking again, went back to the window and looked out.

Her mother was sitting on the caravan steps, a book resting on her knees.

Rebecca burst into tears.

'I can't do it!'

Mum had put some glasses on and looked like an owl, but they hadn't yet made much progress with the reading. Mum read a few words, stopped and tried again. And after just a few sentences she snapped the book shut.

'I know she reads to you, and I've got to do something; I can't just sit here doing nothing! But I can't do it right now!' Mum folded her glasses, the owlishness left her face, and she looked tired. And desperate.

Then she grinned through the veil of tiredness. 'I've got it!' she said. 'You'll be all eyes!'

The sheep were rather concerned that extra eyes were about to be bestowed upon them. Third eyes. Fourth eyes. There'd be no stopping her! Apart from anything else, they would look ridiculous. Mum rummaged around in the shepherd's caravan for a while, then came back to the steps carrying Yves's little box. She placed it on the top step, plugged a plastic cord into it and turned a knob.

Next moment the sheep had taken a few steps back from the steps and were marvelling at the box, which was changing colours and singing!

'Well, what do you think?' said Mum.

When it became clear that the loud box wouldn't move from the spot – presumably because Mum had pre-emptively tied it up – the sheep ventured closer and could see tiny little humans moving about in the box, honking away animatedly in European. Apart from the really rather unusual minuteness of the humans, there was nothing particularly impressive about it.

'You can't smell anything!' said Maude.

The others bleated in agreement. With no scent the Europeans in the box were of little interest – even less so than normal-sized humans.

Mum watched with slight disappointment as the sheep scattered. Only Ramesses and Ritchfield liked the new entertainment offering. For Ritchfield it was like a new window – a window that lit up during the daytime too, and Ramesses liked the music. The music meant that you didn't have to be scared of the scary bits – like the bits with cars in them. Then the humans disappeared – nobody could make out where they had gone – and circles and squares darted through the box. Afterwards, the programme suddenly got more interesting. A woman walked through a vegetable market to heroic music, then you saw her chopping up courgettes and peppers. Some of the courgettes were bigger than the humans from before. A flock of enthusiastic little humans galloped along, then a brightly coloured package filled the screen. The vegetable programme was over far too quickly, but then there was chocolate, bread and a rather exciting fruit programme. Just as the sheep had started to enjoy the box after all, it started coughing and went black.

It was Mopple's fault. He'd sniffed the box to see if you could perhaps get to the shiny green courgette from the back, and in the process, he'd absent-mindedly nibbled the white plastic cord that Mum had tied the box to the caravan with. The box didn't seem to like that. It'd gone black with rage and wasn't showing any courgettes anymore. All that remained was a furry feeling on Mopple's tongue.

The sheep had finally partway digested the huge amount of concentrated feed and were beginning to think about how they were going to get their shepherdess back.

The sky was getting darker, and her sheep were watching television down on the meadow.

Rebecca wondered if she was already in the process of going mad. How quickly did that happen? How much time had passed? What time was it now?

Time was a curious thing.

Rebecca could have sworn that she'd been up here on the third floor for all eternity. Days? Weeks? The only thing that spoke against that was the light. When Rebecca had woken up on her metal bed for the second time, the final patches of sunlight were disappearing from the parquet floor. Early afternoon maybe.

And now the shadows were long, and the blue of the sky was becoming more pensive.

One day. A single, endless day and a quarter of a bottle of water.

How had the day started, out there, before?

With a red coat and Pascal dressed in green, that's as much as Rebecca knew. The red coat was still here; Pascal wasn't.

And then what? The forest.

And after that?

She didn't know.

Rebecca looked down at her sheep. Beside each sheep was a shadow sheep, thinner than the original, with longer legs. The shadow sheep looked fragile. So near and yet so far. Unreachable. Rebecca was afraid for them. Something terrible was going to happen to her sheep down there, and she would have to stand up here and watch, completely helpless.

Rebecca was scared, like a child with a fear of the dark.

'What if there's another reason the walkers shot at the Jackdaw?' asked Miss Maple. 'I mean – it's a bit odd, isn't it? First, they catch deer and play Garou, and then all of a sudden, they're after him?'

Mum was sitting in front of the caravan looking at the forest, chain-smoking. And this time – strangely enough – she carefully picked each cigarette butt out of the snow and put them into a plastic bag.

The sheep had tried to gather ideas for saving Rebecca, but their best – and up to now only – plan had been to bleat 'Rebecca' into the forest. It had soon got boring and Miss Maple was sleuthing again.

'Maybe they wanted to be the only Garou?' said Ramesses.

'Maybe the Jackdaw was competition, and that's why he had to go?'

Maple shook her head. 'The walkers didn't want to be like the Garou. They probably don't even believe in a real Garou. Maybe they were after the Jackdaw all along – and the Garou . . . was meant to be the scape goat!'

The Garou? A goat? That certainly gave them fodder for thought.

'So what?' bleated Heather.

Maple's ears drooped. Heather was right. What use was it knowing what the walkers were up to? They needed a shepherdess.

'We ought to go and look for Rebecca,' she said.

'But if the dogs couldn't even pick up her scent in the forest . . .' said Maude despondently.

The others bleated in agreement. Nobody wanted to go into the forest again.

Over on the neighbouring meadow the goatherder was feeding the goats mangelwurzels, and the sheep looked on with indifference, too stuffed and depressed for the usual fodder envy.

'We know something the dogs don't know!' said Miss Maple, her eyes sparkling.

The others stopped chewing the cud and looked at her.

The door.

The door and the metal bed.

The door and the metal bed were the only things in here that looked more prison than chateau. The only things that weren't lying.

The metal bed was screwed to the floor.

The door was padded and didn't even have a handle.

Now that she had understood that she wasn't going to be able to move forward, Rebecca tried going back. She had been in the forest with Pascal. And then she'd followed the fox, just briefly, but when she'd turned around again, Pascal was gone. The narrow pass had curved and then forked, and she couldn't see very far ahead. And there were so many tracks in the snow – from the shoot probably – that she couldn't find his. Had she been afraid? Yes. She hadn't admitted it straightaway, but she'd already been afraid then. She'd blundered along the narrow pass for quite a while, calling out to Pascal. And then? What then?

The forest disappeared in the mist.

No, it didn't. Not yet! At some point the goatherder had stood in front of her. He didn't seem surprised to see her – as if he'd been watching her for a while, and for a moment Rebecca had been really scared. But then the goatherder had grinned and looked pretty friendly. He had signalled for her to follow him, and Rebecca had walked home behind him, relieved.

Home?

She wasn't home. She was on the third floor. What had happened then? What on earth had happened?

'He's going into the forest!' Maude sighed.

He was indeed.

After the goatherder had finished feeding the goats, he had first walked along the yard wall for a bit. But instead of disappearing through one of the little wooden doors, he had gone left through the gorse bushes and was now stomping through the no-man's-land on the other side of the yard wall, making his way towards the forest.

Maude, Othello and Maple were hot on his heels.

Unlike Mum, Dupin and the dogs, the sheep knew from Lane that the last person Rebecca had seen in the forest was the goatherder, not the Jackdaw. They had decided to shadow him.

It was their best lead. Their only lead.

They still would have preferred it if this particular lead wasn't leading them into the forest again.

Fortunately, the goatherder kept to the edge of the forest. Eventually he stopped and lit a candle beneath a broad horse chestnut tree. He said something in European. The sheep didn't understand it, but it sounded very gentle and very friendly.

Then he carried on towards a birch. At the foot of the birch, a gorse, a hawthorn and lots of brambles had interwoven to form a perfect little hiding place.

The goatherder slipped inside, and the sheep kept their distance behind a big brown fern.

'Do you know where we are?' asked Othello.

Through the bushes behind them you could see a fence that looked just like their meadow fence. And on the other side of the fence stood a sheep, hazy and chewing, that really looked like Mopple the Whale, and behind him, dark as a spider, the branches of the old oak.

'That's our meadow!' said Othello, very quietly and very angrily. 'He's spying on our meadow!'

'Quiet!' whispered Miss Maple.

The sheep retreated behind two silvery beech trunks and waited for the herder to reappear from his hiding place.

Mopple stopped staring into the forest and trotted back to the shepherd's caravan. Staring didn't help at all. No matter how long you stared for – the forest didn't get any greener. Mopple couldn't get the courgette out of his head. It had been such a long time since he had seen something that green, and he wanted to take a bite out of it.

After the incident with the plastic cord, Mum had tidied the box away into the caravan.

Then she had wrapped herself in her coat and was 'going to confront the snob – he couldn't pull the wool over her eyes any longer!' The thought of someone pulling wool over her eyes, whether that be two eyes or three, deeply disturbed the sheep. Luckily, Mum didn't reach for the shears, but she left in a hurry, disappearing through the meadow gate towards the chateau.

For the first time since Mopple could remember – and Mopple the Whale, the memory sheep, could remember further back than anybody else – the caravan door was wide open, and nobody was inside.

Just one step. Just one peek. Half a courgette at most. Nobody would miss half a courgette. Or maybe a whole one would be better so that there were no discernible bite marks. Two! Two courgettes would probably be the best course of action. Nobody would notice a thing!

Mopple the Whale took a deep breath and placed his hoof on the first caravan step.

A phone rang.

Not in the room on the third floor, no, sadly not, the room on the third floor was quiet as a coffin, but in Rebecca's memory. In the forest. It had been a miracle that she'd even had any signal in the forest.

She had stopped briefly – and the goatherder had stopped in front of her too – and she had answered the phone.

It had been the vet. Yes, that's it, the vet!

He'd managed to find an animal transporter and a driver, and he could pick them up tomorrow – or maybe even this evening. Her and all of the sheep. Going to a horse sanctuary! Where they'd be safe.

Rebecca had been happy. Maybe she'd expressed her happiness a little too loudly. Had the goatherder understood? Did he understand English?

No, she thought at first, but then she remembered: Hortense had once told her that the goatherder used to be a teacher before. He'd taught classical languages. Before. Before what?

She remembered that they'd carried on walking, the goatherder ahead, Rebecca behind. More quickly this time. Maybe they'd changed direction.

Rebecca wasn't sure.

And then? Nothing.

What about her phone? Rebecca had put her phone in her coat pocket. Maybe . . . No. Her pockets were empty. Obviously. Where was her phone?

The goatherder didn't stay in his hiding place for very long. He gave the impression of a badger returning to its sett to make sure that everything is still in order. Then he carried on along the side of the apple orchard, making his way towards the chateau again. Dusk was falling. The chateau windows were glowing from the inside, and distant voices mingled, forming a surprisingly insect-like buzz. Outside, between the buildings, everything was still.

The goatherder stopped in front of a metal door, unlocked it and went into a room full of tools and little machines. It was suddenly bright inside.

The sheep squinted through the door and saw the goatherder taking Things out of his coat pockets. Biscuits, a pipe. A flat bottle.

And then: a talking device. Rebecca's talking device! No doubt about it. It was bigger and more cumbersome than most other talking devices, and it smelled of Rebecca, a healthy scent of earth and a whiff of concentrated feed.

The goatherder put the talking device into a drawer.

'He's . . . He was . . . He's got . . .' Othello was beside himself.

Before the others knew what was happening, the black ram had lowered his horns and pushed the heavy metal door shut with a loud bang. The goatherder's key was stuck in the door on the outside, clinking against the metal. Clink. Clink. Clinkety-clink.

The goatherder hammered on the door. Muffled shouts could be heard coming from inside.

'There! Serves him right!' Othello raised his horns proudly. 'He's got Rebecca's talking device! He's been spying on us! He's the Garou!'

'Maybe,' said Miss Maple. 'But how are we going to find Rebecca now? He can't lead us to her anymore.'

Othello looked livid for a moment, then rather embarrassed. 'Maybe . . . We could wait for someone to open the door again!'

They looked left and right across the yard. Maude scented the air. Nothing. All the humans were busy with the green men in the chateau. It might be a while before somebody released the goatherder.

The sheep trotted back towards the meadow. All in all, the mission hadn't exactly been a resounding success.

* * *

Mopple had attempted it from every which way. From above. From below. From the back, where a couple of plastic cords were hanging out of the box. But there was no sign of any courgettes. Maybe they'd fallen out?

Mopple let the box be and looked around.

It had got so dark in the caravan.

And then, it got even darker. Somebody was standing in the doorway blocking the light. Mopple froze.

Mum switched the light on.

Then, nothing happened for a terribly long time.

'Well, I never,' Mum finally said. 'I thought I was drunk for a minute. But I'm not. It's cold in here.'

To Mopple's horror, Mum pulled the caravan door shut and slumped down into a chair.

'Are you drunk?' she asked sternly. Mopple tried his best to look innocent.

'Do you want me to read your cards?' asked Mum. 'It doesn't matter today, you know. They're not telling me a thing. They're not going to help me. To be honest, I could use a bit of company right now.'

Mopple didn't want to be company. He just wanted to get outside, but he couldn't get past Mum, and Mum started shuffling the cards.

'There's fewer every time I shuffle them,' she said.

Then she started laying different cards onto a low table in front of Mopple. Normally it would have been appetising, but right now Mopple just wanted to get away.

'The Fool!' said Mum. 'The World. The Sun. Not bad at all. And here: the Moon.'

Mum frowned. 'The Moon isn't very good here. Illusion.

Confusion. Dream and deception. Lunacy.'

Somebody knocked on the caravan door. Mum jumped out of her chair as if she'd been bitten by a flea and flung the door open.

Outside stood Dupin and two men with sheepdogs.

Long rosy tongues lolled out of the dogs' mouths. Dupin shook his head.

Mopple stared at the cards in front of him. The card with the moon on it looked pale and cold, and Mopple could see wolves howling at the paper moon on the card. The moon! If the card wasn't very good, then it had to go. Plain and simple. There was a moon right under his nose, one he could eat!

Without a moment's hesitation Mopple chowed down.

The card was tough. Mopple was still chewing when Mum came back. Mum seemed strange to him. As if she were made of glass. As if she were about to shatter.

'I know she's not dead!' she said, her voice glassy. 'I can see it! Yes, I know some of what I do is humbug – but not all of it! I know she's alive! And I know she's not far away. I've got this feeling that she's watching me!'

Mopple swallowed. He had done what he could.

Mum opened the door and shooed the fat ram outside.

Night fell. A night with no Rebecca.

Rebeccca only spotted the wolf in the moonlight.

She was lying on the metal bed again, too exhausted to sleep, staring up at the ceiling.

In the wan half-light of the moon, the fauns seemed to finally move, jumping and dancing.

Three fauns.

Three Devils.

The ceiling with the fauns wasn't doing her much good. She continued staring obsessively up at it all the same. There was nothing else to look at, and since the sun had gone down, she didn't dare look out of the window. Rebecca was too scared of what she might see down there.

The longer she stared up at the ceiling, the more certain she was that the fauns weren't really dancing. They were running. Fleeing. Fleeing from something. What were they fleeing from?

Then, as the moon started to drag the silhouette of the French window across the parquet, she spotted the wolf – his eyes first, small and smouldering, then his mouth and his sharp teeth, finally his ears and paws and tail. The wolf was lurking in a bush, ready to strike, and now that Rebecca had spotted him, she couldn't keep her eyes off him.

The wolf was terrible.

No wonder the fauns were fleeing.

Rebecca knew that ceiling frescos were an art form. That people used to find great joy in different effects. Three-dimensionality. Illusion. Painted reality. Who had told her that? Pascal?

The wolf had probably been painted in hues of green, and during the day it blurred into the forest of leaves. Only at night, when the colours disappeared, could you see him. A wolf that only existed by moonlight . . .

Simple.

Rebecca knew that.

But a part of her shuddered all the same.

'And you shut in the Garou just like that?' Heather asked.

The sheep had retreated to the hay barn and were looking at Othello in awe. The lead ram proudly raised his four horns. He knew that it hadn't been very clever pushing the door shut like that, but he still wasn't particularly sorry that he'd done it.

'I don't think the goatherder is the Garou,' said Miss Maple.

The other sheep looked at her crossly. Whenever they were rid of the Garou, Miss Maple came along and ruined it.

'Why?' bleated Maude.

'Why?' bleated the other sheep.

Maple thought for a moment.

'Because of Aubrey,' she said then.

'Aubrey?'

Maple nodded. 'The goatherder reared her, didn't he? Aubrey likes him. She wouldn't be so hell-bent on catching the Garou if *he* were the Garou.'

'Maybe she doesn't know he's the Garou,' Zora argued.

Maple shook her head. 'It's not just that. Do you remember all of the things Aubrey knew about the Garou? Moon and silver and bullets? And how determined she is to find him – so determined that she followed his tracks in the forest! She must have got that determination from somewhere – and I think she got it from the goatherder! That means that the goatherder is the werewolf hunter!'

Maple closed her eyes and could see the goatherder in front of her: grey, invisible and silent. And sad! Why was he always so sad? What had happened to him? Maybe the woman and the girl belonged to him! Maple remembered how he'd trudged through the forest a little distance behind Rebecca and Zach – maybe to protect them from the Garou, but probably just to catch the Garou in the act. Maybe it had happened like this: the goatherder had spotted Rebecca and her red coat in the forest and had followed her. And then something must have happened.

Something that made him think that tracking her wasn't enough.

'Does that mean he shot Yves?' Heathcliff asked.

'Probably,' said Miss Maple, opening her eyes again. 'Can you imagine him sitting in his hiding place night after night, waiting with his silver bullets for the Garou, and Yves always coming along and messing it up? Eventually he couldn't take it anymore and made sure that Yves wouldn't turn up again!'

The flock had huddled around Maple with looks of disappointment. If they had known that the goatherder was responsible, they wouldn't have gone to such pains to hide Yves!

'But,' said Cloud, 'if he's not the Garou – what does he want with Rebecca?'

Maple thought for a moment. 'He doesn't want Rebecca,' she said then. 'He wants us. We're his web! We're here to lure the Garou. He must have heard that Rebecca wants to leave. That's why she can't come back. The goatherder knows that we can't drive a car without Rebecca!'

The sheep looked at one another. Othello had shut in the werewolf hunter instead of the werewolf! Even the less-intelligent sheep knew that wasn't good.

'But if the goatherder is the werewolf hunter,' said Lane, 'who's the Garou?'

In the deep of the night, Heathcliff trotted out of the hay barn to look at the moon, all alone. He didn't really know why, but he got the feeling that goats often looked at the moon.

The moon was round and full and the meadow so bright that you could make out the sparrow's tracks in the snow. Yet Heathcliff couldn't concentrate properly.

That was down to two things.

One of them was an empty space at the meadow fence, the place where Vidocq had spent the whole evening staring longingly into the forest. The sheepdog had probably just disappeared amongst the trees. Heathcliff could understand him. He was just as shaggy as Vidocq and he understood what longing was too.

The other thing was even more unsettling: the doors of the wardrobe under the old oak, which had never moved, no matter how much Mum tried, were wide open. Heathcliff froze. He remembered the book and that there had suddenly been creatures inside the wardrobe that didn't really exist. Half-goats, for instance. Or – werewolves?

But the creature standing in front of the open wardrobe was harmless. So harmless that Heathcliff was sure it was just a dream.

Rebecca looked up.

It was almost light already, and the wolf on the ceiling was nothing more than a feeling. A spectre. Soon daylight would banish it completely.

Next moment Rebecca knew that a noise had woken her.

She spun round and saw the door slowly opening.

This whole time Rebecca had been afraid that the door would never open again.

Only now did she realise how afraid she had been that it would open.

24

RAMESSES BRAVES THE ICE

'Rebecca?'
    'Zach!'

Was he really surprised to find her here? Or had he locked her in here? Rebecca would so dearly have liked to see the eyes behind his sunglasses.

She had considered all the possibilities: the goatherder, Mademoiselle Plin, some nutter. Even Pascal. But Zach? Zach was so obviously round the bend with his whole spy obsession that she hadn't even considered him. But now she remembered what Pascal had said: Zach used to be a patient at the asylum, and he was the only one who hadn't wanted to leave. What was the training he was always talking about? Did he mean here? On the third floor?

She resolved not to make any sudden movements. Instead of going towards the door, she took a few steps back from the door, towards the window and turned away from Zach. It was the most difficult thing she had ever had to do in her life.

'Beautiful view!' Her voice sounded so calm. Rebecca could feel how desperate she was.

Zach nodded and stood beside her at the window.

'This was my room. Back when I was still in training. My first room. I sometimes come back here. Are you in training too, Rebecca?'

'No,' said Rebecca, hoping that it was the right answer.

'Good.' Zach nodded contentedly. 'Training is hard. You shouldn't be here, Rebecca. Did you see the wolf on the ceiling?'

Rebecca saw the horizon turn pink.

'It's just a picture,' said Zach reassuringly. 'No matter what Eric says. Lots of things you see are just pictures. It's important to see the things behind the pictures, that's what the old man used to say. That's what makes a good agent.'

Rebecca couldn't take it anymore. 'Can I . . . go?' she asked, shocked by how shaky her voice was.

'Of course,' said Zach. 'If you're not in training, it's not a problem. You should go, in fact.'

He smiled. A real Zach smile.

Rebecca realised that Zach was still just Zach.

A friendly guy living in a story. A spy story. Weird and odd, but also clever and brave and touching. He hadn't locked her in here. He had just found her. Rebecca suddenly had a lot of respect for Zach. For somebody who had spent so much time on the third floor, he was shockingly stable.

That made her think.

'Was there somebody else here in training?' she asked. 'After you? In this room? Somebody from here?'

Zach nodded. 'The old man always said he was the best. His most interesting case. We were probably all a bit jealous.'

'Who was it?'

'The son of the former chateau owner. Old aristocracy, the old man said, and . . . fragile. He tried to kill himself back then, because of some stupid drug thing, and then he came here for treatment. "Heaven-sent," that's what the old man said.'

'Eric?' asked Rebecca.

Zach nodded. 'We should go. I'll take you back, okay?'

Zach politely held the door open for her, and Rebecca rushed outside. The dark dusty corridor she found herself in was one of the most beautiful places she had ever seen.

'That way?' She had to hurry. Her sheep and Mum were down there, in the dark.

'Can I ask you something?' said Rebecca, descending a steep spiral staircase, slowly, because her head was spinning. Her head hurt. Somebody must have hit her on the head.

'Of course, Rebecca.'

'What about before? Before your training?'

A lost expression crossed Zach's face. 'Before? I don't know. They say I came from a good family. But they gave up on me, so I don't see how that could be true.'

Zach looked at Rebecca, a bit lost.

The sheep were up and about early – almost before first light. They'd barely slept. The moon hadn't let them sleep. The moon – and the howling.

Now everything was still.

The chateau, the yard, the shepherd's caravan. The green men had long since disappeared, and there was no sign of Mum. Yet there was already fodder in the trough, not the usual concentrated feed, but tasty grain that was possibly a shade too bitter.

The sheep chewed sleepily on it, until Aubrey suddenly jumped into the trough and kicked their noses.

'Don't eat it! Whatever you do, don't eat it!' she bleated. The sheep looked at the little goat with indignation.

'Why not?' bleated Heather.

'This is our trough,' said Maude, who wasn't a morning sheep. 'Clear off!'

'But it smells like the powder!' bleated Aubrey. 'In the hut! With the rats! Sleeping rats! Sleeping deer! Sleeping sheep! The werewolf powder – don't you get it?'

'It does smell a bit bitter,' Maude admitted.

Lane looked down at Aubrey, who was still wearing the glowing hat. The hat that had saved them both. 'I believe her!' Lane said.

The sheep stopped eating, and Aubrey told them about the hut in the forest, about the fodder on the table and about the powder, about the rats and the bitter smell.

'I'm quite certain that that's the reason the rats were asleep. And why Mopple saw a sleeping deer. That's how he hunts. He's not a real wolf! He's too slow. He can only catch deer if they're drowsy, so he gives them fodder with powder in it that makes them sleepy. It's the only way he can hunt!'

The sheep abandoned the feed trough. They felt a bit woozy.

'But we're not deer!' said Cordelia. 'Does that mean he's hunting us now?'

Nobody answered.

'But the humans!' bleated Cloud. 'Mum. The humans in the chateau. They'll look after us, won't they? Somebody will!'

'I think we'll have to look after ourselves now,' said Othello quietly.

'Does that mean he's coming?' asked Ramesses.

'He's coming!' said Maple.

Ramesses nodded mutely, and suddenly he didn't just look young and fearful, but also kind of determined.

'When?' asked Zora.

'As soon as it's light,' said Maple. 'When he can see.'

'We ought to hide!' bleated Mopple, trying to make himself thinner.

'Where?' asked Heather.

'Behind the hay barn!' said Ramesses. 'Behind the shepherd's caravan! Behind the feed store – like we did when we hid from the gun!'

'He'll pick up our scent,' said Maude despondently.

'No,' said Zora. 'No, he won't.'

The sheep looked at her in astonishment.

'He was after me,' Zora explained, 'and I ran, and he was still behind me. And then I stood still and he stopped. Just stopped. He couldn't find me! He couldn't find me because he wasn't able to scent me. He was only able to hear and see me when I moved. He's not a real wolf. He can't smell us!'

Miss Maple nodded. 'We can give it a try. If he doesn't see us, he might just go away.'

'And if he sees us?' asked Heather.

'Then . . . then I'll lure him away!' said Othello.

The grey of the sky was gradually getting lighter, and Othello trotted to the drinking pool to banish the fatigue with a cold drink. Mist crept across the ground. The chateau was as still as a stone.

Othello was just about to dunk his nose into the water when he saw the sheep from the depths looking back at him. He looked determined. And strong. Much stronger than Othello felt. He imagined what it would be like to swap places with the sheep from the depths. The sheep from the depths could defend the flock against the Garou while he stood there under the water, completely silent, completely safe. It was just a thought, and yet . . .

Could the sheep from the depths even get out of the water? Could shadows go it alone? Was the Garou maybe some kind of masterless shadow? A creature that had risen from the depths and devoured his human? Or was the human still somewhere beneath the surface, not daring to show himself? Othello was certain that humans had a human from the depths and that they didn't always really understand it. The black ram looked down into the dark water, and Melmoth suddenly appeared beside the sheep from the depths. Melmoth, his teacher. The sheep that had taught Othello the most important lessons of his life. Wind and freedom. When to fight and when not to fight. Melmoth looked at him without saying a word, but Othello knew what he was trying to tell him. No words. More of a feeling for what was important.

The feeling helped and Othello felt more awake.

Othello nodded at Melmoth, and Melmoth nodded back. Then Othello purposefully dunked his nose into the water and had a drink. The sheep from the depths went blurry, and Othello felt better. He looked around. Sir Ritchfield was standing beside him, a tender, lamb-like look in his eyes. Othello knew that he had seen Melmoth too.

'I miss him!' said Sir Ritchfield.

Othello nodded. 'I miss him too!'

'A flock is like a . . . like a lamb,' said Sir Ritchfield. 'You have to protect it. No matter what.'

Othello fell silent.

'*He* would have protected it.'

'I know he would.'

'Evening begins when the nightingale sings . . .' Othello looked over at Ritchfield. Although the old ram was still standing beside him, Othello knew that in his mind Ritchfield had long since trotted off to the fragrant nocturnal meadows of his youth. Othello almost envied him. He was still here, knee-deep in snow, the Garou lying in wait for them somewhere in the dawn.

It had got a bit lighter again. The sheep disappeared behind the hay barn, behind the feed store and behind the shepherd's caravan, where they wouldn't be seen if the Garou came from the chateau. Hopefully the Garou was coming from the chateau!

Heathcliff didn't hide straightaway like the others; he trotted hesitantly over to Othello instead. Mist was rising from the stream, and the horizon was getting light. The world was so beautiful.

'Are you scared?' Heathcliff had to know.

'That's not important,' said Othello. 'It's my flock. That's what's important. A lead ram will defend his flock against anything. Even the sky.'

Heathcliff's eyes widened. 'Against the sky?'

'I once knew a ram who defended his flock against the sky.' Othello's voice was smooth and clear. 'Against a storm. The flock fled into the forest, but he stayed on the hill and attacked the storm. He didn't come back.'

Othello was silent for a while. 'Whether you're afraid or not doesn't always matter.'

The mist had turned golden, the horizon pink as a sheep's muzzle. It was a beautiful moment.

'Go up the oak!' said Othello suddenly. 'He won't look up. Sheep don't climb trees. Go up the oak, Heathcliff!'

'I'm a sheep!' Heathcliff said decisively. 'I don't climb trees!'

'I know,' said Othello. 'You'll be a sheep up in the oak too.'

But Heathcliff didn't go up the oak. He didn't dare. In that moment all he wanted was to be with other sheep. As many sheep as possible. With a flock. His flock.

And then the Garou didn't come from the chateau after all; he came out of the wardrobe. Heathcliff suddenly remembered the dream he'd had last night. The dream hadn't been a dream, and Eric wasn't harmless.

The Garou stretched and looked at the sheep huddling uselessly on the wrong side of the hay barn and the shepherd's caravan. For a moment, before the fear washed over them, they just felt stupid.

The Garou stared. There was a strange glint in his eye that Othello recognised from crazy circus dogs. He wasn't a wolf. He was something completely different. Othello thought that the idea that the humans had of a wolf must be something far worse than the wolf itself. The wolf in the zoo back then had been terrible, but very alive at the same time.

The wolf in the human had something mangy about it, something dead.

The sheep squinted woozily over at the wardrobe, and Othello positioned himself between the Garou and his flock.

A knife flashed.

Then Othello remembered the plan. Lure him away. The black ram scraped his hooves and ran.

The Garou, however, didn't follow him.

Othello turned around in a wide arc and galloped back, but it was almost too late – the Garou was already near the woozy sheep at the hay barn, and he had a knife in his hand. The knife wasn't very long, but it looked sharp and dangerous – like a single tooth.

The Garou stepped even closer. It was the moment before he pounced, the moment when everything stands still.

Hunter. Prey. Time.

Yet something wasn't standing still.

A sheep leapt forward out of the safety of the flock, then galloped right under the Garou's nose.

Running.

Running for his life. For all the sheep's lives.

No wolf can resist a sheep fleeing in panic, not even the Garou.

The Garou spun around and ran after Ramesses.

Across the yard, along the moat, ice sparkling below. Between the hedges. Fingers in his fleece, touching him – to no avail. Hedges, hedges and more hedges. A narrow space. The maze!

Hooves on ice, hooves on snow. Wolf boots on snow.

Mist. Breath. Life.

Boots on snow.

Ramesses galloped between the hedges in a panic. Why had he run off? Why? And why had he run into the maze? Why on earth?

Around the corner. Around another corner. Straight on. Snow spraying everywhere. Follow your left horn. Follow your right horn. Follow the scent of the forest. Around another corner.

Stop.

Ramesses dug all four hooves into the ground and stopped in front of a green wall. The wolf's boots were very close now, and Ramesses was stuck in a prison of evergreen leaves. He felt dizzy. He couldn't breathe. He couldn't think. He lowered his horns. When he could hear the wolf's breathing – terribly quiet breathing – he darted off, straight towards him.

Why on earth?

Ramesses and the Garou reached the bend at the same time. The Garou moved aside – he was so quick, so close and terrible – and his knife darted for Ramesses. Ramesses just carried on running. On and on he went. Around so many corners. Across all the snow. Past the claws of stone beasts of prey. Into the forest. Still running.

The wind sang in his ears. Any fatigue had vanished. Running. Being alive. Nothing could be easier.

Only when more and more trees were blocking his path and his run looked more like the zigzagging of a panicked hare, did Ramesses realise that running wasn't that easy anymore. He had a sharp pain in one of his hind legs and cold in his lungs. He stopped – just for a moment – and scented the air. The forest was confusing: an icy, tangy tangle of scents.

Coming from all directions. Moss and snow. Thousands of strange animals.

Blood.

The smell of blood shocked Ramesses. A sinister, familiar smell.

His own blood.

The Garou's knife had bitten deeply into Ramesses leg and brought forth red droplets.

Red droplets in the snow.

He left a trail, like a cord that tied him to the wolf. A cord that Ramesses had to fight against. A cord that weakened and betrayed him.

It was so early. The light had a whole day to fall on the ground and betray him to the Garou. The Garou, who was bursting through the undergrowth not far away.

Ramesses took a deep breath. Fear surrounded him, big and terrible, even more terrible than the Garou himself. Ramesses had to look through it. Behind the fear there was something that could help him.

Fight.

Running on its own was no longer enough, not with the red trail. What Ramesses needed was a duel space, somewhere a sheep could take a run-up, double back and see the sky. An open space.

Ramesses galloped on. Trees, trees, trees. Trees and snow. Sometimes he heard footsteps behind him, sometimes rustling and cracking. Once he heard breathing. Eventually it went quiet and all that Ramesses could hear was his own heartbeat. He stopped and listened. Nothing. The ground beneath his feet had changed. It was hollow and treacherous; the trees had gone. A dawn sky hung over him, light and wide. Ramesses stood on the ice of the lake, white on white, with wild eyes and two horns. For the first time in his life, he thought about his horns.

The red trail had followed him.

The ice whispered.

The Garou was on the edge of the lake, the knife in his hand, staring ecstatically at Ramesses.

Ramesses stayed calmly in the middle of the lake and scented the air. The wolf would follow him onto the ice; it was obvious. Onto the smooth ice. The wolf couldn't help it. But for now, the wolf was just standing there on his two ungainly, impractical human legs. If he fell, Ramesses would attack. If not . . .

The red trail licked around Ramesses's hooves, enticing the Garou. It finally lured him onto the ice. Seeing his smooth predatory movements, no sheep would have taken him for a mere human. A shudder went down Ramesses's spine, but he stood firm and lowered his little horns. All of a sudden, he heard something . . . music maybe.

Fall! thought Ramesses, as the wolf fell into an easy trot.

Fall! as the knife flashed, grey and clear as the sky.

But the wolf didn't fall. The wolf was running, making his way towards Ramesses.

Ramesses's hooves dug into the ice. Then there was a loud bang. A shot?

A murder of crows cut through the sky.

The Garou stood still. He looked down at where the blind ice was cracking and darkness was welling up.

The Garou made a whimpering sound and sank onto his knees. The ice laughed and broke, a labyrinth of laughter lines on the white skin of the lake.

Then something strange happened.

The Garou's knife had forgotten Ramesses and was hacking desperately into the darkness beneath him. Ice screamed and tore.

The lake stretched out its dark, hungry fingers towards Ramesses, and the young ram forgot the Garou, forgot everything, even the fear, and galloped towards the bank as quickly as he could. The cold reached for his left hind leg, but he shook it off and carried on running, faster than the cold and the ice, until soft snow clung to his hooves.

There was nothing out on the lake anymore. No wolf. No human. Just a hole like a toothed jaw and the red trail disappearing into the darkness.

But on the edge of the lake sat a red fox, gazing over at the hole with a strange look in his eyes.

Ramesses turned his back on the lake and limped away. Out of the forest.

Back to the meadow.

Homeward, where a sleepy flock and an absolutely exhausted Rebecca were waiting for him at the shepherd's caravan.

25

THE UNSHORN RAM GETS SHORN

'That's why he howled at the moon!' said Aubrey thoughtfully. 'The moon's a goat's cheese! A goat's cheese that he couldn't wrap up!'

The sheep made sceptical faces. The goat's cheese moon theory was pretty controversial.

A few days had passed, but the sheep were still ruminating on all the things that had happened on their meadow since the full moon.

'I don't think it was Eric howling at the moon,' said Miss Maple.

'But . . .' bleated Heather. Maple always doubted everything!

'I think it was his dog howling at the moon,' Miss Maple explained. 'The wolfhound Mopple told us about.'

'Because the moon's a sheep?' asked Cordelia.

'Because he was lonely,' said Miss Maple. 'When the Garou was hunting, the dog was left on his own.'

The others nodded sagely, chewing warily and keeping their distance from the meadow fence. They still felt a bit nervous. Over the past few days, it had felt like the devil had indeed been unleashed in the yard, but unfortunately not in the form of the friendly chap with the hooves and the horns.

'The Devils,' Maple muttered suddenly. All this thinking and sleuthing was leaving her no time for grazing. 'Mum was right – the cards really do help you to see things. You just had to know how: three devils – none of them were completely to blame, but each had a part in it. First there was the Garou, who had killed the deer and sheep and humans all those years ago. Then came the goatherder, the Garou-hunter, out for revenge no matter what it took; if something stood in his way, he got rid of it. Like he got rid of Yves and Tess. Finally, there were the walkers. They were on a killing spree of their own and used the Garou as their scape goat. What a mess!'

Dupin had spent a long time talking to Rebecca, explaining everything to her. Then, lots of cap-men had appeared and started taking humans away.

First the two walkers, who had given each other bloody noses, later the Jackdaw with a bandage around his head, Mademoiselle Plin and two days later, Eric, whom they found in the lake, pale and extremely stiff. The sheep had been a little bit worried that in their eagerness the men would take Rebecca too.

But Rebecca was still there.

Hortense had spent a lot of time sitting with her in the caravan and had howled and howled and howled.

Then the cap-men had found Things in Eric's house. Mainly pictures, beautiful and artistic pictures with a lot of red in them, but sleeping powder and diaries too.

Shortly after that, the cap-men had taken the goatherder away too. The goatherder had looked rather happy about it. The goats would be fed by Madame Fronsac from now on, which wasn't a bad outcome for them.

Finally, three burly men showed up and carried the wardrobe off the meadow, into the yard, where they attacked it with axes until just a heap of splintered wood remained. Rebecca and Mum watched from the steps of the shepherd's caravan, clouds of white breath billowing into the frozen air.

'I knew from day one that that wardrobe was trouble,' said Mum, a glint of satisfaction in her eye.

The shepherdess nodded. 'He hid in there. That's what the police said. He was there when the furniture was brought out onto the meadow all those years ago, and he kept the key. That's why nobody saw him coming – he just slipped inside when nobody was looking, biding his time. And then . . .' She shuddered.

'Can't have been very comfy,' muttered Mum. 'Not to mention cold.'

'He must have been freezing,' Rebecca agreed, another cloud of breath puffing into the icy air.

It had been a stressful few days for the sheep, without television and being read to, but now their departure was imminent.

This time they were going to the horse sanctuary. The sheep were excited.

The big shears snapped in the air like an aggressive crow and the sheep shuddered.

'Okay,' said Rebecca. 'Let's do it!'

Together with Zach and Mum, she had driven the unshorn ram into the pen and now he was for the chop. Shearing in the middle of winter, whatever next! The vet was there too. Just a little bit, Rebecca had promised the sheep, so that he could see again. Hoof trim. Eye drops. Calcium tablet. Worming treatment. The works.

But they had to catch him first. The unshorn ram wasn't the quickest, but he was the master of ducking, diving and doubling back. And he was strong. Rebecca was panting. Zach's sunglasses had fallen off and he was squinting.

The other sheep stood on the outside of the fence bleating words of advice.

'Not in the corner!' bleated Cloud.

'A bit to the left!' bleated Heather.

'More to the right!' bleated Maude.

'Watch out, behind you!' bleated Heathcliff.

'Forwards!' bleated Sir Ritchfield.

The unshorn ram stopped and looked confused. Zach pounced and grabbed his hind legs.

'Now it's best if you just keep still and wait for it all to be over!' declared Lane. It was one of those great pieces of advice that everybody liked to dish out and nobody followed.

The shears clattered, and lots of matted wool fell to the ground. Powerful sheep legs appeared and broad, split hooves. Rebecca groaned when she saw the hooves. More wool fell to the ground: a back, a neck, a sheep's head. Alert sheep's ears. Even the biggest sceptic now had to admit that the unshorn ram – the half-shorn ram? – was undoubtedly a sheep, a sturdy ram with round, amber-coloured horns and dreamy eyes. He kicked a bit and bleated a bit, but on the whole, he took it in his stride. Unlike Rebecca. They had never seen their shepherdess shear a sheep – probably because she had never shorn a sheep before. She swore and panted, she lost her bread hat and almost cut Zach's ear off.

Afterwards there were almost two new sheep on the meadow: the strange ram – and Zach, whose black suit was so covered in white wool fuzz that he could have been mistaken for a sheep. The freshly shorn ram himself looked a bit like a cloud – one of the more ragged ones – and there was already a rumour going around that he might be a cloud-sheep.

'Job's a good 'un!' said Rebecca contentedly.

Mum didn't say a word, picking wool fibres from her jacket with her fingertips.

'I need a manicure.' She sighed.

Rebecca grinned and clacked the hoof shears menacingly.

Then the two women sat on the caravan steps smoking and watched the snow thawing.

In silence.

'They still haven't caught the head honcho,' said Rebecca finally. 'He must be important. International. Pascal gave him a new face after a shootout, and then he obviously had to be taken out – so that nobody could describe the new face. I could have told him that. How could he be so stupid?'

'Greed,' said Mum, blowing smoke into the air.

'Debts.' Rebecca sighed. 'Can you believe that those weird winter visitors were really contract killers? They looked so harmless!'

'I had a funny feeling about them all along,' said Mum. 'Anyone who spends that long in the shower can't be normal.'

'You have a funny feeling about everybody,' said Rebecca.

'So? I was right, wasn't I? That goatherder! And bloody Eric!'

'I . . . I kind of get Eric,' Rebecca muttered. 'Obviously not what he did, but . . . I spent a night in that awful room. And he spent half a year in there, staring up at that wolf every night. And going through withdrawal as well. And who knows what the old quack was telling him. He knowingly . . . and the animal on Eric's coat of arms was a wolf too. The old man probably thought it was absolutely hilarious. Everything is so blank and stark up there, you know, you get a real craving for colour and movement.'

'He could at least have left the people alone,' said Mum, flicking her cigarette butt into the snow. 'And the sheep,' she added begrudgingly.

'The police psychologist says he probably tried to stick to deer. But after the shoots he couldn't sedate any deer because they were too timid . . .' Rebecca broke off. 'I hope the police psychologist will leave me in peace now. I just want to get away from here and forget the whole thing.'

'Nonsense,' said Mum, lighting a second cigarette. 'You should write a book. Or at least give an interview. "In the jaws of the werewolf," or something. Believe me, it's compelling stuff.'

'But it was the goatherder who locked me up.'

'A mere detail.' Mum waved her cigarette disparagingly. 'Then later on you can give a second interview, "In the clutches of the werewolf-hunter." What do you think? How did they catch him?'

'He handed himself in and admitted to everything. Now that he knows the Garou is dead, he's a completely different person. He even apologised for clobbering me.'

'I forgive him,' said Mum.

'You do?' asked Rebecca.

'That and Yves as well,' said Mum. 'His wife and child, just imagine. I'm telling you, if anything had happened to you, I'd be sitting in the forest armed with silver bullets too.'

'Tess,' said Rebecca after a while. 'I can't forgive him that as easily.'

'That was the goatherder too?'

Rebecca nodded. 'So that she didn't disturb his werewolf trap. Eric would never have done anything to hurt Tess. He loved her. Weird, huh?'

'Weird,' said Mum, standing up. 'I'm going in. I'm cold.'

And when Rebecca wasn't looking, she flicked the second cigarette into the snow as well.

The sheep watched from the back of the car as the chateau shrank like snow in the sun, only more quickly. Saying goodbye to the red apple in the orchard had been a wrench. They'd never get to eat it now. But they were happy to be moving on. Maybe they would discover George's Europe after all, the Europe resplendent with apple trees, green meadows and long bread! A Europe without wolves and goats at any rate!

'There's Aubrey!' said Heather suddenly.

And a little black goat was indeed running along behind their car. Running like mad.

'I think she wants to come with us,' said Cloud.

The sheep looked at one another silently for a moment, then Lane deftly unfastened the flap at the back of the car.

It fell open. The car slowed down.

Aubrey sped up.

She finally managed it and landed between the sheep in one admirable goaty leap. The sheep looked at her rather awkwardly.

'I think that's a sheep!' bleated Sir Ritchfield suddenly. '

A sheep! A sheep!' the others bleated in relief too. If Aubrey was a sheep, their lives would be that much easier in the future!

'Don't worry,' Heathcliff whispered into her ear. 'It's not that hard to be a sheep. I'll show you what to do!'

'We're a sheep now,' Aubrey said to the little black goat who was always with her. The little black goat looked proud.

The car stopped and Rebecca came and closed the back of the car again.

The sheep peered curiously out of the car, into the forest.

'Look!' said Ramesses.

The sheep looked. Now if Ramesses said something, they always listened very carefully.

'What is it?' asked Heather, but then she saw it too. All of the sheep saw it.

Something quiet, beautiful and important.

Just like every evening, the darkness was creeping out of the forest. But this time it looked as if the light would hold on, to every tree, every stem, every branch, just to stay in the world a little longer, flowing slowly and reluctantly from the road, from the trees and from the sky.

It was the most important thing the sheep had seen for a long time. It meant green and grass and lambs and meadows and gambolling.

It meant spring.

All of a sudden, the sheep could smell something special.

The humans were wrong. The grass growing wasn't a sound. It was a smell.

The most beautiful smell in the world.

'Speusippus!' said Aubrey.

'Hindley, Hareton, Hannibal,' said Heathcliff.

'I don't know,' said the nameless ram, chewing.

'Epicurus?' asked Aubrey. 'Heraclitus?'

'Gorse, Hazel, Daisy,' said Heathcliff. 'Tulip?'

'I quite like Tulip!' admitted the ram, chewing his hay thoughtfully.

There was a haystack at the end of this story too. They had to share it with three brown ponies, but that wasn't a bad thing. The ponies weren't particularly well-versed in grazing with sheep, and up to now it hadn't been all that difficult to filch the hay right from under their noses. But the ponies were catching up.

'I don't think they're sheep!' said eagle-eyed Sir Ritchfield.

'Europe isn't that bad after all,' said Cordelia. 'You just have to get used to it.'

'And I ate the Moon!' Mopple told anybody who would listen. 'If I hadn't eaten the Moon, things wouldn't have worked out quite as well as they did!'

And there was absolutely no doubt about that.

EPILOGUE WITH GOATS

A bored group of goats gazed at an empty sheep meadow, where dead leaves played in the wind. The goats' eyes flickered with ennui.

'They were wanting!' said Calliope.

'But fun,' retorted Calypso.

'An intermezzo!' Circe giggled.

'A thriller!' declared Calypso, dramatically twizzling her ears.

'A thriller with sheep?' asked the goat with only one horn, squinting out of one eye and peering critically through the fence.

'A capriccio!' said Calliope, kicking out.

'A comedy!' sniggered Circe.

'It wasn't really a comedy,' said the goat with only one horn, peeking through the fence again.

'Everything's a comedy!' bleated Calypso. 'It was just a comedy involving a lot of red!'

The goats watched the frisky leaves on the former sheep meadow with barely disguised regret.

'We're just imagining it all, anyway!' said the goat with only one horn.

ACKNOWLEDGEMENTS

Thanks go to . . .
   Werner, Susi, and O, Tanja K. and Jutta R., Ulla K., Micha D., Robert B., and of course my agent Astrid Poppenhusen.

Special thanks go to my US publisher Soho Press and my UK publisher Allison & Busby. I am so pleased that the sheep and goats of *Big Bad Wool* finally had the chance to make a bold leap into the English language.

Big thanks also to my translator, Amy Bojang, who – with the help of a lot of woolpower – made the leap a smooth one.

LEONIE SWANN's debut novel, *Three Bags Full*, was an instant hit, topping the bestseller charts in her native Germany for months and being translated into 26 languages. She has since continued her ovine detectives' investigations in *Big Bad Wool* and introduced a motley crew of senior sleuths in *The Sunset Years of Agnes Sharp*. Swann lives in Cambridgeshire.

@_leonieswann